GET A FREE BOOK

Download The Watcher, a novella exclusive to Ty Patterson's newsletter subscribers from https://bit.ly/3mDhpCO

Check out Primer on Author's store, the next Cutter Grogan thriller

Join Ty Patterson's Facebook group of readers

ALSO BY TY PATTERSON

Zeb Carter Series

Twelve books in the series and counting

Cutter Grogan Series (Zeb Carter Universe)

Seven books in the series and counting

Zeb Carter Short Stories

Three books and counting

Warriors Series (Zeb Carter Universe)

Twelve books in the series

Gemini Series (Zeb Carter Universe)

Four thrillers in the series

Warriors Series Shorts (Zeb Carter Universe)

Six novellas in the series

Cade Stryker Series

Two military sci-fi thrillers

ACKNOWLEDGMENTS

They say it takes a village to produce a book. In my case, many continents have been involved. Sure, an author's job is a solitary one, but writing is just one part of putting out a book.

My beta readers, who are around the world, are my first responders. I owe a debt of gratitude to them for getting into shape all the words I write.

Donna Rich, my proofreader, and Merwie Garzon, my editor, have been invaluable in polishing the book.

Lastly, a special thanks to Debbie Gallant, Tom Gallant, Michelle Rose Dunn and Cheri Gerhardt, who have supported me since the beginning.

To my wife and son, for their sacrifices in supporting me.

Out beyond ideas of wrongdoing and right doing, there is a field. I'll meet you there.

Rumi

AUTHOR'S NOTE

This is a work of fiction and while it is based in real countries and features several landmarks, I have taken considerable liberties and literary license in depicting how the countries work and with their landmark attractions as well.

1

T*ehran*

'Over here,' someone whispered from an alley.

Zohra Hashimi looked over her shoulder and saw the police cruisers behind them. She panted as she ran, clutching her bag like a shield against her chest.

'Over here,' the voice whispered again. 'They haven't seen you.'

She darted into Gholami Street, from where the voice came. Hands caught her wrists and guided her into the darkness. Light reflected off a broken window and briefly illuminated a pale face.

Another woman. There were a bunch of them, hurrying in the darkness, picking their way carefully.

'Where are we going?' her voice quavered.

'To a safe house,' a woman answered. 'We will stay there tonight, until the morning.'

'Don't you know about it?' another woman asked sharply. 'It was shared in the messaging app we use.'

'Is she a protester?' yet another girl asked. 'How do we know she is not the police?'

Zohra was slammed against a car. Someone brought out their phone and lit her up with its flashlight.

'She isn't wearing a scarf over her head.'

'That doesn't mean anything. Search her.'

Rough hands patted her down. They snatched her bag and went through it.

'Where's your phone?'

'I lost it when I was running away from the police,' she lied. 'That's why I don't remember the safe house.'

'Here's her identification card ... oh.' The voice went quiet. 'Search her on the internet.'

Another woman typed her name in a search engine and came up with several hits.

'Not that one,' she muttered, 'not her ... there! I found her. She is not lying. She's a student like many of us. She is from University of Tehran. Come, khahar,' *sister*, 'let's go. We have wasted enough time.'

Zohra fell in with them. Around twenty of them, she counted the shapes. Many of them were in their twenties. *I am older than all of them,* she thought, *but they accepted me for who I am.*

She knew that was down to her identity card. It gave her credibility. And, it wasn't fake.

She stumbled over a tin can which rattled loudly.

They froze. Cruisers went down Sattar Khan Street, sirens wailing. Officers' yells came to them with only a layer of office and commercial buildings as protection.

They turned into an alley, where one of the women went to a building. A bank's sign hung outside it. She fumbled at the door and opened it carefully.

How did she know about it? Zohra wondered. She followed the women into the lobby and down a staircase.

'Here.' Someone turned on the light. 'We will be safe from the police.'

Zohra checked them out. Twenty. Her initial count had been right. All of them seemed to be college students or early in their careers.

'Okay, turn out the lights. Bathroom is upstairs. Go softly without making any noise. This building is safe for tonight only.' The speaker had hard eyes and a tattoo of a dragon on her forearm.

They sat on the hard floor. Some of them sang songs. Others told jokes and stories to each other.

Zohra had no one to talk to. She didn't know any of them. She felt the hard shape of her phone, that she had hidden in her shoes.

Her panic didn't subside.

Will they still protect me if they know who I am?

She slept and woke up to a loud crashing.

'IT'S THE POLICE,' a woman screamed.

'How did they know we were here?' another voice shouted.

'GO!'

They ran up the stairs and there, uniformed officers were waiting for them. Zohra gasped in fear. She reached down to her right shoe, slowing her climb, and brought out her phone from beneath her heel where she had hidden it.

Women shoved past her as they tried to escape through the lobby.

The sounds of the officers' sticks and the shrieks of the women being clubbed, filled the building.

She texted a message with trembling fingers.

Baradar, I don't know who else to reach. I need your help. Please save me.

She hit send and while trying to return her phone to its hiding place, was jostled forward. It fell to the floor and before she could retrieve it, a hand darted, picked it up and it disappeared.

Zohra tried to see who had taken it. There were still a few women behind her. She turned, but her hair was grabbed by an officer who shouted furiously at her and brought his cane down on her head, and she saw and heard nothing else.

2

Tunisia

The heat was oppressive. It hung like a heavy blanket, weighing down life forms especially those that hadn't learned to adapt.

'It's hot,' Bwana complained in their comms.

'It's the Sahara,' Zeb wiped sweat off his forehead. 'What did you expect?'

'A five-star hotel, a pool, jacuzzi, the works,' Beth said sarcastically.

Zeb grinned at Bwana's silence. They were deep in Tunisia, in the desert which was in the south of the country. The nearest town was Tieret, to their left and the Libyan border was to their right.

Dunes, scraggly shrubs and an endless expanse of desert as far as the eye could see.

Except for the camp of nomadic goat herders that were five-hundred meters away. A gathering of tents around which the animals wandered, their bleating audible in the distance.

'Our intel was correct?' Chloe asked doubtfully when a herder came out of one of the tents and drove the animals to the shelter of a large tarp that was spread over poles. The man was dressed in a burnous, a long-flowing cloak that protected the body from the heat and also allowed for air circulation, and a cheche, a long scarf that was wrapped around his neck. He swatted a stick lightly on one of the goat's rumps.

Zeb lowered his binos, wiped his eyes and raised them again. 'Not our intel. CIA's. You read it as well.'

The CIA's dossier had been categoric. Ivan Petrov, a senior Russian general, had fled Moscow after his protests about the Ukraine invasion had made his survival risky. Humint had confirmed his sighting in Tunisia and elint, by way of satellite and drone imagery, had obtained photographs of his presence in the goat-herding camp in the desert.

The Agency operators were enjoying downtime in Morocco when Clare, their director, greenlit them.

'Extract him. You are the only American assets on the ground close to him. He was in the Kremlin's inner circle. What he knows will be invaluable to us. Russia's game plan, which other countries it might invade, troop movements, weapons, their nuclear plans ... all that will help us and Ukraine. On top of that, he sat on the General Staff of the Armed Forces. He will know about GRU operations and assets around the world. He is so valuable that we need to hot-extract him.'

'What if he isn't willing, ma'am?' Bear had objected.

'Don't give him a choice,' she had replied.

With that as their mission brief and the CIA file for more information, the operators had arrived in the country in the dark. They had flown to Douz, a city that was the gateway to the Tunisian Sahara and had driven for over five hours on the C211 highway and had left their vehicles outside a petrochemical plant near Tieret and had trekked over the dunes to where they had made camp, five hundred meters from the collection of tents.

They had dug trenches in the sand, wrapped themselves in heat-protect blankets and lay hidden.

The sheets over them were long-life, battery-powered, that either cooled or warmed the body depending on the ambient temperature. They were equipped with water packs that let the operators sip from them and couldn't be detected by thermal imaging.

The operators had to thrust their heads out of their comfort to recon the camp, which was when the heat of the desert hit them.

'There are twelve bodies in that camp,' Meghan said. 'Our drone launch at the dawn confirmed that many heat signatures. One of them has got to be Petrov.'

'That goat herder is the first dude we've seen,' Roger drawled. 'Why would Petrov come here, in the middle of the desert in North Africa? There's nothing here. It won't be the first time CIA's intel was wrong.'

'You saw the photographs,' Chloe reminded him.

'Those could have been taken in any desert camp in the world. Tents, goats and sand look the same everywhere.'

'We are here, now.' Bear growled. 'You got a better idea of how we could confirm his presence?'

'Sure. Rog will walk up to the camp and say *howdy*, Texan style,' Beth said sarcastically. 'The herders will welcome him. They'll offer him tea and biscuits and tell him, *oh, here's Petrov, the Russian general. Do you want him?*'

'I don't think they have biscuits,' the Texan retorted, but it was a weak protest. No one won in verbal sparring with the twins.

Zeb wriggled out of the comfort of the blanket cautiously to raise his head above the trench for a better look. The goat herder had disappeared into the larger tent which appeared to shimmer as bodies inside it moved. A man poked his head out briefly, shouted at the animals and withdrew.

'That's dude number two,' he said softly. He glanced at his watch. Just past twelve pm. *The heat will only increase from now on. Will anyone come out?*

They could play the waiting game and approach the tents when it grew dark but there was no surety that the herders wouldn't break camp and move.

They're driving those goats to some town where they can trade them. They won't be here for long.

He crawled out cautiously. 'I'm going for a closer look.'

'What?' Beth exclaimed. 'We have no cover. You think they won't spot you?'

'We're coming with you,' Meghan's upper body broke out of her trench. 'Beth and I. Two women wearing headscarves along with a man will be less suspicious than a single man. They might think we're tourists whose vehicle broke down.'

Zeb glanced at her, to his right, and then at her twin who flanked his left. The sisters were tall. Five feet ten, green eyes that were concealed behind brown contacts, looks that drew attention in any part of the world. They were deeply tanned and like the rest of the operators, spoke Arabic fluently.

'Would it make a difference if I said I insisted on going alone?' he asked mildly.

'No,' Beth retorted and crawled out.

Zeb crouched low on the ground and patted his chest to confirm his shoulder-holster Glock was in place.

'We'll cover you from here,' Bwana said grimly.

Zeb nodded and was rising when they heard the chopper.

3

Zeb wriggled back into the trench swiftly and checked that the twins had returned, too.

They had.

'That's a Kasatka,' Bear whispered in their earpieces.

Zeb recognized the chopper as it came into view. The Kamov, Ka-60, helo was also known by the Russian word for killer whale, which was what his friend had called out.

It was painted matte black to prevent any reflection. A serial number on it, no other markings, no flags or lettering.

'I ran that number past Werner,' Meghan's referred to their AI engine which was at the heart of their operations. The software was plugged into national and international databases, some of which were legal and some hacked. It had facial recognition, voice analysis and more features than Zeb could keep track of. The twins kept upgrading it regularly to keep it on the cutting edge of technology. 'Registered to a trading company in Tunis, which is owned by Karim Aziz, a super-wealthy businessman. Dates, meat, carpets, the firm exports just about everything.'

'Doesn't look like it spotted us,' Broker commented when the chopper landed in a swirl of dust.

Goats burst out from beneath their shelter and ran into the desert.

No one's going after them. Zeb shifted in his trench and trained his binos on the chopper. *Two pilots. They're staying inside. Two ... no, three men climbing out.* 'Can you see who they are?'

'Nope,' Beth replied immediately. 'Helo's blocking our view.'

Zeb focused on the men's feet. He stiffened when he made out what they were wearing. *Combat boots!*

The three men emerged from behind the chopper and went inside the large tent.

'Shades. Dark clothes. Were they carrying weapons?' Chloe mused.

'They were,' Bwana confirmed. 'I made them out before they went inside. Why would gunmen come into this camp?'

They got their answer shortly when a bunch of men emerged.

'THAT'S PETROV!' Beth whisper-yelled.

'Yeah,' Zeb nodded.

The Russian was in the middle, being shoved towards the chopper by the visitors. Three more men stayed back watching, all of them armed.

Zeb focused on the man on the extreme left. He's the herder who came out. *He's armed too.*

'That's an AK-12,' he identified the rifle. 'Used by the Russian military. These men aren't friendlies. Petrov isn't going willingly with them.'

'Take them out?' Bwana asked.

'Yeah,' He shoved his blanket back, rested his left hand on the ground, preparing for a lunge. 'I—'

'Meg and I too,' Beth cut him off. 'The rest can provide cover.'

'There will be more men inside the tents,' Chloe warned. 'We haven't seen everyone.'

'Yeah,' Zeb nodded and slung his HK416 over his shoulder and Velcroed it to a pad on his chest. 'But we can't let the chopper fly away with Petrov. On my count. Three.'

He half-rose in his trench and felt Beth and Meghan do the same.

'Two.' He jammed his right leg hard on the ground.

'One.' He burst out of the trench and sprinted towards the camp.

Beth and Meghan fell in alongside him.

Ten meters, then twenty which became a hundred at which one of the herders spotted them.

The man yelled.

He gestured in their direction and then his head exploded and his body fell to the ground.

4

'Got him,' Bwana said in their earpieces. 'We're coming out of our trenches too. We've got to spread out to see around the chopper.'

Zeb didn't reply. His team was a well-oiled machine. They had been working together for several years. They were friends. They didn't need orders and, in any case, they had never worked in a hierarchical manner. They never would. He knew his friends would find the best shooting positions they could and cover them.

He unslung his HK when Petrov stumbled, was yanked up roughly and pushed towards the chopper. The Russian and his captors were blocked from his view by the aircraft.

The helo's rotors started spinning. Its engines whined. Sand swirled.

'That will help us,' he yelled at the twins, gesturing at the dust cloud.

'Yeah,' Meghan gasped, 'but that chopper might lift off any moment—'

'It won't,' Bear said comfortingly.

The cockpit's window shattered. One of the pilot's bodies jerked and slumped. The other man ducked forward which was a mistake. A round took out his head.

'Two down,' Bear confirmed. 'The bird won't fly.'

'Going around, from either side of the chopper,' Meghan panted as she and Beth circled wide of the aircraft.

Zeb kept going straight, using the helo as cover. A round screamed over his head. Another kicked sand ahead of him.

He was a hundred meters away from the chopper. He could see Petrov's legs beneath the helo, kicking and dragging in the sand as he was pulled back into the tent. Sand blasted into his face. He gritted his teeth and considered his options. *Can't go in front of the chopper or behind it.*

He dove beneath the chopper near the rear wheel where the ground clearance was the biggest. The rotor wash sent a blast of wind and sand into his face, momentarily blinding him. He gritted his teeth and blinked rapidly to clear his vision.

The three shooters were close to the tent, pushing Petrov towards its open mouth. The canvas itself was being shredded by gunfire by his friends. One of the shooters turned, as if he felt the operator's presence. His mouth opened to yell a warning.

Zeb stitched him with a burst of fire. The two remaining shooters spun around swiftly. One of them started to bring Petrov around as a shield.

Zeb shot him in the face.

'RUN!' he yelled at Petrov.

The general didn't react, frozen with fear. The surviving shooter was close to the mouth of the tent, several meters away from the general. He sprayed rounds at the American and lunged at Petrov to grab him.

Zeb ignored the sand spraying on his face from the rounds. He didn't hurry as the gunman closed in on Petrov.

Got to make my shots count.

The top of the tent blew away in the wash of the spinning rotors. He heard shots and screaming from inside. He ignored them. His HK was steady in his hands, its sight tracking the shooter who was inches from the general. The gunman's face was twisted with rage as he yelled incoherently, his AK-12 jerking in his hand as he kept firing at the American beneath the chopper.

A round spanged off its body and whined in the air. Another bullet smacked into the wheel next to Zeb. He waited until the shooter's body was fully exposed, and triggered a long burst into the body mass.

The gunman jerked and stumbled and collapsed limply.

Zeb sprang out from beneath the chopper and caught hold of Petrov's collar.

'I'm American. I'm here to rescue you,' he yelled in Russian. 'Do you understand?'

He squeezed the man's shoulder hard to shake him out of his daze.

Petrov nodded rapidly. 'Da, da.'

'Run behind the chopper. My friends are there. They will keep you safe.'

Zeb watched the general stumble away, confirmed the shooters were dead and snuck a glance into the tent.

A herder sprang out at him, yelling furiously, triggering wildly.

Zeb dropped to the ground instantly and fired into his belly. He rolled away, propped himself up and swung his HK in an arc to smash its barrel into the shooter's temple. He got to his feet in the same move, emptied his magazine into the man's chest, slapped a new one and crept towards the tent.

'All clear," Beth announced in his comms.

Her tone sent a warning through him.

He ghosted inside the tent and froze at the sight of the women.

5

Zeb was stunned.

Women? We thought there would be more herders inside the tent.

He checked out the bodies. Two gunmen lay on the sand ahead of him, Beth and Meghan were to his right, their HKs in their hands, hard-faced and expressionless.

'We came up from behind,' the elder twin said. 'Three more herders—'

'They're hostiles,' Beth interrupted bitterly. 'Let's not call them herders. They were at the back of the tent,' she cocked her head to indicate where they had entered from. 'None of them were expecting us. They were focused on your shooting.'

She shrugged as if to say, *it was easy work for us to take them out.*

'How did you get these men?' Zeb indicated the bodies in front of him.

'I did,' Chloe emerged from behind the mass of women. 'I snuck in when the top of the tent blew away.'

Zeb checked out the women who had terrified expressions on their faces. They were bunched close together, seeking comfort from one another's presence. All of them were dark-haired and dark-eyed, dressed in jeans of various colors and shirts or hoodies. Backpacks on most of them.

'Fifteen,' Chloe read his glance. 'I counted.'

'You spoke to them?'

'No. There wasn't any time.'

'Why didn't our drone detect them?'

'They were covered in thermal blankets.'

Zeb glanced back at approaching footsteps. Bwana and Bear entered the tent. They too froze at the sight of the women. They recovered quickly and came to him.

'No one else in the other tents. Food, water cans, cooking oil, feed for the goats, that kind of stuff,' the African American murmured. 'Who are the women?'

'We are going to find out,' Zeb replied grimly. He velcroed his HK and dropped his hands to his sides. 'Where's Petrov?'

'With us,' Broker chimed in his comms. 'You've got women there?'

'Later,' Zeb told him.

'American?' One woman drew closer to them.

'Yes,' he replied. 'Who are you?'

She didn't reply for a moment.

'Who are you?' he repeated in Arabic.

She hesitated and glanced at the rest of the women. One of them whispered to her. Others joined in the conversation. Heads nodded and eyes flashed in their direction.

'You came to save us?' the speaker asked in English.

It was his turn to hesitate. 'No,' he answered truthfully. 'We didn't know about you. We came for Petrov ... the man who was with you.'

Her accent doesn't sound Arabic.

'He wasn't with us. He was a prisoner, but he didn't come with us. They,' she nodded at one of the bodies on the ground, 'brought him to the tent three days ago. We didn't speak to him.'

'Who are you?' Meghan asked her.

The woman considered them. She drew herself to her full height and answered defiantly. 'We are Iranian protesters.'

6

T*ehran*

Zohra Hashimi opened her eyes and blinked against the harsh glare of the fluorescent lights. She was surrounded by a dozen other women, all of them lying on the cold tiled floor of a dull room. No windows. A dirty sink in a corner. Her nose wrinkled involuntarily when she took in the stainless-steel toilet near it. There were thin sheets on the floor on which it seemed the women had slept.

Her head throbbed. She felt it and drew a sharp breath when her fingers came across the swelling on her temple. The night's events came back to her.

She sat up straighter, rubbed her eyes and scanned the room again, recognizing the protesters with whom she had fled from the Tehran street.

'Where are we?' she asked. Her chest started pounding when she realized there were fewer women than there had been in the basement.

'Somewhere in Tehran,' one woman answered. 'We don't know where. We know we are in the city because we traveled only fifteen or twenty minutes.'

'They put us in a closed truck,' another protester added. 'We couldn't see where we went. We arrived in front of a building which was full of guards and we were brought here.'

'Is this a prison?' she asked fearfully.

'We don't know. There was a steel door and what seemed like offices, but we didn't see any prisoners nor did we hear any sounds.'

'I could hear traffic,' a younger woman who had been yelling furiously during the protest while holding a placard, threaded her fingers through her hair. 'I could hear ambulance sirens. You were unconscious the whole time. Your temple was bleeding. We asked the police for medical help but they refused. It seems to have stopped now.'

She drew closer and inspected her head. 'It will heal, but you have an ugly swelling. Are you feeling any pain?'

'Yes,' Zohra blinked rapidly to hold back her tears at her gentleness. 'Like a headache.'

'Hopefully it will go away soon. Here,' the protester offered a bottle of water. 'Drink lots of it.'

'My name is Zohra—'

'I know,' the woman smiled. 'I was the one who checked you out on the internet. I am studying economics at Modares University. Masters.' A shadow crossed her face. 'I hope I can complete it.'

That reminded Zohra. She clutched the other woman's sleeve. 'Where are the other women?'

'Some of them escaped when the police broke into our hiding place. They charged at the officers and ran away. The others ...' her face darkened.

'The police took them away for questioning in the morning. They never returned,' another woman completed in a scared voice.

'They took away our watches, phones, bags, everything,' yet another protester spat. 'They gave us some food and water but didn't tell us anything.'

Zohra inhaled deeply as she tried to control her panic. *In, out,* she recalled her yoga instructor's voice and timed her breaths to the mental voice. 'What time is it?'

'Khahar,' the woman said patiently, 'what did I just say? They took everything away from us. We don't know. We think it is morning, but we aren't sure. It could be late night as well. All of us slept for some time. They came when we woke up, caught hold of some of us randomly and took them away.'

'We tried to hear voices but there is nothing,' Narges cupped her ear to indicate the utter stillness beyond the room.

Zohra closed her eyes and tried to recall the events in the basement. She remembered fleeing up the stairs and losing her phone.

Did my message go out?

She prayed that it did.

Will he remember me?

Another thought intruded.

Do the police have my phone? Did they see my message? Will he be recognized? Will he get in trouble?

Her head snapped up at a sound.

The door was being unlocked.

All the women turned to it with panicked expressions.

It opened.

7

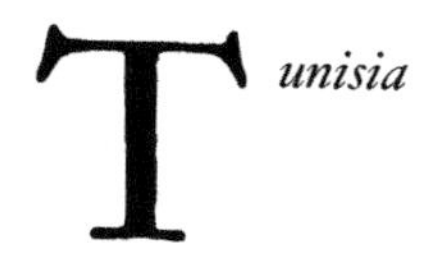

unisia

ZEB STARED AT THE WOMEN IN DISBELIEF.

'You are Iranian?' he slipped into Persian instinctively.

'You know Farsi?' Her eyes lit up. 'Balle.' Yes. 'We are Iranian. We are all protesters. We knew the police and Sepah were looking for us—'

'Slow down, khahar,' Sister. Meghan said with a smile. 'We aren't going anywhere. Tell us how you got from Iran to Tunisia and how you ended up with these shooters.'

'Farideh, don't tell them anything more,' a woman with a guarded expression caught the sleeve of the speaker. 'How do we know you are American?' she challenged the operators.

Zeb hid a grin. *Good question. We are carrying false papers.*

Every Agency operation was a deniable one. They rarely carried their real identity documents with them.

The chopper's engine died down outside the tent. Its rotors

slowed their spinning and came to a stop and with it, the swirling sand disappeared.

'You're welcome,' Roger declared in their comms. 'You don't have to shout over the clatter now.'

'You'll have to trust us,' Zeb mic-tapped, thanking the Texan and replied to the woman.

'We trusted the people back in Iran and this is where we ended up,' her voice was border-line hostile.

'Wait,' Beth ordered when Zeb made to speak. She punched a number on her encrypted phone and turned it on speaker. 'Ma'am, where are you?'

'Meeting with the President,' Clare's voice was loud and clear.

'At the White House?'

'Yeah, why?'

'Can you get to the North Lawn and turn on video with the building in the background?'

Zeb nodded at Beth's request. *Smart thinking. No security conflict there. Clare won't show herself or anyone else on camera.*

'I am guessing there's a reason for this request,' their director answered after a pause.

'There is, ma'am. We are in the middle of the Tunisian Sahara, with Iranian women, protesters, who were captured by a gang. The women don't believe who we are.'

Clare didn't lead with *Iranian women? How did they get there?* She hadn't gotten to her position, one of the most powerful ones in DC, by asking questions at the wrong moments.

'Hold for a minute,' she said mildly.

They waited.

The women drew closer to them. Zeb was aware of their curious looks. He tried to look as non-threatening as possible.

'Video on,' Clare said.

Beth turned her phone towards the women, many of whom sucked their breath sharply at the most recognizable building in the world.

'Khaharan,' Sisters. The Director addressed the women, speaking Farsi as fluently as them. 'Those people with you *are* American government officials. You can trust them fully.'

'Who are you, khanom?'

'I can't tell you that, khahar. Be assured that they will get you to safety.'

'Satisfied?' Beth queried Farideh and the woman who had challenged them.

Both of them nodded.

'I had to ask, sister,' the second woman said. 'We have been through a lot—'

'No apologies needed,' the younger twin grinned. 'I'm Beth, that's Meghan, yeah, we're twins. Chloe and Zeb. Those two big men are Bwana and Bear. Don't be scared of them,' she chuckled. 'We have two more behind the chopper. You'll meet them later. Tell us your story.'

Zeb turned his head and spoke softly in his collar mic. 'Broker, launch the drone. Keep an eye out for any visitors, either hostiles or friendlies.'

'Copy,' his friend replied. 'The horizon is empty, but we'll keep a watch.'

He turned his attention to the women and listened.

The fifteen of them were all university students. A few had fled from the cops after being captured and joined the rest of women who were planning to get away from the country. The women had made contact with a central group of dissidents who had connections with the underworld.

'They gave us false passports and identities,' Farideh Rezaei, the first speaker who had introduced herself, continued.

'You met this criminal gang?' Chloe wrinkled her forehead.

'Na. Our friends, the other dissidents, coordinated with them.'

'We,' Parvaneh Kazemi, the challenger gestured at all the protesters, 'come from families who are well-known in Tehran. They already are being harassed by the government because of us. There is a rumor that we were on a police black list. If the criminal gang knew who we really were, they too might exploit our situation. We couldn't risk that.'

'Our friends,' Farideh interjected, 'the other dissidents, had worked with this group before. They had arranged for several protesters to escape to Europe. That was our plan too. Go to Germany and return to Iran when it was safer, but continue our campaigning from Berlin or whichever city we were in.'

'We went to Varamin, that's—'

'Forty-five kilometers southeast of Tehran,' Beth broke in. She smiled at Parvaneh to remove any sting from her interruption. 'We know your country very well.'

'Balle, it looks like that,' the protester smiled briefly. 'There was a truck waiting for us. It was to take us to Turkey. The driver and his helper had papers for us. They had packed meals for us. We climbed into the vehicle and after about an hour, ate our food. We woke up here,' she said bitterly. 'With these men. They told us we were in Tunisia. They slapped us when we asked why we were here. They punched and beat us for no reason. They gave us water, milk and some food. They told us we would be moved today. When we asked where, they hit us.'

One woman pointed at the bruise on her cheek, another held up her reddened arm. Farideh showed a cigarette burn on her palm.

Zeb felt rage wash over him. He clenched his fist. He saw Bwana's eyes narrow. He made himself relax. 'They spoke in Farsi?'

'No, in English. Not very fluent.'

Zeb could see the desert over the shredded tent. *There's nothing there.*

It came to him suddenly. 'You trust your friends? These dissidents who made the arrangements with the gang?'

Parvaneh, shocked by the cold fury in his voice, replied hesitantly. 'Yes. They are our friends.'

'They too would have escaped if they could,' Farideh waved

her hands despairingly, 'our families could afford the gang's costs, theirs couldn't.'

'You're in touch with the protesters who escaped?'

'Yes, agha. What are you thinking of?'

Zeb surveyed them again. *All of them are young. They would be sold to human-trafficking rings.*

From his friends' expressions, he knew they had the same thought. 'That gang betrayed your friends. They planned to...' He trailed away, unable to express himself.

'We know,' Farideh said softly. 'We worked it out. We would be sold as sex slaves. We—' A muscle twitched on her cheek. Her lips worked but no sounds came out. The weight of the events became unbearable for her. Tears escaped her eyes and when Parvaneh and the other women hugged her, she broke down.

'I don't understand, however,' she sniffled after a while and wiped her face. 'Why was that man, Petrov you said, brought here?'

'We'll ask him,' Zeb said grimly.

8

Bear and Chloe stayed behind with the women while Zeb, accompanied by the twins, went behind the chopper.

Petrov, flanked by Broker and Roger, was sipping coffee from one of the operator's flasks.

Zeb studied him as they neared.

The Russian was as tall as the twins. Silver-hair that was cropped close to his head. Clean-shaven, dark-eyed, he radiated authority even in the middle of the desert.

'We've made the introductions,' Roger's lips twitched. 'He didn't believe us initially until we pointed out that if it hadn't been for us, he would have been back in Moscow, never to be seen again.'

'I have heard of you,' Petrov returned the flask to the Texan with a nod of thanks and shook Zeb's hand with a firm grip. 'SVR, GRU, many agencies and people in my country have you on their hit list.'

'What about you?' Zeb asked him.

'You saved my life. That changes my perspective,' the general said honestly. 'I also know you didn't rescue me out of the goodness of your hearts,' he flashed a brief, wry smile.

'Why did you come to Tunisia? Who are these people?' Zeb pointed to the chopper's pilots.

'Tunisia, because it is an escape route that is not on anyone's radar. I knew everyone would be checking out the normal channels when I escaped. Flights, trains or ships to Europe ... I didn't take those. I drove to Kazakhstan. I had several passports with me and enough dollars to bribe border officials. From that country, I flew to Tunisia. My idea was to circle the Black Sea and the Mediterranean and get to Europe.'

'And this gang?'

'I don't know who the men in the helicopter were. The men masquerading as goat herders, they are from the Casbah Maliks, a criminal gang. They are into human trafficking.' He smiled bitterly. 'My country's agencies have used them before, to move people in or out of countries. I contacted them when I was in Kazakhstan for passage to Europe.'

'Looks like they double-crossed you.'

'Da.'

'The chopper belongs to Karim Aziz, a businessman in Tunis. It's owned by one of his companies.

The Russian's forehead wrinkled as he stared into the distance. He shook his head slowly. 'Aziz. I don't know him. I didn't have any contact with Tunisians except this gang. But I can work out what must have happened—'

'He must have had connections with the Casbah Maliks,' Beth interrupted him. 'He found out about you, negotiated with the gang to give you up, put together a team of shooters and pilots and arranged for them to take you. Any guesses what his intention with you was?'

'Moscow,' Petrov said bleakly. 'He would have taken me back to the Kremlin.'

Makes sense, Zeb thought as he and Roger searched the pilots and the shooters' bodies. *Tunisia has criticized the Russian invasion but many of its people didn't like the government's decision. Aziz must be trading with Russia. He would see this as an opportunity to win favors with the Kremlin.*

He held up one of the pilot's identification documents, felt Beth come next to him, who photographed it.

'It might be fake,' she said, 'but let's get Werner to check.'

Zeb checked the pilots' phones. 'No messages. Calls from unknown numbers.'

'They were pros,' Roger commented. 'Those are from the Maliks?' he asked when Bear appeared at the tent's mouth holding a baggie with several phones.

'Yeah,' the bearded operator jiggled it. 'Some names in there, a few calls.'

'Give,' Meghan demanded. 'We'll check them out.' She nudged Zeb with her shoulder. 'What's up? You've gone quiet.'

He rubbed his jaw pensively. 'What do you think Aziz will do when he hasn't heard from his pilots?'

'He'll send a retrieval team.'

'Yeah,' Zeb agreed and made a circling gesture in the air to get his friends closer. 'And it will come hot and hard.'

9

His words spurred them into action. The twins and Chloe disappeared into the tent while Broker and Bear checked out the chopper.

'You can fly this?' Zeb asked them.

'Never flown a Ka-60 before, but there's always a first time.' He strapped into a seat while Bear got into the copilot's.

Zeb ducked down and stepped back when the rotors started spinning.

'Looks familiar,' Bear told him in his earpiece. 'Not very different from the Black Hawks we have flown.' He checked out the rear of the chopper and leaned out to Zeb. 'We're taking the women and Petrov?'

'Only the women. Petrov comes with us.'

Bear gave him a thumbs up. 'Yeah, better to separate the targets.'

Zeb hurried inside the tents where the twins and Chloe were briefing the protesters.

'We'll put you in a safe house in Tunis,' Chloe said, 'and arrange for you to be flown to—'

'Germany. Berlin,' Farideh answered promptly. 'That's where we were going.'

'Berlin it is. I'm guessing you don't have any money, phones, anything on you.'

'No. We had only our clothes on us when we woke up.'

'We have gathered several phones from their bodies. Check if any of those belong to you.'

Farideh nodded. She listened when several women murmured to her urgently. She gesticulated to them, but they looked unconvinced.

'A problem?' Zeb looked questioningly at them.

'They are asking how we know we will be safe in Tunis,' she twisted her hands nervously. 'I told them we can trust you.'

'There will be other members in this gang, agha,' a woman at the back burst out. 'They will know their members are dead. They will hunt us.'

'They might,' Zeb smiled reassuringly. 'We've thought of that. You'll have protection at the safe house. You will fly in a private aircraft to Berlin. We'll take care of the paperwork needed. We have contacts in Germany. They will coordinate with the authorities there and ensure you are safe. We will also alert Europol about this gang. They will put the Maliks on their most wanted list.'

He grinned at their silence. 'You will be safe, khaharan. I guarantee it.'

'We don't have money,' Parvaneh said embarrassedly, 'but we will find a way to pay you back.'

'No. That's not needed. Please don't worry, khahar.'

'But—'

'We are not doing this for money,' Meghan said firmly. 'We work in an organization that has funds for such events. We've got to go, Parvaneh. Like you said, other members of this gang might wonder what happened. We have to leave from this place before they arrive.'

That spurred the women. They drew together and followed the twins out.

Parvaneh stayed behind. She looked at Zeb and Chloe. 'You

can do all of that? Accommodation, papers, protection, Berlin contacts?'

'Yes,' he replied.

Her shoulders slumped in relief. Her body sagged. She went into Chloe's embrace willingly and shuddered. She straightened when her trembling eased. 'How can we repay you?'

Chloe grinned and pointed at Bear. 'You see that big man? He loves food. All of us do. We'll visit you when you're settled in Berlin.'

'We'll cook you khoresht, polo, kebabs ... whatever you want, khahar.' She hugged her again, smiled at Zeb and went to the chopper.

ZEB SET A HARD PACE WHEN THE KA-60 HAD TAKEN OFF.

'Our vehicles are an hour away. We'll have to go fast. You can do that?' he had asked Petrov.

'Better than dying,' the general had replied.

He's keeping up, he glanced at the Russian in the rear-view of his Raybans. They had cameras drilled into their stems which projected the back view onto the lower part of the lenses, turning them into counter-surveillance devices.

He heard Meghan on the phone, making arrangements for the safe house and protection. They had a network of contacts around the world, former military men and women whose services they tapped into for such exigencies.

His phone vibrated. He glanced at it. Clare.

'Package is safe, ma'am,' he cut ahead so that Petrov wouldn't overhear. 'We're taking him to Tunis.'

'I'll arrange for extraction there. The women?'

'Meg's taking care of that. Safe house, passage, everything.'

'Going to?'

'Berlin.'

'I'll talk to Dieter. Make sure there are no blockages.'

'She's probably spoken to him already but your call will help too.'

Dieter Reinhard, Director of BND, Germany's Federal Intelligence Service. He was not just a professional contact but a personal friend to all of them as well.

Zeb hung up and slowed down to let his friends catch up.

'All okay?' Roger drawled.

'Yeah.'

'Everything's set up in Tunis for the women,' Meghan relayed. 'Khaled Fathi, remember him? Former Tunisian Presidential Guard. He's got his own protection firm now. We have worked with him a few times. He'll set them up in a villa in Le Kram. Clare is diverting a military aircraft which will be landing in the evening. That will fly the women to Berlin. Paperwork at both ends will be taken care of before they depart.'

'They don't have any money,' Bwana objected.

'They do, now,' Beth sniggered. 'I slipped a few dollar rolls in Farideh and Parvaneh's pockets with a note that they are for all of them.'

'They didn't notice?'

Beth waggled her fingers. 'I learned from New York's best pickpocket. Mark introduced me to him.'

Mark, her boyfriend, an NYPD detective.

'And I gave Farideh a burner phone. I told her not to use it until they were in Berlin,' Meghan added.

'What about me?' Petrov asked. 'You aren't interrogating me? No aggressive questioning? You didn't save me to give me the luxury treatment.'

'We didn't,' Bwana gave him his hard face. 'But you're far more valuable to DC than to us, here.'

'You call this luxury?' Roger mopped sweat from his face.

'I have been in worse places,' the general said.

I bet you have, Zeb side-eyed him. As part of the General Staff, the Russian was plugged into every critical operation and decision that his country carried out. He had been part of the

Ukraine invasion's planning and execution. There were rumors that he was one of the few living Russians who knew where the Russian president's palace was, an opulent hide-out which was one of the best kept secrets in the world. He was a widower, which had made escape easy for him. He had left behind no family to be threatened.

Zeb glanced at the sky when they reached their Range Rovers.

Four pm. We got here safe.

The challenge was to reach Tunis unharmed.

10

They saw the chopper at five pm, when they were on the C211, heading north.

Zeb, driving, spotted the dark speck in the sky high above them to their far left. He tracked it until it disappeared from sight.

That's going in the direction of the camp.

'Seen it,' Meghan observed from the shotgun seat. She didn't raise her eyes from her screen. 'Our drone saw it as well. Too far to make out its tail number.'

'It could be anyone's bird,' Beth commented from the rear. She and Petrov shared the bench seat while Chloe was in the far back.

'Bwana,' Zeb eyed the second Range Rover in the mirror, 'you have room to lift the floor board?'

'We have,' Roger replied. 'You think that was Aziz's chopper?'

'Only one way to tell.'

The chopper returned twenty minutes later. It circled them and then followed them from their left, flying at a height of two-hundred meters.

Sun's reflecting off it. Can't make out anyone inside except the pilot.

'That's a Ka-60 as well,' Bwana identified it.

Petrov twisted anxiously as he followed it with his eyes. 'Is it after us?'

'Bwana,' Zeb ignored him, 'do your thing.'

He gripped the wheel lightly while the second vehicle slowed. Meghan stowed away her screen and brought up her HK but kept it below the window sill.

'Beth,' Zeb kept driving, ignoring the chopper. 'Lower your window and lean back.'

'But that will expose Petrov ... oh,' she trailed off when she figured out what Zeb intended. 'You want them to see him. That will force their hand. If they have nothing to do with Petrov, they will fly away, or else they will go hostile.'

'Yeah,' Zeb gassed their Rover which responded with a surge, leaving tar behind them.

There's no one else on the highway. That chopper's got to be Aziz's. There's no other reason for it to be interested in us.

A blast of warm air rushed in when Beth's window slid down.

Petrov made an inarticulate sound but leaned forward willingly to show his face.

The helo reacted after a moment.

It raced ahead of them and spun in the air to face them.

It hovered for a moment and then a figure showed partially from its door who fired at them.

11

Zeb yanked the wheel hard to the right as sand puffs stitched the side of the highway.

'He'll correct his aim.' He didn't realize he had spoken aloud until Meghan nodded. 'He'll expect us to go left.'

He kept going straight. The sand puffs disappeared. A line of pockmarks appeared on the highway. A round spanged off their hood.

'DO SOMETHING,' Petrov yelled in fear and anger.

'Stay tight,' Chloe yelled back at him.

She and the twins thrust their HKs from the open windows and fired at the chopper. They didn't expect to hit it but their action got the desired result.

The chopper lifted high above, but its shooter kept firing at them.

Zeb swerved on the highway, deliberately, erratically. More rounds spanged off their hood and roof.

'Bwana?' He watched the second Rover come to a stop.

'On it,' his friend replied.

. . .

Roger had moved the instant the chopper had spun around to face them. He unsnapped his belt and climbed to the rear where he unlocked the rear seats and rolled them forward on their custom rails.

That made room for the floorboard to be lifted.

He reached inside and removed the case.

'Lift gate,' he grunted.

Bwana activated it.

The Texan dropped the case on the highway and jumped out.

The Range Rover had slowed to a crawl and his shoulder roll minimized the landing impact.

He grabbed the case, unlocked its latches opened it and removed the FIM 92 Stinger missile launcher.

'It's hot,' Bwana reminded him.

Which meant there was a rocket in it.

He got prone.

'They haven't seen you yet,' his friend said impatiently, 'but Zeb hasn't much more time. He can evade the shooter only so much.'

'Patience, grasshopper.' Roger brought the launcher to his shoulder, opened the sight screen and pointed it to the blue sky to give the system the negative contrast for its detection method.

'Move,' he ordered.

Bwana swerved instantly to the left, leaving him exposed on the highway with the launcher to his shoulder.

The chopper is exposed too, to me, he grinned.

He sighted the helo, heard the system confirm acquisition from its tone, and fired.

12

The result was spectacular.

The missile ripped into the chopper which exploded. Its tail blew off and fell a distance away. One rotor blade spun in the air and crashed near them. The rest of the helicopter broke up into pieces with the cockpit falling to the ground two-hundred meters from them.

'Cover us,' Zeb snapped and got Bwana and Chloe's mic-tap in acknowledgement. He, Beth and Meghan, ran cautiously to the wreckage.

'They can't be rescued,' the older twin said bleakly, pointing to the pilot and shooter's bodies, both of which were burning.

'Only two of them,' Zeb searched the debris and didn't find any other bodies.

'Aziz must be running out of heavies,' Beth said drily.

Petrov had emerged from the Range Rover when they returned to it. The Russian's expression of incredulous surprise was disappearing slowly as he took them in, the remains of the chopper and the second vehicle that rolled up. He watched Beth fist-bump Roger.

'Stingers! What else do you carry with you?' he said, finally. 'That's why you weren't worried when the helicopter showed up.'

'I should have noticed your Range Rovers were riding differently on their shocks,' he continued when no one replied to him. 'You must be carrying a small arsenal in these two vehicles.'

Enough to start a war. Zeb didn't articulate the words. He adjusted his shades over his eyes and got behind the wheel. He looked at Petrov speculatively when the Russian and the twins climbed in.

'Why does Aziz want you so desperately?'

The general frowned. 'That chopper was going to kill us all.'

'I'm not sure of that. Their plan could have been to take us out and rescue you.'

'We'll never know, will we?'

Zeb tapped the wheel softly, letting the silence build.

Petrov broke under his gaze. 'I don't know what you're implying.'

'Moscow kills traitors. Your country is known for using polonium, or manufacturing accidents. What was the latest? A critic of the government fell out of a window in India. You see what I am getting to? Why didn't Moscow send killers after you?'

Petrov took in his words. He nodded jerkily. 'Da ... I see what you mean. But Moscow doesn't know where I am.'

'Ka-60 choppers, AK-12s, those are equipment and weapons that the Russian military use currently. They aren't sold to the Tunisian government. How did Aziz get them? I am sure he is in contact with Moscow. They ordered him to capture you.'

'How can you be sure those helos belong to him?'

'We are,' Meghan said flatly.

'Moscow wants you alive,' Zeb insisted. 'We thought you were valuable because of your information. What else are you hiding from us?'

'Nothing!' Petrov protested. 'Your government wants me alive in return for my intel. I am going with you willingly. Protection and asylum in America in exchange for my information. I know how the deal works. Why do you think I am hiding anything from you?'

Zeb believed him. He turned back to the wheel and jammed the gas.

'Aziz," Chloe said after a while. 'We've got to question him.'

'Yes,' he said without looking at her in the rear mirror.

'Shucks,' Bwana complained.

'What's up?'

'He won't have many shooters left. It won't even be a contest.'

13

Tehran

ZOHRA'S HEART NEARLY STOPPED WHEN A POLICE OFFICER entered the cell through the opened door.

'Sepah,' someone whispered behind her, identifying the man's uniform.

Cold dread filled her.

The officer placed his hands on his hips and surveyed them arrogantly.

'You and you,' he pointed at Leila and Aisha, 'and you as well,' he gestured at Zohra, 'come with me.'

The women had introduced themselves in the confines of the cell and everyone knew the other's stories.

'Where are we going?' Leila asked.

He took a long step forward and slapped her hard. His blow felled her to the floor. 'Does that answer your question?'

No one moved in the shocked silence. Leila wept silently and got to her feet.

Zohra fell in behind them as the officer led them out of the cell. A guard locked the door once they were in the hallway.

Breathe, she told herself. *You are not going to die. He's going to question you, that's all.*

Her words sounded hollow to herself.

She could feel her nails digging into her palms as they passed several doors.

The Sepah man shoved Leila through a door.

Zohra saw an officer behind a table in that room and then she was past it. Aisha went to another room.

The officer beckoned her to a third room and just as she entered it, she heard the sounds of blows and voices crying out.

The Sepah man grinned revealing crooked teeth. He shut the door and punched her belly.

14

'Who are you?' he snarled.

Zohra's breath escaped in a gasp. She doubled up in agony and shrieked when he grabbed her hair and straightened her.

'ZOHRA!' she yelled. 'I AM ZOHRA HASHIMI. I AM A STUDENT AT THE UNIVERSITY OF TEHRAN.'

'I know that,' he sneered and pushed her against the wall. 'Who are you really? Are you a protester? What were you doing on the street?'

'I was going home after class,' she cried. 'I live in Teymoori. I didn't know about—'

'LIES!' He slapped her. 'You were in the protest on Sattar Khan Street. Look at your clothes. You wear jeans. Your T-shirt is exposing your breasts. Don't you have any shame? Is this what you learn from watching American TV all day?'

Zohra felt her lips split. She felt a trickle of blood roll down her chin. She fell on the floor and tried to get up when he kicked her in the stomach.

Her vision went dark. She groaned and lay still as the waves of agony raced through her.

'Tell the truth and I might go easy on you,' he crouched over her and caressed her hair.

'I ... am ... telling ... the ... truth,' she forced the words. She closed her eyes and breathed shallowly until the intense pain turned into a dull throb.

'I am a research student at the University,' she panted. 'A PhD student in biochemistry. The kind of research our country needs. I wasn't protesting.'

She cried when he caught her hair and pulled her to her feet.

'I read all that from your student record. I called the university as well,' he cupped her chin and forced her to look at him. 'Do you think we are stupid? I am Sepah. I am not the ordinary police or Ershad,' he referred to the morality police. 'We are responsible for not just the country's security but its safe running as well. Don't underestimate us.'

'I am not, agha,' Zohra forced herself to be respectful. 'But I am just a student. I am not a protester. I leave the university late, after my research, go to my room, go to class the next day. That's my routine.'

'Teymoori is far from the university. Why do you live there?'

'I like to live close to the city center.'

'Who do you live with?'

'I live alone. Don't you know that?'

He slapped her. 'I ask the questions. Clear?'

She nodded through her tears. She felt another trickle of blood from her lips, but she refused to feel it, refused to acknowledge he had hurt her.

'Where are your parents?'

'Sistan. They are dead. They had some land. They farmed. They were killed in a landslide. They wanted me to be educated and escape the village. I sold the land after they passed away, came to Tehran, worked several jobs and funded my education. You are Sepah. Surely you must have read my file.'

She regretted the gibe the moment the words left her.

He slapped her hard and then fist-punched her in the belly.

She fell to the floor gasping and shrieked when he yanked her by her hair.

'You have a spark,' he snarled. 'I like that. I like my women to have courage.' He started unbuckling his belt.

'NO!' she screamed when she read his intention and scrambled away.

'Scream. Shout,' he taunted. 'No one will come to your rescue.' He started unzipping his fly.

'Please,' Zohra cried desperately. 'I beg you.'

'Go ahead. I will ask you to beg in a different way—'

His phone rang.

15

'Yes,' the Sepah officer snarled, accepting the call without glancing at the screen.

He straightened immediately at the voice on the other end. 'Balle, agha. Balle.'

He nodded, ended the call and pocketed the phone. He zipped himself up, buckled his belt and slapped her again in cold fury.

He caught her elbow and marched her out into the hallway.

Zohra whimpered and sobbed as she stumbled along with him. She saw Leila and Aisha brought out of their rooms.

The three of them were shoved into their cell and its door locked.

Zohra took one step inside, then two. Her body throbbed with pain. Her stomach felt like a mule had kicked her. Her lips were swollen, bleeding and her ears rang from the blows. The two other women were in a similar state.

'He,' she swallowed, 'tried to rape me.'

'Me, too,' Leila nodded.

'He threatened me with it,' Aisha said.

Zohra broke down. She fell into their arms and sobbed and

felt them cry too. She felt the other protesters gather around them and hold them close.

'Why,' she asked when she had recovered, 'did they let us go? They didn't let the other women go. They have disappeared.'

'I don't know khahar. My officer got a call and he stopped his questioning after that.'

'It was the same for me as well.'

Zohra didn't know what to make of it. She was alive. Unmolested. That gave her some hope.

I didn't tell him my secret even though he hit me so hard.

Her insides twisted.

Would I have held out if he raped me?

16

'Who asked you to interrogate them?'

The questioner was dressed in military uniform. The two stars and two crossing wheat plants on them indicated he was a major general.

He was that. Mehrdad Gholamreza was the Commander of the Islamic Revolutionary Guard Corps. IRGC to the Western world, also known as Revolutionary Guards. Sepah to the citizens of the country.

It was a branch of the Iranian Armed Forces but in recent years, it had grown so powerful that its influence was apparent in every aspect of Iranian society. It was said to have more than a quarter-of-a-million active military personnel, but the exact figures were a closely guarded secret.

Gholamreza wasn't happy. His office in Tehran was in an anonymous government building in Moniriyeh. Only the armed guards at the entrance and the elaborate security checks indicated that someone of importance occupied the building.

Brigadier General Saeed Naser felt like squirming but didn't show any expression. He was head of Basij, a para-military branch of Sepah, which was comprised of volunteers. The division enforced state control over society, provided law enforcement, enforced morals and was pervasive in every town.

Naser, Deputy Chief of Sepah, was widely regarded as Gholamreza's successor. It wasn't an automatic promotion once the latter stepped down but within the corridors of power and influence, he was a shoo-in.

Basij was a high-profile outfit as well, but despite his seniority, the Brigadier General knew his place. Gholamreza ruled with absolute power and fear. Those who failed were severely punished and often killed regardless of how high up they were in the organization.

He had no favorites and treated all his commanders with the same attitude. Ruthless efficiency and contempt. Respect was an emotion he reserved only for the supreme leader, the president and a few others.

'It was a mistake, agha,' Naser said. 'The Sepah on the street were overzealous. My orders were to hold protesters for the night and release them in the morning.'

'You have seen the American TV news? They are reporting that we assaulted and raped the women on Sattar Khan Street.'

Naser swallowed. 'The women were held, yes. Some of them were taken away—'

'Stop,' Gholamreza whispered. 'I don't want to know the details. Can they be returned?'

'They can, but they might talk about what happened to them.'

'That should not happen. Deal with it.'

Naser nodded. He knew what the order meant. The protesters who had been raped would be disposed of to human-trafficking rings. They would be smuggled to Turkey and various other countries where they would remain as sex slaves. No one would believe their stories even if they talked.

Sepah was good at making inconvenient men and women disappear. Sometimes, children too.

'Where are they now?'

'In Tajrish, in a government office.'

'That's an affluent district.'

'Which is why I chose it,' Naser allowed a trace of pride to creep into his voice. 'No one will suspect we have prisoners there.'

'Move them away immediately. The media is sniffing a story. The reporters will check out every public office to see if the women are there. Take them out of the city and release them. Threaten them that if they go to the press, they and their families will regret it.'

'Yes, agha.' Naser smiled. Threats and violence appealed to him.

'Those officers who questioned them ... transfer them too.'

'They are good men.'

'I don't doubt that, but I don't want the media to know about that. Do you realize how much attention this has gotten?' Gholamreza never raised his voice. His eyebrow lifted and his voice went cold if he wanted to emphasize a point, as it did now. 'I got a call from the supreme leader's office. I had to lie to his people, saying we don't have the women. I am meeting him in the afternoon and I am sure he will ask again.'

He reached for a file and flipped it open, indicating that the meeting was over.

Naser got to his feet, nodded and went to the door.

'Saeed,' the commander said sharply.

'Yes, agha?'

'Monitor the women after they have been released. We need to know what they do.'

'Yes, agha.'

17

'Let's go. Move.' Two guards entered the cell, slapping their canes on the walls.

The protesters got up uncertainly.

'Go where?' Leila asked nervously.

The guard slashed her shoulder with his stick. She shrieked and fell back in the arms of several protesters.

'Don't ask questions!' the guard yelled. 'Do as we say.'

Zohra squeezed herself in the middle of the group and followed the men out into the hallway. They went to the front of the building where a van awaited.

It's some kind of office, she blinked rapidly in the sunlight, taking in the walled yard and the gated security. *Doesn't look like there is anyone else here*.

'Get in. This is not a picnic.'

'Tell us where we are going,' Shabnam asked and got a slap. None of them protested again. They climbed into the vehicle which had no windows. They heard the van start and it shook on its shocks as it drove out of the building.

Zohra tried to find cracks in the body and between the doors.

'What are you doing?' Maryam asked.

'Trying to see where we were held.'

'It's no use. I am sure we are in Tehran but now ...' she trailed off fearfully.

Zohra gave up when she found the van was sealed tight. She tried to count the turns the vehicle took but lost count after a while. Her eyes grew heavy and she dozed for a while when a sudden rattle woke her up.

'Where are we?'

'Still in the van,' Leila said with a half-smile. 'We are still in the city. You can hear the honks. Looks like there's lot of traffic.'

'It must be the morning rush hour,' Abida said, 'which means we spent the entire night in that building.'

'We should try to escape,' Zohra said. 'There are only two men in the van. The driver and the other guard. We can rush them, as soon as they open the door.'

'They might have guns.'

'We didn't see them. They were carrying sticks.'

'They might have hidden them in the cab.'

'Escape and go where?' another woman asked. 'They know where we live. They know everything about us.'

Zohra bit her lip. She hadn't thought it through.

'Let us see where we go,' Shabnam squeezed her forearm. 'We can decide then.'

'What if they are taking us out of town where they can rape or kill us? Or send us to some sex gang? You know what Sepah and Basij are capable of.'

All the women fell silent.

'Let us see what happens when the van stops,' Shabnam said strongly. 'We should be prepared, however, ready to act instantly.'

'Balle,' many of the protesters agreed.

Zohra went back to her somnolent state. Her body ached from the jostling of the road. It felt like they had been on the road for hours.

After what felt like an eternity, the driver slammed on the brakes, sending the van careening.

The women squashed against one another. Some of them cried out and pounded the van's body.

A chorus of horns sounded from outside and something crashed into the side of the van.

Its inside buckled. It skidded sideways.

Zohra clung to a woman, screaming, as she watched in horror the metal of the van tear and felt the vehicle sliding and rising on two wheels. She could hear several horns blaring outside above the shrieking and yelling of the women. A head crashed into her face cutting open her split lips. Someone caught her shoulder and squeezed hard. A woman screamed in her ear. She too was shouting and then she saw it.

'THE DOORS!' She caught hold of the nearest woman and shook her to get her attention. 'They have unlocked. SHABNAM, MARYAM, LEILA, THIS IS OUR CHANCE.'

The women surged towards it and kicked it open.

The doors swung wide to reveal a busy Tehran intersection.

Their van was tipped on its side, resting precariously on a lamppost on the side walk. A truck had plowed into its side which had caused it to slide and its body to twist and tear.

The smells of burning rubber, gas fumes and the city. Shouts from a gathering crowd, many of whom were coming their way.

'Vanak Square,' one of the protesters shouted. 'That's where we are.'

Zohra got onto the street. She stumbled as she lost her footing. She caught hold of the nearest woman to steady herself. It was Leila.

They turned to look at the cab. Its doors were smashed in. They saw movement inside it on the side mirror.

'GO!' Shabnam screamed.

They scattered at her yell.

Zohra caught Leila's hand and ran down Valiasr Street. She heard someone shout behind her, but she didn't look back. They went past fancy stores and barged through pedestrians and shoppers.

'Here', Leila tugged her hand and guided her into Sixteenth Street and then Gandhi Street and into a maze of alleys and busy roads until they came to Nowruz Park where they checked that no one was following them or paying attention to them.

'We got away,' Leila gasped, flopping onto the grass.

'Yes,' Zohra panted. She wiped sweat from her face and looked around.

But for how long? She wondered fearfully.

18

T*unisia*

'BERGES DU LAC,' MEGHAN ANNOUNCED WHEN THEY ENTERED Tunis in the evening. 'Upscale neighborhood. Villas and several embassies overlooking Lake of Tunis. Aziz has got his place there in an un-named alley off Rue De L'lle De Java.'

She pronounced the street name perfectly. All of them were fluent in several world languages and before any mission to a new country, they made it a point to learn conversational skills in the local lingo. Regular visits to linguists in New York during their down times kept their skills refreshed.

'Place!' Beth snorted. 'It feels like a palace.' She held her screen up to show the white-washed villa which was enclosed by a ten-foot concrete wall. Lush front and rear gardens. A large swimming pool at the back, a smaller roof-top pool and a red Ferrari on the driveway.

Zeb took it in briefly and then focused on his driving. Highway A1 that cut through the city and branched out into several arterial roads at a busy intersection. Tunis Nippon Garden to their left. A few villas dotting the landscape. Several signboards in French, a legacy of the country's colonization.

Berbers, the Ottoman Empire, the French, everyone came here. The country had one of the highest per capita GDP on the continent and that showed in the clean, wide streets and the infrastructure in the capital.

'How did you get that photograph?' He overtook a travel coach and entered Avenue Principale, which was a quieter street that ran through the affluent neighborhood.

'Police files,' she chortled. 'The National Guard has an extensive dossier on Aziz. Looks like he isn't as low-key as he thinks he is.'

'His neighbors will know about him. This place is full of embassies and upscale homes. Many places will have private security,' Zeb said, glancing at the street signs. He passed Olympysky Club. The lake to their right. Fancy yachts at their moorings. Brightly lit. He took the next right and entered the neighborhood.

'Aziz might still have some heavy-hitters with him,' Bwana's voice rumbled in their earpieces. 'We should not underestimate him.'

'We won't,' Zeb navigated to the outside of a restaurant on Avenue De La Bourse where several vehicles were parked on the grassy bank off the sidewalk. He turned off the ignition and ran his fingers through his hair. 'Drone recon. We wait for night and then attack.'

'What about me?' Petrov asked.

'You'll stay here.' He sent a pin to Bear and Broker's phones, climbed out and stretched.

'I'll stay with him,' Chloe smiled faintly. 'Y'all go on.'

Zeb went down the sidewalk with the twins who carried their backpacks with them. Bwana and Roger behind them.

None of them carried their HKs. Those would be visible.

They had their Glocks and knives, spare magazines and protective armor beneath their vests.

'Now,' the Texan drawled when a black BMW rolled up to the restaurant and spilled out several attractive women, 'that's the life.'

'You can join them if you wish,' Beth sniggered.

'Let me think,' he looked at the sky and made a show of frowning. 'Taking down some hardcases or charming some beautiful people. The latter ... I can do that anywhere. It comes naturally to me. A cross I have to bear.' He grinned when Meghan made a rude noise. 'But the former ... nope, I'll come with you. You'll need all the help you get.'

Zeb put away his shades and sent the location of Aziz's villa to Broker. He glanced at the lake when a woman's laugh came to them. A soft, liquid sound that took him back instantly to the days when he had a wife and a young child.

We went to Morocco. Same weather. Similar yachts. The world faded as he remembered his wife's dancing eyes and chuckle. He felt Beth's hand on his forearm and Meghan squeeze his right shoulder.

'You have us,' the younger twin said, reading his mind.

He swallowed and nodded. 'I know.'

'We are your family,' Meghan didn't let go of his shoulder.

'I know.'

The memories faded and the world returned. Berges du Lac. Rue De L'lle De Java, ahead of them. They turned into the street. No one else on the sidewalk. Aziz's villa visible, looming over the other residences. The mission returned.

19

'Drone,' Zeb said.

'Way ahead of you,' Beth smirked. 'It's in the air.'

He stiffened when two figures emerged from the shadows of the street and relaxed when he identified Bear and Broker.

'How did you get here so quickly?'

'We've been here for a while,' the elder operator's teeth flashed. 'Beth sent us the villa's coordinates long before you did.'

'You did a recon?'

'We walked past the villa. Metal gate set in the concrete wall. No outside guards. Cameras all over.'

'He'll have firepower inside. He'll be alert since he'll have known by now the second chopper failed. Let's see how many men he has with him,' Zeb leaned against the wall and watched the screen over Beth's shoulder.

'I'll join Chloe,' Bear tapped him lightly on the shoulder and left.

Zeb nodded absently as he watched the drone's feed emerge. The couple, who were romantic partners as well, were the two best close-protection operators he had come across.

The villa came up on the screen. Well-lit from the outside.

No Ferrari in sight. Underwater lights in the pool. A bathrobe on a lounge chair. Trimmed plants and hedges. A fountain in a corner.

An alley at the back where there was a service entrance, another metal gate, set in the concrete wall. *That looks like a privately-owned drive for deliveries to the villa.*

A shadow moved in the front. *That's a guard. Another one near the door.*

'Eight, no, nine men,' Beth was way ahead of him in counting the bodies and their thermal prints. 'Four outside, two at the front and two at the rear. Five inside. Three on the ground floor and two upstairs. A tenth body is in the bedroom that overlooks the pool at the back. From its shape and size that's got to be Aziz.'

'All of them are armed. Look like AK-12s,' Zeb pointed out.

'Why does Aziz need that much protection?' Roger asked.

'He's got offshore accounts,' Meghan coiled her hair behind her head in a pony tail and slipped a band around it. 'We didn't do a deep dive into him, but I'm guessing a lot of his business is illegal. His connections to the Maliks ... he could be into human trafficking as well.'

Zeb tightened his jaw at that. They had come across various criminals and gangs. Russian Mafia, Mexican cartels, arms dealers, killers, money launderers but the people traders were the worst.

'No mercy,' he replied tightly. 'We take the guards out, extract Aziz and get away. We can't get into a firefight. Someone will raise the alarm and given that this is an upscale neighborhood, the police response will be prompt.'

He looked up and down the street, his eyes lingering on a boom lift that was on the left side of the street, near a street light. It bore the name of a local maintenance company.

'Bwana,' he jerked his head at the crane. 'The aerial platform on that one is at a height. It might overlook Aziz's villa. Think you can—'

'I don't think. I *know* I can,' the African American's teeth flashed and he went down the sidewalk swiftly. 'In position,' he confirmed moments later.

Zeb tried to see him on the platform, but its protective railing obstructed his view.

'EMP to take out all cameras and the security system.' He unzipped his vest and removed a Faraday pouch. 'In five beats.' He placed his cell-phone and earpiece in it and pocketed it. His friends mimicked the move. Beth brought back the drone and threw a sheet over it from her backpack to protect it from the electro-magnetic waves.

Broker and Roger hurried to the alley at the back while Zeb and Meghan drifted to the front.

He counted his breaths as they neared the metal gate.

A soft pop came to them from the boom lift.

'NOW!' Zeb and Meghan ran full tilt at the wall.

20

Zeb and Meghan vaulted over it smoothly and landed soundlessly on the other side, ten meters apart.

One body on the front lawn, down from Bwana's shooting.

The guard at the door shot at them, his round flying harmlessly over their heads and slamming into the concrete wall.

Another pop came from the boom lift, audible over the shouting from inside the house and the rifle fire in the rear garden. The heavy at the door collapsed.

'I'll take the door,' Meghan panted and ran towards it, zigging and zagging.

Zeb raced towards a large window, unzipping a pouch from his waist to remove a pair of NVGs and wraparound headphones. He slipped them over his eyes and ears with his left hand.

The window shattered. *That's Bwana's shooting.*

He brought out a flashbang from his pocket, lobbed it through the broken window and looked away. The grenade went off, filling the room with white light and an earsplitting bang that was muffled by his head gear.

The front door blew out from Meghan's explosive while simultaneously another flashbang went off in the living room.

That's Broker or Roger.

Zeb climbed through the window, his HK in hand. A shadow to his right, weaving through the smoke. It was Meghan, identifiable by the markings on her vest.

Another shadow moved at his ten-o-clock. A man yelled and fired. Zeb dropped to the floor and took him out with a short burst into the body mass.

'GO UP,' Roger roared. 'All guards are down here. We'll cover you.'

Zeb hurried to the stairs at the far end of the living room. He felt Meghan close in behind him.

Marbled steps. Ornate metal banister. Shots came down from the landing above.

He felt a tap on his shoulder. Turned back to see Meghan point to his headphones. He slid the switch at the base.

'Jeez, Zeb,' Beth's voice came on exasperatedly. 'Took you long enough. Drone's in the air. I have a front-row view of what's going on inside. Two shooters on the upper floor. Bwana took one out. The other one, who's firing at you, is belly down on the floor. Bwana doesn't have a sight line to him. He's two meters to the right of the stairs. You go up, he'll chop you down.'

'Not if we can help it,' Zeb reached into his pocket and brought up another flashbang.

He hefted it in his hand. *Fifteen steps. They are smooth. Can't risk slipping on them.*

'Where's Aziz?'

'Barricaded in his bedroom,' Beth replied. 'He's tried his phones but they are down. He can't jump onto the rear lawn and escape. Roger and Broker have that covered.'

'We don't have much time,' Meghan warned.

'Yeah,' Zeb lobbed the flashbang up and over the stairs and followed it up with a second one.

They exploded seconds apart. Bright flashes painted the

walls of the house. He went up the stairs, keeping low and Meghan did the same.

A wild burst of firing from the shooter that stitched the wall where the stairs met the upper floor. A picture frame fell off its hanging. A flower vase shattered.

Zeb could hear the guard shrieking and cursing as he triggered.

'Wait,' Beth cautioned.

Zeb and Meghan ducked below the mouth of the stairs, waiting until the shooter's magazine ran out and then they burst up the steps, a meter separating them, Zeb in the lead, his HK swiveling to the right, the rifle bucking in his hand in a long burst as his head cleared the opening and then he saw the shooter through the smoke and his rounds riddled his body.

A bullet buzzed past his cheek and he glanced back in alarm.

'I'm good,' Meghan pushed him lightly forward.

He went onto the floor, crouch-walked to the fallen guard while she covered him.

'Dead,' he confirmed. He scanned the floor quickly. Couches, that were shredded from the shooting, another body on the tiled floor, two open doors which led to bedrooms and a third one to their right which was closed.

'That's the one. He's in there.' Beth guided him. He looked through a shattered window into the night sky but couldn't spot the drone.

'AZIZ,' he went to the side of the door and pounded on it with his HK's stock. 'Give up.'

A curse came from inside.

'Stand back,' he yelled.

'We'll have to do this the hard way.'

'Move,' Meghan ordered and planted a water-tamped explosive charge to the door. They waited at a safe distance on either side of it.

Windows rattled when it went off. The door buckled in from

the detonation, a large, jagged hole from where the charge had been placed.

Zeb heard a scream from inside the room. He kicked the door open and dived inside, firing high into the ceiling to warn Aziz.

He looked up from the plush carpet to take in the room.

Large bed. Mirrored ceiling. Walnut wardrobes on one wall. Half-open door to a bathroom. Soft lighting. A heavyset figure near a bedside table. Aziz!

'MOVE!' Beth shouted.

He rolled desperately just as a heavy chair landed where he had been.

Aziz, in striped pajama pants and shirt, threw himself across the bed and crashed into him.

Zeb grunted from his weight. He fell on his back and tossed away his HK. His head rocked from the man's fist. Another blow slammed into his headphones. Aziz was growling as he struck repeatedly with his bare hands, his eyes narrowed in rage.

Zeb had enough when a meaty fist slammed into the side of his neck.

He knuckle-jabbed into Aziz's throat and followed it up with a brutal side-of-the-palm chop to the man's neck.

Aziz fell back, gasping.

Zeb wriggled out from beneath him, picked up his HK and slammed it into his temple to knock the man out.

He caught the man by his shirt and dragged him across the carpet.

'You can't carry him?' Meghan checked the bathroom to confirm it was empty.

'Have you seen his size?' he protested.

She caught hold of Aziz beneath his armpits and helped him carry the man down.

'Hurry,' Roger joined them. He relieved Meghan and helped Zeb take the unconscious man through the broken door, out into the garden and through the front gate.

Bear and Chloe were waiting with their ride, its doors open.

Petrov made room expressionlessly when they shoved Aziz in the rear seat.

'Rendezvous outside the city,' Zeb told them. 'Beth will find a—'

'Done. An empty warehouse. I'll send the pin to your phones.'

Zeb checked on his friends. Broker and Roger were unharmed.

'Good shooting,' he told Bwana as the operator joined them.

'What's that?' he asked Meghan, pointing at the bag slung over her shoulder.

'Aziz's laptops and phones.'

He grinned ruefully. *They're always a couple of steps ahead of me.*

His smile faded as he led them out of the street at a fast jog. No one looked out of neighboring houses.

'The immediate ones will have lost their power when we EMP-ed Aziz's house,' Meghan read his glance. 'If they heard the shooting, they must have thought of staying indoors.'

A few cars on the Avenue De La Bourse. The restaurant was crowded and sounds of revelry came to them as they climbed into Zeb's ride.

'Our faces will be on some of the cameras,' Broker commented from the rear.

'We'll deal with as many as we can,' Meghan replied absently as she fingered one of Aziz's phones. 'My guess is Aziz is into a lot more than just trading carpets.'

Only one way to find out, Zeb stomped on the gas and drove out of the neighborhood.

21

The warehouse was in El Gorjani, in an industrial district which was filled with auto shops, metal sheet establishments, tire vendors and several other small manufacturers.

'This was on sale,' Beth muttered as Zeb drove into the front yard of the strip-mall-like front of the warehouse.

She went to the three security cameras, set her EMP gun to low range and burned them out. 'Meg and I will find a way to hack into its database and erase our images.'

Zeb went to the shutter and broke its locks with bolt cutters. He and Bwana rolled it up and entered it.

Concrete floor. High ceiling. Empty. Its lights worked.

'Perfect,' Bear said as he and Chloe carried Aziz in.

Roger found a wooden crate on which they shoved the businessman.

'Aziz,' Zeb spoke in Arabic. 'I saw your eyes flicker. I know you are pretending.'

'You could have told us,' Chloe flexed her shoulders, huffing in mock anger.

Aziz didn't respond.

Zeb sighed and emptied a bottle of water on his head.

The businessman jerked in shock. He gasped, spluttered, cursed and wiped his face. He glowered at them savagely.

'Do you know who I am?'

Zeb slapped him.

Aziz fell to the ground. He shook his head dazedly, got up slowly and sat heavily on the crate.

'What do you want?' he asked defiantly.

Zeb hit him again, savagely, remembering Farideh and Parvaneh's descriptions, about how the trafficking gang had treated them.

'We ask the questions. What was your deal with the Casbah Maliks? What did you ask them to do with the women? What were you planning to do with him?' He cocked his head at Petrov who was watching from behind.

'I don't know what you are talking about,' Aziz snarled. 'You kill my guards, kidnap me from my house ... do you know who you are dealing with?'

Bwana came forward before Zeb could respond. He drew out a wicked-looking knife and held it to the light. 'Shall I gut him?'

'No,' he answered himself. 'I'll start with his fingers. Rog, help me, will you?'

The Texan caught hold of Aziz's left hand and forced open his palm.

The businessman struggled and screamed when Roger snapped his little finger.

'Hey,' Bwana protested. 'I was going to cut it.'

'You can still do that.'

Bwana lunged forward and plunged the blade in Aziz's palm.

The businessman howled in agony and writhed on the ground when Roger let him go. He cupped his hand to his chest and rocked in pain as blood streamed from it.

Zeb watched silently. He felt no pity.

'Talk,' he said. 'What's your deal with the Maliks?'

Aziz sobbed louder. He kicked his legs out but didn't reply.

Bwana held up the bloodied knife in the light and took a threatening step forward.

'WAIT!' the businessman shrieked.

He propped himself on an elbow and shuddered. He drank greedily from the water bottle that Roger held to his mouth, swallowed and looked at them fearfully. 'I fund them.'

Zeb nodded. *I thought it would be something like that.*

Beth hissed angrily. Chloe made to go at Aziz, but Bear held her back.

'Keep talking,' Zeb ordered.

The Tunisian businessman jerked his head and spilled.

'They were into drugs and weapons. I used them to distribute those to different African countries, to warlords. I bought them in Europe and used them to move my product.'

'Product,' Broker scoffed incredulously.

Zeb held his hand up to silence his friend.

'Women ... I knew they were more profitable than guns or drugs. I knew how refugees moved from this continent to go to rich European countries. I got the Maliks to get into that line of work.'

'The way he speaks,' Meghan murmured softly so that only the operators could hear. 'It's like he's addressing business executives.'

'There must be some MBA school for criminals,' Bear said contemptuously.

'They kidnapped such refugees initially, from Somalia and other war-torn countries,' Aziz continued, 'and then I told them to look at countries like Iran, where women would be escaping it. I arranged contacts for them, with underground networks there to arrange passage for protesters.'

'How many other Iranian women did you sell?' Broker asked harshly.

'This was the first batch. We delivered several women to Europe safely. That was needed to build trust.'

Bear swore. He caught Aziz and hauled him up easily with

his left hand, slapped him with his right and dumped him onto the crate.

'We got it wrong,' he spun on his heel. 'It wasn't the Iranian gang that betrayed them.'

'Yeah,' Zeb replied. He looked pointedly at the knife in Bwana's hand.

Aziz followed his gaze. His moans died into a whimper and he resumed. 'There are wealthy clients in this continent, in the Middle East, Asia and even in Europe and America for young women. I had them lined up. The Maliks brought them to the desert. They were to be trucked out to Tunis where they would be loaded in a ship—'

'Never to be seen or heard of again,' Meghan cut in brutally.

Aziz didn't reply. His gaze dropped to the floor.

'And what of him?' Zeb jerked a shoulder in Petrov's direction. 'What did you plan to do with him? Where was your helicopter taking him? To the Russians?'

The Tunisian seemed to forget his injury momentarily. He stared at Zeb, perplexed. 'Why would I sell him to Russia? Iran was my client.'

22

'Iran?' Beth asked incredulously.

'Yes. Why did you think it was Russia?'

Aziz wriggled back on the crate when Bear moved threateningly. 'My client was Iran. Their government was interested in Petrov. They told me I should contact them if I came across him.'

'It was just a coincidence that Petrov contacted the Maliks for escape?'

'Yes. The first time I knew about him was when the gang told me they had a Russian passenger. I had Petrov's details with me, which my Iranian contact had sent. I told the Maliks I would take the general.'

Zeb looked at the Russian who looked as bewildered as them.

'I don't know why that country is interested in me,' the general told the operators in Russian. 'I didn't have any dealings with their government.'

'Where was the trade going to happen?' Zeb snapped at the Tunisian.

'In Turkey. I was to hand him over personally. That helicopter was to bring him from the desert to me here, and we were then going to fly to Istanbul.'

'Who would meet you there?'

'I don't know. I was to message a secure number when I flew out from here and confirm my arrival. Someone would contact me.'

'Who was your contact in the Iranian government?'

Aziz looked away.

Zeb lost his patience. He sprang at the Tunisian, caught his wounded palm and squeezed it hard. 'We're this close to killing you,' he snarled over the businessman's agonized yell. 'If you think you're going to negotiate some kind of deal with us, you are wrong. Tell us everything you know and we might let you live.'

'Kamal,' Aziz yelled. 'Major Mohsen Kamal. I've known him for a long time. I supplied him with drugs and women—'

'Iranian Army?'

'I don't know. I saw him in uniform only once and from his badges, I knew he was a major. That was our first meeting. It was arranged by a criminal gang I do business with in Tehran. He didn't tell me which regiment he was. He didn't give me any details. We never met again. All our communication now is through secure messaging.'

'How long have you known him?'

'Three years,' Aziz blew on his wound as if it would stem the bleeding. His pajama top was wet with blood and sweat. 'He pays well.'

'Does he know about these Iranian women?'

'No. I supplied him with Eastern European women.'

'Do you have his photograph?' Beth leaned forward.

Aziz shook his head. 'He would have killed me if I took his photograph. He is a dangerous man.'

'You are confident he was military?'

'Why would anyone wear an army uniform in Enghelab Golf Club? That's an exclusive one, members will know each other.'

'Was he going to meet you in Istanbul?'

'Yes.'

'How much was he paying for me?' Petrov asked.

'Half-a-million dollars.'

The Russian's face twisted in a bitter smile. 'I didn't know I was that important to Iran. No,' he switched to Russian at Zeb's probing look. 'I still don't know why they want me. I haven't heard of Kamal.'

The operators peppered Aziz with questions, but it was obvious the Tunisian had nothing more to give them.

Bwana wiped his knife on the businessman's pants and sheathed it in his thigh holster. He tore a strip off his shirt and bandaged the wound.

'You won't die,' he told the whimpering man.

'Stop,' Meghan told the operator when he was drawing his fist back to deliver a knock-out punch. 'We need to unlock his devices.'

She brought out two phones from the bag and held them to his face. Their home screens opened. She reset their passwords, stowed them away and brought out two laptops.

'Passwords,' she commanded.

Aziz didn't respond.

'You're a sucker for punishment, aren't you?' Bwana reached for his blade.

It got the desired response. The Tunisian typed on them laboriously, moaning and cursing all the while and sat back when he had finished.

Meghan's fingers flew over their keyboards. She slammed them shut after a few moments and got to her feet. 'He's all yours.'

Zeb touched Bwana on the shoulder when the African-American started bunching his fist.

'We don't kill him?' his friend asked.

'No. It's his lucky day.' They zip-tied Aziz and gagged his mouth.

'What do we do with him?' Bwana asked in a low voice when they drew away from their prisoner.

Zeb held his hand up and dialed a number.

It was answered on the second ring.

'Achi,' brother, a strong voice answered in Hebrew, alertly despite the late hour. 'What can I do for you?'

Zeb smiled involuntarily. Avichai Levin, Director of Mossad, always took his call whatever time it was.

'We have a package for you.'

'Dead or alive?'

'Alive. Why would I give you a dead body?'

'Maybe to use us as your personal disposal service?'

'Not this time. He's in Tunisia.'

'That's not far. I have a team nearby.'

Which means he probably has someone in the country, Zeb grinned.

'Who is he?'

'A businessman.'

'Why would that interest me?'

'He does business with the Iranian army.'

Levin's voice turned serious. 'What kind of business?'

'Drugs and women. That's what he claims. We think we've squeezed everything out of him but—'

'We have our ways. Send me the location details. Iran. Zeb, what are you getting into?'

'I don't know. We came here to extract Petrov—'

Levin sucked his breath sharply. 'You got him?'

'Ken, yes, but that led us to Karim Aziz, whose real business is running women, drugs and weapons.'

He broke it down quickly for the Mossad head, who was not only a personal friend but was also security cleared by Clare to receive sensitive intel as long as it was in their mutual interests.

'The women are safe?' his friend asked.

'Yeah. They'll be on their way to Germany in the morning.'

Levin made a relieved sound. 'You'll share Petrov's intel?'

'Clare will. But—'

'Yes, I know. I'll tell you what we get from Aziz.'

'Who was that?' Petrov asked curiously when Zeb hung up.

'Mossad.'

The Russian's incredulous expression drew chuckles from the operators.

'Look at Aziz,' Bear flicked his eyes at the Tunisian who had a horrified expression on his face. 'He's wishing we had killed him.'

23

They secured the warehouse with new padlocks and Zeb led their two-vehicle convoy out of El Gorjani.

'Airport?' Meghan asked him when the signs to Tunis-Carthage International Airport flashed past.

'Yeah,' he said. 'Let's send Petrov home.'

'I hope you don't mean Moscow by that,' the general smiled wryly.

Zeb chuckled. 'No, America. Iran,' he prompted. 'Any recollection? What would be their interest in you?'

'I have been thinking about that. You're aware Iran is supporting my country in the Ukraine invasion.'

'What?' Broker pretended to be surprised. 'You mean they've been lying all along when they said they are neutral?'

Petrov smiled briefly. 'Da. That's their official stance. We all know that's not true. Iran's troops are on the ground in Crimea. They supplied my country with drones which are carrying out attacks in Ukraine. They want NATO to be beaten and America and the West to be humiliated. Besides, they want Russian help with their nuclear weapons program. You are aware that the oil trade between the countries is deepening, despite your country's sanctions?'

'Yeah,' Beth said. 'We might have read some intel on all of that.'

'Which makes me wonder what's Iran's game? Did they intend to return me to Moscow? That would make the Kremlin happy, but the relations between the two governments is already close. There is no need to sweeten ...' He trailed off. His eyes took on a faraway look.

'What?' Zeb demanded. The airport drew closer. An airliner thundered over their heads, heading to its destination.

'There was a meeting,' Petrov whispered. 'Now I remember. It happened late last year, when I was still in the Kremlin's favor. I, along with the SVR and GRU heads and a few other senior generals met with Mehrdad Gholamreza.'

Zeb braked hard in surprise and got a loud, angry honk from a vehicle behind them. The car overtook them with the driver flashing an angry look.

'Gholamreza?' Zeb asked. 'The Revolutionary Guards Corps's commander?' He resumed driving and flashed his indicator to take the turn into the airport.

Petrov nodded. 'Da. It was a highly secret visit. It didn't get any publicity.' He smiled faintly. 'I am sure even your agencies didn't know of it.'

'We didn't. Why was he there?'

'Drones. He was discussing how his organization could deliver them through the Basij network.'

'Their volunteers move freely, often crossing borders. They could transport the drones.'

'Yes, that was his proposal. We accepted it. One of the generals, Kovalev, asked how we could help in return.'

Zeb stopped him with an upraised palm. He took an unmarked lane and parked their Range Rover in an anonymous-looking lot, with Beth guiding him. Bear nosed his ride next to theirs and they made their way swiftly to the VIP terminal, surrounding Petrov.

A uniformed Tunisian officer at the entrance. A suit next to him.

'Bob?' Beth asked him.

'Yeah.' A distinct American Midwestern twang. He didn't offer a second name and neither did Beth ask for one. He showed an identity card which she compared to a message on her phone. She then photographed him and spent a few seconds analyzing his biometrics.

'You're careful,' he grunted.

'Always.'

The Tunisian officer watched impassively as if he had seen several high-value-personnel handovers.

He might have, Zeb suppressed a smile. *Several countries' agencies prefer Tunisia for extraction.*

Bob took them down a carpeted hallway. 'No immigration. I've taken care of that.' He waved at a lounge that overlooked a private runway. 'That's our Gulfstream out there.'

Beth confirmed its tail number, spoke to the pilots and verified their identities.

'All good,' she thumbs-upped at Zeb.

'Will I see you again?' Petrov shook their hands.

'Could happen,' Zeb smiled briefly at him. He checked Bob wasn't in hearing distance and lowered his voice. 'Kovalev.'

'Da, I never finished telling you about that meeting. Gholamreza said our countries were already cooperating. The general then asked him how the nuclear program was coming along. The IRGC man smiled. He said there were some delays but Iran wasn't worried.'

He smoothed his clothing. His expression turned somber, his eyes bleak. 'He said they were working on something that would be better.'

'A better nuclear weapon?' Bwana frowned. 'We or Mossad would have sniffed it out.'

'He didn't say. He didn't refer to it again. The moment he

said it, his expression changed, as if he knew he had said too much.'

'That's why,' Zeb connected the dots, 'Iran wants you. You heard him say it. You are not in Moscow anymore. Iran is worried their secret might leak.'

'Petrov doesn't know anything more than that comment,' Broker objected.

'He doesn't, but that conversation is enough to activate intelligence agencies around the world to sniff in different directions.'

He watched a private aircraft land and taxi to the terminal.

'All of us have been focused on Iran's nuclear weapon program,' he rasped. 'What if this 'something else' isn't one?'

24

They stayed back in the lounge after the Gulfstream had taken off with Petrov.

Zeb glanced around. Bob had left. A wealthy-looking couple at the drinks counter. No one else around.

'Clare?' Meghan guessed.

'Yeah.'

She dialed their boss while Beth brought out her phone and turned on a white-noise-generating app. It turned the space around them into a make-shift SCIF, Sensitive Compartmented Information Facility where they could converse freely with their director. The program would distort their conversation to electronic surveillance or to any recording equipment.

'Petrov's on his way, ma'am,' Zeb began when the director came on line.

'The Iranians want him,' Beth took over. She briefed the Agency head quickly. 'Another weapon, ma'am. Petrov was categoric in what Gholamreza said.'

They waited for Clare to mull it over.

'Petrov is highly regarded by not just the Pentagon but by our allies too,' she said at last. 'He was a moderate amongst a bunch of hawks. No wonder he fell out with the Kremlin. I believe him. We have analyzed Gholamreza to no end. He's smart, very capable, and an ideologist. He has an intense hatred for the West. All that's why he was appointed to lead the Revolutionary Guards. But he's also got an enormous ego which he hides. That boast in Moscow in that meeting ... his mask slipped there. I believe him. We have to take this threat seriously. I'll brief the president right away. I'm sure he'll want to convene the National Security Council. I'll inform Catlyn and Daniel too.'

Catlyn Feder, Director of the CIA. Daniel Klouse, National Security Advisor to the president. Both of them were friends and supporters of the Agency.

'Get back home,' she ordered. 'It won't be hard for the Iranians to work out what happened in Tunis. The National Guard has descriptions out. White men and women and one African American. They don't have photographs, thankfully.'

'We deleted a lot, ma'am,' Meghan offered.

'And I got Catlyn to get her team to do the rest,' she smiled. 'Still, it's dangerous for you.'

'The guard at the airport terminal didn't stop us,' Bear commented.

'That's probably because Bob bribed him. No. Don't stay there anymore. Get back home.'

Zeb didn't reply.

'No!' She picked up on his silence. 'Don't even think of it.'

'Ma'am,' he checked the couple. They were still at the drinks counter. The operators weren't attracting attention. 'We have a way in.'

'How's that?' she asked sharply.

'We go to the Istanbul meeting, capture the handover team and go from there.'

'And then? You'll go to Iran? I will not allow that. Don't you realize you are one of the most wanted men in Iran after you pulled that stunt with Mostofi?'

She referred to an earlier mission when they had captured

the previous head of the Revolutionary Guards in Tehran and brought him back stateside.

'That was a cool mission, ma'am,' Roger drawled appreciatively. 'We got him in their backyard, under their noses.'

'Which is why it isn't safe for you in Iran. They aren't forgetting what you pulled off anytime soon. Do you think Gholamreza doesn't know about you? He'll have extensive files on all of you. Why are we even having this discussion? Even if I greenlight it, the Revolutionary Guards know that Petrov has been captured.'

'No, ma'am, they don't,' Meghan looked up from her phone. 'I checked the news reports. There are reports of a shootout in Berges du Lac, with vague descriptions of us. Aziz's disappearance is not mentioned. I checked the National Guards' system and he's not in it either. The police are keeping the information tight for whatever reason.'

'You hacked into the National Guards system?'

'No comment, ma'am.'

'Why am I not surprised?'

'We have Aziz's phones and laptops. Beth and I could easily make it look like he escaped with Petrov to a safe house and that the Istanbul meeting will happen.'

'What if the National Guards reveal he is missing?'

'That will play in our hands. There's another reason for us to be in Iran.'

Zeb looked Meghan sharply, alerted by her tone. 'What?'

'Werner got a message from one of our burner phones.'

There were a few people around the world who had helped them in their missions or whom they had gotten close to. The operators provided burners to them as a means of reaching out in emergencies.

'In Iran?' Zeb ran down a mental list of people who had the devices in that country. There weren't many. 'Who was it? Shabnam Vakili, the cook who helped us?'

'No, she didn't help us in any mission.'

'She?' That narrowed the names even further. 'It's—'

'Yes. Here. Read it. I had to confirm the burner was still in Tehran and had to run some security checks and then we got busy with Aziz which is why I didn't mention it earlier.

The rest of her words didn't register with Zeb. He read the message.

Brother, I don't know who else to reach. I need your help. Please save me.

'Zohra,' he whispered.

Zeb pictured her immediately. *She was twenty when we met her. First year of university. She was studying chemistry.*

Zohra was the same build as Chloe. Petite. Shorter than the twins by several inches, but what she lacked in height she made up in personality. Her flashing eyes and ready smile warmed those around her.

The details came back to him.

25

Tehran, Past

IT WAS A RECON MISSION IN TEHRAN TO CAPTURE MOSTOFI. They hadn't gone hot yet. They were still in the planning stage.

They had been staying in Jomhouri, a neighborhood near the University of Tehran.

Zeb remembered their going out for dinner. Bwana and Roger arguing on the choice of restaurants. The Texan had finally agreed that they sample local cuisine and they proceeded to an upscale-looking one on Golshan Street.

It was busy. Many men. One family. Two couples, one of whom was Zohra and her boyfriend.

They were seated next to them.

It started off with loud whispers, when they were in the middle of their dinner.

Zeb snatched a glance at the neighboring table.

The boyfriend leaning forward, his face twisted in anger, the woman looking down at her plate.

'Eat,' Beth kicked him beneath the table. 'Not our business.'

He nodded and resumed. Made small talk and laughed at Roger and Broker's jokes but couldn't help overhearing the nearby conversation.

The young man seemed to be insisting that university was corrupting her and she was defending her education.

'You don't respect me,' he slapped the table.

Everyone looked at them. The woman flushed. She gave a nervous smile. 'That's not true. Let's finish our dinner and go. We can talk later.'

'See, you are giving me orders again. All this will change when we get married.'

An older man at another table nodded. 'Yes, that's how it should be.'

'We haven't discussed that,' the woman said softly. Her hands twisted nervously. 'Let's pay the bill and go. Please.'

'We will go when I am ready,' the man snarled, emboldened by the other diner's support. 'And why aren't you wearing your chador? I have told you so many times - WHERE ARE YOU GOING? DON'T RUN AWAY WHEN I AM TALKING TO YOU.'

The woman shoved her chair back as tears ran down her face. She fled the restaurant without another word.

'Teach her a lesson, baradar,' the elder man suggested. 'Women are forgetting their place. They are watching too much TV and Western movies.'

'I will,' the boyfriend said harshly, dropped several bills on the table and went out.

Zeb lost his appetite. He looked at the older man whose companions seemed to agree with him. They were shaking their heads with glances to the door.

He thought he heard a shout from outside and that decided for him.

'I want a hot tea. Quickly. As hot as you can serve it,' he told the server who nodded and disappeared into the kitchen.

'I can't—' he began, looking at his friends.

'Neither can we,' Broker wiped his lips, tossed his napkin to the table and laid several rials on the table enough to cover a generous tip.

Meghan, Beth and Chloe stood up, their faces tight.

'We'll deal with this,' the elder twin said and they went out.

The server returned and poured the boiling-hot beverage in a cup.

'That's too ...oh,' Bear trailed off when he worked out his friend's intention.

Zeb took the cup and headed to the entrance. He made a show of looking through the glass door and tripped. He stumbled and took several fumbling steps to regain his balance.

Hot tea spilled from his cup and splashed on the older men.

They jerked at the contact and shouted in agony.

'I am sorry,' Zeb made a contrite face. 'I am sorry. I was so clumsy.'

'YOU FOOL, CAN'T YOU SEE WHERE YOU ARE GOING?' The man who had commented, yelled, as he dabbed at his face with a wet napkin.

'I am sorry,' Zeb said again and noted with grim satisfaction the reddened skin on the diner's neck and forearms.

He went out of the restaurant followed by his friends.

The loud shouts in the nearby alley guided them. They hurried into it and slowed down at the scene.

The boyfriend was doubled up in agony. His lips were split. His right arm was twisted weirdly.

'He hit her,' Meghan said harshly. 'We asked him to stop and he told us to shut up and go away or he would beat us up too. She asked us to help her.'

'He won't hit her again,' Beth snarled.

'Let's make sure he doesn't have any children as well,' Bwana growled and kicked the man in his groin.

26

The young man crumpled with an agonized groan and lay on the ground curled tightly.

Zeb bent over him and searched his pockets. He withdrew his wallet and photographed his driving license on his phone.

He caught the boyfriend's hair and yanked his head up. 'Stay away from her. We'll come to know if you harass her or even approach her. We'll break more than just one arm if you do that. If you get someone else to hound her, we'll destroy you.' He shook the man's head savagely. 'Do you understand?'

'Balle, balle,' the boyfriend sobbed. 'Please let me go.'

Zeb dropped his wallet on his chest and stood back.

The young man stumbled to his feet, moaning softly. He staggered to the mouth of the alley where Bear and Broker were standing implacably. He shrank, edged past them and disappeared into the night.

Beth, Meghan and Chloe went to the woman who collapsed in their hug. Her body shook as she cried silently against the elder twin's shoulder.

She stood back finally and wiped her face. 'Moteshaker,' thank you. She said it several times. Her body trembled and her hands shook. 'I thought he was going to ... he has hit me before.'

Zeb's fists bunched involuntarily at that.

'He became more and more controlling. Dominating. Telling me what to do and how I should dress and how university was a waste. You heard him in the restaurant,' she sniffled. 'I wanted to break it off. I didn't have the courage. Moteshaker. You helped me.'

'Let's get away,' Bear warned softly from the mouth of the alley. 'We're drawing attention.'

Zeb nodded. 'Is there someplace safe you can go? I don't think you should stay at your place tonight—'

'I will be safe in my home, baradar.' She attempted a shaky smile and went with them out of the alley. 'I rent a small apartment less than ten minutes away, on Molla Ali Street. The landlord is a police officer. He has many brothers, all of them are in the police. Arash won't dare to come to my place.'

'We'll walk you to your apartment,' Beth said firmly in a tone that brooked no argument.

'Moteshaker,' the woman said. 'It's not needed. I will be okay—'

'We're not asking,' the younger sister smiled warmly to take the sting out of her words. 'We'll sleep better knowing you're safe.'

The woman stopped on Golshan Street and took them in. Her hair whipped in the breeze and her body still shook from shock.

Zeb felt her penetrating gaze and imagined how they appeared to her. Five men and three women, all of them dressed casually but there was no mistaking the menacing air that clung to them after the incident. Her eyes lingered on Bwana and Bear, the largest of the operators.

'Who are you khaharan, baradarha?' she whispered.

'Friends,' Beth chuckled. 'Come, let's go to your home.'

She introduced herself on the way. Zohra Hashimi, a first-year student at the University of Tehran. 'I am studying Chemistry,' she said proudly. 'I want to complete my Masters and then maybe a PhD and go into research.'

Her eyes grew wide when they introduced themselves. 'You are Americans? You speak Farsi so well.'

'We travel a lot,' Zeb replied lightly. 'Our work takes us all over the world. It helps to pick up the local language.'

Meghan told her their cover story, that they were security consultants who advised big companies.

Zohra grew animated. She asked about their lives in New York, listening intently. 'Someday I too will travel,' she said determinedly and pointed at her building. 'That's where I live. On the first floor.

'No, you have to come in,' she insisted when they made to leave. She took them up to her first-floor apartment and grinned when Bear and Bwana had to duck through the door.

Zeb looked around appreciatively at the apartment. A living room at the end of which was the kitchen. A bedroom and a bathroom. It was small, but it was cozy and neat. Sheets tidily folded on the bed. No dirty dishes in the sink.

'Your parents?' Broker eyed a photograph on a wall.

'Yes,' Zohra nodded as she served them chai. 'They are no more. We lived in Sistan. They had their farm there. It was a simple but hard life. Agriculture is so dependent on the weather. They always wanted me to get away from the village. Be educated. They died in a landslide. I sold their farm and came here, to Tehran. I worked in a beauty parlor and did several other jobs. Those, along with the small funds I had from selling their estate, paid for my schooling and university. I still work part-time to cover my living costs.'

'You had no help?' Roger asked, impressed.

'No, baradar. I am an only child. My parents didn't have any relatives either. I stayed in a girl's hostel, enrolled in a good school ... I was lucky. I got good-paying jobs. The salon I worked in didn't question how old I was. The owner would have been arrested if anyone found out I was underage.' She eyed the photograph. 'I looked older than my age in those days. Still, I am lucky. There are so many other women in my country who don't have it as good as me.'

'When did all this happen?' Zeb sipped his tea. Zohra had made it just right. Not too sweet and not bland either. He noticed there was no self-pity in her narration. She didn't go into her struggles. *She isn't seeking sympathy.*

'Four years ago. I am twenty,' her cheeks dimpled. Her smile faded. 'Arash wanted me to marry him this year. I was against it. I wasn't thinking of marrying for a long time.'

'Forget him,' Roger said firmly. 'You have a choice. He was in your past. Don't let him affect your future. It's not an easy one to make. I know. Emotions don't always allow us to think rationally. But you can do it. Start your life again with a clean slate.'

Zeb nodded in agreement. They knew their friend's back-story. He had grown up with foster families, none of whom had treated him well. *He's lived some of what she's been through.*

Zohra nodded several times and then she smiled shyly. 'You are very handsome. Like a Hollywood star.'

The Texan was lost for words for once. He smiled embarrass-edly. 'Thank you. Genes. I got lucky.'

'Don't feed his ego,' Bear slapped his forehead theatrically. 'He's already got a big head.'

That drew a laugh.

It was while they were leaving that Beth drew out a phone. 'Keep that with you,' she gave it to Zohra. 'There's only one number on it. Ours. You can message us anytime if you need help.'

The young student took it with trembling fingers. Her eyes brimmed with tears as she hugged each one of them.

'Don't be a stranger, baradar,' she whispered to Zeb. 'Visit me whenever you can.'

'I won't,' he promised.

27

Tunisia, Present Day*

ZEB FINGERED THE PHONE ABSENT-MINDEDLY. 'WE NEVER heard from her after that night.'

'Nope,' Meghan confirmed.

He looked up when voices reached them. Another smartly-dressed couple entered the room, escorted by the guard at the door. The uniformed man looked in their direction, nodded once and left the arrivals.

We'll need to leave soon.

'Ma'am,' he began.

'There's not much point in my objecting, is there?' Clare said resignedly.

Zeb grinned. 'You're our director, ma'am. You can red-light the mission.'

'As if you'll listen! I know how you work. You all will request personal time and the eight of you will do your thing. Alright,' she said firmly. 'Go to Istanbul. At the same time, find out what's happened to Zohra.'

Beth fist-pumped discreetly. 'Yes, ma'am.'

'I'll brief you after my meeting with the president. There might be CIA assets or those of some other agency that might be able to help out in Istanbul.'

'Copy that, ma'am,' Zeb acknowledged and ended the call. 'When did she send that message?'

'Yesterday.' Meghan looked up from her phone.

'When we were in the desert?'

'Yeah.'

'We are leaving?' Bear asked when the new couple eyed them curiously.

'No,' Zeb shook his head. 'There will be cops looking for us on the highways. Our Lear—'

'Is on its way here,' Meghan interjected. 'We go to Istanbul from here.'

'Our rides?'

'We get our go-bags from them. Khaled will retrieve our Range Rovers and keep them safe. He's well-connected. He'll be able to take away the vehicles without anyone asking questions.'

'You have thought of everything,' Roger said admiringly. 'What would we do without you?'

'You would be lost,' Beth snorted.

Zeb was silent when they retrieved their go-bags and returned to the lounge. He went to the floor-to-ceiling windows and watched private jets land and take off.

'You are worried,' Meghan said as the twins and Chloe joined him.

'For Zohra, yeah.'

'We've got Werner running searches. No bodies found in Tehran that match her build. No one admitted to hospital. She's still in university, but she's now enrolled in their doctorate program.'

'Biochemistry,' Beth grinned. 'That plan she had when we met her ... she's executing it.'

'We are running traces on Arash too, but he's dropped out of sight.'

Zeb worked it out in his mind. Istanbul and then Tehran. He wished they could go to Iran right away, but they still had a mission to execute.

'We'll get to her,' Chloe squeezed his forearm. 'Till then, we'll have to trust her to keep herself safe.'

28

Tehran

Zohra looked around Nowruz Park. It was mid-day, but the sun was out, warming up the winter day. A few kids playing in the distance. A suited man reading a newspaper. Another one on his phone.

'We've got to leave,' she said. 'The police or Sepah or both will be looking for us.'

'Yes. Where do you live?'

Zohra hesitated, wondering whether to trust her and then dispelled her doubts. *She was with me all along in that cell. She was threatened too.* 'Teymoori,' she said. 'But I can't go back there. My address is in the university records. They will go there immediately.'

'I too can't go back,' Leila agreed. 'It's the same for me.'

'Where do you live?'

'Vanak, near Alzahra University. I am studying psychology there. It's time we knew each other properly,' Leila stuck out her hand with a grin. 'I am Leila Shokri. I organized that protest on Sattar Khan.'

Zohra stared at her. 'You?'

'Balle,' the psychology student smiled ruefully. 'I am very active in student politics.'

'And I am Zohra Hashimi,' she shook the younger woman's hand as she studied her.

Leila was the same height and same build as her. Her hair was curly and streaked with gold and brunette tones. Her dark eyes moved expressively and her hands were never still. They were continuously gesturing or tapping a rhythm on her thighs.

'Can you go to your friends or parents' place?' she asked the protester.

'I can't put them at risk,' Leila shook her head. 'My parents aren't anywhere nearby. They are in Gorgan. I came to Tehran when I got admission to the university.'

'We have to split up,' Zohra said. 'We can't be seen together?'

'No,' the other student shook her head vehemently. 'We are safer together. We can look out for one another. How can you even think of separating? I agree we cannot join Shabnam, Maryam or any of the other protesters. That will be too big a group. We'll be noticed immediately. But there's no way you and I are going our own ways.'

'Listen,' Zohra caught her shoulder fiercely. 'Being with me is a risk. I am a danger to everyone around me—'

She stopped abruptly. The stress of captivity, lack of sleep and the continual worry had made her reveal more than what she intended.

Leila's eyes widened. 'What do you mean? What are you not telling me?'

She shrank instinctively. 'Are you a spy? Are you an Ershad or Sepah informer?'

'NO!' Zohra said angrily. 'How can you even think that? They beat me and that man would have raped me.' She shuddered in remembrance.

'What then? What are you hiding from me? Why are you a danger to others?'

'You have to go. I can't go into that.'

Leila's face took a determined look. 'No. I am not going anywhere until I know what's going on.'

Zohra felt her heart sink. The weight on her mind grew too much for her to bear.

'Our government is building a secret weapon.'

29

'Secret weapon?' Leila said shrilly. She lowered her voice instantly when Zohra squeezed her shoulder.

'Secret weapon,' she hissed. 'What are you talking about? Aren't you a student?'

'I am!' Zohra slapped her palm on the ground. 'I am a biochemistry PhD student in the university.' She blew hair away from her face in frustration. 'Don't ask me how I found out about it, but it is true. I have seen the evidence.' *I can't tell her all that I know. I have revealed too much as it is.* 'Leila, trust me. What I know can get me killed. Once Sepah finds out I know, they will hunt me down, torture me first to find out how much I know and who else I have told. I cannot tell you anything more. You will be in danger too. That's why I said we should split up. Try to understand.'

'Why will they hunt you for that? What's so special about this weapon. Every country builds weapons. The whole world knows about our nuclear weapons program.'

'Not like this one.' Zohra's voice shook. 'It is an illegal one. I researched it. It is banned by the United Nations. If America or the West find out about it, the kind of sanctions they will apply might kill our country. It's not just illegal, it is so immoral... it's against humanity.'

'Our country is already suffering because of the oil sanctions.'

'These will be worse. Much worse. The entire world will turn against us. Trust me. The people in power won't suffer, though,' she said bitterly. 'They never do. It's us, it's them,' Zohra gestured to the distant people in the park, 'who will pay the price?'

Leila rubbed her eyes. 'When I joined my friends in that demonstration, I never imagined I would end up listening to you about a secret bomb.'

'I know what you are feeling. When I woke up in that cell today, I thought all this was a bad dream. It's only when I felt the pain in my head and the swelling on my temple that it all came back to me.'

'Bomb,' Leila looked away as if to regain her bearings and then turned back. Her eyes probed for what felt like hours until her shoulders straightened and nodded. 'Okay, what's our plan?'

Zohra ground her teeth in frustration. 'There's only one plan for you. You have to leave me. I'll figure out what I need to do.'

Leila grinned. 'No chance. I am sticking close to you. If Sepah starts looking for you, you'll need all the help you get. I am not leaving you alone.'

Zohra stared at her. 'Are you out of your mind? This isn't a game. Didn't you hear what I told you? This is big. It is so enormous that Sepah will kill brutally to keep it secret. How they treated us in that cell shows to what extent they can go.'

'I heard you. I know about Sepah, perhaps more than you,' Leila said grimly. 'I said my parents are in Gorgan. That's not true. I tell that lie because it is easier than telling everyone what happened.'

'My parents are dead,' she looked around casually in the park and drew closer to Zohra. To a casual observer they looked like two young women enjoying the sunshine. 'They both were teachers in a small school in Gorgan. There was a peaceful demonstration in town one day. This was just before I joined university. The town people were protesting against Basij's heavy-handed tactics. My parents joined in. The paramilitary volunteers broke up the parade forcefully and, in the stampede, killed my parents. I found out later they deliberately targeted them because my parents encouraged girls to have their independence and their own voice in school. I wasn't there. I was here, in Tehran, checking out accommodation.'

Zohra watched her, stunned.

'My sister,' Leila continued emotionlessly, 'was raped one night, after that. The police never found out who it was, but I am sure it was Basij. She hanged herself after a week.'

'Basij,' she spat after a moment, 'and Sepah are my enemy.'

30

Zohra squeezed her hand. 'What happened to you is not a reason to be with me—'

'Stop!' Leila's eyes flashed. 'You cannot talk me out of this. I have decided. I am not leaving you.' Her face relaxed into a wide smile. 'I will follow you if you try to escape. You are stuck with me.'

Zohra choked up. She opened her arms and Leila went into her hug willingly. They held together and drew comfort from each another until they parted.

'We can't go back to our accommodation,' Zohra said. 'We have to hide somewhere.'

'I have friends in the protest movement,' Leila said. She made a wry face. 'You weren't in the demonstration that night, were you?'

'No. I was going home and got caught up in it. What I know ... I couldn't trust anyone, which is why I said I was a protester.'

'You didn't say that,' the psychology student corrected her. 'I remember that night. I was one of the women who questioned you. You kept quiet and we all assumed you were one of us.'

'I would have joined but what I found out ... it scared me.'

'I understand. I and my friends, other organizers, have a deep network. But even I don't know everyone. There is a core group that I have never met, but I know they help women escape Iran. They have safe houses. They will shelter us for some time.'

'You trust them?'

'With my life,' Leila said simply. 'But we cannot hide there forever.'

'I know,' Zohra said. She made to say something and then stopped.

'You are hiding something from me again. We have to trust each other if we are going to come out of this alive.'

The sobering comment decided it for Zohra. 'There are some Americans,' she said softly. 'I met them when I was working towards my bachelor's degree.' She unpacked the events of many years ago.

'Arash raped you?' Leila asked harshly.

'No. He never returned after that night, but he tried to force himself on me a few times.'

The psychology student cursed. 'Men!' She ground her teeth. 'This Zeb Carter. Do you trust him?'

'Balle. They said they were security consultants, but I am sure they were from their military. They could even be spies. There was no reason for them to help me. None of the other people in the restaurant came to my aid. They did. Yes, I trust them. I don't care what's between our country and America. Those eight people will come for me. I am sure of it. There was no reason for them to give me that phone. They will know what to do once I tell them about the bomb.'

'American spies!' Leila rolled the words. 'Just what have you got involved with, Zohra?'

'Then, when I met them? Nothing. Now, it is something that can get us killed. That's why you should go—'

'Stop. We had this discussion. It's over. I am not leaving you.'

'You are letting your emotions get in the way—'

'Basij killed my parents. My sister is dead because of Basij. Am I emotional about this? Yes!'

'Our government will consider us traitors once we tell the Americans.'

'Government?' Leila laughed bitterly. 'Our government is doing everything it can to stifle our lives, to make us live the way the clerics want us to. Do we have any freedom? How long do you think I'll live if I am a lesbian? You think I care about whether we are traitors? If our country is developing a bomb that is against the international laws, we should tell the world about it.'

She broke off and breathed harshly.

'We will be the most hunted people in Iran,' Zohra pleaded. 'Think of that. You don't have to do this.'

'I heard you the first time. You don't need to say that over and over again.'

'What can I say or do to make you go away?' Zohra threaded her fingers through her hair in frustration.

'Nothing.'

'Why? Any other woman would have run away after hearing what I said. Many of them would have gone to the police and reported me.'

'I am not them,' Leila said stubbornly. 'And as to why? We spent more than a night in that cell. We almost got raped. We got lucky with that accident. That time we spent, all of us women, it means something to me. I go on protests even though I know I could be arrested, beaten or even killed, because I want to make a change in our country. I have nothing left. My family is dead. I am alone. The only way I can make my life worthwhile is by doing something which will make all our lives better. This, helping you, is it.'

'You are wrong,' Zohra said quietly.

'What about?'

'You are not alone. We are in this together.'

The smile that broke on Leila's face was like the sun rising. 'Now you are talking, Ms. PhD.'

‘Let’s not get ahead of ourselves,’ Zohra said drily. ‘Even if the Americans come, how will they find us?

'That’s assuming Zeb Carter got your message. Come,' Leila got up and dusted her jeans.

'Where?'

'Let's see if we can find your phone.'

31

Istanbul

'This is the life,' Roger threw himself on the bed in his hotel room in the upscale hotel.

They were in Beyoglu, a district in the city center, located on the European side of the Bosporus.

Meghan and Beth had booked seven rooms for them while they were in Tunis. 'No other option than to go with this hotel,' the elder sister had explained. 'We can use a CIA safe house—'

'We won't,' Zeb told her. 'We have no idea how safe it really is.'

He watched the bustle of Istanbul as they filed into the Texan's room which happened to be the largest.

'What are you doing?' Bwana asked when Roger reached for the phone.

'Room service. We need body fuel.'

Zeb went over to Beth who was sprawled on the bed with her laptop open.

'That,' she pointed at a red cross, 'is where the burner was last, when Zohra sent that message. It was in a building in an alley from Gholami Street.'

Her expression told Zeb he wasn't going to like what she was going to say next.

'There was a protest march on Sattar Khan Street that night. There are enough news and social reports that several students were captured by the police that night. All of them women.'

'Do we have their identities?' he asked tightly.

'Nada. The police denied holding them initially, but several Western news agencies challenged them and they finally admitted they had arrested some demonstrators.'

She typed rapidly and brought up a news site. 'Here. A van crashed into Vanak Square earlier today. Several women escaped from it. There are social media rumors that they were the protesters from Sattar Khan. I have proof.'

She opened another website. 'Security camera footage from a store's camera. See those women?' She zoomed in on a few whose faces were clearly visible. 'And this one,' she opened another tab, 'is from a cell phone upload from the demonstration. The same women,' she said triumphantly.

Zeb compared the images. 'Yeah. Zohra?'

Beth grimaced. 'Unfortunately, most of the women have their heads down and many of them aren't in the frame.'

'If she was in the van, she escaped,' Chloe said encouragingly. 'She's out there. She's smart. She's a PhD student! She'll lie low and find a way to make contact with us again.'

'Where's that phone now?' Zeb asked.

'It's gone dead. It has been either destroyed or someone removed its battery.'

They broke off when their food arrived and after the meal, Zeb went to the window.

He saw Meghan's reflection in the glass as she joined him. 'We have sent a message to Kamal. I told him we'll be in Istanbul tomorrow with Aziz.'

'Let's hope he bites.'

32

Tehran

Naser was back in Gholamreza's office. He knew what the meeting was about.

Zohra Hashimi, he thought bitterly. It had taken some time for the Sepah officers to investigate the imprisoned women and find out who they actually were. Once Zohra's details had been known, red flags had gone all over the military establishment and phone lines had burned.

Gholamreza's expression was thunderous when he entered the office.

'How could you let her escape?' he demanded.

'You asked me to release her!' Naser said.

'Did I ask you to let them escape?'

'It was an accident. We couldn't have foreseen it.'

'Fool,' the IRGC leader threw a glass against a wall where it shattered. An aide ducked into the office and retreated swiftly at the director's glare. 'Don't you have any brains? I thought you would have investigated the women before releasing them.'

'We didn't have time for that, agha.'

'First, you capture them,' Gholamreza raised a finger. 'Then you imprison them,' Another digit unfolded. 'Finally, you let them get away. I have killed people for lesser mistakes than that.'

Naser swallowed but kept silent.

'Have you read her file?' the IRGC head challenged him.

'Yes.'

'Then you are aware she might know everything about the program.'

'Yes.'

'I have to meet the supreme leader later today. What should I tell him?'

'That Sepah will do everything to find Zohra Hashimi.'

'No,' Gholamreza thundered. 'Sepah will find her. Quickly. That's what I will tell him because that's what you are going to do. Understood?'

'Yes, agha.'

Gholamreza gritted his teeth in anger when Naser left.

Incompetents, he swore to himself. *I have to do the thinking for everyone.*

He clenched and unclenched his fist several times and slammed a drawer shut.

'Hiram,' he yelled irritably when his eyes fell on the glass shards.

'Clean that up,' he growled when his aide entered his office. His eyes then fell on a file lying on his desk with Emad's name on it. He covered it up with another sheet of paper and when his flunky left, skimmed through it.

Emad. It meant determined. Resolute. It was the name of the project that would make Iran the greatest Islamic nation in the world. Every other country would bow to it.

Now it felt like it would be an utter failure.

Gholamreza had killed several people, many of them painfully.

He wondered if he would meet the same fate if Emad couldn't be revived.

33

Gholamreza paced around his office as he reflected on how he had convinced the country's leaders to accept his idea.

'Think about it,' he had argued passionately. 'The world knows about our nuclear program because we went about it so secretively. America and Israel have tried to sabotage it several times. We need to carry out Emad differently so that no one suspects it.'

'How do you propose that?' Amir Hossein, the president, a hard-line cleric himself, steepled his fingers.

'Do the research in the University of Tehran. Navid Farhad teaches there in any case. I have checked him out. His background and specialism are best suited for Emad. He will handpick a few students. We will create a highly-secure lab there where they will work as well as live. We will have our own people there. Entry for anyone will be impossible. We will get the university to say that the research can win the Nobel Prize. Everyone will believe that. Farhad is famous in research circles. He presents papers and gives talks all over the world. He has several patents. No one will question why the access to the lab has that much security.'

They had debated his proposal at length. A handful of select military leaders had been brought in. They had tried to convince the president and the supreme leader that the research be carried out in army camps, but the spiritual leader of the country had bought into his plan and after that everyone else had fallen in line.

Convincing Farhad was easy, he recalled with a wolfish smile.

The academic was passionate about his country and was a believer about its role in the world order. His eyes glimmered when the IRGC leader laid out his plan. He saw the potential.

Gholamreza wasn't surprised when Farhad didn't show any concern about the ethics or morality of Emad. His psychological profiling of the researcher had shown that the academic had a very low regard for humanity and thought only in terms of success and failure of his research.

Farhad agreed to lead Emad.

'Your wife and children will be in our protection,' the IRGC head told him, 'until this is over.'

You and they will have to be killed once the program is complete. He didn't articulate his thoughts however.

The professor waved a hand dismissively as if his family wasn't important. 'I can't do this alone. I need—'

'Pick two students. Only two. I will vet them myself. They will need to be men.'

'Some of my best students are women.'

'Are you seeing the protesters on the streets? Most of them are women. They are trouble. This is not up for debate. Choose men. They have to be single. Their families have to be far away from Tehran. Leave the rest to me.'

Farhad produced two names, Behnam Ali and Javed Reza.

Gholamreza did extensive checks on them. Both came from good families. Their fathers were government officials and were in fervent support of the supreme leader. He had them followed, checked out their financials, their dating history and dug up everything on them.

They passed his security profiling.

Farhad brought them into the program without revealing its real intentions. They signed up enthusiastically.

An existing lab in the university, at the far end of the biochemistry department, away from main hallways and parking lots, was converted. Reinforced doors layered with steel. Biometric access. Security guards inside and outside. No other exits.

The inside of the spacious lab had living quarters for the three researchers and a dormitory for the five Sepah guards. The men were among the best agents in the Revolutionary Guards. Crack shots, experts in all kinds of weapons and martial arts and highly committed to the cause of Iran. They had an arsenal with them inside the lab.

Bioreactors, chromatography equipment, cell culture media and everything that was needed for the research was procured discreetly either from Iran itself or from Europe and shipped by the Basij network.

Emad started.

The research was going well until Zohra Hashimi turned up, Gholamreza pounded his desk with his fist.

34

Gholamreza remembered how it had happened. He had read Naser's report over and over again until it was burned in his memory.

Women students had protested in the university that day. They had marched the hallways with their banners and placards. Several male students had joined them as well.

The demonstrators had turned violent when several security guards and police officers charged at them. The ensuing fights turned into full-scale riots when more students and several professors joined in as well.

Lecture rooms were destroyed, windows and doors were broken. Several fires started.

Naser hadn't worked out how the conflagration in the Emad laboratory started, but it spread fast with several chemicals exploding.

Farhad and his students and the Sepah agents worked to put it out frantically, but the lab and the accommodation were the size of two basket-ball courts and they were spread thin.

The university's power went down. The research center's back-up kicked in, but that too blew out in the intense heat, as did the battery bank.

That had unlocked the biometric doors, a safety measure in the event of power failure.

Zohra Hashimi was there, Gholamreza snarled silently.

Naser had pieced it together in his report after extensive interviews with Farhad, Ali, Reza, the Sepah soldiers and several students.

Hashimi had been running down the hallway to get away from the riots. She wasn't alone, there were several students with her, but she had been the last in the group.

She had heard the biometric doors open.

It looks like she heard the shouts from inside and saw the smoke, Naser surmised in his write-up.

Whatever the reason, Hashimi darted inside the lab. No one saw her enter. No one saw her leave and she wasn't seen again in the university.

And she left with something that has stalled Emad, Gholamreza thought bitterly.

35

'We need money before we do anything,' Leila said.

'I have some in my bank account,' Zohra replied.

'How will you withdraw it? And, don't you think the police will be monitoring our accounts?'

Leila put on a desperate expression before she could reply and approached an elderly woman in the park. 'Khanom, our bags were stolen in a restaurant. Our phones and purses were in it. We are going to the police station to report it, but can I use your phone to make a brief call? I will ask my friends to meet me outside the park.'

Zohra put on a strained face as well and that seemed to convince the woman.

'Of course,' she reached into her bag, brought out her phone, unlocked it and handed it over. 'What is this country coming to? These thieves are getting bolder every day.'

LEILA SMILED POLITELY AT THE WOMAN AND TOOK THE PHONE. She quickly dialed a number and waited. After a few seconds, she spoke into the phone in a hushed voice, 'Merci, this is Leila.

Don't ask any questions. Can you meet me outside Nowruz Park right away? Balle, at the entrance to the boulevard? Please bring two scarves as well with you. No, don't ask why. I will explain later.'

She hung up the phone and thanked the woman profusely.

'You trust Merci?' Zohra asked Leila as they set off towards the exit.

'Yes. She's my closest friend from university. She is one of us, a protester. She had some family work otherwise she too would have joined us at the demonstration in Sattar Khan that night.'

'I will hang back,' Zohra said when they neared the turnstile gates. 'It's best she does not see me.'

'There's something in your head. It's not just looks that you have.'

She looked at Leila surprisedly and grinned ruefully at her wink. Emotion welled up in her. She caught hold of the psychology student's hand and squeezed it. 'I would have been terrified if I had to do all this alone.'

'You still should be. We might not get out of this alive. We aren't safe, yet.'

Zohra nodded. She rested against a tree trunk and waited for Leila to go out of the park. Her heart thumped when a siren wailed in the distance but it faded away and died.

She peered around the trunk cautiously and saw Leila talking with another woman. They hugged and the psychology student returned to the park.

'Here,' she handed a scarf to Zohra.

The two of them wrapped the garments around their faces to partially cover it and went out to Nowruz Boulevard.

'Head down. Stay behind me,' Leila whispered and flagged a cab.

'Gholami Street,' she told the driver and climbed into the back.

Zohra slid in beside her.

'To that building we were hiding in?' She mouthed.

The student nodded.

Half-an-hour later they were at the mouth of the street where Leila stopped the cab, paid off the driver and they got out.

'No point in letting him know where we are going.'

'How did you get so smart?'

'I have been involved in so many protests. This is like second nature to me.'

Leila's face softened. She tucked a tendril of hair behind Zohra's ear. 'Don't be hard on yourself. We are in this together. We have to rely on each other. We both have our individual strengths. Don't think you are inadequate. That's how men have suppressed us all along, by making us think and feel like that. Besides,' her lips twitched in a sly smile. 'You are a PhD researcher. I am a lowly psychology student. You are smarter than me.'

Zohra punched her playfully on her shoulder and they went down the sidewalk to the nearest store.

They tried out various pairs of goggles and emerged with a new pair of shades over their eyes, purses and bags full of clothing.

'It's a government bank,' Zohra identified the building they had sheltered in as they drew closer.

'Yes. We found that its security cameras hardly worked and that its lock could be picked easily. It lends to other companies so there is nothing valuable in its offices.'

They went through the glass door, with Zohra at the back. She eyed the stairs next to the reception desk. *We went down those steps to the basement.*

Leila smiled at the woman behind the counter. 'We were here a few days ago regarding a loan application. Unfortunately, I forgot my phone and its battery seems to have died. Did you find it?'

'Oh no! Let me see. We have a file for lost items,' the woman pursed her lips and punched keys on her computer. She shook her head. 'No phone. We have an umbrella, a coat, a bag, but no phone.'

'None of those are ours,' Leila thanked her.

They went out, unaware of the newly-installed camera on the ceiling.

36

The cameras in the bank were hooked into a system that had facial recognition. It alerted the police when it matched Zohra to the images in its database. That alert got routed to the Sepah office. Naser was still in the building when an aide rushed to him with the news. He hurried to the lower floor and entered the security monitoring room. The men at the screens stood up at his entrance.

'Sit down,' he frowned and leaned over the aide's shoulder who pointed to an image.

'That's her, agha. Our system says it is a sixty-percent match. You can see her face is half-hidden but our software used the distance between her eyes and ears and the shape and size of her forehead to identify her.'

'Where was this and how long ago was this?'

'Iran Capital Bank near Gholami Street. Half-an-hour ago.'

'Aziz,' Naser rasped at his aide. 'Take a team. Get her if she is still there. If she isn't, find out what she went. Search the neighborhood. You know the drill.'

The aide stiffened. 'Yes, agha.'

. . .

ZOHRA AND LEILA HADN'T GONE FAR FROM IRAN CAPITAL Bank. They had bought clothing, handbags and a cheap phone, all of them cash purchases. They had then stopped at a street vendor for doogh, a yoghurt-based drink.

The researcher stifled a smile when her friend slurped noisily. She looked past the vendor at a store that had fancy dresses on display. Its show windows reflected the street behind her, bustling with shoppers and office-goers.

Two vehicles raced past, their sirens on full blast. She angled her head to watch them through the corner of her eyes.

'Let's go,' she murmured.

'Why?' Leila asked, oblivious as she watched a video on her phone. 'We're still to finish our dooghs.'

'Let's go,' Zohra repeated. 'Don't turn around.'

Her friend picked up on her inflection. She pocketed her phone and followed without hesitation. 'What happened?'

'Two vehicles stopped in front of the bank. I saw uniformed men go inside it.'

'They could have come for any reason?'

'You really think that?'

'No,' Leila shook her head. 'They identified us in the bank somehow. They must have installed security cameras.' She nudged Zohra with her shoulder to take the next alley.

'This is a dead-end,' the researcher objected.

'I know what I am doing. This is one of our escape routes.' The psychology student dragged out a wooden crate from beneath a broken-down car and put it against the wall.

She and Zohra stepped on it, climbed over the wall and entered the backyard of an apartment building. A dog barked from inside and a woman looked on curiously from a window as they hurried out of its gate.

They reached Jalil Pour Street where they took more side alleys and back roads until they reached Mehran where Leila made a call.

'Merci, Iran Capital Bank is no longer safe. I think they have installed security cameras. Spread the word. Our sisters will have to find another building if they have to escape from their demonstrations.'

'How much money did Merci give you?' Zohra asked when she hung up.

'Enough. Why?'

'We'll have to find somewhere to stay.'

'I thought of that. Merci will connect us to the core group of dissidents—'

'No. Sepah will search our apartments. They will question our friends and everyone who knows us. They might even follow them. We need to find somewhere to stay, away from people who know us.'

Leila pursed her lips. For a while they strode in silence. Then she nodded. 'You are right. I'll message Merci, warning her to be careful. Where do we go, then?'

'Pasdaran.'

'What's there?'

'You'll see.'

37

Istanbul

IT WAS EVENING WHEN ZEB TAPPED ON BETH'S DOOR. NO response. He went to Meghan's room. She didn't answer.

'They're here,' Roger whispered from his doorway and raised a finger warningly to maintain silence.

Zeb entered the Texan's room and stayed near the door where the rest of his friends had gathered.

Beth and Meghan were on the bed with their laptops in front of them. Zeb could see their screens from where he was. They were on a video call with someone.

His jaw dropped when he made out one of the faces. *That's Aziz!* The Tunisian businessman's face was blurred but identifiable. *How's he talking? Did Mossad arrange for the call?*

Zeb placed the other man from his accent. *That must be Mohsen Kamal.* The Iranian had a light beard and a scar high on his right cheek. The Iranian flag was his background image.

'What happened in your villa?' Kamal asked. 'There was a gunfight. I thought you were dead.'

'Some shooters attacked me,' Aziz said angrily. 'They must be from some rival gang. I got away with Petrov just in time.'

'Which gang?'

'How do I know? I didn't stick around to ask questions. I escaped, but it looks like they killed all my men. I will return when it is safe and then I'll ask questions. And get my revenge. But we need to meet. I have got Petrov. Let's do the exchange. I don't want to stay here for long.'

'You are in Istanbul?'

'Where do you think I am?' Aziz said irritably. 'Why do you think I messaged you if I wasn't in the city?'

'You arrived earlier than I expected.'

'I told you why. When can we meet?'

'It will have to be tomorrow—'

'It can't be tonight? Someone might identify me or Petrov.'

'No. It has to be tomorrow. I have to make arrangements.'

'What about my payment?'

'We agreed on half-a-million dollars.'

'We also agreed I would get half in advance.'

'I will pay you the full amount when I get Petrov.'

'No,' Aziz's face hardened. 'I want my advance now. I don't like it that you are trying to wriggle out of our deal.'

'I am not doing anything of that sort. That's a lot of money to arrange on short notice.'

'You should have thought of that before you negotiated the deal. Besides, that's pocket change for the Iranian Army. You might spend that much on a missile which might never get fired. Petrov is far more valuable to you than that. You are getting him at a bargain. If you are not interested in him, I can sell him to the Americans for far more money than that. Decide quickly.'

Zeb watched Meghan type furiously on her laptop. He craned his head to look around her shoulder, but Chloe's hand on his shoulder stopped him. *Stay put,* she messaged with her glare.

Kamal remained impassive. 'You will get the entire money tomorrow—'

'Deal's off,' Aziz snarled. 'You are wasting my time. I should have guessed you would turn out to be a slippery customer. I will trade Petrov to another country. But I will also let your superiors know why the Russian General is in a foreign country when he could have been with you. I will name you. You know how your military works. You might not see another sunrise again.'

'Are you threatening me?'

'I am predicting your future if you don't honor our agreement. Threats?' Aziz scoffed. 'You Iranians are the experts on that.'

Kamal's eyes flickered. 'How do I know Petrov is with you? You might be bluffing.'

'Wait a moment. See this?' Aziz held up a newspaper.

'Yes. That's today's edition.'

The Tunisian's face cleared up. His room became visible.

That's not this room, Zeb's eyebrows came together in astonishment. *Where is he? How's this call happening?*

38

'You can see my room?' Aziz asked.

'Yes,' Kamal replied.

The Tunisian adjusted his camera and went to a corner of the room to show Petrov, who was bound in a chair and gagged. He yanked on the Russian's hair which made him blink.

'Can you see him now? This is your confirmation. Make the advance payment right away or I sell him to someone else. I am sure if I go to multiple countries, there will be a bidding war and I will get a much higher price than what I agreed with you.'

Kamal watched the Russian for a long while and then nodded. 'Check your account.'

Aziz bent to his keyboard and after a while a slow smile spread across his face. 'You have paid the exact amount.'

'Bring Petrov tomorrow,' Kamal said expressionlessly, 'to the Grand Bazaar Cafe on Istiklal Street. At noon. Don't be late.'

'You want the exchange to happen in a busy restaurant?'

'Yes. Be on time.'

'You will be there?'

'Yes.'

Aziz frowned and stroked his beard. 'I will have armed men

with me. If you try to take Petrov without paying me ... that won't go so well for you. I will do anything to keep the Russian safe and secure until I get my money.'

'You will get it,' Kamal said coldly and turned off the call.

Zeb stared incredulously at the laptop screens. 'How was that possible? Aziz is with Mossad and Petrov is in some safe house in DC. How did they come together on the video call? Did you—'

'Do you really want to know?' Meghan smirked. 'You are a low-IQ mortal. This might go over your head.'

'Yeah,' Zeb exclaimed. 'You all knew!' He stared at the rest of the operators. None of them looked surprised.

'We worked it out,' Bwana said in a superior tone.

Zeb stared at him. The African-American and Bear were Mensa members. It was no surprise the two had figured it out. He looked at Chloe for an explanation and shook his head exasperatedly at her snigger.

'Tell,' he said defeatedly to the twins.

'It was simple,' Beth chortled. 'We asked Avichai to record Aziz's video. We anticipated the questions Kamal might ask and sent them over to Mossad and then asked Avichai to record Aziz's video. We also asked Clare to make that recording of Petrov. What you saw was very clever editing and VFX by a studio. They gave us instructions on how to run it in real-time along with an AI engine with which we could feed answers. We had Aziz's laptops and phones. He didn't have any great security on them. We got hold of his messages, emails, his bank accounts, heck, we got to know his life! It was easy to figure out his communication style. That helped Meghan write out his answers. That's what she was doing on the keyboard. The AI software got Aziz's render to respond as if he were in the room, along with the right facial expressions.'

Zeb shook his head in astonishment as he took it in. Meghan's eyes sparkled when he looked in her direction. 'Kiwi VFX,' she said helpfully. 'Ring any bells?'

He narrowed his eyes as he ran through names in his memory. 'New Zealand studio? Sought after by big-budget Hollywood directors? Emily Henderson runs it,' he snapped his fingers when it came to him. 'Keke Arono's wife,' he referred to the New Zealand Security Intelligence Service's head whom they had met in a previous mission. The hard-faced, implacable-looking woman had become their friend after their operation and one evening, had introduced her wife to them.

'We know Emily well,' Beth shut down her screen. 'We met her a few times when she visited New York. She gave us a virtual tour of her studio. What they do is just out of this world. You saw their output. Kamal fell for it.'

'Yeah,' Broker agreed. 'He bought it.

'Yes,' the elder sister grinned. 'That's the reason we arranged the call with Kamal this late. We needed time to arrange this for the studio to work their magic.'

Time. Zeb's stubble rasped against his palm when he rubbed his jaw. *We don't have much of it before the exchange tomorrow.*

He brought out his phone to look up Grand Bazaar Cafe.

'I've got it on my map,' Meghan guessed what he was searching. 'It's right in the middle of Istiklal Street. You know how busy that is.'

Zeb nodded. One of the most popular streets in the city. It was a major pedestrian avenue in the Beyoglu district of the city. *Big tourist attraction*, he recalled from their previous visits. *Locals too frequent it,* he corrected himself.

Turkish delicacies, souvenirs, and handmade items, they were all available on the street, with restaurants, cafes, and bars providing both traditional Turkish fare and international cuisine.

'I can see why Kamal wants the exchange to happen there,' he commented, looking at the satellite imagery of the street that Meghan brought up. 'There are quite a few streets near it, Balo and Yesilcam for example. He can take Petrov and disappear into any one of those and get away from there.'

'We on the other hand have to plan for every possible exit,'

Chloe analyzed. 'The bustle will work against us. Shoppers and tourists will get in our way.'

'Yeah,' Zeb pictured Istiklal in his mind. 'They will hamper him too, but he has had more time to work out his exfil.'

'None of you have asked the million-dollar question,' Beth prompted them.

'What's that?' Broker flicked lint, that he alone could see, from his T-shirt. Appearance was as important to him as it was to Roger.

'Who is Mohsen Kamal?'

'Iranian Army. That's what Aziz said,' Bear replied.

'No, he said he was wearing an army uniform. Major Mohsen Kamal is a smart, upcoming officer in the Revolutionary Guards. He is Sepah.'

Why am I not surprised, Zeb thought grimly.

'I know how we can get away from there with Kamal,' he pointed to the satellite images. 'We need to blow up a store.'

39

Tehran

'YOU KNOW THIS IS WHERE THE RICH PEOPLE STAY,' LEILA SAID softly as their cab entered Pasdaran. They had changed taxis twice before, giving random districts as their destinations to the drivers. 'Embassies, businesspeople, politicians, they all have homes and offices here.'

'Balle. That's why it is safer here. Sepah will think we will go to the crowded districts or even leave Tehran.' Zohra leaned forward and directed the driver. 'Drop us off here.'

'Here? On Bathaie?' The man met her eyes in the mirror, surprised at her instruction. The street was a busy thoroughfare that cut across the district.

'Yes, here.'

The driver grumbled beneath his breath at his fare being cut short and sped away as soon as he was paid.

'There's a Sepah office and Army barracks here,' Leila said nervously.

'Stop worrying. I know what I am doing.' Zohra adjusted her scarf to cover the lower part of her face, showing only her eyes which were hidden behind her shades. She nodded approvingly when her friend did the same and led them into a residential street.

They went past the barracks and a fancy beauty salon. The wealth in the district was apparent from its clean streets, leafy boulevard and the absence of crowds. A BMW cruised past, its tires crunching on dead leaves. The smell of fragrance from a perfume store. Two women came out of a boutique, clutching expensive bags.

'We'll have to live long enough to enjoy life like that,' she murmured.

'And get lucky,' Leila sniffed.

Zohra entered a winding alley near Sadr Highway which bordered the district. The small street was lined with small shops and expensive homes. The smell of spices and sweat hung in the air, and the sound of children playing in a school echoed off the walls of the narrow walkway.

They reached a pharmacy tucked away in the dead end.

She climbed the steps, dug out an old prescription from her handbag and gave it to the counter clerk. She waited until the sole customer had left and lowered her scarf and lifted her shades. 'It's me,' she whispered. 'I need to meet Fatima.'

The clerk, a middle-aged woman eyes flashed in recognition and looked pointedly at Leila.

'She's with me. She can be trusted.'

The woman pretended to laugh as if Zohra had made a joke. She came out from behind the counter and looked up and down the street, all the while gesticulating like she was conversing with the visitors.

'Come,' she said when she confirmed there was no one else on the alley.

She took them to the backroom and into the cool store. She went to the rear wall which had floor-to-ceiling wooden racks stacked with medicines. She reached beneath a shelf and yanked hard.

Zohra grinned at Leila's gasp when the entire section swung outwards soundlessly.

'Go,' she told them.

'Zohra!' A stout woman standing inside the brightly lit room hugged her tightly and kissed her cheeks. 'You didn't tell me you would be coming.'

'It's an emergency, khaleh,' the researcher said.

'How many weeks?' the woman looked at Zohra's belly.

'No, nothing like that.'

'Her, then?'

Zohra laughed at the psychology student's expression. 'No, not her either. It's not that kind of emergency. We are wanted by the police. Sepah is looking for us as well. We need a place to stay for some time. It could be a few days or even a few weeks. Can you put us up?'

The woman gazed at them keenly. Her expression cleared. 'Were you involved in that protest on Sattar Khan? I can't imagine any other reason for you to be in trouble.'

'Something like that.'

'We were,' Leila asserted forcefully.

'And you are?'

'Leila So—' the psychology student began.

'Leila,' Zohra interrupted. 'It's safer for you if you don't know her second name.'

The woman nodded and brought out her phone. She consulted an app and nodded. 'I have a spare room. I cannot give that out.'

Zohra's face fell. 'I understand. We'll try someplace else—'

'Dokhtar-e-man,' my daughter, the woman said softly. 'Let me finish. I have to keep that room available for emergencies, but I can make room in my office. I don't use it anyway. We can put in a small bed. It has a bathroom and is at the back. You won't see anyone who comes here.'

'Are you sure? We can—'

'No more discussion,' the woman said firmly. She rang a small bell and two women bustled in. 'Neda, Sahar, prepare my office for these visitors. They will be staying with us for some time. Towels, bedding, toiletries... provide everything that they will need.' She looked at her watch and clicked her tongue impatiently. 'I have to go to the hospital. I have my rounds there.'

'Go, khaleh,' Zohra hugged her. 'Thank you,' she whispered.

'That's not needed,' the woman stroked her hair. 'If I can't protect my own, what use am I?'

She smiled cheekily before she left. 'There's a small modification to this building since you last visited. There's a door built into the wall, next to the closet. The builder made it well. You can see it only if you are very close to it. It opens into the back street. You can come and go without going through the pharmacy.'

Zohra couldn't help herself when she saw Leila's face when they were alone in the woman's office. It was crowded with files and unused medicines and flyers and posters from pharma companies. There was enough room for the bed however and they could move around freely. 'You have so many questions. I can see it.'

'Balle,' the younger student waved helplessly. 'Where are we? Who is she?'

'She is Fatima Jaffari, one of the best gynecologists in Tehran.'

Leila's eyes rounded. 'You called her your aunt.'

'She is. Distantly related to my mother. I found out about her only a few years ago when I was going through some of my mother's old letters.'

'And what's this place?'

'An abortion clinic.'

40

Naser stalked through the corridors of Iran Capital Bank, his gaze flitting from one individual to the next. He was in uniform. He wanted everyone in the office to know he was from Sepah. He wanted them to be scared.

It was late in the evening, but the staff hadn't gone home. *Because of me*, he puffed out his chest. *They know the power I wield.*

He stopped in front of the reception counter where his captain had finished talking to junior officers.

'No luck, agha,' his subordinate said. 'Zohra was at the door. We got lucky that the camera caught her. The second woman was enquiring about a phone.'

'Phone,' Naser mused when the captain finished explaining. 'If they lost it, they could buy another one.'

'We took away all their belongings. They have no money to buy with.'

'Unless their family or friends helped them.'

'True, but in that case, they wouldn't be coming here for the phone. They could restore a lot of their data when they set up a new number. These days everything is in the cloud.'

'There must be something important on it. I can't think any other reason for them to come back for it.'

'I agree.'

'Who was she?'

'She didn't give a name, agha,' the captain made a face. 'She had her face down when she entered the door and the camera wasn't in the correct angle. I got our people to go through the identities of all the women we had taken in. Unfortunately, many of them fit the height and build and as you know—'

'They are all missing. I am aware of that.'

'We searched the neighborhood as well and questioned taxi drivers, but no one saw them.'

'Even if they did, many of them wouldn't cooperate with us. They hate us.'

'Yes, agha.'

Naser's gaze hardened when he took in a woman in the hallway who was talking to other bank officials. 'That's the woman who was at the reception?'

'Yes. I questioned her for a long—'

'I will talk to her.'

'Agha, we can't alienate these people...' the captain trailed off under Naser's harsh glare. 'Yes, I will arrange it right away.'

'Do you know who I am,' Naser growled when he was alone with the woman in a vacant office. It seemed to be that of a senior executive, with just one desk with a computer on it. He hadn't paid any attention to the name on the door. It didn't matter. The bank staff were small fry to him. Meaningless. Irrelevant.

'Yes, agha,' she licked her lips nervously. 'I have seen you on TV a few times.'

The brigadier general straightened his shoulders. Recognition was good for his ego. The woman was stout with henna-dyed hair. She wore the bank's uniform, a dark manteau that fell below her knees, with dark trousers and black shoes.

'What's your name?'

'Parmida Bahrami.'

'What was that woman's name?'

'She didn't tell me, agha. I told all this to your—'

Naser slapped her.

41

The flat of his palm struck her harshly on her face and sent her sprawling to the floor.

Parmida shrieked and lay still for several moments and then felt her lips and her face. She got up slowly and took a step back.

'You can't do this—'

Naser hit her again.

Her head rocked and tears leaked from her eyes involuntarily.

'Don't tell me what I can or cannot do,' he snarled. 'That woman is a security threat to our country. I will use every power I have to find her.'

Parmida looked at the closed door desperately. No one came to her rescue. She shrank when Naser moved threateningly.

'She didn't give any name. She asked if we found her phone, nothing else.'

'Lies,' Naser smacked her again. The sound of the blow was loud in the office. 'You are hiding information from us because you hate Sepah.'

She fell against the desk and cried out loudly.

'I TOLD YOU EVERYTHING I KNOW,' she sobbed. 'Why should I lie?'

A knock on the door. It opened before Naser could respond. The captain stood in the doorway. He took in the fallen woman impassively. 'Let's go, agha. We found a taxi driver who took them.'

'You had better not hide anything from us,' the brigadier general growled at Parmida and left the room.

The captain dropped his expressionless facade. He made to move towards her, concernedly.

'STAY AWAY FROM ME,' Parmida hissed. 'If you touch me, I will scream so loudly the entire staff will come here. Go to your boss and slap that taxi driver. You are nothing but thugs. Pigs.'

The captain left the office.

PARMIDA WIPED HER TEARS AWAY. SHE INSPECTED HERSELF IN a compact mirror from her bag. Her hands shook so hard she had trouble focusing on her face.

Her manager came inside. 'Are you alright?'

'Do I look alright?' she spat. 'Why didn't you come to help me? I am sure you heard me cry.'

'Those men are Sepah,' he shifted uncomfortably.

'So what? Are they above the law? You will allow them to mistreat your employees? What kind of man are you? Go away. I don't need your help.'

The manager slunk away.

Parmida leaned against the desk and let emotion overcome her. She wept for several moments and then fixed her face all over again.

She adjusted her dress and went out of the office. The male staff looked at the floor shamefully and said nothing when she went out and flagged a cab.

'Kaveh,' she called her husband when she got into her ride. 'Are you still communicating with those American journalists?'

She eyed the driver, but he was wearing earbuds and was

engrossed in his own call. He couldn't overhear her.

'Balle, we message one another all the time. I send them information which they publish. Why, what happened?'

Parmida couldn't control the sob that escaped her. She narrated the interrogation and heard Kaveh's inarticulate sound of anger.

'He hit you?'

'Yes, three times.'

'Naser, who is supposed to be the next Sepah chief?'

'Yes.'

Kaveh cursed loudly.

'How badly are you hurt? Let's go to the—'

'I am okay,' she said firmly. 'Tell those American women, those journalists, what happened.'

'I will do that,' he agreed harshly. 'They work for big networks. It will get a lot of publicity there.'

'Balle, but keep my name out of it.'

'Yes, that's the arrangement I have with them. Come home quickly. I will have chai ready.'

Parmida hung up and watched the lights and sounds of Tehran flash past.

Kaveh was a TV host at IRIB, Islamic Republic of Iran Broadcasting, the state TV station.

He also secretly fed news and information to a small, trusted group of American journalists. His tips had focused Western governments and media attention on several atrocities carried out by the Iranian government. Some of the stories, for which he was responsible, had gotten even Iran's allies to have a quiet word with the president.

Many protesters who had been imprisoned for merely demonstrating had been released by the state because of her husband's work.

Parmida's lips thinned.

Brigadier General Saeed Naser had picked on the wrong woman to harass.

42

Istanbul

The Grand Bazaar Cafe was a fifteen-minute walk from their hotel.

They set off early the next day. Seven am. Way before the stores opened and Istiklal got filled.

Tehran's morning air. Crisp and cold with a hint of fog. The ever-present smell of gas fumes but also hints of incense and cooking.

There were a few delivery people on Istiklal when they entered it. A few joggers. A bunch of elderly folks practicing deep breathing.

'It's small,' Zeb confirmed when he peered through the Grand Bazaar Cafe's window. 'Fifteen tables.'

'Yeah,' Beth agreed. 'That's what we figured from the reviews and satellite images.'

'All eight of us in that place,' Bwana spoke from a distance away. It was SOP, Standard Operating Procedure, that they spread out when they were together. It made them less conspicuous. 'We will get noticed.'

Zeb checked out the neighboring stores. A toy shop. An electronics retailer. A leather boutique.

'We still have that safe house in Esenler?

It was an Istanbul district, deeper in the European side of the city.

'Yeah,' Meghan answered. 'We handed it over to the CIA, but it's still operational. I checked.'

'That's where we'll interrogate him.'

'Great, but how do we get Kamal? You have a plan?' Bear asked him.

Zeb regarded his friend. His lips twitched.

'Whoa!' the operator raised his hands defensively, 'whatever's on your mind, I don't like it.'

'There's no other option. You are the closest to Aziz's build. You'll go as him, disguised.'

Bwana and Roger's guffaws drowned out Bear's protests.

'You will pass,' Chloe eyed her boyfriend critically after the twins had finished with Bear.

'Pass?' he surveyed the mirror in Roger's room. 'I look big. That wig on my head looks like his hair. My nose is similar to his but in what other way—'

'Kamal will come to the cafe at the last minute,' Zeb cut him off. 'He might even be late. He will want the advantage and entering after you will give him that.'

'What Zeb is saying,' Roger dumped his go-bag on the bed and began packing it, 'is that he won't have much time to check you out thoroughly. Because of this,' he hefted his bag meaningfully.

'He might have watchers in the cafe before he arrives, to check me out,' Bear objected.

'I'll be there,' Chloe patted his shoulder, 'with Broker. We'll find a way to take them out. In any case, you'll be wearing your scarf, like this.' She adjusted it over her partner's face to cover his mouth and show only part of his nose and his eyes. 'That will fool them. You look close enough to be Aziz. Only Kamal has met him and that too, once. His watchers will be fooled by you. Stop arguing.'

Bear shrugged helplessly.

THEY LEFT THEIR HOTEL AT ELEVEN.

They drove to Balo Street and parked to face Tarlabasi Boulevard, which would be their getaway route.

They strolled towards Istiklal.

Bear went ahead of them.

Zeb, Beth and Meghan followed at a distance.

Broker and Chloe behind them while Bwana and Roger were far back.

All of them in dark or khaki cargo pants whose pockets had spare magazines, flashbangs, teargas and smoke bombs and the various gear they would need. They wore loose jackets beneath which they had their Glocks.

'I'm in,' Bear called out in their comms.

'Their chai is great,' he said moments later.

'No one who looks like watchers,' Chloe said after a while. 'A family. A large man. Some college kids. No one's paying attention to Bear or to us. Bear's right. Their chai is awesome, but their koloocheh is out of this world.'

'Rub it in,' Bwana grumbled.

Zeb chuckled. Beth and Meghan were to his right. They strolled down Istiklal, like other tourists. He eyed the cafe from the corner of his eye and spotted Bear at a central table and Broker and Chloe in a corner.

'Leather boutique,' Roger decided. 'That's the least crowded. 'There's no one in it right now except for Bwana and me.'

'You have a safe place to plant the explosive?'

'Yeah. There's a trash bin at the rear corner. We'll place it there.'

Zeb scanned the street. No signs of police. No one looked at them. A few men glanced at the twins admiringly but not in any way that alerted him.

Will Kamal show up? He wondered.

Mohsen Kamal turned up at twelve pm.

43

'He's here,' Chloe said warningly. 'Three shooters with him. They've taken a table near the counter. One of his men has ordered drinks ... Kamal's checking out all of us. Relax,' she said quickly before Zeb could interject, 'Bear's got his scarf around his face.'

Zeb and the twins were at the toy store, checking its display. They checked the window's reflection for the presence of any hostiles but didn't see any.

'It will be hard to make out any shooters in this crowd,' Beth made a face.

'That's why he chose this place,' Meghan said.

They started strolling back to the cafe as Chloe kept up her commentary.

'Bear has lowered his scarf a fraction and is looking directly at Kamal who looks unconvinced.'

'He's probably looking for Petrov as well,' Zeb murmured.

'He's rising! He's decided to leave!'

Zeb fast-walked to the cafe. The twins kept pace. They were seconds away from its entrance.

Tourists on Istiklal. Shoppers and couples.

He started counting down in his mind as he worked out his moves.

The explosion ripped through the street as if a bomb had gone off.

That's what Bwana and Roger detonated, he thought grimly.

People screamed. They surged out of Istiklal heading to the various exit streets.

Zeb and the twins burst into a sprint.

'TERRORISTS!' he roared. 'THEY HAVE GUNS.

His words spurred the stampede as people fled out of Istiklal, away from the leather boutique and its nearby stores.

'Tear gas going off,' Chloe said calmly on the heels of the explosion.

He could hear their flat cracks in his earpiece over her voice and the shouting in the cafe.

He reached its entrance. Was jostled by an escaping customer. *Not Kamal*, he checked quickly. He shoved the man away and lobbed a smoke bomb inside. Two more sailed in over his shoulder, thrown by Beth and Meghan.

Zeb burst into the cafe with a scarf wrapped around his nose and mouth.

We have to act fast. The tear gas will affect us too. The inside of the restaurant was thick with smoke. Its customers screamed and shouted.

'We are on our seats.' Chloe gasped. 'We won't get in your way. Kamal is against the wall. His men are grappling with other customers to get them out of the way.'

'Take him,' Meghan cried at him, 'we'll get his men.'

One of the Sepah shooters heard her. He was close enough to Zeb, his eyes narrowed, tears streaming from them.

He fumbled beneath his jacket but before he could withdraw his gun, Zeb pounced. He caught the hand and trapped it against the gunman's body and rabbit-punched him in the throat and pushed him backwards to where Beth and Meghan were.

He kicked a chair out of the way. A body slammed into him.

'Get out,' he snarled at the customer. 'Didn't you hear the bombs?'

Kamal was a fast-moving shape against the wall, bending double, blinking furiously, cursing and swearing.

Zeb kicked a chair out of his way and charged at the major who whirled instantly and thrust a knife.

44

Zeb skidded on a broken porcelain plate on the floor and lost his balance. He shot out his left hand to jam it on the floor and stop his fall.

The stumble saved him as the blade's point cut through air inches over his neck.

Zeb was unbalanced however and fell to the floor when Kamal kicked out his legs.

The Sepah man was on top of him instantly, an elbow to his throat, the knife slashing downwards.

The tear gas stung Zeb's eyes. He blinked furiously to clear his vision. A shot sounded from behind him. There was no time to worry about his friends, though. He had to subdue Kamal quickly, before the police arrived.

He caught the major's knife hand when the blade was nearly touching his throat and squeezed hard. He twisted simultaneously to dislodge the elbow to his throat.

There was no give in Kamal. He thrust down with all his strength and kept up the pressure on Zeb's neck.

Last chance, Zeb thought desperately as his vision started blurring.

He jack-knifed his lower torso off the floor, bringing his

knees together to slam into Kamal's side. Simultaneously, he jerked his head to the side violently.

The major yelled from the blow. His blade scraped the side of Zeb's neck and dug into the wood. Sweat fell off his face and onto Zeb's chest.

The operator slammed the heel of his palm against Kamal's ear and then curled his fist and smashed its fleshy side into his temple.

The major fell sideways with a sharp oath. Zeb reared upwards and knuckled him in his throat.

MEGHAN SAW THE TWO SHOOTERS REACH FOR THEIR WAISTS. She and Beth were bunched too closely together. The escaping customers and the layout of the tables had hemmed them in.

Can't allow them to fire.

She caught hold of a chair's back and flung it at the men. She sensed Beth dive at a table.

'Duck!' her sister yelled.

She bent low when her twin threw several plates at the men which crashed into their chests.

'Stay down,' Broker shouted from behind them.

Meghan caught Beth's shoulder and pushed her to the floor just as a heavy table slammed into the men.

'You couldn't do that before?' she snarled at her friend.

'I had to finish my chai.'

Meghan plucked her scarf from her back pocket and wrapped it around her mouth and nose. Someone had broken the cafe's windows and the effects of the tear gas and smoke were dissipating, but her eyes still watered.

She checked out Zeb. He had knuckled Kamal and as he rolled away to get to his feet, Bear lunged out of his seat, caught hold of the major and hurried him out of the restaurant.

. . .

Zeb scanned the cafe swiftly. It was wrecked, with its broken furniture and shattered plates on the floor. A few customers remained on the floor, rubbing their eyes, crying. Its staff seemed to have taken refuge in the kitchen since no one was visible.

'Let's go,' he rasped. He went to the serving counter and grabbed two jugs of water and raced out of the cafe behind his team.

He jerked in shock when Bwana poured cold water over him from a bucket he had procured.

'Let me take these,' his friend relieved him of the jugs.

Zeb continued jogging on the near-deserted Istiklal. The leather store was to his right, its front door shattered.

'That sounded like a big explosion,' he commented as he wiped his face and dried his eyes.

'We used an extra C4 slab,' Roger smiled with his eyes. 'We told the store staff very politely that we would bomb their place. They quickly agreed to vacate it. No injuries to anyone. Now if he,' he cocked his head at Bwana, 'had asked them, they would have called the police. That's what good looks and manners get you. Instant respect.'

'You are saying I don't have either?' the African-American growled.

Zeb ignored their bickering as he hastened his pace and followed his team. Bear was far ahead, dragging an unresisting Kamal with the twins just behind.

'How long were we in there?' he grimaced at his wristwatch which had broken during the fight.

'Seventy-eight seconds,' Roger told him.

'It felt longer,' Chloe tossed a wet paper towel in a trash bin and turned into Balo Street.

'You know what combat does. Time becomes elastic.' Zeb said absently scanning the street quickly. Cars parked on either side, narrowing the road. Balo looked deserted. A few stragglers hurrying away in the distance. Bear was nearing his Range Rover, his hand in his pocket for the key fob.

They heard the whine first, of several engines.

A bunch of bike riders came into view from around the turn.

Helmeted. Black leathers and there was no mistaking what they cradled in one hand.

'SHOOTERS!' Zeb yelled a warning.

45

Zeb ducked behind a car for cover, his Glock materializing in his hand. Bwana, Roger and Chloe had already taken position behind three other cars, their handguns trained on the bikers.

'Ten of them,' Meghan said in a clipped voice. 'Armed with AK74s. They are firing!'

Her last words were needless as the chatter of guns filled the street. A side mirror blew away and fell at Zeb's feet. The car he was sheltering behind lowered several inches when one of its tires hissed with air escaping it. Car alarms blared and sirens wailed in the distance.

Zeb crawled to the front wheel and tried to peer around. Concrete chips from the hostiles' bullets smacked his face.

His inner radar pinged, warning him of danger. He glanced back and swore at the sight of the police cruiser entering Balo, its siren wailing and lights flashing.

Istiklal is a pedestrian zone. Where did it come from?

He erased the thought instantly from his mind. The where and how weren't important. What was obvious was that they were trapped between the cops and the bikers.

Zeb peered out from behind his cover and tried to shoot out

the cruiser's tires. Rounds from the hostile gunmen clipped the street and made him duck.

Both the bikers and the police vehicle were about two-hundred meters away and gaining slowly on them.

A man behind him ran down the sidewalk and key-fobbed his car open.

Zeb saw his chance.

He burst out from behind his cover, crouched low and sprinted down the sidewalk.

'SORRY!' He shouldered the car owner and sent him sprawling to the sidewalk.

Zeb snatched his keys, dove into the car, fired it up and spun the wheel hard to get the vehicle to move out on Balo at a right angle, blocking the approaching cruiser.

A cop leaned out of the vehicle and shot at him. The car's windshield shattered. The police officers from within the cruiser came out of it and ducked for cover when the bikers' shots peppered their ride too.

'Smart work,' Meghan said breathlessly. 'That car will block the shooters too. They have already slowed. But they still can tear up every car we are hiding behind and get us.'

Zeb nodded bleakly. He had bought them time from the cops, not from the bikers.

46

Bear was with Beth, the two of them flanking Kamal, ahead of the rest of the operators, sheltering behind a Hilux. The vehicle's tires had burst from the oncoming bikers' rounds.

Its body bucked and shuddered on its shocks as the riders shot it up.

'You know what I'm thinking?' Bear eyed his Range Rover which was fifty-meters ahead.

'Yeah, let's do it.' Beth clubbed Kamal with her Glock and the two of them pushed and shoved their hostage down the sidewalk as they laid down long bursts of fire over the roofs of the cars.

'Come on,' Bear swore when the major stumbled and caught his shoulder to straighten him.

A round tugged Beth's sleeve. 'I'm alright,' she reassured him instantly and then they were at their ride which too was shuddering from the impact of the rounds.

Those bikers are barely forty meters away, Bear grunted while he and the younger twin opened the Range Rover's rear door and shoved Kamal inside it.

Bear dove behind the wheel and without waiting for his door to close, fired up the engine and stomped on the gas.

The SUV exploded forward with a squeal of its tires.

His door slammed shut from the momentum.

'GO!' Meghan yelled in his earpiece. 'Beth has found cover.'

His windscreen starred and cratered from shots but none got through the thirty-millimeter-thick armored glass.

He rammed through the riders who, because of the narrow street and the parked cars lined on either side, were crowded together.

His fender caught a shooter and sent his bike skidding between two vehicles. The other bikers tried to get onto the sidewalks.

Bear felt his wheels crunch over something. He wasn't sure whether it was body or a bike and then he was past them.

He didn't go far.

He turned around fifty meters away and parked crossways to block Balo Street. He reached behind him, caught his HK, lowered his window a few centimeters and fired at the riders from behind them.

'Take them out,' he said grimly. 'I've sandwiched them.'

Zeb darted to the next vehicle's rear, peered around it and shot into the mass of approaching bikers. Bwana from the other side of the street thumbs-upped at him with his left hand as his Glock bucked in his right.

The shootout was brutal and swift.

The bikers had nowhere to go, caught in the withering fire from the rear, front and sides. Their bodies jerked from the shots. Some of them leapt onto the sidewalks where they were brought down by the Agency operators.

'Let's go,' Zeb grunted when he heard the cops behind them use a bullhorn, demanding them to surrender. He heard more sirens in the distance.

'Some of the gunmen on the street might still be alive,' Broker objected.

'We'll have to risk that.'

He crab-walked sideways along the sidewalk, using the parked vehicles for cover.

Beth joined him and then Meghan. He saw Bwana, Broker and Roger through the gaps on the opposite side.

He keyed open his ride and slid in. The twins climbed in.

'Chloe, where are you?' he asked.

'Ahead, three cars down.'

Zeb crunched over a fallen bike, steered to the right where Beth opened the door to let in Bwana, Broker and Roger.

A shot slammed into their rear window. His friends' Glocks opened up instantly and the AK74 fell silent.

'Told you,' the elder operator said. 'Some of them might be faking it.'

Zeb didn't reply. He accelerated and glimpsed Chloe keeping pace with him to his left. She shook her head when he pointed at the door. He used his ride as her cover to ensure she got into her partner's Range Rover and then accelerated behind his friend's ride.

'Safe house?' Bear asked from ahead.

'Yeah,' Zeb grunted. 'Esenler.' He frowned at his rear-view mirror when a leather-clad biker got to his feet and stared at their departing vehicles.

Can't do anything about him, his eyes narrowed harshly. *We can't risk going back to take him out. We have got to get away.*

47

Tehran

ZOHRA WOKE UP BEFORE LEILA THE NEXT DAY. SHE STARED AT the ceiling for several moments and then glanced over at the younger woman who had her sheet drawn over her head and was breathing softly.

She picked up the phone from the floor and brought up an app. She entered another number on it and held her breath while the app reloaded and then showed a green dot.

It's still there, she exhaled softly, *where I hid it.*

It had been random luck. She had bought a new phone on the day she had been captured with the intention of having a new number and canceling her old one.

She had grabbed the package in the laboratory when she had come across it, realizing instantly what it was from the research papers scattered on the floor.

She had taped the new phone to the stolen item and had

hidden it in the most secure location she could think of and had then fled.

And got caught along with Leila and the other demonstrators, she clicked her tongue silently at the turn in her luck.

She removed the number from the app and returned the phone to the floor just as Leila yawned and stretched.

'Let's get ready,' the younger woman mumbled and went to the bathroom. They freshened quickly and left the clinic through the rear door.

Leila gave the driver the destination and turned to her when they climbed in.

'That clinic is illegal?'

'It has to be.' Zohra nodded. 'You know the laws and how it is in our country.'

Leila shook her head in wonderment. 'I googled your aunt in the night. She's so well-known. Why does she run it? She's risking her life.'

Zohra sighed and leaned back against the seat of the cab. 'Because of her daughter. Her story is similar to your sister's. She too was raped. No, not by Sepah but by a boyfriend. She became pregnant.'

'Three doctors and a medical examiner have to certify that the abortion can happen. Balle,' Leila said bitterly. 'I know how the system works.'

'She could have gotten all of that because of my aunt's connections, but the social pressure was so much that she too killed herself.'

Leila surged across the seat and hugged her tightly. She blinked away tears. 'I don't know if I could be that brave.'

Zohra looked at her in astonishment and burst out in laughter. 'Leila Shokri, you go on protests knowing what the risks are. You are helping me knowing that we could both die. There's no difference between my khaleh and you. Now, where are we going?'

'Jordan,' Leila said. "Some of the protesters who were with us. To see if anyone knows where your phone is.'

'Do they know we are coming?'

'No. The fewer calls we make, the better.'

They stopped their cab at Mellat Park which was the neighboring district and proceeded on foot.

Zohra wrapped her scarf loosely around her hair and draped it over her nose and mouth, which made Leila do the same.

Anyone looking at us will think we have covered our face from the pollution.

She followed the younger student as they crossed Pahlavi Street and entered Jordan.

'Mehrdad Street,' Leila pointed with her shoulder at a tree-lined avenue. 'That's where they are.'

They went down the sidewalk. A car opened ahead of them and a family spilled out.

A bouquet on the ground. Zohra picked it up meaning to throw it in the nearest trash bin when the police van rolled up with their sirens blaring.

'Stay down,' Leila hissed when the vehicle went through a building's entrance.

'Is that—' Zohra began with a lump in her throat.

'Balle, that's where the students are staying.'

They joined a group of onlookers who watched officers jump out of the vehicle and go inside.

Zohra wiped her sweaty palms against her jeans. She thought everyone around her could hear her thudding heart, but no one was paying her any attention. They were all focused on the officers who returned twenty minutes later pushing five women ahead of them.

'Some of them were with us!' Zohra pointed with her chin at the women.

'Yes,' Leila replied shakily. 'Farida, Pari and Shaheen were with us.'

'Can we do something to get them out?'

The psychology student looked at her consideringly. 'Do you realize what you are saying?'

Zohra shrugged. 'We are already wanted by the police. What difference does it make if we break some laws?'

Leila smiled slowly. 'Zohra Hashimi, you surprise me every day.'

She beckoned discreetly and they went to the sidewalk where she brought out her phone and messaged someone. 'That's a secure app. All of us organizers use it to communicate with one another. I have told the group about the police.'

Zohra pictured the neighborhood in her mind. 'Pahlavi Street, the way we came, or Modares Highway. Those are the only two major routes that van can take and to get to either of those, the van will have to go to Ansari Street. All other routes are residential.'

'Come,' Leila caught her arm and hustled her to the intersection of Mehrdad and Ansari Streets. 'We are lucky.'

'How?'

'There are a bunch of protesters nearby. They were having a meeting in a safe house. They will do something about the van.'

48

Istanbul

ZEB FOLLOWED BEAR AS THEIR RANGE ROVERS SURGED OUT OF Balo Street.

A sharp turn to join Tarlabasi Boulevard where the traffic moved faster.

'Got to change our rides,' he muttered. 'Ours are bullet-ridden and those cops behind us would have noticed our vehicles.'

'Kasimpasa Stadium,' Meghan told him sharply. 'Go there. There will be enough vehicles there. We can swap ours.'

Zeb checked his rear-view mirror. No signs of pursuit. He lowered his window and above the whipping sound of the wind, could hear police sirens.

Will we get there in time?

He overtook a slower-moving truck, missing its fender by inches. He got an angry honk in return.

'How's our prisoner?'

'Barely conscious,' Chloe replied evenly. No panic in her voice. 'That tap Beth gave him ... it wasn't the lightest.'

The boulevard curved. The stadium came into sight. Zeb felt Broker and Bwana shift in their seats to look out of the rear mirror. He heard magazines slap into their Glocks.

'We can't fire at cops,' he warned and turned on the radio for a local news station.

Excited commentary filled the air as the host rattled off the events. The explosion and fight in the cafe and the shootout on Balo Street. 'Terrorists have struck Istanbul,' he yelled.

Zeb winced and made to lower the volume when his voice rose. 'There are more attacks in the city. A car exploded in Taksim Square. There are gunmen shooting people on Nevizade Street. Reports are coming in of a hostage situation in Cukurcuma Street. Our city has turned into a warzone. Where are the police?' the radio host thumped his desk loudly.

So many incidents? That can't be a coincidence! Zeb wondered and then it came to him.

He adjusted his rear-view mirror to focus on Beth who grinned at him and raised her laptop. 'That was me. I create those fake reports and witness sightings and got bots and false accounts to spread them on Twitter. Those will draw away the cops.'

'You are a genius,' Bwana summed it up for them.

'I know.'

THEY ROLLED INTO KASIMPASA STADIUM.

Zeb cursed beneath his breath when he saw a couple of men stop and stare at their rides as they rolled into the enormous parking lot.

He followed Bear to the far end of the lot where they circled a few times.

Meghan pointed with her forefinger at a Toyota whose driver was approaching it.

'Beth and I will deal with it,' she said and climbed out before he had rolled to a full stop.

Zeb watched the sisters smile at the man, gesture at their Range Rover, talk for several moments at the end of which the man nodded, gave the elder twin the key and walked away.

'What did they tell him?' Roger asked bemused.

Zeb didn't answer. He was observing Bear who had stopped next to a Ford. The operator took the direct approach. He jammed his Glock in the man's belly and Chloe did the rest by zip tying his wrist and gagging him.

They moved swiftly once they had possession of the new rides. Broker and Bwana went to Bear's Ford while Zeb got behind the Toyota and drove out of the stadium.

'What did you tell that man?' he asked when Meghan had finished punching the safe house's coordinates into the navigation system.

'That he would get a better price for our Range Rover.'

'He didn't see that it was bullet-ridden?'

'He did. He said we were terrorists. I asked him if he had seen any killers like the two of us.'

'We can be convincing,' Beth said straight-faced from the back.

'He bought that?'

'Yeah, especially when we told him that we could report his drug dealing to the police.'

'He's a dealer? How did you know that?'

'We were close enough to see the baggies in his jacket pocket,' Meghan chuckled.

'That will stop him from going to the cops,' Broker said admiringly.

'Yeah,' Zeb agreed, 'and hopefully by the time the second driver is discovered we will have left Esenler too.'

. . .

THE DRIVE TOOK HALF-AN-HOUR FROM THE STADIUM TO THE safe house which was on 544 Street.

'They are numbered in this part of Istanbul,' Meghan commented and gestured to a white residence at the far end. 'That's our safe house.'

It was behind a sports complex, from within which they could hear a crowd cheering. The driveway was lined with tulip trees which had grown tall and hid large parts of the approach from the street.

Zeb waited while Meghan used a key code to unlock the door and was the last to enter after Bear and Chloe had hustled Kamal inside.

He surveyed the modestly furnished living room. *No TV,* he registered while he and the team swept the living room quickly for electronic surveillance.

'Clean,' he announced in Farsi.

'WHO ARE YOU?' Kamal yelled. The major looked at them furiously and eyed the door. 'ARE YOU FROM AZIZ? DO YOU KNOW WHO I AM?'

Roger smacked him in the face and shoved him on the solitary couch.

'I am an Iranian army officer,' Kamal wiped his mouth. 'I don't know who you are, but you are in deep trouble unless you release me right away.'

He looked at them consideringly and then his eyes lit on Zeb.

'YOU!' he snarled and lunged off the couch.

The Agency team leader deflected his punch, caught his waist, spun around and threw him onto the sofa again.

'You are the one who attacked me in the restaurant,' Kamal said menacingly once he had recovered. 'And you,' he looked at Bear. 'Now I recognize you. You pretended to be Aziz.'

He took them in. 'Are you Petrov's people? Where is he?'

'You are SVR?' he asked when they didn't reply.

'Try again,' Broker smirked.

Kamal's eyes narrowed. He searched their faces, his gaze lingering on the twins.

Does he know about us? Zeb pursed his lips. *Sepah has files on us, but he's a major. Would he have access to them? He's supposed to be a star, though. He might have heard of us.*

His guess was correct. Kamal jerked backwards as if he had been stung.

'You're them,' he whispered. 'You are the Americans. I heard about you. Naser briefed me on you. He said you can speak several languages. I can see that for myself.'

Naser. That must be Brigadier General Saeed Naser.

'You report to him?' Zeb asked.

Kamal's face hardened. 'I don't cooperate with Americans.'

Bwana snorted and drew his knife. He wiped it against his T-shirt and inspected its point.

Kamal smirked, seemingly unaffected by the intimidating gesture. 'Torture will not work on me. I have endured much worse than what you can inflict. I will not break.'

'Why did you want Petrov?' Beth asked him.

'You will get nothing from me,' the major folded his arms insolently.

Zeb nodded at his friends. 'He's right. He's a battle-hardened Sepah veteran. That's why Naser sent him on this mission. You heard him. He won't break. We'll be wasting time if we try to interrogate him.'

He smiled at the questioning looks on his friends' faces. 'Let's go.'

49

'Go?' Bear's face darkened. 'What do we do with him? We went to all this trouble just to release him?'

'Yes. Leave him here. He'll get back to the city and return to Iran.'

'Yes,' Kamal nodded rapidly. 'That's the best course of action for you Americans. You should have realized I wouldn't work with you. I will not betray my country ...' he trailed off when Meghan snapped her fingers.

'I get it. We'll let it be known that he cooperated with us. We'll spread that message through intelligence circles, secure channels. Heck, even Twitter. We'll say a certain promising major in the Revolutionary Guard is a traitor. Beth and I can write up some fancy stories on the intel Kamal has leaked to us.'

The major's puzzled expression cleared up as he worked out the implications.

'That's right,' Zeb took the knife from Bwana's hand. 'There's no need for this. Those rumors will get back to Naser and Gholamreza. You failed in your mission to get Petrov. They will believe that false information. I wonder what they'll do to you.'

'Is it true that Gholamreza likes to torture prisoners himself?' Broker asked with an innocent expression.

'He rapes the wives and daughters of traitors,' Bear added.

A thin line of perspiration appeared on Kamal's forehead. He grew alarmed when Zeb turned away and headed for the door along with the operators.

'Wait!' His voice cracked.

Zeb paused.

'You can't do this. No one will believe you.'

'There's only one way to find out.'

Beth and Meghan brought out their screens.

'STOP!' Kamal yelled. 'What do you want?'

Zeb turned back to him. 'Why did you want Petrov?'

The major's lips twisted. 'I'll be killed for this.'

'Not if you cooperate with us. We'll put you up in a safe house in Europe or America. You'll be a traitor to Sepah but at least you'll be alive.'

Kamal looked at the door wildly as if considering his chances of an escape.

'Nope,' Chloe shook her head. 'You won't get past us.'

'Send it,' Zeb said impatiently to the twins. 'We have to move. We can't spend any more time with him.'

'HE KNOWS ABOUT THE WEAPON!' Kamal yelled.

50

'What weapon?' Zeb asked him.

Kamal licked his lips nervously. 'Didn't Petrov tell you?'

'Why would we be asking you if he did? Why would we capture you?'

'I am a valuable asset—'

'You are a lowly major, dude.' Roger snorted dismissively. 'You really think we would explode bombs in Istanbul just for you?'

'Kamal,' Zeb said harshly. 'Tell us about this bomb or get back to Tehran.'

The Iranian major met his implacable gaze. His eyes fell away.

'The Russian general knew about our secret weapon. We couldn't risk him talking about it to anyone else. That's why I had to get him from Aziz.'

That tallies with what Petrov and we figured out.

'What's this secret weapon? Another nuclear weapon?'

'I don't know.'

Bwana snatched the knife from Zeb and was on Kamal in an instant. He thrust the blade down to his throat.

'I DON'T KNOW!' The major reared back. 'Only two men in Sepah know about it. Gholamreza and Naser. My boss told me this much only because I had to bring in Petrov otherwise, I wouldn't even have heard of it.'

Zeb believed him. 'Such a program cannot be kept secret forever. Something always leaks. There is always some rumor.'

'Not in my country,' Kamal said proudly. 'People know better than to talk. They know the consequences. Everyone fears Sepah.'

Zeb heard a siren in the distance. It faded away eventually but it reminded him of the time. *We have to move out of here quickly*.

'Still,' he snarled, 'you would have picked something up. You are close to Naser. You might have heard him say something—'

'Emad. That's the program's name. I heard him speak to someone on the phone once. He hung up immediately when he realized I was in his office.'

'Emad,' Zeb repeated. He knew what the word meant. 'You are sure he was referring to the weapon?'

'Balle. The way he said it, I knew it was a weapon.'

'Great,' Chloe said encouragingly. 'There must be more information you can remember.'

'That's all I know,' Kamal said sullenly. 'I'll get killed for this.'

'Only if you go back.'

'Where is this being developed?' Zeb asked him.

'How many times do I have to tell you? I don't know anything more.' His angry expression faded. A thoughtful look appeared.

'What?' Zeb demanded.

'Because I am on a fast-track within Sepah,' Kamal said arrogantly, 'I travel all around the country. I have visited all our military bases. I have even been to the nuclear facilities in Arak and Natanz. Nothing is happening there.'

'They are secret for a reason,' Roger drawled. 'And you are only a major.'

Kamal flushed angrily. 'Yes, I might be kept out of top secret programs, but I will know about troop movements, security arrangements and logistics. Part of my job is to work with the military and protect our establishments. I know where our best soldiers and agents are deployed.'

'What are you saying?'

Kamal sucked a breath. 'Emad is not being developed at any military installation.'

51

Tehran

ZOHRA AND LEILA BROKE INTO A FAST-TROT WHEN THE VAN emerged from the building and drove down Mehrdad Street.

Dark windows. We can't see inside it, the research student observed. She and the younger woman hustled down the sidewalk.

'It's stopping at the traffic light,' Leila exclaimed.

They reached the busy intersection. The van was behind a couple of cars. No one was paying it much attention.

The suddenness of the demonstrators shocked Zohra.

They streamed out of cafes and restaurants, their faces covered by shawls and scarves, chanting slogans and holding banners and photographs of arrested or dead women. They surrounded the van and pelted it with rocks.

The light changed but traffic didn't move as it was blocked by the protesters and a growing crowd of onlookers.

The van honked and inched forward, but the demonstrators held their ground.

More rocks shattered the vehicle's windscreen.

'Stay back,' Zohra commanded. 'This could turn violent. We can't risk being arrested again.'

They sheltered behind a stationary car and watched the protesters break the van's windows. Several molotov cocktails exploded against its front and sides and it lowered several inches when someone punctured its tires.

Zohra could see a scuffle when the demonstrators forced open the driver's door and dragged him out. A cheer burst out when more students went to the rear, battered the back door and fought with the police officers.

Her breath caught when a shot rang out but the round seemed to go harmlessly in the air.

The report spurred the protesters who attacked the officers. A louder cheer rang out when there were crashing sounds from inside the van and five women burst out.

'Come,' Leila caught Zohra's arm as soon as a cruiser rolled up and officers burst from within. 'More police will arrive. We have to get away.'

They ran after the escaping women on foot, their hearts beating fast. The women were led by several of the demonstrators who seemed to know where they were going.

Zohra was impressed by the way the rest of the protesters had melted away in the side alleys once the women had been freed.

'No one got arrested,' she panted.

'No,' Leila huffed. 'They were very quick to break into the van. I think the police inside it had orders not to shoot. There is a lot of Western media interest in the protestors, so that helped as well.'

'Do you know where the women are going?'

'No,' the psychology student waved her phone in the air. 'I

know the core group has several safe houses. They will put up the women there.'

They slowed to a walk when they reached the National Library. Zohra's eyes bulged when the five women turned into a building adjacent to the Shahid Hemmat Metro Station and disappeared inside.

'Wait here. I don't want you to be seen,' Leila crossed the street and messaged rapidly on her phone.

A young man came out of the building, looked casually in her direction and gestured discreetly.

Zohra cut through the traffic and joined Leila when she beckoned with a nod. 'This looks like an office building,' she whispered, eyeing the man who ignored them and spoke in his phone.

'I have never been here before.' The psychology student punched the button to the top floor.

Another man greeted them in the hallway once they exited the car. 'Mehdi!' Leila embraced him. She kissed him on the cheeks and spoke softly. He looked at Zohra and then nodded at a door.

'Go inside. Don't stay long, though.'

They went through the door into a large open space.

'It was an office but it's unoccupied,' Leila explained rapidly. 'Mehdi converted it into a safe house.'

'He did that? How did he get access to the building?'

'Rich father who's into property. Mehdi manages his portfolio. Dad knows about his son's involvement in the protests. He is supportive.'

'How do you know him?'

'He's in my class.'

The three women who had been with them in the cell came out of a make-shift room.

'Leila, Zohra! ' Shaheen cried out and hugged them. 'We were so scared. Mehdi said you alerted them otherwise we would have been in prison by now.'

'We got lucky,' Zohra explained briefly.

'Your phone?' Pari shook her head. 'We don't have it. I know who has it, though. It was Mina. She was directly behind you and I was by her side. She picked it up and pocketed it. I saw it.'

'Where is she?' Zohra's heart sank.

'That's the problem,' Shaheen replied grimly. 'No one has heard from her.'

52

Istanbul

'EMAD,' ZEB SAID REFLECTIVELY. HE EYED HIS FRIENDS AND knew what they were thinking. *We should get this intel to Clare right away.*

Kamal sat on the couch, his expression a mixture of fear and anger. 'I told you everything I know,' he said defiantly.

'What you told us is jack—' Roger began.

'Yeah,' Bwana growled. 'You gave us a name. If your country wasn't developing some top-secret weapons all the time, now, *that* would worry us.'

'I can only tell you what I know.'

'We've been soft with you,' Bear hauled Kamal up easily with his left hand and his right fist drew back.

'I HAVE NOT!' The major tried to free himself and punched the operator on his chest.

His blows had no effect. Bear shook Kamal disgustedly and

flung him back on the couch. The furniture's springs squeaked from the impact. It slid on the floor several inches.

The Sepah man's harsh breathing and furious mumbling filled the room.

'He doesn't have anything else with him,' Beth whispered.

'I think we can safely assume that,' Broker uncapped his water bottle and drank deeply.

'Where were you taking him?' Zeb asked the major.

'To Tehran,' Kamal said wearily. 'Don't you get tired of asking the same questions?'

'Where?'

'A safe house in Niavaran.'

Zeb's eyebrows rose. 'That's a fancy neighborhood.'

'That's why we chose it,' the major sneered.

'You were going to interrogate him there?'

'Not me,' Kamal shook his head. 'Naser, my boss. I was to hand Petrov over to him.'

'Brigadier General Saeed Naser, in person?'

'That's what I said.'

Zeb turned his back on Kamal and took in his friends.

'Naser?' Meghan read his expression.

'Yeah,' he whispered. 'Let's get him.'

53

Tehran

'WHAT DO YOU MEAN NO ONE HAS HEARD FROM HER?' ZOHRA asked shrilly. She broke off from her angry words when Leila tugged her t-shirt.

The researcher drew a deep breath made an apologetic gesture to Shaheen. 'She must be living somewhere, with someone—'

'Her apartment is empty, khahar,' the other protester replied patiently. 'I personally went to her place. It was locked. We tried her phone. It is dead. She hasn't showed up in university. She hasn't posted anything on her socials and isn't responding to messages.'

'What about her parents?'

Pari, who had joined them along with Farida, gestured expressively. 'They don't get along. They disowned her when they found out she was a protester. Her father owns several restaurants and other businesses. He is close to the government. I am close to Mina. I was with her in their house when she and her parents fought. It was ugly. They accused her of betraying them, of being a traitor to the country. They asked her to leave their home.'

Zohra was stunned. 'That must have been tough on her.'

'We helped her find an apartment. Her university was paid for. Her family is very rich. Her grandparents had gifted her a lot of money. She wasn't struggling financially, but we were her only family and now we don't know where she is.'

'Don't give up hope,' Leila consoled Zohra when they were back in the abortion clinic.

The PhD student lay on the bed staring at the ceiling.

'Zohra?' the younger woman repeated. 'Did you hear what I said?'

'Balle. But what can we do? Without that phone there is no way for Zeb to contact me.'

'I will ask the core group if they have heard of Mina. She can't disappear just like that.'

Zohra turned on the bed listlessly and watched her type out a message. 'We will be killed,' she said despairingly.

'Stop talking like that.'

'No,' the older woman shook her head. 'For a moment I thought we would survive. We could shelter here until the heat died down. Then, when I saw that van take away the women in Jordan, I realized Sepah won't give up hunting me.'

'They will sooner or later. Yes, they might not stop but they won't put in so much effort.'

'No, they will only increase it.'

Leila looked up from her phone. 'Why will they do that? That doesn't make sense.'

Zohra wet her lips and looked away.

54

'I trusted you. It was your idea to develop the weapon in the university. Everyone objected to that. The generals said they could provide a secure military base. I believed you, however, and convinced the generals to go with your plan. What do we have to show?'

Gholamreza didn't say anything. He stood ramrod straight, his eyes on the carpeted floor as the supreme leader verbally lashed him.

'I wanted to destroy that Jewish country. I wanted to humiliate America. With this weapon, we could do whatever we wanted with any country. What are we left with, now?'

The supreme leader sat in a throne-like chair in the large reception room. His seat was simple. No fancy decorations, no gold or silver trim. His black robe was plain and his white beard caught the light. His hawk-like eyes were focused on the only other person in the room, the IRGC head.

The Sepah boss heard faint voices outside the reception hall. He knew there were guards outside the door, who, if the supreme leader wished, would kill him without hesitation.

'I will put this right, agha,' he said respectfully.

'Do you know where the stolen material is?'

'My people are searching for it.'

'Why don't you take the police or the military's help?'

'The fewer people who know of it, the better, agha.'

Gholamreza felt his soul was being inspected by the beady eyes.

The supreme leader nodded finally.

The Sepah head inhaled deeply once he was out of the room. His skin crawled as he was followed by the guards and escorted to his car and only once he was outside the supreme leader's palace, he allowed himself to relax.

I still have my job. I am still alive, he thought. He felt his forehead and it came away clammy. He knew he couldn't afford to be complacent however. His fate could change in an instant, on the supreme leader's whim.

'Sa'dabad Complex,' he told his driver. 'I have a meeting with the president.'

'YOU HAVE LET US DOWN,' AMIR HOSSEIN GLARED AT HIM.

It felt like a repeat of Gholamreza's meeting with the supreme leader. He and the president in his office, with guards outside the door.

The country's executive head was dressed in a Western business suit. His beard was neatly trimmed but in contrast to the supreme leader, the president's eyes didn't hide his fury.

'We should never have agreed to your plan. We spent so much in turning that university laboratory into a manufacturing center and one girl destroys the entire mission? How is that even possible? What's even worse, no one knows where she is or what she has done with the material. She could be in the British embassy or any other country's—'

'She isn't, agha,' Gholamreza interrupted the president respectfully. 'We have been watching every country's diplomatic office not just in Tehran but all over the country. Bus stations, train stations, ports, we have eyes everywhere. I am confident that she is still in Tehran.'

'Confident!' the executive leader shouted. 'You were confident when you came to me with your proposal too. Do you know I have to report to the Supreme Leader every day and tell him we still have no progress?'

'I just met him, agha.'

'I am surprised he didn't sack you.'

I am too, Gholamreza bit his lip.

'Find her, Mehrdad,' Hossein sighed, taking his first name. It was the president who had recommended him to the post and given him glowing references which had gotten the supreme leader to approve his appointment to head the Revolutionary Guards. 'I don't need to tell you how precarious your position is. We were counting on this weapon to restore our national pride, our position in the world, and now ...' he trailed away. 'What are you doing about getting new material?'

'We stole it last time from a German lab. We can't return to that place again. I have got our agents to try in other places and other countries too, but that is a rare—'

'I know,' the president said coldly. 'It is not something you can buy in a shop. Our diplomats in various countries have made discreet enquiries too. We can't go to Russia either, our ally. Even they will not support us in this weapon. All foreign doors are closed to us.'

He slapped his desk. 'You. Have. To. Find. That. Material. There. Is. No. Room. For. Failure.' The words sounded like bullets.

'I understand, agha,' Gholamreza said. No one knew better than him that it was not just his life but those of his wife and children that hung in the balance as well.

The punishment for failure at that scale was brutal and ruthless.

55

Gholamreza didn't take out his frustration on his aides. He didn't slam the door when he entered his office nor did he yell when his chai wasn't the way he liked it.

He told his flunky to get another cup, leaned back and brooded for several moment and then summoned Naser.

'One more cup,' he ordered his aide when the Basij head entered.

'Sit,' he told his visitor. 'Any news?'

'Nothing good, agha. We got a tip-off that some women were hiding in a Jordan apartment. We raided it, captured five protesters. None of them were Hashimi.'

'Did you question them?'

'They escaped, agha. A violent mob attacked their van and set them free.'

'We can fail only so many times, Saeed,' Gholamreza said harshly.

'I am aware of that, agha. I am tracking down those who escaped. In addition, teams are going out to raid the apartments of every student, every woman who-ever she is, who might be involved in the demonstrations. We will question them. I am sure we will find her soon.'

'Her friends?'

'We interrogated them and her classmates and professors too, soon after she escaped. They don't know where she is. I believe them. We were persuasive.'

Gholamreza looked at a map of the city on the wall. 'About nine million people in Tehran. Seven-hundred-and-thirty square kilometers. She is there somewhere, with the fate of our country in her hands.'

56

'YOU DID WHAT?' Leila yelled.

Zohra buried her head in her hands. 'I stole something without which the weapon cannot be developed.'

She looked up fearfully when her friend didn't respond for a long time.

The psychology student's mouth was open in astonishment. Her eyes were round. No words came out of her and when she reacted Zohra was stunned.

Leila laughed. Her body shook as she rolled on the bed and pounded the mattress.

'What's wrong with you? Didn't you hear what I said?' Zohra asked her angrily.

'I heard,' the younger woman wheezed and wiped her eyes. She giggled. 'That's the best news I have heard for a long time.'

'Are you alright? What's there to laugh about what I did? We are in intense danger.'

'My hero,' Leila kissed her on the cheeks, 'I know what you did. I now know why you are terrified. When I first met you, I thought you were just another academic, a research student who is more interested in theory. But over time I have realized what a deep person you are and now with this ...you said your khaleh and I were brave. Pah,' she snorted scornfully. 'We have nothing on you.'

'You are taking this too lightly,' Zohra said disbelievingly.

'I am not. I know how serious this is. But your stalling their evil weapon,' Leila hooted in laughter again, 'I don't have words. How did you manage that? Where is it? What is it? What's the weapon? You never told me about it?'

'Leila,' Zohra caught her chin and forced the younger student to meet her eyes. 'This can kill us. In fact, it will. I am sure of it. We can't hide forever. Sepah is too big. The Revolutionary Guards have so many resources. They will find us.'

'I know,' Leila said soberly. 'I am not out of my mind.'

Zohra stared at her for long moments and then released her. 'I can't tell you anything more. I can't put you in danger as well. No,' she said firmly when her friend made to protest, 'we are not debating this.'

'How do you know whatever you stole is still there?'

'I know.' Zohra said firmly. *I can't tell her I check my new phone's location every day.*

Leila eyed her for a long time. She fingered their phone and smiled as if she had worked out how Zohra knew. She crossed her legs, pulled a pillow over her thighs and rested her elbows on it. 'If Zeb Carter cannot reach you on your phone, then we must find a way to contact him.'

'How?'

'Why don't we email the CIA?'

57

Istanbul

'WHERE'S THE SAFE HOUSE IN NIAVARAN?' BETH APPROACHED Kamal.

'I can't tell you,' the major stuck his jaw out obstinately.

She slapped him.

'What?' She snarled at his shocked expression. 'You think only men can hit? Oh, I forgot, you are Sepah. That's what you do. Target women.' She kneed his groin and while he writhed and shrieked on the couch, searched his body, found his phone and held it to his face to unlock it.

She tossed it to Meghan who caught it expertly and caught Kamal's shirt and righted him. 'I won't ask again.'

'He's going to be a liability,' Broker drew his Glock. 'Let us finish him here and get going.'

'It's on Niayesh Street,' Kamal shouted. 'A walled house in a dead-end off that road.'

'Who is in it?'

'No one. I rented it specifically for Petrov.'

Roger drifted over to Zeb who was chewing his lip thoughtfully, observing.

'You don't think he's confessing too easily?' The Texan adjusted his shades on the bridge of his nose.

'Yeah, I do. But there's a way to check if he's telling the truth.'

Zeb's face was mirrored on his friend's shades when Roger turned to him. He grinned at the operator's look. 'You'll see in a moment.'

They turned back to Beth who was drawing out responses from Kamal expertly, asking few questions and letting his fear do the heavy-lifting.

'I was to message Naser when I arrived in Tehran and he would come to the safe house.'

'Message how? On this?' Meghan joined her sister and held up Kamal's phone.

'Balle. We have a secure app.'

The older twin scrolled through the phone's menu and showed him a program. 'This one?'

'Anything interesting on it?' Zeb asked her.

'Nah! Routine stuff. Meet me here. Go there. Why are you late?'

'We don't keep anything important on our phones,' Kamal boasted.

'When were you to return to Tehran?'

'Tomorrow. I was going to drug Petrov and we would catch a commercial flight.'

'What about your shooters?'

'My men? They would come with us.'

'How were you to confirm that you had Petrov with you?'

'I was to message him once I had the Russian.'

Meghan gave him the phone. 'Do it. I have read your communication. I know how you write. Don't play tricks.'

Beth jammed her Glock against his temple.

'There's no need for that,' Kamal yelled. 'I am cooperating. But I need something in return.'

'What?' the younger twin demanded.

'A life in America. A new identity. Protection until the threat against me goes away.'

'That can be arranged,' Zeb agreed.

Kamal looked at him suspiciously for a moment and then took the phone and wrote out the message. He showed it to the twins who nodded and pressed send.

Meghan took the device from him, pocketed it and she and her sister returned to Zeb.

'We're really going to ship him to Clare?' Beth asked him.

'No,' Zeb said. 'We'll ask Mossad to pick him up.'

'MOSSAD?' Kamal screamed. He shot up from the couch. 'I TOLD YOU EVERYTHING. I DID NOT LIE. I THOUGHT YOU AGREED TO TAKE ME TO AMERICA.'

'I lied,' Zeb shrugged. His voice was sand-papery, his eyes flinty. 'I have read your file, what we could get on you. You and your men raped women in detention centers.'

The major's face lost its color. 'That's ... not true,' he blustered. 'That's propaganda from your media.'

'Mossad will find the truth.'

Kamal launched himself like a missile. He lunged across the floor and got an arm around Zeb's neck, turned him around expertly to face the operators. He used his body as a shield, his free hand darting beneath Zeb's jacket to draw his Glock which he jammed against the American's temple.

'DROP THEM!' he roared.

'I thought he was smart,' Bwana crossed his arms. 'Beth, didn't you say he was a rising star in Sepah?'

'He is,' she bobbed her head. 'He's got favorable media coverage as well.'

'No doubt for assaulting those women,' Chloe said harshly.

'DROP YOUR WEAPONS OR I WILL SHOOT HIM!' the Sepah man shouted.

'That's why he,' Bear pointed to Bwana, 'said you weren't smart. If you shoot Zeb, you have lost your leverage? Did you work that out?'

Kamal trained the Glock on him in a flash and triggered it.

It clicked on empty.

Zeb unwrapped the arm around him easily. He snatched the Glock from Kamal, who stood immobile, shocked. He reached into his cargo pants, brought out a magazine, removed the existing one in his Glock and slapped in the new one. 'It's loaded now.'

He spun Kamal towards the couch, twisted his left arm behind him and broke two of his fingers.

The major screamed and staggered towards the sofa at Zeb's heave.

The team lead punched numbers on his phone and looked out through a window. *We have stayed too long here. We need to be on the move.*

'Avichai,' he said rapidly when the Mossad director took his call. 'I have another package for you.'

'Another one? We have not even finished interrogating Aziz.'

'Anything interesting from him?'

'Gang stuff. Nothing that threatens your, my or European security. But,' he said bleakly, 'he spilled a lot about women trafficking. That will interest law agencies in many countries. Where's this package? Tunisia?'

'No, Istanbul. Major Mohsen Kamal of the Iranian Revolutionary Guard Corps.'

'Sepah,' Avichai breathed. 'We will be delighted to get our hands on him. We will treat him like a valuable guest.'

'Why aren't you believing me?' Kamal moaned as he nursed his injured hand.

'Is that him in the background?' the Mossad head asked.

'Yeah,' Zeb replied. 'This needs to happen quickly—'

'In the next hour. I have a team there. People you know. Send me your coordinates.'

'He has a meeting with Naser tomorrow.' Zeb laid it out to him swiftly.

'We'll confirm if he was speaking the truth,' Levin said brutally. His tone softened. 'I know what you are planning. It's not a mission even we would take on.'

We have another reason to go there, Zeb thought bleakly of Zohra's message.

'Travel safely, achi.'

'NO!' CLARE SAID FIRMLY WHEN ZEB OUTLINED HIS PLAN. 'You are not going to Iran to capture Naser.'

'Ma'am,' he argued, 'will we get another such opportunity? He's the number two man in Sepah. He will know of Emad. We cannot lose this chance.'

'Zeb, you know what will happen if the Revolutionary Guards suspect that you are in the country. They will lock Iran down. It will become a giant prison.'

'We have to take our chances, ma'am. Do you want to risk not knowing what Emad is? I am sure Petrov briefed you as well.'

'He did. If Iran is working on another weapon—'

'A weapon of mass destruction in the hands of a not very trustworthy government which is openly hostile to the West,' Chloe cut in. 'Do we want to risk not knowing about it?'

'Why does it have to be you?' their boss said.

'Does the CIA have any assets that can find out? That agency didn't know of Emad. No one did, until Petrov told us.'

Clare brooded for a moment and then said wearily, 'It's a go.'

58

Tehran

GHOLAMREZA LOOKED UP FROM THE FILE HE WAS READING.

The Revolutionary Guards had highly sophisticated IT systems with multiple levels of firewalls and security built in, but for the most sensitive information, the organization preferred either verbal or paper reports.

'You are still here?' he asked Naser. 'What is it?'

'You should see this, agha,' the Brigadier-General brought out his phone, scrolled through it and pulled up a video.

'I don't have time for junk videos.'

'This will interest you.'

Gholamreza glowered at his subordinate and then nodded curtly. He watched the first second and then he inhaled sharply, took the phone from Naser and watched closely.

The clip captured a bunch of people who were escaping to a parked vehicle on the side of a road. There were bodies on the street. Another vehicle that had been parked crossways and was straightening. The video ended when the two rides went out of sight.

'Where was this taken?' the Sepah head barked.

'Istanbul. Earlier today.'

Gholamreza's head snapped up. 'Istanbul? Isn't that where your man was to get Petrov?'

'Balle, agha. This was taken by one of Mohsen's men. The mission was a failure. I don't have all the details. This man was in the back-up team. He doesn't know what happened at the meeting. He and the other Sepah men with him went to the rendezvous when Mohsen didn't check-in. Those people in the video had captured the major. They took out most of our men. Our man, who recorded this clip, was one of the few survivors.'

'Where is Petrov?'

'We don't know, agha.'

'Mohsen?'

'He is unreachable. His phone can't be tracked.'

'You lost Hashimi and now you are telling me you lost Petrov, too!' Gholamreza hissed.

'Yes, agha. And Mohsen too, most likely. He is one of our best officers.'

'You don't look particularly upset about these losses.'

'I am, about Hashimi,' Naser said gravely. 'But not about Petrov. He didn't know about Emad.'

'He knows we are building it.'

'He doesn't know what, though. You ordered me to find him and bring him to prevent him from speaking to Western countries. We knew the risk but it isn't as great as it would have been if he knew about Emad.'

Gholamreza steepled his fingers and pondered for a moment. 'I don't like it that he's out there somewhere, knowing what he does.'

'What exactly does he know, agha? You are aware I was against getting him back right from the beginning. So what if he tells America that we are building some secret weapon? Every country is building something secret.'

'We have debated this several times,' the Sepah head said sharply. 'There was a lot of value to getting him back. It was how we would have maintained total operational secrecy. Who had him? Some Tunisian you told me.'

'Karim Aziz, one of Mohsen's contacts. He is a shady businessman, but he has been useful to us. Petrov landed in his net by coincidence.'

'Ask him about Petrov.'

'He too is missing.'

Gholamreza slammed his palm on his desk. 'Do you have any good news? Give me one reason why I shouldn't sack you?'

'You didn't ask me the most important question, agha. You didn't ask me who those people are, who took Mohsen.

The Sepah leader played the video again and shook his head. 'Their faces are not clear. There seem to be some women but even that's not clear.'

'Go to the next video, agha. I got our technicians to enhance it and do whatever they could to clean it up. You will see their faces.'

Gholamreza played the next clip. He shot up from his chair when he recognized one face and cursed loudly. 'Do you know who that is?'

'Yes,' Naser replied. 'That's Zeb Carter. He has Mohsen.'

59

Gholamreza worked out the implications. 'Which means he might have Petrov too.

'Yes, agha,' Naser replied.

'Which also means,' the Sepah head said through gritted teeth, 'the Russian would have told him what he knows.'

'Yes, that's a safe assumption.'

'WHY ARE YOU SO CALM? AREN'T YOU WORRIED THAT I MIGHT FIRE YOU OR COURT-MARTIAL YOU? YOU HAVE FAILED ON SO MANY OCCASIONS. IS THERE ANY REASON WHY I SHOULD KEEP YOU IN SEPAH?'

'I am not worried, agha, because you are angry right now. Your rage is preventing you from thinking what this means.'

For a brief moment Gholamreza thought of snatching his handgun in his desk drawer and shooting his subordinate.

Naser stood ramrod stiff, his face attentive, no trace of insolence in his eyes.

The Revolutionary Guards leader forced himself to calm down. He drank a glass of water and occupied his chair. He played the enhanced clip again and focused on Carter. His fists curled instinctively.

And then it came to him.

'You told me you were going to interrogate Petrov personally.'

'Yes, agha,' Naser's eyes glimmered which told Gholamreza he was thinking in the right direction.

'The Americans will make Mohsen talk. Everyone has a breaking point. Our man would have told them about where he was going to take Petrov and that you would be going there as well.'

'You got it, agha,' Naser smiled. 'You know Carter as well as me. We both have read his files. We know what he did to the previous Sepah head. You know what the American will do.'

'Yes,' Gholamreza smiled wolfishly. 'He will come to Tehran. He will come to our country to capture you. But this time you will not fail, will you, Naser?'

'No, agha. It is our turn to set the trap and we will succeed.'

60

Istanbul

ZEB CROSSED HIS ARMS AND LOOKED OUT OF THE WINDOW OF the safe house. He ignored Kamal's protests in the background when his phone buzzed again.

'Yeah?' he growled without checking who the caller was.

'I have arranged four cars for you in Litros,' Clare said crisply.

'Four ma'am?' He straightened.

'Yeah. The police have clamped down on Istanbul. They are looking for eight people. They don't have your exact descriptions, but it will be better if you split up. I am still working on your exfil.'

'I have that in hand, ma'am.'

'You do?' Beth sidled next to him.

'Yeah.' He grinned when a car rolled up in front of the house and two figures climbed out. 'Those two look familiar.'

Beth hugged the Mossad operatives in delight when they entered.

Carmel and Dalia were as tall as the twins, olive-skinned, sharp-features and alert, dark eyes. They were dressed like the Americans, in jeans and T-shirts, with hands close to their loose jackets.

They were kidon, elite operatives within Mossad's famed covert unit of the same name which carried out high-risk operations around the world.

Zeb had come across them in a previous mission in Tel-Aviv. The initial encounter had been hostile since the agents weren't sure of identity and believed him to be a threat. Since then, a close friendship had developed and the kidon had often collaborated with the Agency on specific missions.

The visitors high-fived and embraced the Agency operators and came to Zeb.

'Of all the gin-joints, you came to the one we have set up shop in,' Dalia, the elder Mossad agent grinned and hugged him hard.

'You are looking good,' Carmel, who was her romantic partner as well, surveyed him critically.

'We keep him on his toes,' Meghan said straight-faced.

'I am sure you do. That's him?'

'Yeah,' Zeb nodded. 'Major in Sepah. Avichai briefed you?'

'Ken. Yes.' She looked at him sharply. 'You know the police are looking for you.'

'Yeah.'

'You need help with exfil?'

'Hold up a moment,' Zeb told her when a squeal sounded. He looked around to see Dalia was duct-taping Kamal's wrists with Bwana's help. His protests muffled when they applied the tape to his mouth as well and shoved him back on the couch.

'What's this plan you have in mind?' Meghan narrowed her eyes at him.

'Yeah,' Broker added as the rest of the operators joined them. 'Do tell us. It's only our butts on the line.'

Zeb grinned and dialed another number.

A voice picked up.

'Brat,' brother, a strong voice in Russian answered. 'It's been a long while.'

'I have a couple of Mossad kidon with me,' Zeb answered quickly in Russian, smiling broadly at the expressions on Carmel and Dalia's faces. *They are trying to work out if they can identify him by his voice.*

'They know the language?' Grigory Andropov, the speaker, headed a covert outfit similar to the Agency. It wasn't as well known as the SVR or the GRU which was how he wanted it.

Andropov didn't share his president's world views and was opposed to the Ukraine invasion - feelings that he shared only with highly-trusted friends. Zeb and the Agency team were among them.

The American outfit and his unit had established a discreet back-channel for communication which helped intel flow at a time when Russia was shunned by most of the Western world.

'Da, we do,' Carmel and Dalia chorused.

'Two women, Mossad agents who know Russian.' Andropov's smile was obvious in his voice. 'I bet you are kidon. You wouldn't be Carmel and Dalia, would you?'

The Israelis were stunned. Carmel gave a questioning look to Zeb who read it correctly.

'You can trust him,' he murmured. 'We do. He might be on the opposite side, but he is an ally.'

'You have the advantage on us, sir,' she replied. 'Who are you?'

'And that's how it will remain. Allow an old man some advantages, especially given where my country is politically.'

'Old man,' Beth snorted. 'You'll outlive us all.'

Andropov chuckled and then turned serious. 'Brat, I am sure

you didn't call me for a catch-up. Not with Mossad around. How can I help?'

'Do you have contacts in the Bolshoi Ballet?'

The Russian thought for a moment. 'I might. Why do you ask?'

'We need to join them.'

'Of course,' Meghan's eyes lit up. 'Their posters are all over Istanbul. They are leaving for Tehran today to start their Middle-East tour. They are going by car. Why didn't I think of it?'

Andropov heard her whisper. 'You are going to Tehran? Are you out of your mind?'

'Yes and no,' Zeb replied, 'there are reasons. Call Clare after I hang up and she'll lay it out for you. Can you help me with the Bolshoi?'

'Of course, I can,' the Russian spymaster said irritably. 'Its director is a close friend. Give me a few minutes and I will get back to you.'

'Makes sense,' Dalia tucked her hair underneath her ballcap. 'That ballet company is treated like royalty, here. Their people will be checked cursorily only when leaving the city and country.'

Zeb nodded absently when Andropov texted him back with a name, phone number and an address in Taksim Square.

'You have your gear with you?' he asked the kidon.

'We have lots of equipment,' Dalia grinned. 'What do you want?'

'Explosives?'

'Ken.'

'Can you follow us till we get to the border?'

She and Carmel eyed him speculatively for a moment, trying to read his mind and then they both nodded. 'Yes.'

'That's a good ten-fourteen hours away depending on traffic,' Bear exclaimed. 'You don't have people to spy on, follow, kidnap or extort?' He snapped his fingers.

'Who do you think we are?' Dalia dead-panned. 'We are tourists in this country.'

'Sure!' he scoffed.

'We have work but nothing that can't wait. Anything for you.' Carmel said. 'You plan to blow something up?'

'Maybe,' Zeb replied.

61

T*ehran*

THE INTERNET CAFE WAS ON MERAJ BOULEVARD NEAR AZADI Square.

Zohra and Leila had checked out various such establishments on their phone and had finally settled on that particular one.

'It's a busy part of the city,' the elder woman outlined its advantages. 'There will be police on the street, but they won't be paying attention to a single woman.'

'We hope,' Leila said. She tried on the chador they had borrowed from Jaffari. 'How does this look?'

'It does what it's supposed to,' Zohra said drily as she took in the black robe that covered her friend's hair and the rest of her body. 'What about your face?'

Leila wrapped a black scarf around her nose and mouth which left only her eyes exposed. 'This is better than a disguise. I have the identity card of an employee in Mehdi's father's company. If anyone calls them, they will confirm I work there.'

'Be careful,' Zohra said.

'I will.'

LEILA TOOK A CAB TO AZADI SQUARE AND JOINED THE CROWD of tourists who gawked at the tower that was built to commemorate the two-thousand-five-hundredth anniversary of the Persian Empire.

Azadi Tower was a city landmark and attracted visitors from all over.

The psychology student pretended to gaze at the construction for several moments while she checked out the crowd. There wasn't anyone interested in her.

She broke away from a bunch of tourists, hurried down the park and made her way to Meraj Boulevard.

Government offices and stores. Busy traffic. Honks and the smells of food from street vendors.

She went down the sidewalk and passed the cafe a few times before entering it.

She ordered a chai, paid in cash and found an empty computer and occupied it.

She hunched over the screen, her heart pounding.

It had been her idea to email the CIA, but now that she was at the computer, her palms sweated.

She clenched her teeth and downloaded a VPN. She knew from her protester friend that the cafe was one of the few in the city that allowed a VPN to be installed on the local machine.

She went through the setup and held her breath when she typed in the CIA's website.

It loaded.

Her fingers trembled. She navigated to the *Contact* page and filled out the online form with the message she and Zohra had thought up.

This is for Zeb Carter. This is from the person you met in Golshan Street. I have something very important for you. I am in trouble. I am being hunted. Please post a message on social media when you are in Tehran, flagged with #TehranProtests, something that only I will understand.

I need your help urgently, baradar.

She sent the message, memorized the reference number that the website gave, closed it, uninstalled the VPN, cleared the cache and fled the cafe without drinking her chai.

Leila fast-walked down the street and entered a garment store. She bought a white chador, changed into it in the trial-room and emerged out of the store.

'Hold me!' she said breathlessly when she reached the abortion clinic.

Zohra hugged her until the younger woman's trembling eased.

'Did it work?'

'I sent the message. No one arrested me. I am still here,' Leila smiled wanly.

'Sit,' Zohra ordered and directed her to the bed. She brewed chai for the two of them and they sipped in silence.

'CIA must be getting thousands of such messages,' she said. 'I don't even know if Zeb works there.'

'Don't think negatively,' Leila said fiercely. 'We have to be positive.'

Zohra nodded. *Hope is all that we have.*

62

It took a while for Kaveh to arrange his call with the American journalists. There was a protocol to be followed.

He posted a message on a real-estate agent's website, in a property that hadn't sold, a fake house that was put up for such correspondence.

One of the journalists, Ellen Ronning, checked the site and replied to him a couple of days later and they agreed to a secure video call.

He briefed her about Naser's assault on Parmida and told her why the Sepah officer had been in the Iran Capital Bank.

He and his wife watched the story break on Ronning, the TV show that the journalist hosted. It was live on YouTube which was the only way they could get it in Tehran.

'If you didn't believe that the Revolutionary Guards are a violent, brutal force who terrorize women and vulnerable people, here's a news flash that might change your mind. And if you already know of Sepah's evil ways, then this will be another example on why the United Nations has categorized that outfit as a terrorist organization.'

Ronning took a breath.

Kaveh held Parmida's hand.

'Brigadier General Saeed Naser, widely rumored to head the Revolutionary Guards once its current head Gholamreza retires, assaulted a woman. A bank employee. A highly-respected staff member who has been at the institution for years.'

'Why? Just because he could. Just because he wanted to. And because he wanted to strike fear. There was no other reason.'

She went on into the details of the violent interrogation without naming Parmida.

'Brigadier General Saeed Naser,' Ronning pointed her forefinger at the camera, 'my show is watched by four million people in America. After tonight, every one of them will know who you are.'

Kaveh grinned when Parmida kissed his cheek when the program ended.

'Will you get in trouble?'

'No,' he shook his head. 'Only Ellen knows I am the source and she will never reveal my identity to anyone. But will you get in trouble?'

'No,' Parmida said confidently. 'Naser might suspect I found a way to leak that information, but I was not the only one in the bank that day. Anyone could have done it. Besides, he will not risk anymore negative publicity.'

63

Navid, the internet cafe's owner allowed his customers to download VPNs and do whatever they wished while online. It wasn't his job to monitor their activity and he wasn't sympathetic to the government.

Their hard-handed approach had cost him business several times.

He had cameras discreetly hidden in the ceiling and in his office, he idly watched the feed. His attention was not fully on it. Esteghal and Persepolis, the two biggest soccer clubs in the country, were playing and he was focused on the match.

Navid couldn't help noticing the woman, however. He could only see her back, but she was stiff-backed and tense. Every other customer was relaxed while several of them had their headphones around their ears. She was wearing a chador as well and had covered her face.

That was unusual in a cafe.

Not my business, he thought irritably when Esteghal scored. He cursed. The woman shifted momentarily in her seat, enough for the camera to view her screen. He had fitted HD devices with zoom capability ever since some patrons had stolen his mousepads.

He frowned uneasily when the logo on the website looked vaguely familiar. His fingers twitched. Persepolis were back to defending. 'You had better score quickly,' he snarled at the screen and twirled the button on the control panel.

The ceiling camera did its thing.

He froze when the CIA's website became clear. The woman typed rapidly, closed the website did something else on the screen that he couldn't see and when she got up, he got a closer look at her.

Dark eyes that flashed and then she was gone.

Navid lost interest in the match when Esteghal scored again. He swallowed. His security system had automatically backed-up his zoomed image as well. The police would see the image if they raided his cafe.

His mouth tasted bitter. He had no love for Ershad, Sepah or any law enforcement agency, but he could not risk his business.

Why did she have to come to my cafe to go to that site? He swore and dialed the number to the police.

64

Istanbul

MAXIM IVANOV, THE DIRECTOR OF THE BOLSHOI BALLET checked their passports and compared them to their faces.

The Agency operators had disguised themselves to match their fake Russian documents. Zeb had a false nose, ears and green contacts.

They had applied their new looks at the safe house in Esenler where they had left their rides. The Mossad operators had dropped them along with their gear near Taksim Square and then they had disappeared into the city taking Kamal with them.

The police presence was noticeable, with cruisers and command vehicles traversing the city and at various checkpoints but they hadn't been stopped.

'Da,' Ivanov said handing back their documents to him. 'You can join us, but I don't have enough space in the coaches.' He nodded at the two vehicles parked near Taksim Metro station.

The ballet company's members were climbing into them as they watched.

'We have our cars,' Zeb told him in Russian as he handed his friends their documents. 'Do you have any other vehicles?'

'Da, vans, trucks and cars. They are behind the coaches. The dancers are only one part of our company.'

'We'll join your convoy. What will you tell the border police if they ask you about us?'

Ivanov, burly, thick-haired, bushy-eyebrowed, in a dark suit scratched his cheek. He had been expressionless throughout the exchange. 'That you are set designers and builders. That's what you are, aren't you?'

'Da,' Zeb agreed, equally straight-faced.

'I have never designed a set in my life,' Bwana murmured beneath his breath as the operators broke away and went to their cars.

'You are there for the heavy lifting,' Bear grinned. 'You and I. That's our role in the ballet company.'

'I knew it. We would get the jobs no one else wanted.'

Meghan sniggered and pointed at the four cars. 'How did Clare wrangle those?'

There were two Toyotas and two Renaults, all of them white and nondescript. They sat low on their shocks from the weight of the operators' gear.

Zeb shrugged. 'Probably got Catlyn's people to arrange them.' He put on his shades and got behind the wheel of the first Toyota.

'Gurbulak,' Meghan got into shotgun and adjusted her earpiece. She had gone brunette and looked very different from her sister. Her eyes were brown from the contacts and cheek-pads gave her face a fleshier look. 'That's the border crossing closest to Istanbul. That's where we are going. Dogubeyazit is the closest town on the Turkish side and Bazargan is on the Iranian end.'

Zeb fired up his ride. Broker and Beth behind them in a

Renault, Bwana and Roger in the second Toyota and Bear and Chloe in the last Renault.

He fell in behind an equipment truck as the ballet company's convoy rolled out of Istanbul to cheers, clapping, handwaving and approving whistles from the crowd that had gathered.

'Smile,' Meghan ordered.

He smiled and waved at the onlookers and in twenty-minutes they were on the O-7 with Istanbul behind them.

'We won't make the safe house tomorrow,' the older twin mused. 'We will reach the border around midnight and from there, Tehran is another twelve-fourteen hours by car.'

'Message Naser. Set up the exchange for the day after.'

'Yeah,' she agreed. 'I know how Kamal communicates.' She held up the major's phone. 'Everything is on here.'

Her fingers flew on the keys while Zeb followed the convoy. A long ribbon of asphalt flowing beneath them. Small towns and villages in the distance.

He knew the landscape would change. There would be mountains and rolling hills as they reached Dogubeyazit.

We won't see much of them. We'll be passing through it at night.

He made a mental checklist of what they would need in Tehran. *Weapons. Those will be in our Range Rovers that Hassan is maintaining.*

Hassan Ghafouri owned an auto-shop in the city and maintained the Agency's Range Rovers in immaculate condition for whenever the operators needed them.

Of Kurdish descent, the garage owner's family had been rescued by Zeb from militant groups in Syria. He had helped them relocate to Tehran where they had family.

Hassan knew of the vehicles' deadly contents and kept them securely in his establishment and personally serviced the rides.

Recon of the safe house, Zeb added to his list. *We may not get time for it, however.*

He knew what they were heading into. A hostile country with the Revolutionary Guards desperately hunting him.

Will we be able to capture Naser, rescue Zohra from whatever trouble she is in and get out alive?

He gripped the wheel hard.

We have to.

Failure isn't an option.

65

T*ehran*

NAVID'S CALL MOVED UP THE TREE QUICKLY AS SOON AS HE mentioned the magic acronym, CIA.

Within the hour Naser was in his establishment along with his team.

'Show me,' the Brigadier General demanded.

Navid, bitterly regretting his informing the police, led the Sepah team to his office where he opened the videos folder, selected the right one and played it.

Naser motioned brusquely at him and took over the computer's controls. He replayed the video several times and then straightened. 'Do you have any more angles of her?'

'No, agha,' Navid forced himself to be respectful. 'The cameras only cover where the computers are. We don't have them at the entrance.'

'That woman could be anyone.'

'Yes, agha.' Navid didn't know who the officer was looking

for and didn't care. He was aware of the news reports that Sepah had arrested several women, who had then escaped, but he didn't want to get involved.

He stiffened when Naser looked at him.

'You didn't ask for her identity?'

'No. We don't do that for anyone. She paid in cash.'

The Basij head stared at him for a long time and then nodded approvingly. 'You did well by informing the police. I want a copy of this video and that computer.'

'I can arrange that.'

The brigadier general gave him a card. 'Call me if she returns. Me, not the police.'

'Yes, agha.'

Navid sighed in relief when the Sepah team left.

To add to his woes, Persepolis had lost. He cursed the day and wondered about the woman briefly.

I hope she stays out of Sepah's clutches.

'It could be her,' Naser briefed Gholamreza in his office when they had finished watching the video. 'Our technicians compared her face to Hashimi's photographs. They have only the eyes to go with. The distance between that woman's eyes matches that of Hashimi.'

'Are they confident it is her?'

'No, agha,' Naser didn't allow his disappointment to show. 'It could be of the other woman too, the one who was at the bank. Or any number of women because that distance is not unique. But she looks similar aged.'

'Did you retrieve the message she sent?'

'No. Our people are working on it, but they are saying chances are very low.'

'She could have told the CIA about the weapon,' Gholamreza reflected.

'We don't know that, agha. Hashimi might not even know of

the weapon. We know she has stolen the material but that could be for any number of reasons.'

'Saeed,' Gholamreza snarled, 'we have to assume the worst case.'

'I agree, agha, but that's not what you are going to tell the supreme leader or anyone else, are you?'

The Sepah head grimaced. 'No. This has to remain between us.'

'It will. I am confident though that we will find her soon. Teams are interrogating every store on Meraj Boulevard to see if anyone spotted her. I have people interviewing taxi drivers. Hashimi and this other woman cannot stay in hiding for long.'

A PREMONITION CAME OVER ZOHRA IN THE EVENING.

She sat up abruptly and went out of their room.

Leila followed her curiously to Jaffari's office which was nothing more than a small, cramped room stuffed with medical equipment and in one corner was a table on which was a computer.

'Khaleh,' the research student asked, 'what happens if the police raid this place?'

The gynecologist removed her reading glasses and rubbed her eyes. 'That hasn't happened before. I have well-placed contacts in the police, Ershad and Sepah. I know several high-ranking politicians as well. They have always warned me of a raid. We have gotten enough notice to move the women out to one of the hospitals I consult at. The staff here are very good at folding the beds and putting them in a nearby warehouse. The police, when they come, find only the pharmacy and my office where I do private consultations which is legal. Why do you ask?'

'Clean up,' Zohra urged. 'Right away. I have a bad feeling.'

Her aunt looked at her for a long time while the clinic went about its business. Someone laughed outside in the hallway. A pan clattered somewhere.

'You have felt this before?'

'On a few occasions. It feels like ... I can't describe it ... it's as if I feel I should run away. Whenever I felt like this, something bad happened. If I had paid attention to my instincts, I could have saved myself from getting into trouble.'

'Bad feeling?' Leila echoed. 'I don't understand.'

'I do,' Jaffari said softly. 'Your sister was known for her feelings. They were like a sixth sense, warning of danger. She stopped your father several times from going out and on each occasion, something bad had happened. A bridge collapsed on the route he would have taken, or some other disaster had occurred. Dokhtar-e-man, when any woman in your family gets these feelings, I take them very seriously. Besides,' she got to her feet and rang a bell, 'we have a quiet night. We don't have many patients.'

'Neda, Sahar,' she told her assistants when they arrived. 'Evacuate immediately.'

66

Zohra made a face when they were back in her room. 'Don't look at me like that,' she said as she quickly folded her clothes. 'As if I am some curiosity.'

'People in my village used to speak of elders who felt like this,' the psychology student grinned as she too swiftly gathered their belongings and stuffed them in her bag. 'I didn't believe them. But your khaleh took them seriously.'

They could hear the sounds of hurried movement from outside, the sounds of hushed voices and furniture being moved.

'It's the first time I have acted on it,' Zohra said drily. 'If I felt like this every time something bad was going to happen, I wouldn't have joined that protest march!'

She sat on the bed when they had finished packing and dangled her legs. A vehicle started outside. The sounds quietened.

Was I wrong? she wondered when the silence deepened. The evacuation had taken forty-five minutes.

She made to speak, intending to joke that she had overreacted, when they both heard the fierce pounding at the front door that reverberated throughout the clinic.

Neda entered their room, her eyes wide.

'You have to leave. Right now!' The assistant scattered medicines and files on their bed. She reached beneath it on the floor and dragged out a trunk full of old clothing and laid them out for drying.

'GO!' she said fiercely.

Zohra grabbed her backpack and beckoned at Leila. They opened the door cautiously and peered out into the dark street. It was empty.

'Don't waste time,' Neda pushed them from behind.

They stumbled out, adjusted their chadors about them, wrapped their faces in their scarves and hurried down the street.

They heard the door lock behind them and could hear loud shouting.

Zohra's palms grew clammy. She wiped them against her body.

'Your khaleh will be fine,' Leila smiled weakly. 'She has dealt with these raids before.'

The older student nodded uncertainly. 'Where do we go? I didn't think this through properly.'

'I have. We go to Mehdi's place, where Shaheen, Pari and Farida are hiding.'

They walked swiftly through the quiet streets of Pasdaran, cutting behind the pharmacy until they came to Sadr Highway from where they took a cab.

'That's how they must have found out about the pharmacy,' Leila whispered when they were in the back seat. 'Someone at the internet cafe must have seen which site I was on. I know it had ceiling cameras but they couldn't have captured my face. I had covered it. But Sepah must have questioned taxi drivers until they found the man who picked me up from here,' she gestured to the busy highway.

'Balle,' the researcher agreed. 'They must have raided many other places until they came to the pharmacy.'

Her eyes widened with fear. 'Did they find out about your message to Zeb Carter?'

'I don't know,' Leila's voice shook.

Did I get him into trouble? Zohra felt her nails dig into her palms and then another thought spiked her fear.

Will Sepah arrest my khaleh?

67

Naser entered the pharmacy as if he owned it. He watched with satisfaction as the dozen officers with him, spread out through the rear of the building and checked rooms.

He pointedly ignored the three women who stood watching in the hallway.

Fatima Jaffari, he identified the older one. He had seen her on TV a few times talking of women's health.

'No one is here, sir,' one of his officers came up to him. 'There are some rooms with beds, there is an office, but no one is hiding here.'

The Basij leader's face darkened. His mood soured. One of those taxi drivers said he picked up a chador-wearing woman from Sadr Highway. They had raided homes, clinics, salons and other establishments before coming to the pharmacy. They hadn't found any protesters.

'Why do you have a bed in your office?' he asked Jaffari insolently as he inspected the room from the doorway.

'I see patients here. Sometimes they have to lie down,' she said calmly.

It angered him that the doctor showed no fear.

'You are running an illegal clinic?'

She laughed contemptuously. She made a show of leaning forward and reading the name on his chest plate. 'Saeed Naser. You didn't introduce yourself. Your men said they were Sepah as if that was enough and barged in. You didn't have any search documents.'

'I don't need one—'

She raised a hand imperiously to cut him off. 'I have heard that before, that your organization does not need to follow the law. I am a licensed doctor. I do private consultations here. I have a permit to practice here. There is nothing illegal here. Why would I hide demonstrators here? I have everything to lose if I did that.'

Naser's face burned at her scornful tone. 'Why are there beds in the other rooms?'

'For my assistants. I sometimes take on temporary staff, like when we have vaccination drives. Those people stay here, too.'

She didn't say *you fool*, but he could sense the words were on her tongue. His face flushed.

He raised his hand to strike her.

'You will regret that,' she warned him. She didn't flinch. 'There are cameras in the ceiling,' she pointed. 'Do you know how well-known I am? The interior minister's wife is my patient. Several other ministers' and senior Sepah officers' wives and sisters come to me. You are already in trouble,' she smiled wickedly. 'Have you seen the news about you? That you assaulted a bank employee? Think what will happen if you hit me and the camera footage leaks? You will never get the promotion you desperately want. You won't head Sepah. In fact, you might be charged and prosecuted and might go to prison.'

The Basij leader's rage consumed him, but a thread of reason held his control. His hand dropped. 'I will be watching you,' he snarled.

'I will report you for watching women,' Jaffari retorted.

The brigadier general knew when he was beaten. He ordered his men sharply and they left the building.

'IT'S GOOD THAT YOU DIDN'T DO ANYTHING TO JAFFARI,' Gholamreza commented when he reported to his boss. 'She is well-connected. She is popular. Even my wife talks of going to her.'

'Yes, agha,' Naser swallowed his anger.

'That incident with Iran Capital Bank's employee—'

'Parmida Bahrami. Only she could have leaked the information to the Western journalists. I will teach her a lesson.'

'You will do nothing of that sort.' The Sepah head's voice cut like a whiplash. 'You will leave her alone. I have had a lot of explaining to do to the president and the supreme leader because of you. Don't force me to take disciplinary action. Are we clear?'

'Yes, agha.'

'Any update on the stolen material?'

'No. It is a five-kilogram box. Similar to the coolers they sell in the shops to keep drinks in. We have searched the university and nearby buildings. We have even searched the shops on Sattar Khan where Hashimi was in the protest. We will have to search every residence and every office building in Tehran and even then, we might not find it.'

'Keep going and keep the hunt for her. I don't need to tell you the consequences.'

'Any news from Carter?'

Naser smiled for the first time that evening. 'Mohsen was to handover Petrov to me tomorrow. Carter has moved it back by one day.'

'Why?'

'I don't know, agha.'

'Do you think he suspects we know?'

'I am sure he doesn't. I responded normally to him.'

'Don't let him escape.'

'I won't.' Naser hesitated and then asked the question that was bothering him. 'What about Emad, agha? Is there a way to progress it without finding the material Hashimi stole?'

'No,' Gholamreza said bitterly. 'Our people stole it from a lab in Germany. They have increased their security. We can't try that method again. Our network in Europe is trying for alternate sources, but it is practically impossible without arousing suspicion.'

'Don't we have our own vaccine manufacturing capability?'

'Yes. But what we are developing requires that chemical—' the Sepah boss broke away and eyed him coldly. 'Naser, I don't have to tell you all this. You can read Emad's project report. But better than that, why don't you find Hashimi and capture Carter?'

68

Turkey

FOUR HOURS OF NON-STOP DRIVING. THE SMALL TALK THEY had made with their friends in the other vehicles had dried up. Even Roger had run out of jokes.

They were deep into the country, making steady progress, heading east towards the Iran border.

Meghan had offered to spell Zeb at the wheel but he had refused.

She side-eyed him as she uncapped a water bottle and drank deeply.

He sat relaxed, one hand guiding the Toyota, his left shoulder against the window.

She knew the look was deceptive. He could explode into action at the first sign or sense of danger.

He smiled when he felt the weight of her gaze.

'Do you miss that?' he pointed two fingers at a billboard on the highway.

She wiped her lips and took in the business woman in the poster. 'Our life in Boston? No. It was hard work.'

'This isn't?' He laughed.

'You know what I mean,' she grinned. 'Sure, the business made good money, it gave us a fancy lifestyle, and when Beth and I sold it, it was for a great valuation. But money,' she shrugged. 'None of us lack it.'

Zeb nodded. Each of the operators had done well during their time as private military contractors.

And then the prince had come along.

The Agency operators had helped a Middle-Eastern royal family during one of their missions and in return, the grateful prince, the heir to the monarch, had written a nine-figure check.

Clare had turned the payment down.

The monarch refused to tear it up.

Zeb and his friends wanted no part of it.

The prince got his way, however. He got the team to accept it as their personal operating fund, separate from the Agency's budget that Clare managed.

The team used the gift to buy their office in New York from which they ran their cover business, that of a corporate security consultancy.

The royal also gifted them their Lear, an aircraft that he renewed every few years with the latest model.

Over time, Broker and Roger, savvy investors, had placed part of the fund in the stock market for each one of them. 'No, we don't lack it,' Zeb agreed.

'Money buys comfort,' she stretched her legs, 'but this,' she gestured at the landscape around them, 'gives me purpose.'

'Spending days in places where there might not be sanitation, going after stone-cold killers, knowing you could die any moment ... that's meaningful for you?'

She grinned. She knew he was being deliberately provocative. She shifted to face him, her eyes sparkling. To strangers, Zeb came across as remote, expressionless, a person of few words.

We know him better. He is funny. He can talk on just about any topic and that too in great depth.

'You think I am an adrenaline junkie?'

'You aren't?' he retorted.

'Nope. Sure, there's the mission rush but that's not what drives me. What we do here, in the field, makes a real difference to people's lives. Heck, Farideh and Parvaneh in Tunisia and the other women with them. They are why I don't mind spending hours in places with little sanitation, like you said.'

Zeb's face lightened with a smile. He leaned across to high-five her. 'What about a special someone in your life?'

'What's this? Twenty questions? No special someone. Y'all know that. I am not the white-picket-fence kind.'

ZEB WAGGLED HIS FINGERS WHEN BROKER'S RENAULT overtook them and remained in the lead.

Meghan's reply didn't surprise him. *She's like me. Not interested in romantic relationships.*

'My turn,' she said.

'Ask away.'

'Not a question. More of an observation. You have changed. Back when Beth and I joined, you were all about America and our national interests. You are more nuanced now.'

He laughed. 'That's a neat way of saying I have persuaded Clare to hand over some of our missions to other outfits.'

The Agency was unique in its operating model in the US black-ops space. It could decline any operation without being challenged. Clare had a very close, high-trust relationship with President Morgan who never questioned her decision.

'We have been to every continent,' Zeb continued. 'Several countries in Africa, Asia, South America and Europe. We have carried out missions just about everywhere. Meeting the people on the ground, interacting with civilians ... it gives a different perspective. America is not the center of the universe.'

'That's an interesting perspective from someone whose moral code is black and white.'

'I have added some gray in it,' he grinned.

'This works because of how well Clare gets along with the president. He will not be around forever. What if the next executive is someone whose values are different to Clare's and ours?'

'She and I discussed this,' he said slowly. 'She's clear about it. She'll quit. She might go freelance. She's the most networked person I know. She's deep with European Union leaders. Not just them, every allied country respects her and would snap up the opportunity to have her services as a consultant.'

'What will you do if she quits?'

He side-glanced her. Meghan had straightened in her seat and was observing him expressionlessly.

'I will join her. Clare and I go way back.'

'What happens to us?'

'Your lives aren't tied to mine or Clare's. You might want to continue in the Agency. Beth might want to quit and be with Mark. Bwana—'

'She doesn't. Bwana won't. I will not. Broker, Bear, Chloe, they won't either.'

'Won't what?'

'Stay in the Agency,' she said icily. 'If you and Clare set up shop independently, we go with you. We were, are and always will be a team.'

'I was hoping you would say that.'

'Zeb,' she exploded, 'why would you even think we wouldn't join you? After all—'

'Punch him!' Beth interrupted. 'Seriously. Knock some sense into him, sis. Go on.'

Zeb touched his earpiece in astonishment. 'You have been listening all along?'

'I patched them in when this subject came up,' Meghan said smugly.

'Zeb,' Chloe said angrily, 'you and Clare have been having cozy talks—'

'We haven't!' he said firmly. 'This was one discussion, in passing, and I would have told you when the time was right.'

'When would that have been?' Roger challenged him.

'This is a hypothetical discussion!' He defended himself. 'It is an event that might happen way down in the future. It might not, either. There are many ifs and buts attached to it. The next executive might be someone who works just like President Morgan. Nothing might change. Why are y'all rounding on me?'

'Because you are keeping secrets from us,' Chloe yelled.

'And you weren't? Looks like you folks too have been discussing this.'

'Of course, we have,' Bwana rumbled. 'Zeb, listen clearly. What Meg said, goes. The eight of us, nine, counting Clare, we are one team, wherever we work. Is that clear?'

'Yes, sir,' Zeb mock-saluted even though his friend could not see him.

'No more such secret conversations—'

'It wasn't secret, for Chrissakes!'

'You tell us when they occur. Understood?'

'Yeah.'

'Alright, back off,' Meghan grinned. 'He knows when he's beaten.'

69

They stopped near Tahir, a small village in Agri province, in the night. The coaches broke away from the highway and drove a kilometer to a clearing in the forest.

Zeb breathed the clean air and stretched. The smell of mountains and pine trees around them.

'Mount Ararat is over there,' he nodded at the dark outline of the range in the far distance. 'Highest peak in the country.'

'You have climbed it?' Meghan asked him.

'Not all the way to the top. A long time ago. When...' he trailed away knowing she would understand.

When I had my family.

'We made good time,' Ivanov came to them. 'We'll stop here for dinner for two hours and then continue to the border. We should reach Dogubeyazit after midnight. You will join us, da?' He cocked his head to where his people had made a fire and were dishing out plates.

'We have our provisions,' Zeb declined with a smile. *The fewer of his group who see us, the safer it will be for them.*

Ivanov eyed him keenly and nodded. 'Ask me if you need anything.'

'We will.'

'What's the plan?' Beth demanded when they finished their cold dinner. She, like the rest of the team, was sprawled on the ground.

A ballet group member had brought out a guitar and several people from the troupe were singing lustily. A couple of women were dancing to the tune.

'Or is that a secret as well?' Roger drawled.

Zeb sighed. 'You aren't going to let that go, are you?'

'Nope,' Beth chortled.

'I don't have a plan right now. We recon the Niavaran safe house and then we work out how to hit it.'

'You are forgetting that shooter saw us,' Broker reminded him. 'Back in Istanbul, on Balo Street. He pretended to be dead and was watching us when we drove away.'

'I haven't forgotten.'

'He might have photographed us. Naser will know we are coming. He will look to ambush us.'

'That's what I am hoping for.'

70

Zeb strolled away from their camp to take in the mountain air and headed to the outline of the woods.

He stopped when he was four-hundred meters away from their vehicles, looked up at the vast canopy above and inhaled deeply.

Stars were tiny pinpricks of light in the sky. An airliner was a slow-moving light as it carried its travelers in its aluminum shell, traversing the curvature of the earth.

The mountain peaks were dark and majestic in the horizon, rising imperiously. *They were there before we arrived, they will still be standing after we are gone.*

He grinned ruefully at what the twins would make of his philosophical reflection and turned back to the camp.

A guitar twanged in the distance. Someone bellowed a laugh. Someone cried, the sound muffled.

He spun around instantly, crouching, his eyes searching the darkness. *That cry didn't belong to the camp. It came from within the woods.*

He couldn't be sure, however. He eyed the tree line. Less than a hundred meters away.

This won't take more than a minute. He hustled to the edge of the woods, his Vibram-soled shoes barely making any noise on the thick grass underneath.

The scent of pines grew stronger as he got to the woods. His eyes had adjusted to the darkness and he made out a dim trail.

He froze at the sounds of scuffling. *That's not an animal.*

He went down the track, careful not to step on any twigs and fallen branches in the barely-visible light and froze when he came to the edge of a clearing which was deep inside the woods.

Three Hiluxes parked with their hoods pointing towards a wider track that seemed to exit the forest. The vehicles had their lights turned off and from what he could see, didn't have any occupants.

What got his attention however, were the bunch of people lying on the ground.

He watched for several minutes. The forest was silent. The sounds from the camp barely filtered faintly to where he was.

Twelve of them. Most of them are women! Their hands and feet are tied and their mouths gagged. They must have made the sounds I heard.

A woman kicked out even as he watched and moaned softly. A man grunted.

They are asleep or drugged.

Where are their captors?

He circled the clearing to get a better view, his peripheral vision alert for any movement.

There wasn't anyone else in the vicinity.

He darted towards a Hilux, keeping out of sight of the captives, crouching low, his Glock ready.

Its cab was empty, its hood was cold, as were the two other vehicles.

'RED!' Meghan snapped in his earpiece.

Zeb moved instantly, racing around the vehicles and towards the trail he had taken while entering the forest.

Code Red was Agency speak for *operators in danger.*

71

Zeb sprinted once he was clear of the woods. Details registered on him automatically.

The guitar and singing had stopped.

He could make out a bunch of people crowded around the fire.

Can't make out details. Still too far away.

He broke away to loop around their rides which were the closest to him. He bent double as he neared Bear's Renault and crouched behind it.

They stood out. They had bunched the ballet troupe together with his friends among them.

The gunmen had scarves and shawls wrapped around their faces, AK47s clutched in their hands. One of them was interrogating Ivanov while two more were going through the troupe's bags.

Highway bandits!

A shine at their feet caught his attention. His friends' Glocks. He cursed beneath his breath.

The shooter slapped the director. A woman screamed.

One of the searchers turned at her voice and approached her.

Zeb moved up to his Toyota. He tried its door and then

remembered it squeaked when it opened. He released the handle.

I've my Glock and several magazines. Those will have to do.

His eyes narrowed when the searcher caught the dancer and ran his hands over her body roughly.

She slapped him.

The thug felled her with a blow and spat on the ground.

Zeb could see Bwana's face flickering in the campfire. Granite hard, as if waiting for the right moment to attack. The rest of his team had similar visages.

Need to check there are no other hostiles.

He circled back to Bear's ride and crouched-ran to the nearest coach. He went around it and checked it out swiftly. Empty. The other coach and other vehicles were empty too.

They don't have any shooters on the outside perimeter. They're all bunched together along with the troupe and my team.

A muscle on Zeb's cheek twitched.

They too are trapped with their prisoners.

72

I need a distraction.

The shooters were too close to the troupe and his friends. *I can't shoot them from behind. Some of them might fire loosely and hit the civilians.*

Zeb returned to the nearest coach and climbed in silently. He drew out his phone, brought up an app, selected a voice, put it on timer and placed it beneath a seat.

He got out and rolled underneath the vehicle, just beneath its steps.

A woman shrieked from his phone.

Zeb could see the hostiles' legs and lower bodies from beneath the coach.

They spun around at the scream.

'There's a woman in it. Didn't you search the vehicle?'

Zeb understood what the voice yelled from the passable Turkish he had picked up.

'I did,' another man protested.

'Go, get her,' the first man snarled.

He saw a pair of legs come towards the bus. The shooter cursed beneath his breath as he circled the front and climbed inside heavily.

The coach rocked from his movement.

Zeb rolled out from beneath the coach and stood to the left of the door.

'There was no one inside—' the gunman began as he stepped out.

Zeb struck him savagely on the head with his Glock's butt. He caught the falling body, confirmed he was unconscious and stripped his AK.

The takedown wasn't as quiet as he had hoped. The thug's body had rocked back against the coach before Zeb caught him.

Got to move fast before other shooters come this way.

He took the man's shawl and wrapped it around his face and rolled his body beneath the coach.

'What happened?' a gunman yelled from the campfire.

Zeb went around the front of the coach.

His pulse slowed.

He worked out his moves as he approached the fire.

He was still in the coach's shadow.

The shooter was the same height as me. They will see the shawl over my face. That will allay any suspicions they might have.

Five shooters facing him. Three of them clutched their AKs loosely while the searchers had their rifles slung on their backs.

The troupe and his friends behind them. The line of coaches, vans and smaller vehicles, at his back. His team's Toyotas and Renaults were shadows to his right.

'Where is she?' the gunman who had spoken, asked irritably.

Thirty meters separating him from the shooters.

One of the men was glowering at him.

He must be the one who was yelling. I will have maybe two or three seconds of surprise.

He had to make the most of them.

Zeb's Glock was in his right hand, pointing down.

Fifteen rounds in his magazine. One round in the chamber.

He took a step to his left. If he missed, his rounds would miss the troupe members, but they could hit his team.

That was a risk.

It was acceptable.

Protecting civilians was more important.

I don't plan on missing.

His next step forward brought him out of the coach's shadow.

The camp fire illuminated him.

'Why aren't you talking? Where is the woman? Who screamed? Who are you—'

Zeb's double-tap smashed into Glowering Man's chest.

His left arm flung the AK over the shooters' heads.

Bwana took three steps to his right, caught it and swung it to crash the barrel onto one gunman.

Zeb shot another thug in the shoulder.

Men and women screamed.

The troupe members scattered.

Ivanov dived to the ground.

Those details registered dimly on Zeb whose universe was the shooters.

He dropped to a knee when one gunman fired wildly, spraying the side of the coach.

A round whistled past his face.

He didn't flinch.

He triggered softly and red blossomed on the thug's shoulder.

Meghan lunged forward, got an arm lock around another shooter's neck and dislocated his shoulder.

Bear took out the searcher who had slapped the woman. The operator kicked his groin from the back and broke his wrist.

'CLEAR!' Beth yelled when every shooter was on the ground and disarmed.

Zeb rose to his feet and holstered his Glock. His world expanded.

He helped Ivanov up. 'Are you hurt?'

The director was in shock. His eyes were wide. His lips worked, but no words came out of him.

'Are you hurt?' Zeb repeated.

'No, no,' he breathed harshly. 'What ... who ... who are they?'

'We'll find out.'

Zeb made to go to the troupe, but Chloe and Beth beat him to it. The women talked softly, reassuringly with the company members, many of whom were weeping in relief.

He went to Bwana and Bear and helped them carry Glowering Man's body away into the darkness while Roger, Broker and Meghan moved the captured gunmen to behind the last Renault.

One of the thugs shrieked.

'What's happening?' Ivanov clutched Zeb's sleeve when he returned to the campfire.

'He's talking.'

73

'Turkish gang,' Bwana said.

They were assembled at the camp fire forty minutes later. The ballet company's cook had made hot chai for everyone which they were drinking from paper cups.

The operators had gone to the woods and returned with the prisoners, whom they had freed and who too were drinking the beverage.

'Spasibo,' Galina, the woman who had been slapped, had thanked them several times, sentiments that were echoed by many of the members.

'Who are you?'

'Set builders and designers,' Ivanov replied before Zeb or his team could respond.

Galina traded glances with the director and then nodded.

'Please give me your card,' she said straight-faced. 'Next time I need set building of this kind, I will know whom to call.'

That drew wry smiles and laughs from the troupe members until Bwana broke down what they had learned from the interrogation.

'They are into people trafficking,' the African-American said bleakly. 'Those are Afghans,' he gestured with his cup at the twelve people from the woods. 'They paid a lot of money to escape their country and get passage into Europe. This gang decided to extort them for more money. The women would be sex-trafficked.'

Zeb read his look. *Similar M.O. to the Casbah Maliks.*

'We should call the police,' Ivanov said.

Zeb didn't reply. Neither did the rest of the operators.

'You don't agree?' the director asked.

'We are your guests,' Zeb said with a small smile. 'You should do what is most appropriate to you.'

'We are a famous company. We have a reputation. We can't break the local laws.'

'You shouldn't,' Zeb finished his chai, threw the cup in the plastic waste bag and wiped his hands on his jeans. 'We will part from you here. When the police arrive, please tell them everything. That we joined you in Istanbul as temporary set builders and then we left you here.'

Ivanov's cup was half-raised to his mouth as he took in the words. He blinked.

'You are leaving?'

'Da. When the police come, they will ask many questions which we don't want to answer. We don't want to trouble you however.' He looked at his friends who nodded in agreement.

Galina spoke sharply and softly to Ivanov. Many of the troupe members murmured in support.

'If we don't call the police, what would you advise?' Ivanov asked.

'Take them to the border and hand them to the guards there. Say that you didn't get a good phone signal here to call the police and wanted to get away from this place quickly.'

'How will we explain the dead man and the shooting?'

'Blame it on us. We will go ahead of you and clear the border. They won't be able to stop us after that.'

Ivanov conferred with his members. Heads nodded. Hands

gestured. Galina looked their way several times and spoke insistently.

'Da,' the director looked up finally. 'We will do it your way. Otherwise,' he smiled, 'I will have a revolt on my hands. The dancers won't perform at the next show.'

THE OPERATORS WRAPPED THE BODY IN A LARGE SHEET AND stuffed it in one of the troupe's vans along with the rest of the thugs. The Afghans went into one of the coaches.

'Stop at Bazargan,' Ivanov said before climbing inside the vehicle.

'We won't be stopping anywhere once we cross,' Zeb said.

'Stop at Bazargan. Meet us there. You can't miss our coaches,' Galina came behind him and insisted. 'Our company's name is on the sides.'

'Da,' the director added. 'Wait for us there.'

Zeb shrugged. *We'll have a long drive ahead of us to Tehran. A half-an-hour stop won't hurt.*

'Remember Rukhsar?' Bwana's voice in Zeb's earpiece when they were on the highway.

'Yeah. She ran that cafe in Sori.' A village in the Afghan Hindu Kush Mountains that had been a terrorist stronghold.

It still might be, Zeb grimaced. *The Taliban are back in power.*

'She had a daughter—'

'Nazia,' Meghan replied. 'I remember. Cute as a button.'

'She would be the same age now as those women in the coach.'

Zeb nodded in the Toyota. He didn't reply. There were times when words were meaningless.

THEY REACHED GURBULAK AT DAWN.

A line of trucks and passenger vehicles in separate lanes at checkpoint.

Zeb fell in behind a BMW. He looked in the rear-view mirror to see Bwana's Toyota roll up and behind it he could see the Renaults' outlines.

'The ballet company is way behind,' Meghan stifled a yawn, 'maybe an hour away.'

They had overtaken the troupe at Dogubeyazit and had sped up to reach the crossing in the morning.

Zeb handed his and Meghan's passports to the border guard. He checked them, inspected their faces, stamped them and waved them on and they were into customs-free zone before the Iranian checkpoint.

He watched Bwana produce his and Roger's document in the mirror.

The guard took longer.

His eyes lingered on his friend's face.

'We can't shoot our way out of here,' Meghan whispered.

'Yeah.' He punched a number. 'Carmel, it's show time.'

'Will this work?' Meghan asked.

'Only one way to find out.'

The explosion happened just as the guard bent down to Bwana's window.

It was loud and forceful enough to rattle windows at the check post.

The guard straightened in alarm. He pointed at a plume of smoke in the distance.

The official tossed Bwana's passport back and waved him away distractedly as he yelled at other guards.

Zeb tensed when the Renaults rolled up. This could go either way. They could take a harder look at their passports or wave them through cursorily.

Chloe handed her and Bear's documents.

The guard became excited when other officers joined him. He glanced at the credentials, laughed at something the men said and stamped them.

Zeb sighed in relief and fired up his ride when Broker's ride made it without incident.

The Iranian guard was stoic.

'Tourists?'

'Balle,' Meghan smiled at him through the window. She had covered her hair. 'We are learning Farsi to make our visit easy.'

'What was that explosion?' Zeb jerked his head at the smoke.

'An oil tanker.'

'They explode like that?'

'I don't know. That's what the news said.'

He stamped their passports and they were through.

'That helped?' Carmel voice-smiled when their convoy resumed their travel to Bazargan on the Iranian side.

'Ken,' Zeb replied. 'You blew up an oil tanker?'

'Yes. It went up nicely. We spread it on the internet along with pictures and videos.'

'Tankers burn. They don't explode.'

'We might have done something to make it go *boom*.'

'I thought I heard shots too,' Beth interjected.

'You did. We fired several cartridges as well and reported that the vehicle was carrying illegal weapons. It has drawn police. Several border guards have come too. The border post is practically deserted. It's a good day for criminals to get through the check post.'

'Which you are,' Dalia chuckled. 'Criminals, I mean.'

'Thanks,' Zeb grinned. 'Yeah, we heard they are looking for someone like us.'

'No thanks. You have done far more for us. We are returning to Istanbul.'

'Share whatever Kamal spills.'

'We will.'

'They were too far behind to help with that gang,' he commented once the Mossad agents had checked out of their comms.

'I figured,' Meghan snorted. 'Good thing, too. Knowing them, those shooters would have been lucky to be alive.'

THE BALLET COMPANY ROLLED IN AFTER AN HOUR AND ITS vehicles stopped at a gas station.

'We got caught up in the traffic,' Ivanov ran his fingers through his hair as they drank chai while the company's rides fueled up. 'There was an explosion and then the guards questioned us about the gang and the Afghans. All that took time.'

'They are safe? The Afghans?' Zeb asked.

Ivanov and Galina were with them while the rest of the company was a distance away, out of earshot.

'Da. The guards said they would send them to Istanbul where they would be processed.'

'The police will be looking for you,' Galina said. 'We had to describe you. We could not—'

'Yes, we understand,' Meghan assured her.

'There are other reports. News of eight people wanted for Istanbul's explosions.'

'Relax,' Ivanov said hurriedly when the operators didn't react. 'You see those cars there?' He pointed to four sedans, Fords, in parking bays at the gas station. There are keys inside them. They have full tanks and all their papers are in the glove boxes. Leave your cars here and take them.'

Zeb looked at the Fords. *We had planned to swap our rides. Those will help*. 'Why?'

'Why what?' Galina asked.

'Why are you helping us? You don't know who we are.'

'You saved our lives. Isn't that enough?'

'Our *mutual friend*,' Ivanov said softly, 'told me something about you. This is a small way we can help. Galina is our lead dancer. I don't keep any secrets from her.'

He's referring to Andropov, Zeb made the connection. 'He arranged the cars?'

'Da, after I told him you might need new vehicles.'

'You know how it is with our country,' Galina reflected. 'Everyone looks at us with contempt.'

'I know.'

'But what our government does is not the same as what many of our people feel.'

'I am aware of that.' *They share Andropov's views on Ukraine.*

'We have few friends today, brat,' she smiled briefly. 'We can't even tour Europe. That's why we go to Turkey, Iran and other Middle-Eastern countries.'

'Yes.'

'So,' her smile bathed them in its warmth. 'When we make new friends, we try to hold them close and protect them.'

74

T*ehran*

ZOHRA WOKE UP AND STRETCHED. THE BLANKET AROUND HER felt warm and comforting and for a moment, she was tempted to burrow in its warmth and forget that the real world existed.

The sounds from the outside reminded her that she and Leila weren't alone in the safe house. She thought of waking up the psychology student who was sleeping on the next bed. *No, let her sleep. She is exhausted.*

They were in Mehdi's office-turned-into-safe-house. It had been the only option for them once they had fled from the abortion clinic.

Leila had called him when they were in the cab. The demonstrator had told her there was a spare room and had assured her they would be safe.

They had reached the building at midnight after changing several taxis. They checked the street carefully, splitting up to stroll down the sidewalks and had confirmed there weren't any police.

They had then waited for a wave of commuters to emerge from Hemmat Metro Station and using the cover of the crowd, had entered the building.

Shaheen had opened the door for them and had taken them to a room which had two make-shift beds and a bathroom.

Zohra freshened up and went out into the open space which doubled as the living room. There were a few couches scattered on the tiled floor, a TV on the wall and a kitchen counter on another wall.

She heated water and made chai for herself and went to the glass windows and looked down at Hemmat Expressway that ran alongside the Metro station. She forgot her predicament for a brief moment as the drink warmed her.

The illusion broke when Leila shoulder-bumped her and smiled tiredly.

'There's some more hot water,' the older student told her. 'I can make—'

'You stay where you are. I can make chai.'

The younger woman joined her, cupping her mug in both hands. They sipped quietly until Leila shrugged her shoulders. 'What do we do now? I have run out of ideas.'

'I checked the hashtags when I woke up. There wasn't any message from Zeb. I searched using all words that would make sense. Golshan Street. My apartment building, that date when we met ... there isn't anything. If we only knew where Mina was,' Zohra ground out in frustration.

Leila slapped her forehead dramatically. 'I keep meaning to message the core group about her.' Her fingers sped on her phone. 'There! I enquired about her. Let's see if they know where she could have gone.'

'If Shaheen didn't know—'

'Shaheen is not as well-connected as me.' Leila squeezed her shoulder comfortingly. 'We can stay here for a while. Mehdi says we will be safe.'

Zohra nodded bleakly and looked down at the traffic. *Baradar, come and find me. Before the police do.*

THE MESSAGE FROM THE CORE GROUP CAME AN HOUR LATER.

'Germany.' Leila spoke around a mouthful of cereal.

'Germany?' Zohra asked absently. 'What's there?'

'Mina is there.'

The older student's head shot up. She stared at her friend. 'How did she get there? When?'

'Germany?' Shaheen, who had joined them for breakfast along with Pari and Farida, exclaimed. 'Are you sure?'

'Balle,' Leila smiled at their expressions. 'I heard from the central group. They arranged for several women to escape Tehran. You know Farideh Rezai and Parvaneh Kazemi?'

Shaheen scrunched her face. 'From Kharazmi University?'

'Yes, that's them. You might have met them at some demonstrations.'

'They are rich, aren't they?' Pari interjected.

'Their families are. Politically connected, too. Their participation in the protests was becoming a serious risk to their families which is why fifteen of them escaped the country. Mina was among them. The central group has contacts with people who do this kind of business. Arrange for people to escape. In fact,' Leila snapped her fingers and turned to Zohra, 'they can arrange a call with Mina if you want. They will not give us her contact details in Germany but will coordinate on our behalf and set up a video call over a secure link.'

'Set it up,' Zohra nodded eagerly.

'Rich people,' Farida scoffed. 'They always find a way to get away lightly.'

'Some of them do,' Leila said sternly, 'but every one of them who is in the protests are risking themselves. I can't blame them if they flee because their participation is a threat to their families. I might have done the same in their situation. Don't forget we are staying in a rich person's building right now.'

Zohra hid a smile. It would have surprised her if Leila hadn't spoken up for Mina.

'It's done,' the psychology student said when her phone buzzed. 'Call is in one hour.'

THEY MADE THE CALL ON THEIR PHONE.

Mina appeared on its small screen, petite, frizzy-haired and seemed to bounce on her bed. Her background was fuzzy and indistinct and only her face and upper body were clearly defined in the video.

She waved when Leila introduced Zohra.

'Do you have my phone,' the research student asked. 'Shaheen said she saw you pick it up.'

'Balle,' she nodded. 'I picked it up when you lost it and when the police beat you, I rushed through them with a few other women and escaped. But,' she bent down, straightened and showed them the broken phone. 'It shattered when it fell to the floor.'

Zohra swallowed her disappointment. 'What about the sim card?'

'No, I don't have it. It must have slipped out when it split open. Can't you transfer the number to another provider?'

Zohra felt a sense of crushing defeat sweep through her. She let Leila answer for her as she stared blindly at the woman in Germany, none of the conversation registering on her until the younger woman jabbed her.

'Did you hear that?' the psychology student looked at her excitedly. 'Mina and the other women were going to be sold into sex trafficking gangs in Tunisia before they were rescued.'

Zohra pretended to be interested while the woman in Germany broke down how that had transpired.

'If it hadn't been for Zeb and his friends,' Mina shuddered, 'I wouldn't be on this call.'

The name cut through the older woman's despair.

'Zeb?'

'Zeb Carter, balle. He is an American. He seemed to be the leader of that team, but it was hard to tell. They behaved like close friends.'

'Zeb Carter,' Zohra repeated again, stunned by Mina's revelation. She looked at Leila whose eyes were wide, a look of astonishment on her face.

'Yes,' the woman in Germany said impatiently. 'That's the name—'

'Were there twins with him? Sisters?'

'Balle!' Mina's voice rose in surprise. 'How do you know? There were eight of them. Those two were Beth and Meghan. Are they your friends? How is that possible? How did you meet them?'

She trailed off when Zohra raised her hand to stop her flood of words.

'Tell me again what happened from the time you left Iran,' she begged and listened intently when Mina broke it down again.

Her palms fisted the bedspread when Zeb Carter made his appearance in the narration.

'It's them,' she breathed.

Leila nodded.

'Do you know who they work for?' The older woman asked the protester in Germany.

'They never mentioned that. We spoke to their boss who was at the White House.'

Zohra thought her heart would rip through her chest, so hard was it pounding and so fierce was her excitement.

'Do you have their number?'

'No,' Mina replied.

75

Langley

LEILA'S EMAIL WAS ONE OF THOUSANDS THAT THE CIA received every day. All messages were scanned by an AI program for context, tone, IP address and keywords.

The software determined that it was sent from Iran and that the sender was in a highly stressed and emotional state. It didn't flag Zeb Carter since that name wasn't in its keywords.

However, since the email was from a country of interest, it forwarded the message to the Iran desk.

Amir Rahimi was on duty at that desk.

The analyst was tired as his night shift was ending. His belly was grumbling from stale food and soda. His wife was unhappy with him since he had forgotten their anniversary and his kids weren't talking to him because he had to cancel going to their school play. *Urgent work at Langley* didn't impress them.

His temperament had further soured when the urgent work

turned out to be his performance review with his manager which had been long overdue.

'This could have waited another day,' he grumbled as he sat down with his superior.

The review went well. He returned to his desk with his mood marginally improved.

He was the first human to read Leila's email. He scanned it automatically while reaching for his desk for a bottle for Tums, shook one out and swallowed it.

Rahimi knew where Golshan Street was. He had been to the neighborhood when he had visited the city of his grandparents.

He hadn't heard of Zeb Carter.

He guessed the sender was a woman. In his experience, men didn't call other men baradar in an email unless they were blood relations or extremely close.

Nothing actionable here, he decided and forwarded the email to a generic address which was SOP for messages from that country.

He didn't know that generic address was for several covert outfits, one of which was the Agency.

76

Iran

Zeb was on the Tehran-Tabriz Highway with the early morning sun bathing the country.

Route 32, which was what the expressway was also called, started from the country's capital, ran to Qazvin and from there to Tabriz and further to Bazargan.

It was a scenic place. Mountains in Tabriz. Forests and rolling hills and then down to vast plains.

Zeb was driving automatically, with his fingers lightly steering the wheel, his thoughts on their upcoming recon and on Zohra.

He overtook a truck. Confirmed that the three Fords his friends were driving were strung out behind him.

A jolt over a crack in the road woke Meghan. She rubbed her eyes, stifled her yawn and stretched beside him. 'Where are we?'

'Past Tabriz.'

'We made good time.'

'No traffic. We didn't stop anywhere.'

'Stop by the side. Let's switch seats. I'll spell you.'

'Later. I'm good. Go back to sleep.'

'I've had enough.' She fired up her screen and went silent.

Zeb sensed her tense. She straightened.

'We'll be stopping somewhere?'

'There's a rest area coming up. There's a food stand. Twenty kilometers away.'

She frowned and checked the map on her screen. 'There's a bigger services area not far ... we can't risk being seen in larger crowds,' she answered herself.

'Yeah.'

GRAVEL CRUNCHED BENEATH THEIR TIRES WHEN THEY ROLLED up in the rest area.

A small house which also doubled up as an indoor dining area. Shaded benches on the gravel in front. Enough parking for two coaches and several cars.

Their Fords were the only other vehicles at the rest stop.

Zeb climbed out and stretched. He fist-bumped Bwana and the two of them went inside the dining room and returned with cups of chai and ajeel, a mix of nuts, on a tray.

Something's up, Zeb guessed when the twins conferred in low voices. *They'll tell us when they're ready.*

'Ellen Ronning,' Beth brought it up during their second cup.

'The TV host?' Bear sipped. 'Cutter's contact?'

Cutter Grogan. Former Delta Forces, who had served with Zeb, Bear, Bwana and Roger. He had set up his PI practice in New York after leaving the military and was a close friend to them.

'Yeah, her. She broke a news story about Saeed Naser assaulting a bank officer. This was when we were in Istanbul.'

Zeb cupped his paper cup in both hands and inhaled the chai's fragrance. He didn't hurry Beth. None of them did. *We have time. She'll get to it.*

'Parmida Bahrami was the employee he slapped, but that's only a rumor on the socials. Naser, the bank or she haven't confirmed the identity of the staff member. The socials also say Sepah was there because two women showed up, looking for a phone they had lost in the bank.'

Zeb stiffened. Hot beverage splashed over his wrist. He mopped it up with a paper towel absently. 'Two women? Any descriptions?'

'No. This is social gossip spread by accounts that seem to be anonymous.'

'It could be Zohra and a friend,' Chloe articulated what was on their minds. 'The time line fits. She sent the message to us and then her phone goes silent.'

'There are several other reports,' Meghan said somberly, her eyes flat, hard, 'that several women escaped from Sepah's custody on two occasions. The Revolutionary Guards are looking for them, but in the socials the rumor is that Sepah is looking for one woman in particular.'

'Any description?' Zeb asked.

'No.'

'They are still looking for her?'

'Yeah. Socials still going around. There was a raid on a pharmacy, here, look for yourself.'

Zeb looked over Chloe's shoulder as they crowded around Meghan's screen.

Who is this mysterious woman Sepah is looking for? Is her hunt related to the raid on Fatima Jaffari's property?

There were several other messages in a similar vein.

'Who is Jaffari?' Bear rasped.

'Well-known gynecologist in Tehran.'

'Any relation to Zohra?'

'None that we know of.'

Zeb crushed his paper cup and tossed it in the bin. 'Let's go,' he said in a clipped voice.

He got into shotgun while Meghan took the wheel and they drove out of the rest area.

'She's smart,' she told him firmly. 'She's resourceful. She's evaded the Revolutionary Guards so far. We'll get to her.'

'That's not what I am worried about,' his voice was brittle. 'I am wondering what she's gotten herself into.'

77

T*ehran*

SAEED NASER HAD A MULTITUDE OF RESOURCES AT HIS command. He had highly-trained and experienced agents who wouldn't hesitate to use deadly force on his orders. He had satellites, entire regiments, tanks, missiles and the best cryptography and technology teams in the country.

He also had the police. That organization didn't report to Sepah but there was a very close collaboration between the outfits.

Naturally, since the Revolutionary Guards wielded enormous power, the information flow was one way only but such trivial matters didn't concern Naser.

The police had vehicles equipped with cameras that captured street views and crowds.

One such cruiser was passing Hemmat Metro Station when Zohra and Leila entered the building.

The women were covered in their chadors and shawls.

The camera recorded them.

The video got uploaded to the police servers which Sepah was hooked into.

A gait analysis software compared the two women to the footage it had from Iran Capital Bank.

Major Abid Khan, another of Naser's promising officers, read the report and raced up the stairs to knock on his boss's door and entered it.

NASER LOOKED UP AND FROWNED. 'WHY ARE YOU SWEATING?'

'I took the stairs, agha.'

'Why didn't you take the elevator?'

'The stairs keep me fit.'

The brigadier general didn't show his approval but inwardly he was pleased. It was just the answer he wanted. *Abid and Mohsen are two of my best men.* Then he remembered that the latter was captured by Carter and his face darkened.

'What's the hurry?' he growled.

'I know where Hashimi and that other woman are.'

Naser shot up from his chair. He took the report and read it swiftly.

Abid came to his side and leaned over his laptop. 'Allow me, agha,' he requested and typed swiftly to bring up the video.

'Those two,' he said triumphantly at the clip of the women entering the building. 'That's them.'

'We can see nothing except their backs,' Naser objected.

'We have several seconds of them walking towards the entrance. That was enough for our software to assess their gait and come up with a high percentage match.'

The Basij leader's fists curled. 'Whose building is it?'

'Merwan Ali.'

'The businessman?'

'Yes. He is supposed to be close to the president.'

'He is,' Naser scratched his cheek. 'We have to move carefully, but if protesters are hiding in his office, then even his connections won't save him.' He drew out his revolver from his desk drawer and holstered it. 'Get your four best men. You and them. No one else. Let's go get Hashimi.'

78

'You don't have a number for Zeb Carter?' Zohra asked despairingly.

'No, khahar,' Mina replied. 'Those people gave their names only.'

'Describe them.'

The protester in Germany pursed her lips.

'Please,' Leila read her questioning look. 'This is important.'

'Those twins had green eyes. Bwana is African-American. Broker and Roger are like Hollywood ... are you alright?'

Zohra nodded rapidly as she wiped away her tears, smilingly. 'Balle, balle. I am crying in relief. I know them.'

'You do?' Mina exclaimed. 'How?'

'We can't get into that right now,' Leila cut in before the older woman could respond. 'Do you remember anything that could help us contact them?'

'No. Parvaneh and I have talked about that several times. They even gave us money. We were flown out of Tunisia in an American military flight. The crew didn't know anything of Zeb Carter. They didn't speak to us at all except to offer some food and drinks. We were met in Germany by the police and they too didn't know of our rescuers. Is there a problem?'

'No, Mina,' Zohra smiled at her. 'You have been very helpful.'

Leila ended the call after small talk and regarded the researcher seriously. 'Don't get your hopes up. He is in Tunisia. He could be anywhere.'

'Balle,' Zohra nodded. 'But now you know he isn't an American tourist. He must be some kind of special agent.'

'Let's hope that email gets to him.'

MEHDI ALI WAS AWARE OF THE RISKS OF HOUSING THE demonstrators in his father's building, which was why he had a couple of guards patrolling the entrance continually. Round-the-clock vigil by experienced and trusted people.

One of them spotted the SUV crawl to the curb and spill out five men who were in plain-clothes but moved determinedly towards the entrance. He also noticed the second SUV which had darkened windows but no one emerged from it.

He lifted his phone casually and uttered a single word. 'Police.'

MEHDI REACTED INSTANTLY.

He rushed into the safe apartment. 'Get your bags,' he yelled at Zohra and Leila. 'You have to leave right now.'

He pounded the doors of the other womens' rooms and repeated the instructions.

'What happened?' Zohra asked fearfully as she caught her backpack, shoved her clothing in it and strapped it to her back.

'Police,' Mehdi snarled. 'They are entering the building.'

'Relax,' he said reassuringly. 'I have planned for this eventuality. I have blocked the elevators from working. They will have to take the stairs. That buys us time since we are on the top floor. But we have to move right now.'

'Where?' Leila asked shakily as the seven protesters followed him into the hallway where he unlocked another apartment.

'This elevator is secret,' he punched the code to the car and gestured to them to get into it. 'It goes into the basement car park, into the maintenance room. Only I have the key to that.'

The car reached its destination noiselessly and its doors slid open. Mehdi unlocked the maintenance room cautiously and peered outside.

Zohra and the women followed him rapidly at his signal.

'Get inside that truck,' he hissed, jerking his head at a pickup, 'and pull that tarpaulin over your heads.'

The researcher, the tallest of the women, got in quickly and helped the other demonstrators. They lay on the bed of the truck and pulled the sheet over themselves.

Zohra closed her eyes when the vehicle moved. Shaheen started praying. Pari joined in. The older woman felt Leila's hand seek hers in comfort, the psychology student's palm clammy with fear.

'We will be alright,' the researcher said, hoping her voice sounded calmer and more comforting than she felt.

The truck jolted on its shocks when it joined the street. *Won't the police have blocked all exits from the building?* she wondered and strained her ears to hear shouts or loud voices.

Only the sounds of traffic came to her.

The truck rolled on for forty-five minutes, turning several times. The hard bed rattled underneath them, juddering their body, but the women lay quietly with their teeth clenched and their hearts in their throats until the vehicle stopped on what felt like a quiet street.

'We are safe. You can come out,' Mehdi called out softly.

Zohra climbed out stiffly and rubbed her hips. 'This is a hospital?' Her eyes widened when she took in the building in whose parking lot they were.

'Balle,' Mehdi grinned. 'A private hospital run by one of my friend's family. You can stay here as patients. You won't be recorded in the system and all of you will have rooms.'

'How did we get away? I thought the police would stop us.'

'I built another exit from that basement in the building. It opens into the next building's parking lot. Sepah is looking in the wrong places.'

'Won't they find our rooms? You don't seem to be worried.'

'No,' Mehdi smiled. 'My staff cleaned up after we left. They changed the sheets, towels and pillow covers and dumped the ones you used in the common washing machine. There's no trace of your presence left.'

'Won't you and your father be questioned, though? The police will ask you why you have those beds.'

'For construction workers. We are still fitting out that floor. I will even produce the men who are genuine builders.'

Zohra looked at him gratefully. 'You thought of everything while risking—'

'Stop. This is something I and my father do willingly. No one has forced us into it. And no, if I had thought of everything, I would have found a way to beat Sepah's cameras!'

'Cameras?' Leila exclaimed.

'Balle, I figured out how they suspected you all were hiding in the building. There are no cameras pointing at the building's entrance. I made sure of that when I took over its management. But the police have these patrol cars. You might have seen them. I am convinced one of those would have captured you.'

'But all of us were in chadors with our faces covered when we were out in public,' Farida pointed out.

'They have software that analyses body movement.'

'Balle, some of the other protest organizers mentioned that to me. We have yet to work out how to beat it.'

Leila stood on her toes to peer over the compound wall.

'Pasdaran,' he guessed she was trying to locate where they were and made to lead them inside the hospital.

Zohra met her eyes and had the same thought as the younger woman. 'Mehdi, we will leave you here. Leila and I have another place nearby.'

He frowned. 'But—'

'Trust me,' she smiled. 'We will be safe.'

'Safer than here?'

'Balle. Go, get inside.' She hugged him hard and embraced the other women and went out of the parking lot swiftly along with Leila.

'Sepah won't go back to my khaleh's clinic,' she murmured.

'Smart minds think alike,' the younger woman said smugly. Her smile faded. 'I was so scared back there.'

'So was I.' Zohra covered her face and entered the sidewalk.

Zeb, she prayed. *Please find us quickly.*

79

The Agency team stopped for their final rest break on the outskirts of Tehran.

Zeb patted the false beard over his chin and looked in his Ford's side mirror to confirm it was in place. He didn't like facial hair and had gone in for a fake one that was little more than a stubble. His nose was crooked and a small scar adorned his forehead.

His friends had gone for thicker beards, contacts and various prosthetics. The women too sported different looks.

Except Bwana. *There's nothing we can do about him. He'll stand out anywhere in Iran, however he is disguised.*

It was a risk they had to accept.

We managed in China on several missions. We'll get by here too.

He took the paper cup from Broker and sipped the chai his friend had poured from a flask and studied their surroundings.

They had broken into a used car dealership which was closed for the day. There were abandoned buildings on either side of it which made it suitable for their rest break. Bear had made short work of its padlock with his bolt cutter, the twins had fried its cameras and then they were in.

'This is Kamal's safe house,' Meghan opened her screen to

bring up satellite images of the building. 'On Senobar,' she stabbed her finger on the residence. 'One house to its right and then the street joined Fereshteh.'

Zeb studied it silently. *All of those houses are villas.* That wasn't surprising since Niavaran was an upscale neighborhood. The homes had front yards and behind them were woods that separated the homes from the ones on Fereshteh.

'Naser won't be inside. He will be in some command vehicle from where he can watch the take down,' Chloe observed.

'Yeah,' Zeb tapped the intersection of Senobar and Fereshteh. 'There. That's my guess. He can watch both those streets from that point. He will have several other vehicles on those routes to stop us from escaping.'

'We will be trapped,' Bwana commented.

'You want to nix this operation?'

'When did I say that?' the African American's teeth gleamed. 'We'll have to find a way to trap them with us.'

'There will be too many of them,' Roger objected.

'You didn't hear what I said,' Bwana growled. 'I said trap them. Not capture them.'

Zeb tuned out their bickering and studied the map. 'That building,' he pointed to the one on the intersection, 'looks like an office tower. It is the only commercial establishment there. Check out its roof. It's flat, with a parapet. It could have a great view of the street.'

'A sniper could do lots of damage from there,' Beth agreed.

'We'll need a truck,' Zeb thought aloud. 'With construction material.'

'What for?' Broker asked him, astonished.

His surprise cleared up when Zeb explained.

'That could work,' Meghan agreed.

She folded away the screen and minutes later they were driving into Tehran.

Zeb felt the familiar tightening inside him, like a predator awakening.

He was in mission mode and when he glanced at Meghan, sensed the change in her too.

He hadn't needed to outline the objective to his friends. They had been working together as a team for so long that they could often read one another's thoughts.

Capture Naser and extract the weapon's information from him.

80

'WHERE ARE THEY?' Naser shouted at Merwan Ali and his son.

He was leaning against a desk in Mehdi's office which was near the elevator bank. He could hear his men ransacking the large space which contained several beds.

'We told you several times,' Merwan Ali's Farsi was polished, his tone bordering on contemptuous. 'There are no women on this floor. Those beds are for those builders. Mehdi paraded them in front of you. What made you think we are sheltering dissidents here?'

'I saw them! They entered the building. ABID!' Naser roared.

'Show them the video,' he ordered when the major hurried into the room.

The entrepreneur and his son watched the clip on Abid's phone. 'Sorry, agha,' Mehdi said politely. 'I have never seen them before. I spend some time here when I am not in university. I know all the tenants in this building. I haven't seen any women wear chadors here.'

'THEY ARE BREAKING THE LAW BY NOT WEARING IT. THEY COULD BE ARRESTED.'

'I will remind them of that,' the son didn't flinch from his outburst.

'Those women could have entered the wrong building,' Merwan suggested. 'Your video does not show them leaving. It is very short. Maybe they returned after a couple of minutes. And,' he frowned, 'how do you know they are dissidents? I can't make their faces out.'

'I know,' Naser snarled. He wasn't going to tell them about the gait analysis software.

'Who are they, agha?' Mehdi asked respectfully.

The Basij leader itched to slap him. He knew the son was laughing at him beneath his polite expression. 'You don't need to know that.'

'You break into our building, you threaten our tenants, you destroy this floor,' Merwan polished his glasses and slipped them back on again, giving him a distinguished look. 'The least you can do is tell us who you are looking for.'

'It is a matter of national security,' Naser hissed. 'Why do you need to know?'

'We could ask our tenants and staff to see if they know the women or be alert for them. I could make a phone call and find out. I am sure you are aware of my contacts. My company is building military barracks for our army.'

'And I could take away that contract easily,' Naser shook his finger threateningly.

Merwan brought out his phone and made a show of pressing a button on it. 'I didn't hear you. Can you repeat what you said? It sounded like you were threatening an innocent civilian.'

The Basij chief was aware of Abid's fearful look. Merwan Ali was a very high-profile entrepreneur who had won several awards for his service to the community.

'What about what you said?' Naser spat. 'That wasn't a threat?'

'No, Brigadier General, I was merely pointing out facts to you.'

'Zohra Hashimi,' the Sepah leader barked.

'Who's the other woman?'

'We don't know who she is.'

'Why are you interested in these two? There are so many women protesters out there. What makes these two so special that the next leader of Sepah comes in person to investigate.'

Naser ground his teeth. He snapped his fingers at Abid who stood to attention. 'I can't tell you that,' he snarled, 'but be sure you are on my watchlist and if I find you have been sheltering them, you will face my anger.'

He brushed past them, barked orders at his men and left the office.

MERWAN WATCHED THEM GO AND WHEN HE HEARD THE elevator door close behind them, turned to his son. 'Do you know where they are?'

'No, baba.'

'Don't lie to me.'

'I am not. I can go into details but that will put you into risk. I don't know where those women are.'

'They are safe?'

'I think so.'

'You are right. I don't want to know what you are involved in. I can guess, though,' Merwan squeezed his son's shoulder affectionately, 'and I am proud of you. But be careful. Be very careful. Sepah is the most dangerous enemy to make.'

81

Hassan Ghafouri's garage was near Mehrabad International Airport. It was surrounded by container storage warehouses, aircraft rental outfits, logistics companies and was nestled between Lashgari and Fazlollah Nuri Expressways.

'He's busy,' Bwana whistled after they had parked their Fords and walked into the forecourt.

The establishment was similar to a million others around the world. A large front yard where customers rolled up, an aluminum-sheet covered work area where eight cars were raised on jacks and next to it an office.

Eight workers, Zeb counted. He could see Hassan through the glass window that looked into the work area.

A bell rang when they went through the office door and approached the reception counter. They could hear Hassan on the phone. He hung up swiftly, came out and halted abruptly when he took them in.

The garage owner was short and stocky with an unruly clump of hair on his head. In his forties, he had a perpetual smile on his lightly-bearded face.

'Zeb!' He whooped and rushed across and hugged them hard.

He smacked the twins and Chloe on the cheeks and inspected Beth critically.

'Have you agreed?' he asked her gravely.

'Agreed to what?' she smiled.

'To marry me. I am ready to leave my wife and kids for you.'

He guffawed when he picked her up and swung her around.

'Hassan—' Zeb began.

'Wait,' the garage owner cut him off with an imperious wave. He pressed a buzzer and one of his mechanics came in, wiping his hands on a rag. The man took them in, startled and looked questioningly at his boss.

'Faraz,' Hassan commanded. 'Get chai from Akbar's. The special one. None of the nonsense he serves to his customers. With almonds. Remind him about the nuts or else he can find another garage.'

Faraz disappeared with a nod.

'They are all family,' Hassan told Zeb proudly referring to his employees. 'Nephews and distant relatives. I trust them. They won't mention your presence to anyone.'

'Hassan,' Broker tried.

'No. We have tea first and then talk. Now, Chloe,' he gave an exaggerated wink, 'if you are tired of that man,' he pointed to Bear, 'I am available. I have a fancy house, many cars, I even have goats. You will live a better life with me than with him.'

'What if Beth agrees?' the petite operator chuckled.

'No problem. I will marry her too.'

'Does Parveen know you talk like this with other women?' Meghan asked amusedly.

'Of course! She wants someone to say yes so that she'll be free of me.'

'Why aren't we surprised?' the older sister snorted.

Faraz returned with the chai. Hassan served it to them and watched like a hawk when they sipped.

'It's good,' Zeb reassured him. 'I can taste the almonds.'

'Good,' the garage owner rubbed his hands, raised a finger

and hurried out. 'Faraz,' he bellowed, 'I am not to be disturbed. Deal with any customers if they come.'

'Balle, amoo.' Uncle.

'Now tell me,' Hassan returned. His smile dropped. 'I am sure you aren't here just to visit me.'

'We have four Fords outside,' Zeb jerked his thumb at the forecourt. 'They need to disappear.'

'No problem. No one will recognize them once I am done with them. Are they stolen?'

'No.'

'That's even better.'

'We need an open bed truck filled with timber or concrete bags. Anything, as long as we can make a hollow in it.'

The garage owner scratched his cheek as he sipped his tea. 'When do you need this?'

'Tonight.'

'It will be done.'

'We need three vehicles. Sedans. They are going to be wrecked so their condition does not matter as long as they are drivable.'

'I have enough of those,' Hassan snorted.

'Can you arrange to drop them off in Niavaran? We'll give you the address. The drivers have to park them in a particular way tomorrow and disappear. They cannot be identified.'

'It will be done.'

'Our Range Rovers are ready?'

'Balle.'

'Hassan,' Meghan told him soberly, 'none of these vehicles can be traced back to you.'

'They won't be,' he smiled faintly. 'You need anything else?'

'No.'

'Money? I don't have much cash, but I can empty my bank account—'

'Hassan, we don't need anything else.'

'You just have to ask. This garage. I will sell it. My house, that too. Parveen's jewelry, I can pawn those.'

The operators didn't move. The twins didn't roll their eyes. They listened expressionlessly.

'Baradar,' Zeb said softly, 'we need only the vehicles.'

The garage owner's eyes grew wet. 'My wife and children are alive only because of you. Know that there is nothing we won't do for you. Our house, this garage, everything is meaningless. You want me to join you? Help you out in some way? I have never fired a gun but I will learn. Anything—'

Bwana moved. He went to Hassan and hugged him hard. 'There is nothing else we need.' He rumbled.

'You know that you can ask and I will never refuse?' Hassan lifted his wet face to him.

'We know.'

'You should know you are our family—'

'Hassan,' Bwana said threateningly, 'I will knock you out if you don't stop talking.'

The garage owner looked deep in his eyes and then surveyed the rest of them. He nodded, wiped his face and finished the rest of his chai.

'You are aware I was joking, khaharan?' he addressed the women. 'I have never looked at other women—'

'Jeez, Hassan,' Beth's patience broke. 'We have known you long enough.'

The garage owner nodded, went to his office and returned with an ornate wooden box. It was velvet-lined when he opened it and filled with seeds.

'Pomegranate,' he handed a few to each of them. 'Keep them in your pocket.'

'For good luck,' Bear said.

'Balle. Now,' he closed the box and put it away, 'let's get your vehicles.

. . .

MEGHAN WAS SILENT WHEN ZEB GOT BEHIND THE WHEEL OF his Range Rover. Broker and Beth got in the back row.

The elder twin stirred when Zeb got onto Lashgari Expressway and drove to the city's center. 'What we talked of when we were coming to Tehran ... purpose. Making Hassan and Parveen's family whole again, that's why we do this.'

82

'That's the one,' Meghan murmured when Zeb entered Senobar. 'The third one on the right.'

He flicked his eyes to take in a white villa with concrete columns at the decorative entrance. A tree-lined hedge separated its front garden from the sidewalk.

'That's a fancy safe house,' Beth drawled.

'Sepah,' Broker shrugged. 'The organization must have flexed its muscle to acquire it.'

'The streets are narrow enough for what we have in mind.' Zeb observed. 'Any info on who are in the neighboring homes?'

'The one next to it close to the Fereshteh intersection has a For Sale sign. It's empty. We didn't get anything on the one to its left,' Beth observed.

Zeb checked out the commercial building on the intersection, flicked his flasher on and turned onto Fereshteh. 'Narrow V-junction. Traffic bottlenecks as a result. It is perfect.'

The adjoining street had similar looking homes. A BMW passed them and then a Mercedes. Our Range Rovers won't look out of place here.

He made way for Bear's vehicle that approached and passed them, doing the recon circuit in reverse.

'Looking good,' Bwana commented in their comms.

'Yeah,' Zeb agreed.

THEY GATHERED AT EIGHT PM AT THE V-JUNCTION ON FOOT after parking rides on Shafei, the larger street to which Senobar and Fereshteh joined.

The neighborhood was quiet. Sounds of children from a nearby park. A couple strolled past, engrossed in a deep conversation.

Meghan launched her drone when they were deep in cover of a parked van with no streetlights nearby to illuminate them.

'Ten-floor building,' she navigated the bird over to the commercial complex. 'Software companies, trading firms, real-estate—'

'How do you know?' Broker exclaimed.

'Saman,' she explained patiently, 'It's their land registry database. It lists ownership of properties.'

'That, and a simple Google search of the building's address,' Beth smirked. 'It's not hard.'

'Great view!' Meghan showed her screen to them.

The drone's camera streamed a live feed of Senobar and Fereshteh from its roof.

'Two shooters on top of that building can cover their sidewalks,' Zeb looked consideringly at Roger and Broker, who nodded. 'Bear, you'll drive the truck. Bwana, you will be in the hollow. The rest of us will be spaced out on Senobar to take advantage of the chaos. Is there anyone in the safe house?'

Meghan navigated the drone to the residence and hovered outside its windows. 'There's a crack in the curtains,' she murmured. 'Three men in the dining room. No one else there.'

Zeb watched them for several moments as they ate and talked among themselves. *They are young, short haired, fit.* 'Sepah operatives,' he guessed. 'Can we hear them?'

'Nada,' she shook her head. 'Good sound-proofing inside the house. 'They're Naser's decoys.'

'That's how I see it too.'

Meghan piloted the drone to the rear of the house and whistled when its feed appeared through another crack in the curtains. 'KL-103s,' she referred to the rifles stacked against the wall. 'Those are Iranian versions of the AK-103.'

'That confirms it,' Zeb commented. 'Those are Revolutionary Guards men. Who owns the safe house?'

'An Iranian businessman,' Beth made a face. 'Who else could it be. He's into real estate. From his wife's socials, looks like they are vacationing in Europe. He has connections to the government.'

'Which explains why Sepah shooters are treating his house as their own,' Roger drawled.

At ten pm, Meghan fried the commercial building's cameras with the drone-mounted EMP gun.

Broker and Roger scaled its fence and climbed up the drain pipes at the rear.

'We have padlocked the exit door,' the Texan reported. 'No one can get to the roof from the building, not without us hearing about it.'

Bwana and Bear went to the truck that Hassan's man had parked on Shafei.

'Hollow is big enough for my act,' the African-American grinned.

'What's on the bed?' Roger queried.

'Sand bags. There are sufficient gaps for my weapon. Y'all are aware everything hinges on me?'

'That's a big responsibility, Bwana,' Beth said solemnly, 'are you up to it?

He didn't have a retort.

Zeb rolled beneath a low-hung pickup on Senobar that didn't

look like it had ever been driven. It was two houses away from their target residence. His HK was next to him and his pants' pockets and backpack were filled with the gear he would need.

The rest of his team were spread out beneath various other vehicles, all of them similarly geared up.

He looked up at the chassis of the truck and ran through the take down in his mind again.

Meghan interrupted his thoughts. 'I messaged Naser for the exchange. He responded. We are on for tomorrow noon.'

'Can it be this easy?' Bear queried from the tower.

It never is, Zeb thought. He cleared his mind, breathed easily to slow his pulse down and rested.

NASER WAS MAKING HIS PLANS WITH ABID AT THE SEPAH headquarters.

'I'll be here,' he rolled a model command vehicle on to the 3-D scale model of Niavaran on his desk. 'On Senobar. Two or three doors away from the safe house.'

'I have filled the neighboring houses with our shooters,' the major replied.

'Not too many,' the Basij chief warned. 'We don't want to kill our own in the crossfire.'

'Yes, agha. There is one house for sale. I have left that empty. People would get suspicious if they saw our men in it. We need to have an exit for you however, in case things go hot.'

'I will be in the command vehicle. It is armored. I will have three or four men with me. I don't need another exit.'

He snapped to attention when Gholamreza entered his office.

'Everything is in place?' the Sepah leader asked.

'Yes, agha. It will be simple. Carter will arrive at the safe house expecting to capture me. We will ambush him.'

'Nothing is simple with him. Remember,' Gholamreza shook his finger, 'I want him alive. I don't care if you have to kill the others. The women ...' he paused for a moment, 'see if you can capture them alive as well. They will be good for leverage. You intend to be there, Saeed?'

'Yes, agha. Carter is a big prize for us. I can't leave this operation to others.

'Don't underestimate Carter. Be prepared for anything.'

Naser looked at Abid when Gholamreza left. 'What did you have in mind for an alternate exit for me?'

83

Zeb woke up early and lay still. Six am. A car drove past. A few scattered leaves blew underneath his truck.

'Anyone else awake?' Roger drawled from the top of the tower.

'All of us,' Beth replied grumpily. 'Broker, remember the spiel you fed us when Meg and I joined the Agency? See the world. Make a change. You never said anything about sleeping beneath a Hilux with gas fumes in my face.'

'I did not give you a recruitment speech,' the elder operator retorted. 'You both insisted on joining.'

'Quiet,' Meghan snapped. 'Launching the drone. Those three dudes are still in the safe house. Sleeping,' she added after a moment.

'On soft beds,' her sister grouched.

'Bear, Bwana?' Zeb called out.

'We're good to go,' the African-American operator checked in.

Zeb peered out beneath the truck. He saw the door open on the opposite house. A couple of children came out, dressed in their school uniforms. Their father helped them in their car while their mother stayed in the doorway until the vehicle backed out and drove away.

He dug his thumbs in his thighs when the memory vault in his mind threatened to open. *Not now,* he told himself.

The moment passed. He pictured the street. Meghan, Beth and Chloe were closer to the safe house than he was, towards the V-junction, on either side of the street.

It will work, he told himself. *There won't be anywhere for Naser to escape.*

With Broker and Roger on the tower, they had the high ground which gave them a significant tactical advantage.

AT TEN AM THE COMMAND VEHICLE ROLLED UP ALONG WITH two SUVs.

The larger vehicle stopped one vehicle behind Zeb. From beneath his truck, he could see debris spray out from its tires as they slowed and were hidden from his view by the civilian vehicle's wheels.

The SUVs went ahead and stopped on the other side of the street close to the safe house.

That's where Beth, Meghan and Chloe are.

'Police or Sepah?' he whispered. The Revolutionary Guards' emblem had a rifle in it while the police had no weapons in their symbol.

'Sepah,' Meghan replied. 'No marking on the command vehicle, but the SUVs are clearly marked.'

'It is armored? The command vehicle?'

'Looks like it. Dark windows. Riot-protection grills over them. Even the windscreen is tinted. Our drone can't see through and I can't risk lowering the bird to run the thermals.'

'Naser is in it.'

'Got to be. There's no other reason for that vehicle to be here. The SUVs are packed with soldiers.'

Senobar seemed to suck in its breath at their arrival. The

kids' mom opened her door, looked at the arrivals and went back inside hastily. Passing cars slowed fractionally before speeding up.

'Several shooters have come out of the cruisers,' Roger commented from the tower. 'They've gone to the larger vehicle ... its rear door has opened. A uniformed man has come out. Can't see his face. His head is down. He's surrounded by the officers. They've escorting him to the safe house.'

'Is it Naser?' Zeb saw their shod feet go past his truck.

'Could be. His build—'

'It isn't,' Meghan said confidently. 'I've got the drone's camera on him. He's of the same height and weight but it isn't him.'

'A decoy,' Zeb guessed.

'Yeah. He'll have figured we're watching. Smart move.'

AT ELEVEN AM, HASSAN'S DRIVERS LEFT HIS GARAGE BEHIND the wheels of three sedans.

'Message from Naser,' Meghan said tautly. 'He's asking where Kamal is. I have responded with *on the way*.'

'I'VE HEARD FROM HASSAN. SEDANS ARE IN PLACE,' MEGHAN observed at fifteen minutes to noon. 'They have blocked Senobar and Fereshteh. They won't be moved for at least an hour, they've created that much damage.'

'We're on the way,' Bear replied laconically.

84

Zeb heard the truck before he saw its wheels appear from beneath his vehicle. Its engine growled, fumes from its tailpipe smothered him momentarily before the light breeze dissipated it.

The lumbering vehicle slowed as it approached the safe house. The clash of its gears was audible even from a distance.

BWANA WAITED. HIS EYE ON THE M320 GRENADE LAUNCHER that he had tripod-mounted in the hollow. He was surrounded by sandbags which shielded him. His beat was low, his breathing steady, he was in his element.

'Go,' Bear whispered in his comms as the truck ground to a halt. They had worked out where it would have to stop the previous night.

His friend had jammed the brake on the exact position.

The safe house's entrance filled his eyepiece. He feathered the trigger and absorbed the recoil against his padded vest.

. . .

THE GRENADE RIPPED THROUGH THE DOOR AS IF IT WERE MADE of flimsy cardboard. Its explosion rocked through the street.

Simultaneously the flashbangs and smoke bombs that the Agency operators had placed beneath vehicles or hidden behind street lights, went off, detonated remotely by Beth and Meghan.

Zeb rolled out from beneath the truck, a scarf covering his nose and mouth, shades over his eyes.

He got to his feet lithely as thick smoke enveloped the street. Screams could be heard from within homes. Car alarms went off.

He heard shouts and exclamations as he felt bodies move in the thick haze. Shots ripped through the smoke curtain.

'THERE ARE SHOOTERS IN THE NEIGHBORING HOUSES!' Beth yelled. 'THEY'RE POURING OUT.'

'Pull back,' Zeb growled. 'Naser suckered us in. Get away.'

'Copy,' Meghan said calmly.

He heard HK's chatter and the returning fire from the Sepah men. He crouched low next to the truck, his HK in hand as he ran through his options. A shadow loomed through the smoke. His finger tightened on the trigger and then the man jerked and fell from one of this team's shots.

'We're laying down fire,' Roger, cool, emotionless, 'but you folks need to get out of there before it gets hotter.'

'We aren't staying to take in the sights,' Chloe snarled.

Zeb heard the command vehicle's engine fire up.

He knew he hadn't been spotted. No shots or gunmen had come his way.

I still have a chance.

85

Bear yanked the wheel hard as soon as he heard Zeb's Pull Back. 'Bwana,' he said tautly, 'blow up the bags.'

The truck's tires burned rubber as it turned and mounted the sidewalk.

He jumped out of the cab, bent low and fired at any shadow who wasn't wearing the green shoulder, chest and back patches. They were visible only through the operator's shades and identified their team members as friends.

He felt a step behind him, ducked and spun around.

'It's me,' Bwana held up his palm with a triggering device. The truck shuddered when a contained blast ripped through it. Sand sprayed out of the bed and rapidly filled the street.

'Smart thinking,' Chloe gasped as she came around the front of the truck and joined them. The twins followed her.

They retreated rapidly towards the V-junction.

'Zeb, where are you?' Meghan searched through the smoke.

'Near my truck. I have a window—'

'YOU'LL BE TRAPPED!'

'Get away.'

. . .

ZEB KNEW THE ODDS WERE AGAINST HIM. THE STREET WAS littered with bodies but there were still hostile shadows moving in the smoke.

I've got to try and get Naser.

The command vehicle had turned in the street to back up and u-turn.

He broke cover, running fast and low and shot its tires. They hissed but the vehicle kept moving.

He tossed a grenade under it and leapt towards the sidewalk.

The explosion rocked the vehicle.

A shot zipped through the smoke, inches from his face. Another smashed into a street lamp.

He ignored the rounds and fired at the rear window of the Sepah vehicle. Star bursts appeared on it. He kept shooting at the pockmarks.

My rounds may not get through, but Naser will get nervous.

'Behind you,' Broker warned.

Zeb threw himself to the pavement, spun around and shot the two approaching men, rolled back and continued shooting at the vehicle which looked like it had stalled.

Its door cracked open.

He shot a long burst at it and changed magazines swiftly.

'LEAVE!' he snarled at his friends. 'We have lost our advantage.'

His earpiece clicked in acknowledgement.

He lobbed a grenade at the partly-opened door and spun behind it using the rest of the command vehicle as cover. It shuddered from the explosion.

He thought the blast was echoing from the residences but then shook his head.

That's a chopper!

86

The sound grew louder as the helo appeared in sight.

Bell Cobra, he peered around the vehicle. It hovered just over the treeline, its rotors sweeping away the smoke, exposing the street which showed the devastation the operators had wreaked.

Sepah gunmen on the ground. Bear's truck sideways, sand spilt on the asphalt. No other shooters in sight. *They're probably behind cars.*

The vehicles on the street were parked where they were, their windows shattered, their bodies dented and marked from the shooting.

A gunman appeared in the chopper's open door and tossed down a rope ladder. He laced the street with fire.

Zeb crawled backwards to shelter behind a car.

The command vehicle's door opened and a figure appeared.

Naser!

The Basij head ran towards the ladder, his hands outstretched.

Zeb calculated his chances. *About fifteen meters between us.*

He lunged out from cover, firing rapidly at the open door of the command vehicle. He didn't need to aim. The opening was large enough for him to empty his magazine in it. He slapped a new charge on the run, his hands moving expertly. A round from the chopper nicked his sleeve. Another one blew past his face. A face appeared in the Sepah vehicle's door. It disappeared in a blossom of red when his rounds ripped through it.

Naser yelled in rage and caught onto the ladder and started rising from the ground.

And then Zeb was onto him.

He latched onto the Basij chief's leg and yanked hard. Shots eddied around him, but he knew he was momentarily safe since the helo shooter wouldn't fire at him and risk accidentally injuring Naser.

The Sepah man kicked at him with his free leg. Zeb clung on. He felt himself rising as the chopper lifted. He hauled himself up and caught Naser's holster.

He ducked at a wild fist and punched the Basij chief in the belly. They grappled wildly, fists swinging, a few punches landing, while the helo rose.

Naser held on desperately to the ladder, making inarticulate sounds of rage until one of his kicks connected with the operator's head.

Zeb lost his grip. He fell to the ground and rolled away instantly when searching bullets from the chopper followed his move. He dove behind the car and lobbed a grenade at the command vehicle to deter anyone who might be inside it.

He missed. It clattered against the body and fell to the ground.

Zeb looked up for a moment and saw Naser's mocking face and then he ducked down from the explosion and when he raised his head again, the chopper was disappearing with the Basij leader being winched inside rapidly.

The grenade seemed to have done sufficient damage to the command vehicle's occupants however, since no one showed themselves.

Got to get out of here, Zeb panted. He took a moment to

regroup himself. A barrage of shots struck his car as the Sepah killers trained their weapons on him.

They know I'm alone and on this side of the street. They've license to kill now that Naser's gone.

He had three more grenades left.

He tossed one where the firing was most intense on the other side of the street and sprinted on the sidewalk, towards the truck.

The smoke had cleared up from the chopper's arrival though wisps remained in the air. There was no one blocking his move.

He burst past the gap in between cars, firing wildly at the opposite sidewalk.

They will try to trap me at the truck, which is the bottleneck on the street. They might ambush me beyond it, too.

To his left was a grassy bank, separated from the sidewalk by a metal railing. Children's slides and play equipment on it.

No kids, no families, he scanned it quickly. It was day time. Adults had gone to work, children had gone to school.

He vaulted over the railing and sprinted up the bank, extracting a grenade from his pocket.

He came parallel to the truck and saw shooters crawling across the street, towards the sidewalk he had been on, hoping to trap him.

One of them saw him and yelled a warning, but it was too late.

Zeb's grenade detonated among them.

He ran to the end of the bank, his HK in one hand, the last remaining grenade in the other. Three soldiers behind the truck, were peering beneath it trying to see where he was.

His burst sent them scattering and then he had vaulted over the sidewalk, sprinting towards the V-junction.

Zeb threw his rifle away, snatched his scarf away from his face, pocketed it roughly and ran down Senobar where Hassan's sedan had blocked the road.

A crowd had gathered behind it with several police officers gathered.

'RUN!' he screamed, waving his hands. 'TERRORISTS! THEY ARE KILLING EVERYONE. WHY ARE YOU WAITING HERE? DIDN'T YOU HEAR THE SHOOTING? DO YOU WANT TO DIE?'

'STOP!' an officer roared.

Zeb leapt over a fallen bicycle and ran down the sidewalk towards Kaj.

'STOP?' he shouted furiously without breaking stride. 'I don't want to die. They have grenades. RUN, YOU FOOLS. WHAT ARE YOU WAITING FOR? THOSE TERRORISTS ARE COMING.'

The crowd scattered with screams and yells. The officers tried to control them but the mob wasn't listening.

Zeb merged with them. He cut into Jebeli where several civilians had gathered around a radio on the sidewalk. He wiped his sweat discreetly and slowed to a walk.

A boutique caught his eye. The store was far enough from the firefight that it was business as usual for trade. He hurried inside, returned with a blue jacket which he paid for in cash, slipped it on and ambled with his hands in his pockets.

He caught sight of himself in a store window and wiped away the soot and grime on his face.

How did I survive without even a scratch? he wondered but he knew the answer to that. The flashbangs, smoke, and the covering fire from his friends on the tower, all had played a role.

'Check in,' he spoke softly in his throat mic and grinned at the long burst of relieved curses from his team.

'Bahonar Street,' Beth said furiously. 'Get your ass here, right away. We are scattered near the bank. You can't miss it.'

It took him fifteen minutes to get there during which he bought another jacket and a pair of jeans, changed into them, disposed his combat pants in a bin and pocketed the last-remaining grenade.

He spotted the twins and Chloe underneath a cafe's umbrella on the sidewalk. Their headscarves and shades gave them a chic look as they laughed and conversed.

Beth saw him approaching. She ordered a chai for him and when he joined them, caught his wrist and poured it over his hand.

87

'That's for the stress you put us through,' Beth whisper-yelled at him. 'WHAT DID YOU THINK YOU WERE DOING?'

'Trying to capture Naser,' Zeb winced at the burn and snatched his hand away. He dabbed at it swiftly with a paper towel while Meghan and Chloe watched with amused grins. He uncapped a bottle of water on the table, poured it over his wrist and closed his eyes in relief.

'Capture him? You asked us to leave and then stayed back. Did you know how many shooters were out there? There must have been over thirty. They were disoriented by the smoke and bangs and Bwana and Roger's fire helped—'

Bear's cough was loud in their earpieces.

'And Bear and Bwana's move with the truck and the sandbags was genius,' Beth continued without missing a beat. Her voice rose. 'You were alone out there. We had no eyes on you. We couldn't help you. They would have killed you.'

'I am aware of that. But—'

'But what? You asked us to get away and threw yourself in danger? You got lucky, you idiot. Plain, sheer, dumb, unexpected luck.'

Chloe made to speak. She stayed quiet when Zeb gestured discreetly. *Let Beth get it out of her system.*

'Do you know how we felt out here when you were over there?' the younger twin raged. 'We heard grenades and shooting, that was our only clue you were still alive.' She punched his burned hand with a bunched fist angrily. 'Do. Not. Do. That. Again. You. Hear. Me?'

Zeb winced and cradled his wrist. 'Yes, ma'am,' he said placatingly.

Beth sat back with an angry huff. Silence fell over their table until Meghan stirred.

'They wouldn't.'

'Who wouldn't what?' Beth snapped at her.

'They wouldn't have shot at Zeb. That's why he took the risk.'

'How do you know that?'

'Work it out,' Meghan told her. 'He is far more important to Sepah alive than dead. Gholamreza and Naser must have given explicit orders not to kill him. They might have wounded him, but the Revolutionary Guards want him alive.'

'Yeah,' Chloe nodded. 'It makes sense.'

'Correct,' Zeb inspected his reddened hand. 'Besides, in the chaos of the smoke, the bangs and the sand dust, the shooters didn't know where we were and then their primary responsibility became protecting Naser.'

'If they knew where we were hiding,' Bwana said softly, 'we wouldn't be sitting here.'

Zeb nodded. 'Which was why we had to have surprise on our side, which we had.'

Beth's shoulders relaxed after a while. She wet a paper towel and dabbed Zeb's wrist with it. Her gesture of peace. 'Naser outsmarted us. Those gunmen in the neighboring houses ... we didn't expect them. We thought those SUVs were all that they had.'

'Yeah,' he agreed.

'He got away. We blew the only chance we had.'

'We thought we heard a chopper,' Bear asked.

'There was. Naser's getaway ride. A rope ladder from it for him to climb on. That was another smart move that we didn't anticipate,' Zeb said bitterly. 'I tried taking him down,' he briefed them quickly about the Basij leader's escape.

'I knew they wouldn't shoot at me,' he said hastily when Beth's face tightened, 'I was too close to Naser.'

'There could have been gunmen inside that command vehicle,' she said savagely.

'They didn't show themselves. I had grenaded it earlier and killed at least one shooter in it. I don't know if anyone else was alive in it.'

'The rest of the Sepah gunmen—'

'He's here,' Meghan said sharply. 'Yeah, I agree it wasn't smart of Zeb to go it alone, but he got away.'

Beth's face darkened but she held back her words.

'How did you folks escape?' Zeb asked.

'Easy enough for us,' Chloe shrugged, 'Bear and Bwana provided covering fire, Broker and Roger from the tower. There wasn't a crowd at the V-junction when we reached it. People had panicked and run away. We threw our weapons and split up.'

'We had the easiest escape,' Roger drawled. 'No one from that office building stopped us when we came down from the tower. The gate was open and we strolled out.'

'Our scarves,' Meghan touched her face. 'Hid our faces. No one's got a description of us. I've been following the chatter.' Her eyes fell to her phone on the table. 'It's chaos out there. Some people are saying terrorists. Some are saying Kurdish rebels. Naser and Gholamreza know it was us, but they won't admit it.'

'It would be humiliation for them,' Zeb figured. 'A bunch of Americans attacked their safe house and got away despite all the men they had ... the president and the supreme leader will be merciless with them. My guess is they will go with the terrorist angle.'

'Why are you smiling?' Beth challenged him.

'I might have put that notion in the onlookers' heads,' he shrugged his shoulders and recounted his escape from the V-junction.

He scanned the street which was crawling with police vehicles. *We'll have to leave soon. It's a matter of time before officers do a door-to-door questioning of every house and store within a two- or three-kilometer radius.*

'We were this close,' Bwana growled savagely. 'We would have ended the mission by now.'

'Yeah,' Zeb agreed. He didn't allow disappointment to sweep over him. Few missions ran to plan.

'You don't sound too upset,' Roger guessed.

Zeb scanned the street and spotted the Texan along with Broker at another cafe. Both men were reading newspapers, with coffee mugs on the table.

'What did you do?' Beth demanded, reading his expression.

Zeb opened his right palm and unpeeled a plastic film that had stuck to it.

'You stuck a tracker on him?' the younger sister breathed.

'In his holster, while we were grappling. His service revolver is for show. He rarely removes it. We know that from our files. He won't detect the tag for a while.'

88

'Don't say a word,' Gholamreza snapped when Naser entered his office with Abid in tow. 'You have the scale model of Niavaran on your desk?'

The deputy nodded and led his boss to his office.

'Now tell me,' the Sepah leader barked, 'what happened.'

'They were hiding beneath cars and trucks, agha. Carter was two vehicles away from me. At the agreed time, a truck filled with sand bags drove in.'

Gholamreza listened silently at the narration. He kept his face expressionless, not showing his fury but he knew the Basij leader could read his emotions.

Naser continued steadily, pointing with a finger on Senobar and Fereshteh. 'They had shooters on Kian Tower. Two of them. They had Barretts which ripped through our soldiers. That was the advantage they had.'

Gholamreza displayed his anger. He stabbed his finger in Naser's chest. 'The advantage they had was they planned it better. Did you expect the truck? No. Did you expect the bombs? No. Did you think Carter and his team would throw grenades? You didn't even search the street—'

'We were there early, agha,' Abid began.

Gholamreza spun on his heel. 'Was I speaking to you?' he asked icily.

Abid shook his head.

'Then be quiet!' Gholamreza barked. He resumed his diatribe at Naser. 'You didn't even anticipate that Carter and his team would know we had set a trap? How many men did the Americans kill?'

'Eighteen, agha,' Naser replied stiffly.

'Eighteen! That's like it was a war out there. In fact, that's how the media are describing it. Have you seen how it's being covered on TV? Are you aware of how many phone calls I got? The president is furious. The Supreme Leader's Office has demanded a meeting.' Gholamreza grabbed the model of Niavaran and slammed it on the desk. It cracked but didn't break.

'And you still don't know what happened to them?' he yelled. 'Where are they now?'

'We locked down the city, agha, but they got away. Those sandbags and those three cars that blocked Senobar and Fereshteh—'

'WHO DID THAT?'

'We don't know, agha. The drivers were three men, but no one has clear descriptions for them.'

Gholamreza rarely cursed but his iron control broke. He swore for a long time, pounding his fist on Naser's desk. 'You don't know this; you don't know that ... what do you know?'

His eyes blazed furiously, but Naser didn't reply.

'You did two or three things correctly,' he said after a while. 'That helicopter was a genius move.'

'It was Abid's idea, agha.'

The Sepah leader glowered at the major. He noticed the bruises on the man's face. 'What happened to you?'

'I was in the command vehicle. Carter threw a grenade ... its shock wave threw me inside and knocked me and another shooter out.'

'The second correct thing you did,' Gholamreza continued without complimenting the major on the chopper move, 'was to spread the story that they were terrorists, possibly Kurdish rebels. I repeated that to everyone who called me.'

'The third right thing you did was to transfer all the surviving soldiers far away, immediately.'

'I have warned them, agha,' Abid said. 'They will be arrested; their families will be in danger if they leak out that those attackers were Americans. I am confident they won't talk.'

Gholamreza nodded. Everyone in Sepah understood the language of fear.

He brooded for several moments as he looked at the scale model. 'He came to our country without our knowing how,' he said viciously. 'He destroyed our soldiers. He outwitted us and he's out there somewhere laughing at us. GET HIM!'

'Yes, agha,' Naser straightened.

'But remember,' the Sepah leader growled, 'we will survive even if Carter escapes. But Hashimi and the stolen material ... that will get us killed if we don't find them quickly. Where are you on that?'

'We are still searching the city—'

'YOU HAVE BEEN TELLING ME THAT FOR DAYS,' Gholamreza bellowed. 'GET OUT. FIND HER. FIND THE MATERIAL. COME BACK TO ME WHEN YOU HAVE SOME GOOD NEWS.'

Gholamreza returned to his office and drank water from the glass on his desk.

A few drops spilled.

He stared at them and then at his fingers. There was a barely perceptible tremble in them.

I am angry. Furious at Saeed, he told himself.

He knew deep inside however that he was fearful.

Just that morning the supreme leader had warned him of the consequences of failure.

He didn't even bother to veil his threat, he thought bitterly.

The spiritual head had told him bluntly that Gholamreza and his family wouldn't be seen again in Iran if the material wasn't found.

His face had been dispassionate, his eyes emotionless, as if he had dispensed a death sentence.

Which it was, Gholamreza wiped the drops of water on his desk and sat in his chair heavily.

Project Emad was in limbo. He had met Farhad just that morning and the professor had told him until he got replacement material, there was nothing he could do.

The lab was rebuilt, its security re-installed and reinforced and he and his two research students spent their time in it.

It was for show, however. 'Get me the material and I will give you a weapon. We can do nothing until then.' Farhad had told Gholamreza.

First, Hashimi. And now, Carter.

Saeed, the Sepah leader mouthed silently, *bring me some good news.*

NASER STORMED OUT OF GHOLAMREZA'S OFFICE WITH ABID IN tow. He was seething inside, but he kept his composure and hid his anger from the younger man.

'You heard what he said,' he said curtly to Abid. 'We have to find Hashimi no matter what.'

He brought out his phone and started punching a number when he stopped.

Phone! Hashimi and that woman were in Iran Capital Bank searching for one!

'They must have bought one,' he hissed.

'Bought what, agha?' Abid queried.

'A phone! Hashimi and that other woman must have—"

'Our people searched the neighborhood, they questioned taxi drivers—'

'I know all that,' Naser cut him off angrily. 'But no one asked the shop owners if they had sold any phones! Take a team and ask them. Threaten them. Do whatever you have to and get the numbers of all the devices that were sold.

'Yes, agha. They could have bought them somewhere else as well.'

'DO YOU THINK I AM A FOOL?' Naser roared. 'I know they could have bought anywhere else. Put yourself in their place. They came there to search for their lost phone. What would you have done in their place? Bought another one immediately, with cash, because without a phone you can't do anything these days. GO!'

89

'Do you think Kurdish rebels could have done all of that?' Zohra asked as she and Leila watched the news coverage in the small television in the clinic.

'Who else could it be?' Leila drew a sheet around her and folded her legs.

Her head snapped up instantly. 'You think it was Carter?' she asked incredulously. 'Zohra, that's a stretch. We don't know where they are. We don't even know if they got our message.'

The older woman nodded as she kept watching the TV. Fear was ever present in her. She woke up to it. She lived with it. Sometimes it overpowered her and left her gasping. Leila held her close in those moments, murmuring softly in her hair until the panic attack passed.

Both of them had taken to checking the socials several times a day. They both were aware of what the other was searching for on the phone but never spoke of it as if words would add weight to the silence from Zeb.

'Do you know ... is the ...?' Leila licked her lips and trailed off.

Zohra looked at her and caught on. 'What I stole? It is still there, where I hid it.'

'In that case,' Leila shivered and drew the blanket tighter

around her, 'Sepah won't give up hunting for us.'

'Balle,' Zohra reached out, caught her wrist and swallowed her fear. 'CIA will have software to read emails. I am sure Zeb's name will be flagged. If he hasn't come...' her breath caught.

'It's because he can't or won't.'

'He was in Tunisia,' Zohra said weakly.

'And now he could be anywhere, even back in America.'

'You should go,' the older student squeezed her friend's hand.

'Go where?'

'To Germany. Where Mina and the other women fled. I have some money. I can pay for your passage. You can start over again over there. Their universities are very good. You can resume your psychology course.'

'Don't look at me like that,' she said fiercely. 'Many of the protesters have gone back to their lives. The police have stopped harassing them. You told me that even Shaheen, Pari, Farida and the two women with them went to university and nothing happened. Your life is stuck if you are with me.'

'Go to Germany?' Leila asked disbelievingly. 'And what will you do?'

'I can't leave Iran,' Zohra said helplessly. 'My fate is tied to what I stole—'

'If you are staying here, I am, too.'

'We will die! Sepah will find us.'

'Then we will die together.'

'You have been watching too many movies.'

'STOP!' Leila shouted. 'I am not going anywhere. We will wait one or two more days and if there is no response from Zeb, we'll go to the German Embassy.'

'It will be watched.'

'We have to try something.'

Zohra nodded. She tossed the TV's remote to Leila and went to their room where she lay on the bed and drew the sheet over her head.

It didn't help in reducing her fear.

90

L*angley/Washington DC*

Clare had an assistant, Nicole Rios, who was on emergency time off since her father had suffered from a stroke.

In her absence, the Agency chief dealt with administration matters herself. It was a minor inconvenience that she didn't mind. She had others on her staff to whom she could delegate but other than the Tehran operation, there wasn't anything else on her plate and she could handle routine matters herself.

Her email had automatic sorting. It read key words, flags and senders names and highlighted the urgent ones for immediate attention. The rest went into a different folder which she cleared out regularly.

Those who had her number could reach her instantly.

It was a system that had worked for years.

There were two reasons why Amir Rahimi's email didn't get her immediate attention.

There was a protocol. Any message that got forwarded from the CIA was automatically encrypted.

Clare's email sorting system couldn't read those and this was designed deliberately since there could be a moment when her device was in someone else's possession and such a failsafe contained intel spread.

To bypass it, CIA analysts had to mention keywords in the subject line. It wouldn't matter much if those references were read by the wrong people since the forwarded message was still encrypted.

All that Amir Rahimi had to do was mention a name in the subject line. Zeb Carter.

He didn't because that night, when he had analyzed the message, his indigestion had threatened to humiliate him and that had distracted him.

The second reason was Clare's workload. The Tehran operation was of such critical importance that she spent most of her time at the White House or in Langley, conferring with the president, the National Security Council and with Catlyn.

Which is why Rahimi's forwarded message that contained Leila's email to the CIA, was unread by Clare.

91

Tehran

'We can't attack Naser immediately,' Zeb surveyed his Range Rover from a distance of two-hundred-meters on Shafei.

They had broken up soon after his revelation and had made their separate ways to where they had parked their rides.

There was a significant police presence on the streets by then. Cruisers used loud hailers to warn civilians to remain vigilant and report any sightings of threatening-looking people.

Several stores and offices had closed but there were still a few open inside which citizens gathered and gossiped about the terrorist attack on Senobar.

'We'll have to take him down when the location is right.' He searched the opposite sidewalk and spotted Meghan and way beyond her, Beth. Both women were talking to civilians, catching up on the latest rumor about the shootout.

'Clear,' he said softly and moved casually to the Range Rover.

He got behind its wheel and drove to Meghan who shotgunned swiftly, followed by her sister and Broker who climbed in the back.

'We are rolling,' Bear checked in.

'That could be days,' Chloe objected. 'Naser might not leave the Sepah headquarters.'

'He will,' Zeb said grimly. 'It will be a matter of pride to him. He won't stay hidden.'

'We twiddle our thumbs till he emerges?' Bwana asked sarcastically. 'While every police officer and Sepah soldier hunts us?'

'Something like that,' Zeb grinned, 'and talk to Parmida Bahrami.'

'Who?'

'Of course!' Meghan exclaimed. 'She's the one Naser assaulted in the bank. She might know who the two women were, who Sepah are hunting.'

'Why will she talk to us?' Roger brooded.

'Because of Ellen Ronning.'

92

Before they could get to the TV host, they had to talk to Cutter Grogan whose friend she was.

Zeb grinned at Beth and Meghan's call, on speaker, to their friend in New York while he drove away from Niavaran.

'Cutter, we need your help,' the younger twin began.

'Wait,' he yelped. They heard scrambling sounds. Something fell.

'We need your help,' Meghan said sarcastically. 'We didn't ask you to demolish your office.'

'I was enjoying my burger,' the PI complained, 'when you shocked me.'

'Shocked you how?'

'You said you need my help?'

'That's right.'

'There,' Cutter sighed. 'I have recorded that for posterity. Beth and Meghan Petersen need my help -'

'Quit being a smartass,' Beth snarled. 'We need to talk to Ellen Ronning.'

'Ellen doesn't interview ordinary people even if they happen to be twins—'

'Cutter,' Zeb broke in. 'This is important.'

Their friend's tone changed instantly. 'I'll message her number to Beth. I'll brief her to expect your call.'

His voice lightened. 'Are you in trouble? Should I come wherever you are? I am so honored that you came to me when you were in need—'

Meghan hung up. Her phone buzzed. 'We got her number.'

Zeb continued driving. A cruiser raced past them its lights flashing. A chopper circled the sky.

We are safe for now. We've changed our appearances again and are wearing different jackets. We dumped our weapons way back.

They had replacement weapons in their rides and wouldn't be staying in any hotels.

It would be street accommodation until they captured Naser. Sleeping in abandoned cars or trucks, freshening up in hotels where they could pay in cash. It would be inconvenient, but it would reduce their risk.

'MA'AM,' MEGHAN'S VOICE BLASTED THROUGH THE RANGE Rover's blue-tooth connected speakers. 'I am Meghan Petersen—'

'Cutter told me,' Ellen Ronning said warmly. Her voice rich, perfectly modulated, that could either put nervous guests at ease or verbally rip apart politicians. 'How can I help?'

'Ma'am, you reported on an incident at Iran Capital Bank. Sepah officers assaulted Parmida Bahrami.'

'Please call me Ellen, and it was Brigadier General Saeed Naser. Yes, I broke that news. I don't recognize that name however.' The warmth left her voice. It became hard-edged.

'Ma'am, it's all over social media.'

'That might be the case. I will not comment on internet gossip.'

'Ma'am,' Meghan ran her fingers through her hair frustratedly. 'I get it that you want to protect her identity but we need to talk to the woman who was assaulted.'

Ronning stayed quiet while Tehran flashed past them. Zeb circled wide and came to Tajrish and sped out of the city heading north-east.

The Alborz Mountain Range in the distance, standing proud and tall, overlooking the city. Less than a hundred kilometers from Tehran. He checked his mirrors. Bear's ride was following him.

He drew to the foothills and started climbing. Side-glanced at Meghan who was frowning at the phone.

'Why?' Ronning asked finally.

'She might have information on someone we are seeking.'

'This is Iran. I'm sure you are aware of the risks to her—'

'Ma'am, we are in Tehran. I don't know how much Cutter told you about us, but we are the good people.'

'He hinted at what you do. I'm a journalist. I have seen enough in the world to know there is no black and white, and our country and its agencies haven't always acted in the best interests of other nations.'

'Yes, ma'am. We can discuss politics when we're back in New York. Right now, we need to talk to her. It will be a discreet meeting. We are good at that,' Meghan said wryly. 'She won't be in any danger. All we need is one piece of information from her.'

'If you think she's Parmida Bahrami, you can find a way to make contact yourself. Her name is out there, like you said. If you are as good as Cutter hinted, I am sure you can get her details.'

Meghan pursed her lips.

Zeb grinned. *This is why her show's so highly rated. There's no give in her.*

'She doesn't know us, ma'am. She wouldn't trust us if we made cold contact.'

Ronning did the silent act again. Zeb stopped at a viewpoint that overlooked the city. Several other cars and tourist buses crowded it, everyone busy with selfies and cameras. No one paid them any attention.

'This woman can't be endangered,' the TV host's voice was a whiplash.

'She won't be.'

'If she is, I will expose you. I believe you are with some covert outfit. Moreover, I will do everything in my power to bring criminal charges against you.'

'Yes, ma'am.'

'Leave it with me. I will get back to you. How do I contact you? Your call has its number withheld.'

'I'll message you. Ma'am, it has to be today.'

'You don't ask for much, do you?'

'It's important.'

'That's what everyone says. There was a firefight earlier today in Tehran. A bunch of terrorists is what the authorities are saying. That was you?'

'No, ma'am.'

Ellen Ronning gave a disbelieving snort and hung up.

Meghan huffed and sagged against her seat. 'I wouldn't want to be grilled by her,' she chuckled.

She frowned when Zeb opened the door and got out. 'It's safe to step out?'

'It's safe for me,' he emphasized. 'You all stay inside. I'll get chai for everyone.'

Zeb returned with the beverage in paper cups and handed it out to his team.

'I'm not good with this,' Bwana growled when he went to Bear's ride.

'Good with what?' He ducked his head inside to give his friend the drink.

'Waiting.'

Zeb grinned. 'You remember that time we waited in that wadi in Iraq for thirty-six hours?'

'It was the desert! Where would we have gone?'

Zeb went to the waist-high concrete parapet that was the only protection from the steep drop and drank slowly.

Chloe joined him. 'No,' she smiled when he started turning towards their rides. 'It's just me. They're all staying in the vehicles.'

They watched the setting sun bathe Tehran in orange and gold.

'The wound is the place where light enters you,' she said softly.

'Rumi,' Zeb nodded, recognizing the Persian philosopher and poet's couplet.

'You know how awkward Bear was when he and I started dating.'

'He still is!'

She laughed throatily. 'He quoted Rumi's *the minute I heard my first love story*.'

Zeb nodded. He didn't tell her his wife used to write the poet's words and leave them in the most unexpected places. In his jacket pocket. In the bathroom cabinet. In his holster.

'This,' he pointed his cup in the general direction of the country, 'was one of the cradles of civilization.'

'Enough philosophy,' Meghan said from behind them. 'Ellen came through. We have a meeting.'

93

Eight pm. A Hyperstar, a supermarket, in Eram, in the northwestern part of the city.

Zeb jammed his ball cap low over his head as he pushed a shopping cart ahead of him. He went down the snacks aisle and selected several brands, his eyes moving continuously.

Families. Couples. Single parents, office workers and students. Several of them were talking about the attack in Niavaran, speculating on where the terrorists could have escaped. A lone security guard was at the drinks aisle, scanning the brands. The continual announcement of deals on the speakers and the buzz of conversation and checkout tills pinging.

Zeb went to the women's section and browsed through the cosmetics range. Meghan at the far end, filling her cart. Unrecognizable from her American passport. Beth in the middle of the aisle and Chloe, closer to him.

Two women approached the shelves, stocked their carts and hurried away.

There had been several police officers at the entrance of the Hyperstar when they had arrived, clearly bored at patrolling a supermarket. None of them had glanced twice at the operators.

'Parmida!' Zeb whispered when he identified the single

woman who entered the aisle hesitantly. A middle-aged man was way behind her, peering at the frozen food section.

'We'll take it from here,' Meghan told him.

SHE PUSHED HER CART CLOSER TO THE WOMAN, HER EYES ON the shelves. 'This place doesn't have the brand I want,' she grumbled.

Parmida Bahrami, in her bank's uniform, a shawl over her head, smiled politely.

'Are you a regular shopper here?' Meghan inched closer. She showed her phone's screen on which was a message.

We have a mutual friend. She would have told you about me.

Parmida's eyes widened. She sucked her lip and glanced up and down the aisle.

My name is Meghan.

The operator sprayed perfume on her wrist, sniffed it and presented it to the Iranian woman to check out. She discreetly showed Parmida her driving license.

The Iranian woman didn't comment that the operator looked nothing like the photograph on her identity document.

I sent my current disguise to Ellen. She must have forwarded that to Parmida.

'That's good, isn't it?' Meghan smiled.

'Balle,' Parmida said nervously.

'We are safe,' the American said softly. 'Those two women on either side of us are with me. I have friends around the store. They will warn us if there is any danger.'

'This will have to be quick,' Parmida licked her lips. 'I wasn't ready, but our friend convinced me.'

'Naser was looking for two women in the bank?'

'Balle.'

'Did they give their names?'

'No,' the bank employee recounted the incident quickly.

'How did they look?'

'I spoke to only one of them. I wasn't paying attention to the second one who was at the door. The one who came to me looked like any university student. In jeans and a shirt, with her hair covered. There was nothing special about her looks that I can tell you.'

Meghan watched Zeb cross the end of the aisle. Chloe was pretending to be on a call while Beth was humming loudly as she filled her cart.

'Did Naser say why he was looking for them?'

'No.'

'You never found their phone?'

'No. I have to go,' Parmida said in a scared voice.

'Was she this woman?' Meghan brought up Zohra's photograph on her phone.

'No,' the Iranian woman looked at it quickly. 'She wasn't the one who came to me.'

'What about the second woman?'

Parmida looked closely at the image and then nodded. 'Yes, that's her. I remember her from the CCTV videos in our bank.'

Meghan couldn't contain her fist-pump. 'Wait,' her grin faded when the other woman's words registered. 'You have CCTV?'

'Not anymore. Sepah took away that day's recording.'

'We have confirmation,' Meghan spoke in her throat mic.

Beth's shopping cart clattered loudly behind her. Her humming stopped. Chloe winked.

'We still don't know where she went from the bank,' Zeb said disappointedly in her earpiece.

'We'll figure that out later,' Meghan told him. 'We've got confirmation she's still out there.'

'Who are you talking to?' Parmida's caught her arm, her fear returning.

'My friends,' the elder twin smiled reassuringly at her and pointed at the flesh-colored miniature bud in her ear.

'Can I go now?'

'Balle, khanom. You can't imagine how relieved your information makes us.'

ZEB FOLLOWED THEM DISCREETLY OUT OF THE STORE.

He frowned when he saw a middle-aged man exit the store ahead of him. *That's the same dude who was at frozen foods.*

The supermarket had an enormous parking lot which was dimly lit. Parmida hurried across to her vehicle which was in the distance.

The man followed her.

The twins and Chloe had broken away to return to their Range Rovers.

'Did Parmida come alone?' he asked sharply.

'We didn't ask. Why?' Meghan picked up on his tone.

'There's a man behind her.'

She cursed. 'Coming,' she snapped.

Zeb skirted a car which was pulling out.

The man got closer to Parmida who unlocked her car with her fob.

No light posts where she's parked. No other vehicles nearby.

The man was barely ten meters behind her. He reached into his pocket.

Zeb lunged at him.

⸙ 94 ⸙

His left arm went around the man's throat in a choke hold. His right hand caught his wrist which was emerging from his pocket, and squeezed.

Parmida turned around at the scuffling sounds. Her eyes widened, her mouth dropped open in shock.

'Khanom,' Zeb grated as he dragged away the struggling, gasping man. 'Get into your car and drive away. I'll deal with him. My friends will follow you to make sure you are safe.'

'NO! That's Kaveh. My husband!' Parmida shrieked.

Zeb released him instantly. His face burned. 'I am sorry, agha. I didn't mean to ...' he trailed off when the twins and Chloe joined them.

'No one heard Parmida's yell,' Roger said in their comms. 'You folks are good. We are on the perimeter, on overwatch.'

'Sir,' Beth looked concernedly at Kaveh, 'are you okay? Did he hurt you? I am sorry, but we had to be careful. We had to protect your wife.'

The man rubbed his throat ruefully and hugged Parmida who rushed to him. 'I am fine. He has a strong arm but I am not hurt.'

'Khanom,' Meghan put her hands together in a praying

gesture, 'we didn't have any information on you or your husband otherwise Zeb wouldn't have acted in that manner. He thought Kaveh was a threat—'

The husband reached across and put her hands down. 'It's okay,' he said gently. 'There is no need to apologize. I am glad you were looking out for Parmida's safety. When Ellen called me, I was reluctant to set up the meeting, but she was persuasive.'

Ellen called him? Zeb frowned.

'Kaveh,' Meghan said slowly. 'There's a Kaveh Behrooz, a well-known IRIB presenter.'

'That's me,' the husband's teeth flashed in a smile. 'I am lucky to be Parmida's husband.' He hugged her again. 'I get a lot of threats so Parmida has kept her maiden name and the authorities make sure there is nothing much on us on the internet. Those who are in government know of course as well as many others in the TV world, but ordinary people don't know we have different names.'

Zeb eyed Kaveh. *IRIB presenter. He's Ellen's source. That's why she called him.*

'He was watching me to make sure I would be safe,' Parmida smiled wanly.

'I am sorry, khanom,' Zeb said sincerely.

'No baradar,' Parmida's eyes sparkled in the dim light. 'Like Kaveh said, I am happy you were looking out for me.'

'You got what you were looking for?' Kaveh asked.

'Zohra Hashimi. Yes,' Zeb nodded.

'Who is she?'

'She was one of the women who came to my bank,' Parmida interjected.

'Did she do something? Is she a terrorist?'

'Terrorist? No, agha,' Zeb chuckled. 'She's a PhD student in Biochemistry at the University of Tehran. She's a friend. We have lost contact with her and are trying to find her.'

'Biochemistry ... university,' Kaveh stroked his beard and looked at the store. 'It might be nothing.'

'What, agha?' Zeb asked him urgently.

'There was an explosion in a biochemistry lab some days ago.'

'Explosion?' Meghan asked tightly. 'There was nothing on the news or socials. We have been monitoring them continually.'

'I heard about it from my sources, but I couldn't find anything more. I made discreet enquiries but got nothing. The lab was where Professor Navid Farhad does his research, which was why I got interested. He is very famous. Many say he will win a Nobel Prize in chemistry.'

'When did this happen, agha?' Beth asked sharply.

'There is no confirmation it happened. But I heard about it a week ago.'

Meghan sucked her breath sharply. She looked at Zeb who made the connection.

'That's the day Zohra messaged us.'

95

'Sir,' Zeb scanned the parking lot again. His hands were loose and close to his body, ready for instant, explosive action. 'Where is Professor Farhad now?'

'He's still at the university,' Kaveh replied. 'He gave an interview just this morning about some new vaccine he was working on for avian flu. I can try to find out some more information on his work and what happened at the lab—'

'No, agha. You shouldn't put yourself at any more risk. You made enquiries once, you were told there was no explosion. People might wonder why you are asking again. Leave it alone. You need to go,' Zeb moved deeper in the shadows when a car's headlights flashed their way and disappeared when the vehicle drove out.

'Whoever you are, whatever you are doing, will it hurt Naser?' Parmida hissed.

'It might, khanom.'

She came over to him and gripped his wrist hard. 'Make him regret.'

'We'll try, khanom,' he bowed his head to acknowledge her rage.

He stood aside for them to get in their car and when they had driven away, watched until their tail lights had disappeared.

'What did Rumi say about women?' Chloe chuckled wryly.

'Never underestimate her power or you will be defeated by her anger,' Zeb recited automatically, his thoughts far away.

'What's on your mind?' Beth shoulder-bumped him.

'Lab explosion. Zohra's message. Navid Farhad. Gholamreza's comment about a better weapon.'

Silence engulfed them.

'It's got to be a chemical weapon,' Broker said grimly in their comms.

'Yeah,' Zeb agreed. 'But not something like nerve gas. Something far more dangerous.'

'And evil,' Meghan's face was drawn tight when a pair of headlights fell on her.

'There's a hospital not far from here,' Beth suggested, looking up from her phone. 'Near Bakeri Expressway. It has its own maintenance unit.'

Zeb nodded approvingly. 'We can hunker down for the night, there. I checked the tracker. Naser is still in his headquarters. It'll be like a fortress. We can't touch him there. Let's figure out how to get to him and to Zohra in the morning.'

THE HOSPITAL WAS BUSY. A STEADY STREAM OF EMERGENCY vehicles and concerned people at the large portico.

The operators parked their Range Rovers, paid for their stay and spread out.

'What you would expect,' Bear was a dim shadow against a medical supply vehicle when he led them to the rear of the hospital after their recon. 'Two police cruisers at the entrance. None of the officers are alert.'

'The maintenance bay is at the back,' Broker commented, 'where we are going. Closed down for the night. It has cameras, a shutter which has padlocks. The hospital's compound wall is at its rear. We can go over it if we have to escape fast.'

'*Had* cameras,' Chloe corrected her partner. 'We shot them out.'

'The padlock is scrap metal.' Roger said languidly. 'The shutter is rolled up—'

'Welcome to Le Five-Star Garage,' Bwana interrupted expansively when they entered it.

Zeb checked it out quickly in the illumination from their flashlights.

Five ambulances in various states of disarray, some with their engines taken apart, some with no wheels.

Metal tables with tools along the side and rear walls. Tires, wheels, jacks and various other equipment on the floor. Faded posters and calendars hung on nails. The smell of oil and grease strong in the air.

'This will do,' he nodded.

'We need cameras,' Beth murmured as she unzipped her backpack and removed several devices. Zeb went out with the sisters to mount them discreetly on the walls of the neighboring buildings, with their feeds going to their screens.

Bwana and Bear rolled up tires to block the approach of any intruders while Broker and Roger grunted and heaved as they rolled mobile tool racks out to the front. They drew wires across the approach road and rigged the racks to empty their contents on anyone who tripped them.

Zeb returned to the garage and knocked out the rear windows. The sounds from the nearby-expressway came to them. *That's our getaway route.*

He checked out the contents of several drawers and removed plastic sheets and handed them to his team. 'Bedding.'

'ZEB!'

His eyes snapped open at Beth's yell.

His inner animal reacted instantly.

He rolled out from beneath the ambulance he was sleeping under. His Glock came to his hand without conscious thought, his eye to the sight, seeking targets until they rested on his friend who was propped up against another vehicle and his brain did its computations and told his synapses there was no threat in the garage.

'Put the gun away,' she told him impatiently. The light from her phone's screen illuminated her smile.

Zeb holstered the Glock. Felt shadows behind him. His friends looming in the darkness of the garage.

'What's up,' he checked his wrist. Twelve am. He had been asleep for just over an hour.

'It's Clare,' Beth motioned for him to get closer and put the call on speaker. 'She's got news for us.'

'Ma'am?' Zeb rasped.

'It's my fault,' their Director began distractedly. 'I should have checked my email.'

Zeb looked at Beth and Meghan who both shook their heads. They had no clue what their boss was talking about.

'It wasn't flagged—'

'Which email? From whom?'

Clare's voice sharpened, became professional. 'From Zohra.'

Zeb shot up straight. He winced when his head bumped the side of the ambulance. 'She emailed you?'

'CIA. I forwarded it to Meghan.' She broke it down for them while the operators crowded over the elder twin's phone and read the message.

'That was two days ago,' Zeb worked out the timeline. 'She must have gotten desperate to risk sending that email.'

'She's smart,' Bear said admiringly. 'Using the protest hashtags is a genius idea to filter our response among all the social messages out there.'

'Chemical weapon, ma'am,' Zeb explained their meeting with Parmida and Kaveh. 'That's what we figure. That's Project Emad, probably being developed in the university's lab. Zohra got wind of it somehow and sent us the first message.'

'Find her,' Clare ordered. 'Find out what this is all about. Get her out safely.'

'Yes, ma'am.'

Zeb squinted at Meghan whose fingers were flying on her phone when the call ended.

'Responding to Zohra,' she explained and showed them what she had typed out.

Enjoyed great food on Golshan Street some time ago. Am in the mood for another awesome meal tomorrow. Suggestions? #IranProtests #IranVoice

Zeb grinned. 'That should work. She'll make the connection to that street.'

He fingered his Glock absently as he returned to his luxury bed, the plastic sheet, beneath the ambulance.

One more night, Zohra. Stay free for that much longer.

96

Zohra couldn't sleep.

She tossed and turned and checked the phone several times until she sat up with a sigh.

'You'll wake up the entire clinic,' Leila said irritably in the dark.

'I can't help it—'

'Let's go for a walk.'

'Walk? At this time of the night?'

'This is Pasdaran, where the rich live. We'll be safe. Come. You have disturbed my sleep anyway. Some fresh air will clear your head.'

Zohra followed her out through the office door. She shut it behind her softly and breathed deeply as she and Leila walked away on the rear street.

The neighborhood was quiet. Tehran was sleeping. A dog barked faintly but there were no other sounds.

'Don't,' Leila snatched the phone when Zohra brought it out of her pocket. 'Searching the internet, waiting for a reply ... the worry will consume you.'

'Aren't you scared?'

'Very, but I am forcing myself to think of other things.'

'Like?'

'What I will specialize in once I finish my degree.'

Zohra looked at her friend who was a step behind her. She didn't have to tell Leila that finishing the degree was a remote possibility. *We'll have to stay alive, safe and resume our lives for that to happen.*

She shook her head to clear away the despairing thought and walked faster.

She had barely gone a few paces when Leila shrieked.

She spun around, her heart in her mouth, expecting to see police officers surrounding them.

The psychology student was beaming, her hand high in the air with the phone in it.

'What happened?' Zohra asked fearfully. No lights had gone on in the surrounding homes. It looked like no one had heard Leila's yell.

'Zeb replied!'

The older student stared at her until the words finally registered. She rushed to her friend and peered over her shoulder.

'It's him. Golshan Street. That's where we met. It can't be anyone else. Zeb saw your message. He replied. It's him—'

She stopped and took a deep breath when Leila squeezed her arm. She knew she was grinning stupidly and saw the relieved smile mirrored on her friend's face.

'What do we reply?' Leila asked.

'Suggest a meeting tomorrow night.'

'Night? Shouldn't we meet him and his friends as soon as possible?'

'No,' Zohra shook her head. 'They need to prepare for it. We need to give them as much time as possible.'

'That makes sense. Where?'

'Here, Pasdaran.'

'No,' Leila objected. 'We'll put your khaleh in danger.' Her frown cleared. 'Let's meet in Niavaran. The police will have filled it with officers. No one will suspect we will dare to go there.'

'Good thinking,' Zohra agreed. 'Which account sent that message?'

'It feels like a bot account with all those numbers and letters in it.'

'No. That's how they want it to look like. Add it as a friend and once they accept, message them.'

Leila sent the request and pocketed her phone. 'We are saved,' she smiled.

'Almost,' Zohra replied and prayed that they hadn't jinxed their luck.

97

Abid had personally led the team of officers who had questioned every store keeper on Gholami Street.

The first interrogation hadn't been successful.

The Sepah men descended after the Niavaran attack and that was all that was on people's minds. The shop owners, their staff and the customers distracted the questioning with their own enquiries.

Abid's bruised face didn't help. The cuts above his eyes and the purpled mottling of his skin attracted the wrong kind of interest. Several customers snapped his photographs and said he was a hero to engage with the terrorists.

He didn't confirm or deny that he had been at the shootout but his ego swelled. His questions were less brutal but they didn't get the answers he was seeking.

He returned the next day, determined.

He stomped into the first store as soon as it opened at ten am.

'I am not here to drink chai,' he flung the cup away that the owner offered.

That set the right mood.

. . .

'I DON'T LIKE THIS,' ZEB WHISPERED AS HE STROLLED DOWN Seventh Street in Niavaran the next day. He was far ahead of his scattered team, every one of whom was on foot.

It was bright, the morning air was crisp, the sun doing little to warm them up.

He had changed his looks from the previous day. His nose was dented. He had grey streaks in his hair. He walked slowly as if he had a limp.

'It's a dead-end alley,' Bwana grouched. 'Residences. One exit to Zeynali and the other ends in a cul-de-sac. Why did Zohra suggest this place for the meeting?'

'Because this is where she feels safe,' Chloe said.

Zeb walked on. The houses were set back from the street. A Land Rover drove out of a driveway, a mom hunched behind the wheel as her daughter chattered. Neither of them paid him attention. *Zohra mentioned an abandoned building, where is it?*

There!

It too was set back from the street and was hidden by a clump of leafy plane trees. Its entrance was blocked by a rusty metal fence on which was a *Private Property. No Access* sign.

The front yard was littered with debris. Plastic bags, rotting newspapers, scraps of cloth, a bicycle wheel, an upturned bucket in which weeds had grown. Grass all around which hadn't come across a mower's blade in years.

'I looked it up,' Beth commented. 'It's tied up in legal cases and remains unsold and unoccupied. The locals say it's a haunted house and no one goes near it.'

Zeb grunted in acknowledgment. The end of the cul-de-sac was marked by a thick growth of poplars that were over twenty-meters high. Traffic sounds from Khodaverdi, a busy street that marked the rear boundary of Niavaran.

He eyed the opposite house. Two-storied, concrete structure. Curtains drawn tight over windows. No vehicles in the driveway or in the columned-portico.

'Bwana, Roger, you'll get into the house. Find shooting positions and cover the entrance. Bear, you and Broker cover the Seventh-Street and Zeynali junction. Meg and Chloe—'

'We'll be in the woods,' the elder sister cut in.

'Yeah. Beth and I will meet her.'

'I still don't think we should meet her here,' Bwana grumbled.

'Jeez,' the Texan scoffed, 'we heard you the first time.'

Zeb returned the way he had come. He passed the twins and Chloe who were deep in a low conversation and ignored him. They looked older, carried large bags slung over their shoulders and spoke in fluent Persian.

They'll check out the house, too.

'Yeah,' Meghan said when he had reached Zeynali. 'Those woods beyond the dead-end, are thick. Chloe and I can hide in there, easily.'

Zeb passed Bear who was leaning against a lamp post, reading a local newspaper. He got into his Range Rover and waited.

Life in Niavaran flowed around him. Fancy cars rolled up on Zeynali, stopped in front of boutiques and disgorged their elegantly-dressed women who swept into the stores.

Meghan climbed into shotgun. Broker and Bear occupied the rear seats. Zeb eyed his side mirrors and swung out. Light reflected off Bear's ride as his vehicle merged into the traffic.

Zeb dialed a number.

'Baradar,' Hassan answered instantly. 'How can I help?'

He grinned. 'You might withdraw your offer once you hear what I want.'

'That will never happen. My entire family will help in whatever—'

'Don't start. I need four cars in good condition. Two will be parked on Zeynali. One each beyond the Seventh Street junction. The other two will be on Khodaverdi.'

'Four cars, good condition, full tanks,' Hassan repeated. 'No problem.'

'I need two buses. Two large vans or pickup trucks will do as well. Both near the Seventh Street junction, but they cannot block the four cars.'

'I can arrange those. Full tanks?'

'No. Barely any fuel in them.'

'Okay, so they won't be going anywhere.'

'I need a few other cars or bikes ... any kind of vehicle, which will be parked on Zeynali, again, without blocking the four cars.'

'I can arrange those as well. Full tanks or no fuel?

'Just enough gas to get them to Zeynali.'

'No problem.'

'You have a fleet of vehicles, Hassan?' Broker gave astonished.

'No, baradar,' the garage owner laughed. 'But I have a network of friends who own auto shops. I can easily procure cars, trucks, buses, vans and high-performance bikes.'

'With false plates and no way of tracing them back to you?'

'Balle. A lot of our business is done in cash. We buy and sell several used vehicles. Hiding the trail is easy.'

'Can you arrange these by afternoon?' Zeb asked. 'We need to work on them before they are driven to Zeynali.'

Hassan paused for a moment. 'I can message you the locations of the vehicles. Can you go to them, do whatever is needed and then my people can deliver them?'

'Yes, that will work. Don't get into trouble—'

'Don't start, baradar,' Hassan hung up.

'We need to pay him,' Zeb said absently.

'We will,' Meghan nodded, 'when we are done. He will return it right away if we pay him now.'

ZOHRA AND LEILA LEFT THE CLINIC AT TWELVE PM.

They wore shades and were dressed in older clothes. They had hugged Jaffari earlier in the day before she left for her hospital rounds.

The doctor was perceptive. 'You won't be coming back?'

'We don't know, khaleh,' Zohra admitted.

'Something is going to happen?'

'It's best you don't ask,' she kissed her aunt on her cheeks and embraced her hard.

The research student was jumpy when they hit the street. She looked around at the slightest honk or squeal of tires.

'Stop that,' Leila said beneath her breath. 'You will draw attention to us.'

'I can't help it. I am nervous. How will we spend time till eight pm?'

'We will go around the city randomly. We will have food. We discussed this yesterday.'

'That didn't help my fear.'

'I am scared too.'

Zohra sighed. She caught Leila's arm and led her to Bathaie where they got into a cab. 'Azadi Tower,' she told the driver and mopped perspiration from her forehead.

It was going to be a long day.

IT WAS THE LAST ELECTRONICS STORE ON GHOLAMI STREET. IT was nondescript in appearance. *Kareem's Mobiles*, the fading sign announced. It was narrow and had none of the opulent looks of upscale retail outlets.

Abid surveyed it when he got out of his Sepah ride.

'They wouldn't come here, agha,' his officer commented. 'That shop is so small that the owner might remember all his customers. They wouldn't take that risk.'

'Stranger things have happened,' Abid replied grumpily. He was tired of hearing negative answers. That's what he had been hearing all day long. Naser kept messaging or calling him every hour and he didn't like giving the same update, that no store had sold a phone to Hashimi or even to two young women on that day.

He straightened and put on a grim look. He climbed up the concrete steps and went inside the store.

It didn't surprise him that the establishment had no air-conditioning. A single row of tube lights in the ceiling. A glass counter and shelves in which were phones of different makes. Faded lettering declaring deals and discounts.

'You are Kareem?' he asked the stocky man behind the till. No other employee was in sight.

'Balle,' the man replied.

'I am Sepah,' Abid thrust his chest forward to draw the owner's attention to his name plate.

'You need a phone, sir? No one on this street sells them cheaper than me.'

Abid slapped him. 'Do I look like I need a phone?'

Kareem howled. He clutched his cheek and stood up. 'I AM SORRY, AGHA. HOW CAN I HELP?' He yelled.

'Did this woman come into this store a week ago?' Abid slapped Hashimi's photograph on the counter.

Kareem picked it up and squinted.

'Balle,' he nodded.

98

Zeb rolled out from beneath the pick-up truck and wiped sweat from his forehead.

'I am done, here,' he told his friends.

An aircraft took off from the nearby Mehrabad International Airport.

He wiped his hands on his pants and checked out the large yard he was in. It was a long-term private parking area which Hassan had assured him was secure and discreet.

'So are we,' Meghan replied from Dabestan. 'Beth, Broker and I have moved all our gear to the four cars. They are good to go.'

'Rog and I will need some more time,' Bwana said from Shahrara. 'This van is low-slung. We would have jacked it up but we don't have that.'

Five pm. Zeb worked it out in his mind. 'We'll need to be in Niavaran in another hour.'

'We'll get there.'

'We're through,' Bwana checked in.

The sun was a low-hanging reddish orb by the time Zeb got into the Ford that he had arrived in. His Range Rover was with the twins.

He eyed the van as it receded in his rear-view mirror.

Mayhem, he thought.

He didn't know if they needed the distraction but it was better to be prepared.

'I GOT IT,' ABID YELLED IN HIS PHONE.

'Got what?' Naser replied sharply.

'Hashimi's phone number, agha,' the major controlled himself and motioned for his driver to roll out of Gholami Street. 'She and the other woman bought it in a small shop. They didn't provide any identification and paid in cash. But the owner remembered. He is one of those men who pays more attention to women's looks.'

'Where are they now?'

'Azadi Park. I am heading over there. I will arrest them.'

'NO! Do you have their real time movement?'

'Balle. Our screen in the SUV is showing it.'

'Don't arrest them in the park. We know they are smart. They might be there with other protesters. Observe them and see where they go. Take them where it is less crowded. We don't want any more negative publicity.'

'Balle. We will go to Azadi Tower and I will get men to watch them.'

'Use your head, Abid,' Naser snarled. 'I said I don't want to create a scene. Be near the tower but don't show yourself. Don't let your men be seen. You have got her phone. You can track her from your vehicle. How many men do you have?'

'One team. Four in my SUV.'

'I will send another one and come out myself.'

'Agha, you know what happened last time, in Niavaran.'

'They are women,' Naser said scornfully. 'What do they know of dealing with Sepah? Carter has nothing to do with them.'

'Don't come right away. Wait till I tell you where I will arrest them. Come there.'

The Basij leader thought about it for a moment and nodded. 'Balle. Let me know. I will come with the second team.'

He hung up and made a fierce sound of celebration.

Once we have Hashimi, it will be all over. I can then focus on Carter.

99

Zeb entered Seventh Street at six pm. Evening time. Parents walking ahead of him with their children. Lights in the houses, the smells of cooking.

Dusk was turning to dark swiftly. Street lamps had come on, illuminating the sidewalk. Vehicles entered the street and rolled into driveways.

'In position,' Meghan checked in. 'The woods are dark, deep, silent and empty but for us,' she paraphrased with a chuckle. 'We have eyes on you.'

On the other sidewalk, Beth was level with him, speaking animatedly on her phone, her colorful, sequined headscarf catching the light.

Bwana tapped his mic to acknowledge he and Roger were in the building.

'All vehicles in place,' Bear confirmed from Zeynali. 'Everything is set. Can't see any more cops than normal.'

'We should have insisted she share her phone number,' Zeb murmured, his eyes flicking continually.

'We did,' Beth retorted. 'She refused to give it. She said she wouldn't until she saw us in person.'

'Can't blame her,' Roger said laconically. 'She's scared. She wants to control the meeting.'

Zeb grunted. He reached the cul-de-sac. Knew his friends in the abandoned house would be watching him. He crouched between two parked vehicles. Beth mimicked his move on the other side of the street and gave him a thumbs-up.

We'll give an awkward smile and move out if the owners come to their rides.

'THEY ARE ON THE MOVE,' ABID YELLED.

Naser winced. 'Do you have to shout every time?'

'Sorry, agha. They took a taxi. We are following them several vehicles behind. They are going to the north of the city.'

'Did you see them?'

'Only from a distance. Two women, but we didn't see their faces. We didn't come out of our SUV.'

'Keep your distance. I am coming.'

Naser snatched his cap, jammed it over his head and barked an order to his aide. By the time he got to the elevator car, his driver was at the wheel of his ride and when he reached the parking lot, the second team in another SUV was waiting alongside his vehicle.

'GO!' He ordered.

'Go where, agha?' His driver asked.

'North. Keep going. I will tell you where exactly.'

'DO YOU REMEMBER WHAT TO DO?' LEILA ASKED WHEN THEIR taxi stopped on Zeynali.

Zohra paid the driver and nodded. 'Balle. I will enter the street alone. You will enter that empty house which is opposite our meeting place.'

'I will enter it from behind, from Gorji and hide in its front garden.'

'How do you know of that house?'

'I told you,' Leila said impatiently. 'Some of my university friends used to meet their boyfriends at the abandoned house. They knew people kept their distance from it because of the haunted rumors. They discovered that the opposite house was empty too. No one ever saw the owners. The lights were always on, however.'

'Why can't we go down Seventh Street together?'

'Because, PhD Research Student who doesn't seem to be thinking properly at the moment, until we see Zeb, we don't know who we are meeting. This way, I can cause some distraction if it turns out to be Sepah and you can escape.'

'How? We have no weapons. If it is the Revolutionary Guards who faked those messages, then we are trapped.'

Leila held her hand up. 'See how my fingers are shaking. I am scared too. Do we have a choice? We have to trust someone. If it is Zeb, he will protect us, especially once you tell him about the bomb.'

'If it isn't him?'

'Then we will be together whatever happens.'

Zohra gave her a tight hug and went down Zeynali. She didn't look back at Leila. She knew her fear would make her cry if she saw her friend disappear into the crowd.

Deep breaths, she told herself. *This will be over soon.*

'Zeb.'

He cocked his head up at Meghan's tone. 'Yeah?'

'Naser's on the move. Our tracker is still on his holster. He's heading north.'

North. Zeb pictured the city and placed Sepah's headquarters in his mental map. *He could be going anywhere. Can't do anything about him. Meg or Beth will warn us if he gets here.*

'Everything's still quiet on Zeynali. No Sepah vehicles have come close to the Seventh Street junction,' Bear added.

'What about Zohra?'

'Evening crowd is thick,' Broker observed. 'It's impossible for Bear and me to see individual people. We can't get too close to the junction without exposing ourselves.'

'Stay where you are,' Zeb told them. From their earlier planning, he knew Bear was at a kebab stand while the older operator was at a barber shop, both of them vantage points from where they could watch the intersection as well as good sections of Zeynali. *We decided against launching the drone since we are spread out.* 'We wait.'

His senses sharpened as the night deepened. He went into the zone, identifying and cataloguing every night sound. A faint siren. A car's honk. A child's loud squeal from some house.

A shoe scraped after long moments while the earth rotated and revolved incrementally and somewhere in the world sunrise happened.

Zeb raised his head at the sound.

He was aware of Beth's soundless tensing from across the street.

A figure walked past him on the sidewalk, barely a few meters away.

A woman. Black chador on dark, loose trousers. Head scarf. She stood in front of the house and looked uncertainly around. Her face caught the light.

Zohra!

100

Yet, Zeb didn't rise.

'It's her,' Beth too gave visual confirmation.

Yet, neither she nor Zeb rose.

He could feel her fear. He could see it in the nervous twitching of her hands and sharp jerky motions of her head.

He waited, listening intently for the night sounds and only when he was sure there was no other danger did he stand from behind the car.

She drew a sharp breath.

She stared at him.

Her eyes widened.

Her hand flew to her mouth in the universal gesture of shock and fear.

Zeb heard the pounding of footsteps behind him.

Beth's exclamation.

Something hit him even as he was turning.

'ZOHRA, RUN! I WILL KEEP THEM OCCUPIED. GO!'

He took the second blow on his shoulder and then he caught the weapon.

A fallen branch wielded by a woman who was the same height and build as Zohra. Her eyes were stormy, her head scarf had fallen away and her hair was swirling around her face. He controlled his smile but couldn’t help his lips twitching.

Beth, her hands on her hips, was watching with a grin.

'RUN, ZOHRA!' the woman yelled as she struggled to draw back the branch and kicked at him.

'Khanom,' he said softly, releasing her make-shift weapon. 'Please don't shout. You will draw attention.'

Her eyes flicked over him uncertainly as she panted harshly. Zeb took a step back on the sidewalk, his move drawing both her and Zohra's attention.

He removed his prosthetic nose. 'It's me. Zeb. That's Beth,' he nodded in her direction. 'We have to be in disguise because the police are looking for us.'

'Zeb,' Zohra said in a choked voice after tense moments. Her fearful expression receded. Relief set in. Her shoulders relaxed. 'Baradar, we hoped and prayed you would show up. We lived in fear every day.' Her face crumpled.

She rushed into his embrace and trembled.

'I am sorry, baradar,' she said tearfully when she stepped back.

'No, don't say that,' Zeb reapplied his disguise and looked at Beth who nodded, confirming it looked right.

'Who is your protector?' He grinned at the second woman who still gripped the branch.

'My friend,' Zohra beckoned at her and caught her wrist. 'Leila. Leila Shokri. She's a psychology student at Alzahra University. She's also a student protest organizer. She's been with me ever since we both were captured by Sepah.'

'Khanom.' He smiled at the younger woman, 'you have a strong arm.'

'I am so sorry, agha,' she dropped the branch contritely. 'I was hiding in that garden,' she pointed to the opposite house. You didn’t look like Zohra’s description. I thought you were Sepah.'

'Please don't be so formal.'

'Only if you don't refer to me as khanom,' her eyes flashed.

'All this is very touching,' Chloe said sarcastically in their comms, 'but this isn't the safest place for a reunion meeting.'

'Yes,' Zeb agreed.

'Who are you talking to?' Leila's eyes narrowed.

'My friends. They are around us,' Zeb pointed to his ear. 'We are in contact. Let's go—'

'SEPAH VEHICLE!' Bear said sharply. 'Approaching the intersection. It's turning in.'

101

'Let's go!' Zeb caught Zohra's arm and burst into a sprint towards Zeynali.

'What happened?' she gasped as she and Leila raced to keep up with him.

'Sepah.' He pointed at the pair of headlights that had turned into the street.

'We should go into the woods,' her voice broke. 'Why are we going towards them?'

'Trust me. We have planned for this,' he said grimly. 'Stay behind me. Close.'

Beth kept pace with them on the other sidewalk.

Zeb unholstered his Glock. Glanced back to check Zohra and Leila were following him. Took in their expressions. 'Nothing will happen to you.'

'We can cover the street and the sidewalks from where we are,' Meghan said.

'We are coming out,' Bwana checked in. 'Rog and I will back up Meg and Chloe. We'll get away through the woods.'

'TWO MORE SEPAH VEHICLES!' Bear called out sharply. 'They are racing towards the intersection.'

'One of those is Naser's,' Meghan confirmed.

Zeb didn't reply. *How did Sepah know where we would be?*

No, he answered himself. *Zohra and Leila. That's who they are coming for.*

He increased his stride and hoped the students would keep up. He heard their harsh breathing and knew they weren't far behind.

The headlights grew closer. It threw shadows of the parked cars. It didn't look like its occupants had seen them yet since it hadn't slowed.

'Stay to my right,' Zeb whispered to the women and snatched a backward glance to confirm they followed his instruction.

Everything depends on timing.

The SUV was one car-length away from them.

He was sure its occupants could now see their bobbing heads.

The intersection was four car-lengths away.

'Those two vehicles are slowing, their flashers indicating their turn into Seventh,' Broker said.

Zeb drew abreast of the Sepah vehicle. Its driver's window was rolled down. The man was staring at him. A look of recognition flashed on his face when he took in Zohra and Leila.

It was the last look his eyes registered.

Zeb shot him with a double-tap and without breaking stride, raked the side of the vehicle. He heard the women shriek behind him. He slapped a new magazine. 'Keep running,' he grated.

The night opened up in a hail of fire when the Agency operators from behind cut loose at the SUV.

'On the count of five,' Zeb grunted.

'Copy that,' Bear acknowledged.

'Your phone,' Zeb reached out behind him with his left hand.

'What?' Zohra yelled.

'Give me your phone.'

He took it from her fumbling hand. 'Stay close. Cross the street with me.'

They were on the right sidewalk. Beth was on the left. Their getaway vehicle was on her side of Zeynali, which meant they would have to get in front of the turning, incoming, Sepah vehicles.

And Naser, he thought savagely. He counted down.

Five.

One car-length from the intersection. Honks from the bigger street.

Four.

He saw an SUV appear in the junction, its flasher blinking. It waited for a car to pass.

Three.

Zeb and the women passed the last parked vehicle on Seventh. They were visible from the intersection.

Two.

The SUV started turning in.

One.

Zeb sprinted across the street with Zohra and Leila close behind.

A siren rang out shrilly from Zeynali.

A second later, one of Hassan's vans exploded and several other blasts occurred simultaneously.

Zeb raked the front of the SUV with his Glock.

Beth's HK chattered and blew holes in its sides.

It careened. The driver lost control and crashed onto the sidewalk they had left behind.

Another round of explosions went off on Zeynali from the vehicles they had rigged. Dense smoke settled on the street, obscuring the streetlights and reducing visibility.

'COVER YOUR FACES,' Zeb yelled when he heard the women cough. 'IT'S HARMLESS.'

A shadow loomed by his side.

The second SUV.

Its passenger window was rolled down.

A face appeared.

Naser!

The Basij man's face was twisted in anger. He seemed to be reaching for the door when Zeb and the women registered on him. His mouth opened in a yell.

Zeb threw a smoke bomb at him.

'Grenade!' He heard the brigadier general shout.

Can I take him as well?

No, he decided instantly. *No time. I don't know how many men are with him and how many other Sepah vehicles are arriving. I'll blow the shock advantage we have if I make the attempt.*

He was past the intersection, his boots slapping on the side-walk, Zohra and Leila sobbing but keeping pace.

Someone stumbled and fell ahead of them. A civilian.

A dark shape moved determinedly.

Beth. He recognized the way she ran.

She heard their pounding. Raised her hand and pointed towards a sedan that was barely visible in the smoke.

A cacophony on Zeynali. Car alarms. Frightened screaming from civilians. Shouts from several men.

And then Zeb had opened the rear passenger door to hustle Zohra and Leila inside and Beth spun the wheel hard and raced out even before he had settled in shotgun.

'Check in,' he snapped.

'We got away,' Meghan confirmed.

'So did we,' Roger grinned. 'Those two Sepah vehicles ... I don't know how many are alive in them. We poured enough rounds even if they were armored.'

'We're driving away,' Bear spoke.

Zeb sighed in relief. He put in a fresh magazine in his Glock and reloaded Beth's HK which was in between them. He mopped his face with his sleeve. 'I saw Naser, in the second SUV. He thought the smoke bomb I threw at him was a grenade. There was no time to grab him.'

'Yeah. We'll get another chance,' Meghan said.

'We were lucky this second time as well,' Bwana rumbled.

'The Revolutionary Guards weren't expecting us. The dice won't always roll in our favor.'

He's right, Zeb checked the side mirrors. There was no sign of pursuit. Several civilian cars were fleeing the smoke-filled center of mayhem.

'Listen to him,' Roger scoffed. 'The voice of cheer and optimism.'

Adrenaline pumped in the immediate aftermath of an extreme incident. The surge of chemicals in the bloodstream affected people differently. Some became jumpy, others became hyperactive, many others became talkative.

The Agency operators had their way of dealing with it as a team. They used humor, with Roger, Broker and the twins usually providing it, to blunt the effects of the *supply*, as Bear phrased it.

'Slow down,' Zeb told Beth and pointed to the fire truck that was racing towards the intersection. He took Zohra's phone, leaned across her to roll down her window and timed his throw to land the device on its rear.

He didn't know if it would stay on the vehicle or bounce off onto the street. It didn't matter either way.

He looked at their passengers in the rear-view mirror. 'Sepah must have found out your number. That's how they could track you. They must have discovered it very recently otherwise they would have arrested you a long time ago.'

Zohra shivered. 'Are we safe now, baradar?'

'Yes,' Zeb replied. *For now.*

102

'Safe,' Zohra repeated. Her face twisted. Her control broke. She started sobbing and clutched Leila.

They cried, their bodies shaking as they held each other for emotional support.

Zeb didn't speak. It was intense relief that had triggered their weeping. *Let it come out.*

'Sorry,' Zohra sniffled. 'We didn't mean to—'

'There is no need to apologize,' he said gently.

'I cried at the house and now, here. You must think—'

'Zohra,' he turned around at them. 'I feel admiration for both of you. Nothing else.'

'I promised to cook khoresht for you,' she smiled through her tears. 'There is no need to flatter me for that.'

'I mean it.'

'He's right,' Beth said. 'You both have evaded Sepah for so long ... believe me. That takes courage, determination, smarts—'

'We didn't feel any of that, khahar,' Leila wiped her face. 'We were just trying to survive.

'You're here, now. We will protect you.' Beth reached behind her with one hand and squeezed their palms.

She drove randomly in the city, jumping from one neighborhood to another, taking sudden turns and on a few occasions even driving through red lights.

'Clear,' she said after a while.

The radio broadcast running commentary of the explosions. Terrorists had struck Tehran, the reporter emphasized time and again. He speculated it was the same group that had attacked Niavaran.

Several vehicles had been damaged and Sepah officers had been killed and injured but there didn't seem to be any civilian fatalities.

Hassan's people placed the rigged vehicles in low-congestion areas. Over stinking drain-hole covers or overflowing trash bins. The siren was an early warning for civilians to get away. Zeb shrugged. He had wondered how effective the placements had been since the blasts had followed soon after. *It seems to have worked, however. No innocents died.*

His lips tightened. He knew how Gholamreza's mind worked. *He'll announce that several civilians were ruthlessly targeted by the terrorists.* It was about optics and getting public support.

'Zeb, where are we going?' Zohra asked from the rear.

He turned to look at her and Leila. Their fear had subsided but their nervousness still showed.

'We have a safe place nearby,' he said reassuringly. 'We will spend the night there.'

'And after that?' Leila asked.

'That will depend on what you tell us.'

'There's a—' Zohra rushed to speak.

'Not now. Later.'

She nodded and settled back in her seat.

'Mina said you were always calm,' Leila said. 'All of you. You didn't raise your voices. I can see what she meant by that.'

Zeb's forehead wrinkled. 'Mina? Who's that?'

'The student you saved in Tunisia. She was with several others—'

'You know them?' he asked in astonishment.

'Balle,' she nodded. 'They are student demonstrators. I know Farideh and Parvaneh better than her, but yes, I know Mina as well.'

'You spoke to her?'

'Yes. She's in Germany.'

He stared at her and Zohra for long moments while Beth eyed them in the rear-view mirror as she drove.

'You have lots to tell us,' he said finally.

'THIS ... IS A HOSPITAL GARAGE,' ZOHRA SAID CAUTIOUSLY when they arrived at their safe house.

'It's where we will be safest,' Bear grunted as he and Bwana cut through the new padlock that the workers had installed.

Zeb turned on a flashlight and helped his friends set up their security, the tires and the trip wired tool racks that they had removed before leaving that morning.

'Cold food,' Broker said apologetically as he handed out their packets. 'Zeb told me we would be staying in five-star hotels and flying business-class, when I joined him. I didn't know this was what he meant.'

Leila grinned. She leaned up and kissed him on his cheek. 'It's alright, baradar. There were times when Zohra and I didn't know if we would live or if we did, we were sure we would be raped.'

'Tell us everything,' Zeb said after a long silence.

'There's a—' Zohra began again.

'From the beginning, from where we met on Golshan Street all those years ago, to today. Everything.' Meghan interrupted her with a smile. 'We have time. The night is with us.'

'I never saw Arash again after that night,' the research student started. 'I heard he left the country to go to Dubai, but I didn't follow it up. I wasn't interested. I completed my Bachelor's degree and then my Masters and got into the PhD program.'

Zeb listened quietly as he plugged in an electric kettle from their gear and brewed chai for them. He poured it in paper cups and distributed them and sipped his drink.

Leila introduced herself. She took them through her story. Bwana's face turned granite when she mentioned her parents' murders and her sister's rape.

'I became a student protester that night, it feels like years ago now,' she half-smiled, 'I met Zohra at the Sattar Khan demonstration,' she waved her cup around to include the garage, 'which led us to being here.'

'What happened that night?' Bear stretched his legs on the plastic sheet they were sitting on. 'The night you sent us that message?'

'We were hiding in Iran Capital Bank where Sepah captured us.'

'That's when our nightmare started,' Zohra said and recounted what had transpired in the cell they had been held in, their escape and every event from then on.

Zeb refilled their cups when she finished. He crossed his legs and leaned against a tire.

'What was the message for?'

'My country is building a secret chemical weapon.'

'We guessed it would be something like that.'

'No, baradar,' her face scrunched with worry. 'This isn't nerve gas or anything like it. It's horrifying to even say it.' She licked her lips. 'You have heard of MRNA vaccines?'

'Yeah.' Beth waved in the air. 'Everyone in the world has heard of them.'

'This weapon will lower the human body's resistance and cause death in two weeks.'

Zeb hunched forward. His palm squeezed his cup instinctively.

'Wait,' Zohra said when Beth made to ask a question. 'It gets worse. Professor Farhad has weaponized a specific MRNA that codes for proteins found on pathogens. He has got the chemical weapon to fool the human cells and instead of producing anti-bodies, the immune system does nothing and over time, just two weeks, the human body is flooded with this virus, which then kills.'

'And it is airborne,' she continued in a shaky voice. 'It can be transmitted by coughing and sneezing.'

Zeb crushed his paper cup. His words sounded as if coming from a distance. 'Flu? He has weaponized flu?'

'Yes, baradar. The chemical weapon is an MRNA flu vaccine.'

Meghan rubbed her eyes. 'Many countries and pharma companies are researching into MRNA flu vaccines. They are all in experimental stages.'

'Balle,' Zohra nodded. 'This is not a vaccine, however. It is a weapon.'

Bear cursed loudly and immediately apologized.

'It's alright,' she smiled tiredly. 'It is truly horrific.'

'It's being developed in the university's biochemistry lab?' Zeb asked, recollecting Kaveh's words.

'Yes. It has been converted into a secretive research center. Only the professor and his assistants, Javed Reza and Behnam Ali are allowed entry into it. There is lot of security. Sepah soldiers are inside it. We were told that the professor is working on a breakthrough biochemistry innovation that could win him the Nobel Prize and make the country proud and the security is because other countries should not steal his idea.'

'You were not in his team?'

'No. I was in some of the courses he taught, but I didn't know he was putting together this *research* team,' she emphasized the word, 'and if I had known what it was for, I would have refused it.'

'How do you know about it, then?' Zeb spread his hands. 'Why is Sepah after you?'

'I was near the lab that day when a fire started in it and its doors opened. I could hear shouts and smoke and went in to see if I could help. The smoke was so dense that I could barely see, but I bumped into what I think was Professor Farhad's desk. His notes, his computer ... they were there. I intended to put them away safely, when the word *weapon* struck me and then I couldn't help reading them. The hand-written notes were brief but there was enough in them for me to understand.'

'They are after you because you know about it.'

'Not just that, Zeb,' Zohra glanced sideways at Leila. 'I stole something as well.'

'You stole his laptop and his notes?' Beth guessed with a wide grin.

'Balle, but also a chemical without which they cannot progress.'

103

'You did what?' Zeb exclaimed.

'I stole a container of Xenosine. This is a very rare reagent that a German lab produces. I looked it up later. The professor's notes had a drawing of the various components. He had marked Xenosine in red and written critical underneath it and underlined it several times. The box, the size of a small cooler. You know the kind where people put in juice or alcohol bottles. It was right beneath his desk, sealed. He must have kept it there because it was so important that he had to manage it himself.'

Zohra's words rushed out at their expressions. She looked uncertainly at them when they had finished.

Bear was the first to break the silence. He threw his head back and guffawed. Bwana joined in.

'That!' Leila said excitedly, 'was how I reacted too when she told me. Xeno ... whatever it is, she didn't tell me that. But she said what she had run away with had stalled the program.'

'Yes,' Meghan looked up from her screen. 'Zohra is right. Only one German company makes it.' Her face tightened. 'BND alerted Europol that a five-kilogram consignment was stolen last year. They reported it because Xenosine is a classified chemical because it can be misused.'

'Balle,' Zohra nodded. 'Not much of it is required. Five kilograms would have been more than enough. The professor wasn't developing production ready chemical weapons. He was making a prototype that would be mass produced somewhere else.

'Marketed as flu vaccine and deployed on suicide squads that would go to different countries and spread the virus,' Roger said bitterly.

'They wouldn't be suicide squads,' Zohra corrected him. 'The next step for the professor would have been to develop an antidote, a counter-vaccine.'

'You stole a laptop, his papers—'

'His notebook,' she interrupted Zeb.

'His notebook,' he continued, 'and this container and walked out. No one saw you?'

'No. It was chaos. The fire was spreading fast. There was too much smoke. I could hear people shouting inside the lab. Remember, there was a student demonstration in the university at the same time. Many fires had broken out in the campus as well because the protest had turned violent. I stuffed everything in my backpack and ran.'

'Where are they?'

'Yes,' Leila side-eyed her friend with a sly smile. 'You never told me that.'

Zohra's eyes sparkled. 'In a place no one will think of looking. In the university's sewage tank.'

104

'Zohra Hashimi, Leila Shokri,' Bwana got up and bowed before them. 'You are the most amazing women I have met. Sewage tank! Attacking Zeb with a branch!'

Zeb sobered after the round of laughter. 'We need to recover those. The notebook and laptop might be damaged—'

'They won't be,' Zohra cut in with a grin. 'There was a very large plastic sheet in the bin beneath the professor's desk. I rolled them several times in the sheet. The cooler is water-proof, air-proof, many-proofed. I have seen those before. Nothing can go in it once it is sealed, and I applied that before hiding it.'

'She's a PhD student,' Leila shoulder-nudged her friend. 'She's smart.'

'Yeah,' Beth grinned. 'Why did you think of that place?'

'One of the tank's covers is always a little loose,' Zohra replied. 'The area around it stinks. It was an obvious choice. I know it is shallow. One student had dropped her phone in it once,' she made a face. 'The maintenance man reached into it with his hand. It went up to his elbow.'

'I don't want to think or imagine that,' Beth said hurriedly and dialed a number. 'Let's call Clare.'

'Ma'am,' she said when the Director came on video call. 'We

have Zohra and her friend Leila with us. Yes, we are safe ma'am,' she anticipated their boss's question. 'You should hear this out.'

She outlined Zohra's revelations briefly.

Clare remained expressionless when she had finished. 'I'll consult a few people right away. Hold till then.'

Code for *I'll brief the president, check out whether Xenosine could be used to make a flu weapon and get back.*

It wasn't that they didn't believe Zohra, but the Agency needed independent verification.

'Yes, ma'am.'

Zeb rotated his shoulder as he thought quickly when she hung up. 'Two-person retrieval team. Me and Zohra. We will need a—'

'Maintenance van,' Meghan snapped her fingers. 'Two pairs of coveralls. That will not arouse any suspicion. The rest of us will arrange exfil.'

'Who are you?' Leila burst out. 'Mina said your boss, was that her on the call, works at the White House.'

Zeb chuckled at her incredulous look. 'Yes, that was Clare. She spoke to Mina and the rest of the women. She doesn't work at the White House but meets the president often.'

'Are you CIA?'

'No, but we are a secret American agency.'

'Like in the movies?'

'Which Hollywood movie shows agents sleeping on plastic sheets in a garage, drinking out of paper cups and eating cold food?' Broker said mournfully.

Leila grinned. 'I get it. You don't want to reveal all your secrets.'

'It's for your safety,' Zeb smiled.

She nodded. 'That's what Zohra said too when I asked about the weapon. She didn't say much.'

'Van, coveralls, exfil,' Meghan reminded him about the planning.

'Didn't Clare say you should wait?' Zohra asked curiously.

'Yes, but her answer will be to retrieve what you hid,' Zeb said confidently. 'And we need to be ready.'

Are you awake? He messaged Hassan while Meghan and Beth huddled over their screen.

'What can I do?' the garage owner called immediately.

'I need a van with the logo of a well-known facilities maintenance company. You choose which firm.'

'When?'

'As quickly as you can arrange it.'

'Full tank?'

'Yes. False plates and papers. I need two pairs of coveralls too with the company's logo on it. One should be smaller size.'

'I have standard sizes that will fit most body types. Khaki color. That's what we use in my garage. I can paint the company name. Two or three hours will do?'

'Yes. Leave it in the Hyperstar's parking lot. The one in Eram. I'll pick it up from there.'

He thought for a moment as he went to the twin's screen and looked over their shoulder at the satellite images of the university. 'You said you can arrange high-performance bikes too?'

'Will a Ducati Panigale do?'

Zeb looked at his phone as if he could stare at Hassan. 'You have a Panigale?'

'I am looking at it right now. Police confiscated it from a criminal gang and auctioned it. The buyer went bankrupt and pawned it to another garage. A long chain of transactions happened and I got it because someone owed me and could not pay me and gave me the bike instead.'

Zeb whistled and then shook his head. 'No. That is an expensive super bike. I can't—'

'Zeb Carter, my baradar,' Hassan's voice boomed in the garage. 'I will decide what I can or cannot do. Not you. Where should I deliver the bike?'

Zeb gave up. 'Can you extend its seat to accommodate a passenger?'

'I can. I run the best auto shop in Tehran. There is very little I cannot do. I will add foot pegs too.'

'Just inside the university campus. Can you deliver it there?'

'University of Tehran? Balle. I will have it chained to something with a number lock. I will message you the code.'

Zeb hung up. Rubbed his jaw. *Did I think of everything? Meg and Beth will arrange the exfil.*

The older sister's phone buzzed.

'Clare,' she said and put the call on speaker.

'My consultations didn't take long,' their boss said tautly. 'Xenosine can be mis-used in that manner and apparently Professor Farhad has been on a particular alphabet agency's radar which didn't think it was worth mentioning its suspicions to the rest of us. That's DC politics. Nothing to do with you. Greenlight. Get the package. Get Zohra and Leila out of the country. It won't be safe for them in Iran anymore. Clear?'

'Clear,' Zeb said.

'Naser is no longer a target. What Zohra has hidden is more valuable.'

'Copy that.'

'Out of the country,' Zohra said hesitantly when the call ended. 'What did she mean by that?'

'We'll take you to America,' he replied. 'You will have new lives there. Is that okay?'

'Balle,' she nodded vigorously, her eyes shining.

'Me also?' Leila asked timidly. 'Zohra is your friend.'

'Yes, you too,' Zeb said surprisedly. 'You are Sepah's target too.'

'You don't want to come with me?' Zohra asked her friend.

'How can you say that?' the psychology student said heatedly. 'I don't want to be a burden on Zeb, however. It may not be easy for him or his boss to arrange for—'

'Leila,' Zeb interrupted her. 'When Clare said we should extract both of you, she means it. She will arrange for you to have new lives, a fast-track to citizenship.'

'She can do all of that?' Leila's eyes rounded.

'Balle, she can arrange all of that. We have done it before, several times.'

'Will we be together?' Zohra asked. She glanced sideways at her friend. 'That is, if Leila wants to be together.'

Zeb made to speak. Felt sharp knuckles dig into his ribs. Beth. 'Keep quiet,' she hissed.

He looked at the students, read their expressions and body language and remembered the way Zohra had held Leila's hand at the rendezvous. *They haven't had the talk yet. They haven't acknowledged what they feel for each other and maybe even to themselves.*

He stayed silent.

'Why wouldn't I want to be with you?' the psychology student blazed. 'If I wanted to leave your side, don't you think I would have done it in Nowruz Park, when you told me about the bomb? Did I leave? No. Why are you doubting me now?'

'You are younger than me.'

'What's that got to do with anything?'

'I don't want you to feel you have to protect me forever,' Zohra said weakly.

'Protect you?' Leila yelled. 'Is that what you think I have been doing? Why I have been staying with you?' Tears shimmered in her eyes. 'Don't you want to be with me?'

'There is nothing more than I want than being with you,' the older student said softly. 'You attacked Zeb with a branch ... it came to me how important you are to me. Do you know what I am saying? But I don't want you to be—'

'I LOVE YOU, ZOHRA HASHIMI ,' Leila shouted, her face red with anger. 'Haven't you worked that out by now?'

The research student's face turned wonderous. A smile trembled on her lips. It widened. Her hands spread open. 'Balle,' she nodded rapidly, 'I feel the same. I was afraid it was just me—'

'Stop talking,' Leila rushed into her embrace, her words muffled against Zohra's shoulder.

'Will we be together, Zeb?' Zohra said after they had separated, their faces glowing.

'Yes,' he replied simply.

Beth rubbed her hands and danced a jig. 'I love a romance and happy ending,' she rushed to the women and hugged them hard.

'You fools,' Meghan chuckled affectionately, addressing the students, 'it was so obvious to us. The way you leaned into each other, looked at one another.'

'Sorry to be a buzzkill,' Bwana said solemnly.

'Here goes Mr. Cheerful,' Roger sighed.

The African-American ignored him. He eyed Leila. 'Zohra promised us a fancy dinner. I want you to know, you are now bound by that too.'

'I cook better than her,' the psychology student said equally solemnly.

'There's only one way to know that.'

'You'll find out in America.'

'I'll hold you to that.'

She grinned and high-fived him. 'Deal.'

105

Zeb woke at five am, rolled up his plastic sheet and stuffed it in the large bag. He brewed tea and by the time he had poured it in his cup, his team and the students were ready, freshened and prepared.

'Exfil?' he asked Meghan.

'Don't worry about it. We will guide you once you retrieve the package.'

'Leila?'

'Will be with us.'

Zeb rotated his neck. His back felt stiff. They had been in mission mode ever since Tunisia with very little downtime. They had rested and slept whenever they could but his body was a mass of aches and pains.

None of them were severe, however. They didn't hamper his movement or his edge. He would compartmentalize them once he was in the zone.

He applied his false nose, a different set of ears and looked at Beth who confirmed his look.

It won't matter for long. The bike's helmet will cover my face. He filled his backpack with several spare magazines for his HK, grenades, smoke bombs and ammo for his Glock.

'Wear this over the coveralls,' Meghan gave him a large jacket.

'I have my armor,' he patted his chest.

'Don't argue. It's a prototype. Wear it.'

'I am the guinea pig?' he smiled to take the offense out of his words and folded it over his backpack.

'Make sure he wears it,' she told Zohra who nodded.

The students were watching silently as the operators went about their prep. They took in the array of weapons and the way the Americans handled them expertly.

'Have you lost anyone?' Leila asked softly.

'In our team?' Zeb asked. 'No. We started off as six and then Meg and Beth convinced us we couldn't survive without them. They were right.'

'Have you been injured?'

'Many times.' *I have been tortured too.*

'You all are American soldiers?'

'Not us,' the elder sister said. 'We were civilians. Long story. We will tell you once we are in New York.'

'We can go there?' Zohra asked.

Meghan stopped cleaning her HK. She looked at her and Leila seriously. 'You can go anywhere in America once we get there. You can stay wherever you want. I am sure Clare can help you get into good universities where you can complete your research and degrees. It will be a new start.'

'You all live in New York?'

'Yes. We have our office there. Our apartments are in the same building. Zeb has his own place which he goes to sometimes, but yeah, we are all in the city.'

'Don't forget these,' Bwana dropped several pairs of long plastic gloves on Zeb's backpack.

Roger dumped bottles of water. 'Wash,' he warned with a wink. 'Don't come near us if you haven't.'

Zeb shoved them in his backpack, searched the garage and found several canvas belts that he packed as well.

He heaved it up over his shoulder and picked up his HK. Shoulder-bumped his friends and smiled as reassuringly as he could to Zohra and Leila who were embracing.

'We'll be with you in less than an hour. This won't take long.'

He knew his words weren't true. No operation went to plan.

ZEB LED ZOHRA OUT OF THE GARAGE, TO THE PARKING LOT and climbed into his sedan. He wheeled out quickly and followed an ambulance to the exit.

They drove swiftly to the Hyperstar where Hassan's maintenance van was parked. Its key was on top of the rear tire.

Zeb unlocked its rear, drew out two coveralls and inspected them swiftly. *They will do.*

He handed one to Zohra and drew up the other one on him. He slung his HK over his back and wore the jacket that Meghan had insisted on. It was large, heavy, but he zipped it up dutifully.

And then unzipped it, removed his rifle which was hampering his movement and put it back on again. *I'll have to carry the HK.*

He stuffed his ammo and grenades in the coverall's cavernous pockets and tightened its belt around his waist.

He smiled when he took in Zohra. Her coveralls were a larger size and hung loose around her body.

'It's better,' he told her. 'It will hide you.'

He got behind the wheel and when she was shotgunned, sped out.

Zohra fidgeted nervously beside him as he drove. She licked her lips. There was a streak of gold on the horizon where the sun was rising, visible through gaps in the skyline. It contrasted with the dark-blue sky but she wasn't entranced by it.

'I checked it daily to see it is still there,' she chewed her lip.

His eyes narrowed as he merged onto Bakeri Expressway.

'You checked the stolen material? How? You went to the university?'

'No, Zeb,' she exclaimed. 'I had another phone.' She explained how she had plastic wrapped it and taped it to the container.

'You checked its location every day on your other phone? The one we threw away?'

'Balle. Is there a problem?'

'Nothing that we can't handle,' he smiled reassuringly and tapped his throat mic. 'Meg, Zohra has a phone on the package. Can you trace its location?' He broke it down quickly.

'We can try. We have some fancy apps that could allow us to hook into its GPS feed. But would it still have charge?'

'Is it charged?' Zeb asked the student.

'Yes. Fully charged when I taped it.' She mentioned a model that was known for its battery management. She gave the number which he recited to the twin.

'Leave it with me.'

From the background sounds, Zeb knew she was in a vehicle.

He gripped the wheel hard and coaxed more speed out of the car.

Meghan came back to them when they were crossing Teymoori on the Fazlollah Nuri Expressway.

'Phone's still there,' she said in a clipped voice. 'You know what that means though?'

'Yeah,' he grunted. *If Naser found Zohra's spare phone, Sepah can easily find out what Zohra was checking every day.*

He saw several police cruisers but none of them slowed as they passed. Traffic was increasing. Delivery trucks, cars and buses on the highway. The sun's rays were piercing through the light fog that enveloped the city. Visibility wasn't bad but it wasn't ideal either.

Those conditions are good for us. We'll be less identifiable.

The fog wouldn't last for long however, and with that in mind, he stomped on the gas.

. . .

NASER HAD SLEPT IN THE OFFICE. HE HADN'T RESTED WELL. Gholamreza had chewed him out for yet another failure to apprehend Hashimi and when the Basij leader told him that he suspected Carter had rescued her, his boss had gone ballistic.

He had made Naser listen into his call with the president.

Hossein had been cold and harsh. He had given Gholamreza an ultimatum.

Find Hashimi and the stolen material in twenty-four hours.

He hadn't spelled out the price of failure. He hadn't needed to.

So, when Abid rushed in to wake Naser up at six am, the Basij leader was in a foul mood.

'If you don't have good news—' he snarled.

'I have. I think we know where Hashimi hid the Xenosine.'

106

Zeb rolled into the university's gates. A guard, who seemed to be sleeping at the check post, didn't stop them. A large visitor parking lot.

He slowed and inspected the few vehicles and did a mental fist-pump when he saw the black-and-white Panigale chained to the bicycle stand.

Hassan had come through.

'Follow this road,' Zohra indicated the concrete drive they were on. Large concrete buildings on either side of them. Well-maintained lawns, ponds and maple trees lining the wide routes.

'Those are my lecture halls,' she pointed to another building.

'Where's Farhad's lab?'

'It is at the back of the campus. We don't need to go all the way there. We need to go to the women's dorms.' She gestured at the sign board.

Zeb hung a left, drove past several buildings. His eyes were scanning ceaselessly. No sign of threats.

'Stop here,' she told him.

'Where's the sewage tank?'

'Behind that building,' she pointed to an industrial-looking shed. 'That's the water treatment plant. The dorms are the blocks on the left.'

'The road seems to go there.'

'It does.'

'In that case let's drive right up to it. We are maintenance workers. We should park on the lawn.'

'Balle,' she agreed. 'I don't think like you.'

He chuckled and went past the dorm, drove over the curb, onto the thick grass and circled the treatment plant.

The sewage tank was unmistakable. It was circular, concrete, a meter high and had signs nailed to its side.

Zeb got out of the vehicle, rummaged through his backpack and put on a mask. He drew the long gloves over his hands and gave her the water bottles.

He hurried over to the tank and saw why Zohra had been able to hide her package.

The stench was unmissable. A swarm of flies over it.

'No one gets close to it,' she told him.

'I can imagine why,' he said dryly. He held his breath and climbed onto the tank. A rusting metal door, two meters wide. Hinges on one end and a handle at the other.

He gripped it and almost fell back when it lifted easily.

'It is never locked.' Zohra said from a distance away. 'I threw it right beneath the door.'

Zeb grimaced and dipped into the gunk. He touched bottom and searched.

'NASER! HE'S ON THE MOVE!' Meghan yelled in his earpiece.

'I'm at the tank,' he said through gritted teeth, searching desperately, his body twisted to keep his balance. 'Where is he headed?'

'The university, if he maintains course.'

What was that? It wasn't the circular side of the tank. It moved when his fingers touched it.

He couldn't grip it. It kept sliding in the thick waste.

He tuned out Meghan and ignored Zohra. Reached down with his left hand and turning his head away, grabbed what felt like a container and brought it out with a loud squelch.

'That's it!' Zohra shouted.

She ran forward, uncapping a water bottle and poured its contents over the package and his hands. She emptied another bottle over them for good measure to ensure the plastic was clean and then wet her scarf with the third bottle and wiped his coveralls. She reached deep inside her pocket and sprayed him with a perfume.

Zeb threw away his gloves and with her help, unwrapped the covering.

The phone fell to the ground. She picked it up. 'It's still working.'

Zeb riffled through the notebook swiftly. The pages were dry and the writing and drawing was legible.

The Xenosine container was made of aluminum and had steel clamps with the locking seals on all four sides. He hefted it.

'Got it!' He confirmed. 'Can we open the box to check—'

'You'll never be a scientist, Zeb,' Zohra clicked her tongue impatiently. 'This is a temperature-controlled container. See this?' She pointed to two gauges on the sides that he had missed. 'One of those is the inside temperature. It's minus thirty degrees Celsius inside. Look at the other dial. That's the weight of the Xenosine inside. It's all there.'

'I heard all that,' Meghan snapped. 'Get away. NOW! Naser is eight minutes away. We don't know how many shooters he has with him.'

Zeb got to his feet. He picked up the box while Zohra took the notebook.

'No,' he told her when she bent to pick up the phone. 'Leave it. Naser will know we have the reagent if he sees the phone moving.'

'Naser?'

'Yes, he's on his way.'

She sucked a breath sharply and stumbled towards the van. He steadied her with a hand and shot the vehicle out of the lawn even before their doors had closed.

One minute to the parking lot where there were more vehicles. A suited professor looked curiously at them when they hustled out of the van and to the bike.

Zeb checked his phone, spun the dials on the padlock to get the code Hassan had sent and threw the restraining chain away. He searched beneath its tank and found its key.

He jammed it in the ignition.

One minute to familiarize himself with the Panigale and unlock the two helmets which dangled from the handle.

'Sit in the front,' he told Zohra.

He helped her onto the bike.

'Hold the box and the notebook to your chest.'

He rummaged in his pocket and came out with duct tape with which he fastened the two together. He retrieved the canvas belts from his backpack and strapped the package to her chest securely.

'Comfortable?' She nodded.

He could sense her growing fear.

'You can breathe?'

'Balle,' she gasped.

'We are going to escape,' he squeezed her shoulder. He taped the HK to the tank and put the helmet over her head fastened it securely.

He donned his and lowered his visor.

'Can you hear me?' he asked her through the helmet intercom.

Hassan's got high end ones and has already paired them.

'Balle,' she said, her surprise coming through her fear. 'I didn't know we could talk through these.'

'The volume controls are on the right side. You can feel them with your fingers. The mic is always on. You don't need to do anything.'

'FIVE MINUTES!' Meghan yelled. 'HE'S TURNING INSIDE THE MAIN GATES. GET YOUR ASSES OUT OF THERE.'

Zeb climbed onto the bike and jammed himself close to Zohra. He reached over her side and caught the handle and punched the ignition button.

The Panigale throbbed to life, a deep purr that he could hear above Zohra and his breathing.

'Bend your head to the left.'

Her helmet moved, giving him a clear view ahead.

'Are you comfortable?' Zeb fingered the HK with his left hand. *Yeah, I can snatch it free if I have to.*

'Baradar,' her voice shook, 'get us out of here, please.'

He engaged the gear, revved the throttle and sped out of the parking lot to Zohra's accompanying scream.

107

Naser was in the lead vehicle with Abid beside him. Both of them in the rear bench seat. His driver and a shooter at the front, two more soldiers behind them.

Two other SUVs followed close behind, all of them packed with the best Sepah killers.

They turned inside the gate, siren wailing, lights flashing, the full works. There was hardly any traffic to scatter. A student on a bicycle, cleared away hurriedly.

A motorbike flashed past them with two helmeted figures on it, disappearing in a blur in the side mirror.

'Rich kids,' Naser snarled.

'Yes, agha,' Abid agreed.

'Go over the lawn,' the Basij leader shouted. 'We don't have to follow the drive.'

Their SUV cut over the grass and raced over the expanse, past buildings and round trees until it came to the tank.

Abid was first out of the SUV!

'IT IS OPEN!' he yelled after clambering over the tank.

Naser got out. He scanned the campus with his hands on his hips. He saw Abid pick a phone up from the grass. He noticed the wet plastic.

It came to him.

'THE BIKE! CARTER IS ON THE MOTORBIKE!'

108

Zeb spotted the three SUVs. They were on his right one moment and then they were in his rear-view mirror and out of sight when he turned on Enghelab Street.

'Where to?'

'Niavaran,' Meghan told him. 'We'll guide you. Don't waste time trying to set up navigation on your bike.'

Zeb cocked his head trying to identify the background noise coming through her comms and then shrugged. He needed all his attention to drive the Panigale.

Zohra was a hunched figure in front of him. He felt her shivering but wasn't sure if that was from the bike's throbbing or from her fear.

Probably both, he figured.

He cruised.

'Were those Sepah vehicles?' she asked.

'Could be anyone,' he said evasively. *Anything to calm her.*

He knew she could hear his side of his conversation with Meghan. *Can't do anything about that.*

'Take the next exit,' the twin told him. 'That will take you onto Modares Highway.'

He followed her instructions and got onto the expressway. Larger road. More traffic. He weaved in and out, overtaking slower vehicles, the Panigale responding smoothly to every command.

We have a five-ten-minute lead, he worked out, *before Naser works out we are on the bike and then he'll activate the entire police force.*

Eight minutes later, when he was on Sadr Expressway, he saw the flashing lights in his mirror.

'You have company.' Meghan said.

'I see them.'

He felt Zohra turn her head.

'Don't move,' he told the student. 'Close your eyes if you have to. I need to maintain balance.'

The Panigale obliged when he kicked up the throttle. One hundred and ten kilometers an hour. A notch above the speed limit, a pace the super bike would scoff at if it was sentient.

The lights stayed far behind.

'Next exit to Kamraniyeh Boulevard.'

He navigated the bike. Got a red light at the junction. Looked left, then right and blasted through without waiting for it to change.

'A convoy behind you.'

The cruiser shot out from a side street. It raced right ahead of them, sideways, blocking their route.

Zohra screamed.

Zeb calculated rapidly as he neared it and at the very last minute, twitched the handle to cut around the rear of the cruiser and carried on.

The bike didn't skid. The Panigale's tires gripped asphalt smoothly as if the tight, bending turn was child's play.

He heard a siren go off. He thought he heard shots but couldn't be sure. The helmets deadened everything but the loudest and closest sounds.

'Let her rip,' Meghan commanded. 'You have pursuit. I

expect choppers will join too but not as long as you are in the city.'

'Where do we rendezvous?'

'Working on it. Plan was to pick you up in Niavaran but that's changed. I can see many roads blocked by cruisers.'

How can she see that? Zeb shook his head. It wasn't important.

The bike surged forward at his throttle command. Buildings blurred. Vehicles whooshed behind.

Zeb and every operator had been trained on high-performance bikes. They practiced on race tracks and in cities during their downtime.

His instructor's words came to him. *Think as if you are in a tunnel. Nothing else matters except what's ahead of you.*

His vision narrowed, the universe receded. Zohra's panicked breathing became background noise. His own breathing remained steady as he drove through the city, past lights and signboards and buses.

A cruiser fell behind and then went out of view, unable to keep up with his speed.

Another Sepah vehicle appeared at a junction. Rifles chattered. Rounds missed them and the shooters went out of sight.

A road block ahead, which he navigated around, drifting through side alleys, his bike making easy work of the smaller streets.

He used larger vehicles for cover when he could, leaning forward, making Zohra bend too, to present the narrowest possible profile, not just to reduce drag but also to minimize their target surface.

His left-side mirror blew out.

Zohra shrieked.

Zeb saw the shooter crouched behind a SUV and then he was past it, riding close to a bus which blocked them from firing line and they were ahead.

He was in the zone.

Meghan's voice remained with him.

'Left ahead.'

'Next exit.'

She guided him to avoid the police blocks that she seemed to see, to take abrupt, stomach-clenching turns with him and Zohra dipping down at steep angles, the Panigale perfectly balanced and rising when they sped up.

He heard Zohra dry-heave.

He heard her pray.

'Follow the road to Artesh Highway.'

He dimly realized that the highway was out of Tehran, towards the mountains and when he blinked, the world returned and with it, the knowledge that they were heading to the Alborz Mountain Range. They were already high up, with the city far behind them, the air thinning around them and the road narrowing.

'CHOPPER!' He heard Broker yell.

Zeb looked backwards. Didn't see anything.

'DRIVE,' Beth screamed at him. 'WE'LL DO THE WORRYING.'

He drove. A landslide which blocked most of the road, but the Panigale's tires crunched over the debris easily and found purchase. A line of flashing lights in his mirror.

'Rocket,' Meghan said calmly. 'On my three, swerve to the right.'

Zeb checked the mirror.

Nothing.

If she says there is a rocket, there is.

'One.'

He increased his speed at the plain stretch of traffic-free highway.

'Two'

A parked car flashed past. Its occupants stared at him and they too disappeared far behind.

'Three.'

Zeb swerved hard and ran parallel to the steep cliff.

A flash. An explosion and the protective barrier ahead of them burst in smoke and dust.

Zohra jerked and shouted in fear but Zeb kept going. Climbing.

He knew where they were heading to.

Mount Damavand. The highest peak in the Alborz Mountain Range.

The road became narrow, single lane. Pot holes and piles of rock.

There's no way we can rendezvous here.

Not his problem.

Meghan would figure it out.

A line of rounds stitched the road to his left.

He didn't swerve.

He heard the pursuing chopper however and then, when another burst came closer, a second helo came into view ahead of him from behind the mountain peak. It spun in the air almost lazily to face them.

No, not us. To face the other chopper.

And then he knew why it hovered rock-steady in the air, away from the cliff.

It was piloted by Broker and Roger who had ice in their veins when it mattered and Zeb risked a glance to see that its door was open and even as he watched, a flash emerged from it and then he had to return his attention to the drive, but he heard the explosion behind them and felt a shock wave reach them, but at their speed, it didn't buffet them.

'Tell Zohra I like sohan with my khoresht,' Bwana said as the operators' chopper went high over and out of sight.

Zeb, going at a hundred-and-fifty-kilometers-an-hour, on a narrow, cliff-hugging road, at over three-thousand-meters from sea level and still climbing, couldn't help grinning.

'We have a problem,' Meghan said calmly. 'There's been a landslide where we were going to put down, a kilometer away. There's no other place for us to touch down.'

'Okay,' Zeb said.

'Keep going.'

Zeb ducked when flashes appeared in his mirror but the rounds went wide. He knew Sepah wouldn't give up. Naser and Gholamreza would summon airpower.

We don't have much time either. We have to get onto that chopper before their reinforcements arrive.

'Here's the plan.'

'I'm listening,' he grunted. Loose and ready. His thighs hugging the bike, his chest against Zohra's back who was discernibly trembling. The road was straight even though it was narrow. There was no traffic. In the far distance he saw it turn around the cliff and go out of sight. Some kind of crash barrier that was fast approaching.

'Go straight. Don't follow the bend.'

Zeb kept going.

'Go faster.'

The Panigale ripped through the mountain air. The needle hovered around two-hundred and crept higher.

The crash barrier loomed ahead and grew sharper.

'You got the idea?' Meghan asked.

'Yeah,' Zeb said tersely.

He saw the gap in the metal barrier. A boulder or some accident had torn it partly away, leaving it exposed to the steep drop beyond.

Timing, his control of the bike and Meghan's calculations mattered.

Of the three, only his riding was down to him. He trusted the twin for the others.

The Agency chopper came into view, about thirty meters from the edge of the road.

Its door opened.

A rope ladder fell out.

'NOOOO! Zohra screamed when she realized how their escape looked.

Zeb maxed the throttle.

The bike ran out of road.

It went on the small patch of gravel.

Its tires retained their grip.

His aim was true.

The bike arrowed through the torn barrier and leapt into the sky.

Zeb let go of the handles and kicked away from the bike.

The Panigale fell. It had served its purpose.

He curled his left arm around Zohra and wrapped his legs around her waist, all in a nano-second after shooting off the cliff.

Gravity pulled them down.

The chopper followed, and then his right hand was grabbing at the rope ladder and had curled around it and he groaned at the savage yank in his shoulder but held on.

'We're safe,' he panted at Zohra.

Wind buffeted them as the chopper rose unsteadily.

A blinding flash from its door when Bwana fired another missile at the cliff.

The helo swayed ungainly.

Zeb looked up at the strained faces of his friends peering out of the door and knew what the problem was.

That's a Bell 206. It's already overloaded. We are additional weight.

He looked down.

Polur Plain far below, dusty, brown with patches of green.

The chopper jerked.

The research student yelled in fright.

'Zohra,' Zeb told her, 'put your hands through the ladder and wrap them around the step. I have got you. I won't let you go.'

'What?'

'Put your hands through the ladder and wrap them around the step,' he repeated, injecting as much calm as he could in his words.

She fumbled and then he saw her hands go through and grip each other.

'Hold tight. Don't let go, whatever happens. Promise me.'

'I will,' her voice shook.

'Now, put your legs through one of the ladder's loops. Again, I am holding you.'

He felt her wriggle as they swayed in the air with the chopper trying to rise.

'I have got them through.'

'Curl them up so that your knees are around it.'

'Balle,' she panted.

'Don't let go, whatever happens.'

'I won't. I promise. Why are you saying—'

Zeb unwrapped his legs from around her waist. He removed his hand from the ladder.

He fell.

109

Zohra screamed.

Zeb ignored her.

He felt the wind rushing as he plummeted.

The chopper rose smoothly now that it was free of his weight and it circled high. His friends' faces grew distant as he fell faster.

Zohra's body disappeared through its door as they winched her up and then Zeb closed his eyes.

If he was to die in Iran, splattered on Polur Plain, so be it.

His friends were safe. Zohra and Leila and the package were safe.

Nothing else mattered.

'Pull the cord.'

His eyes flared open at Meghan's words.

Cord? What cord?

'PULL THE FRICKING CORD THAT'S IN YOUR COLLAR,' Beth yelled. 'THE LOOPHOLES ARE BENEATH THE TABS.'

Zeb searched for them, found them after a second during which his body was speeding towards the earth at terminal velocity of one-hundred-and-ninety-three-kilometers-an-hour.

He tugged hard.

His jacket, the weighty, cumbersome one that Meghan had made him wear, jerked and something released behind him.

His fall slowed abruptly.

Zeb looked up to see a parachute canopy open above him, its Technora cords attached to the custom jacket on his torso.

Dying would have to wait.

110

Zohra's throat was hoarse from screaming and praying. Her hands ached. Her arms felt like they would rip out of her shoulders, but she clung onto the ladder and kept her legs looped like Zeb had instructed.

Her eyes were squeezed tight. She didn't dare look down as she was hoisted and felt strong hands catch hold of her and then she was pulled inside the chopper.

She promptly threw up and lay on the Bell's floor, shuddering and heaving with Leila's arms around her and Beth bathing her face with a wet towel.

The world returned slowly as the pounding in her chest eased. She was safe.

Someone kept murmuring that until she believed it and when she struggled upright, she saw for herself that it was true.

Bwana was stretched out at the door, with some kind of missile launcher at his shoulder. He gave her a lazy grin and a thumbs-up. Bear was next to him with a pair of binos to his eyes and a large rifle. Chloe and Beth were with her, along with Leila while Meghan was behind Broker and Roger who were piloting the helicopter.

'Zeb!' she shouted and peered over the edge of the door

with her heart in her mouth. She saw the small speck of his parachute hundreds of meters below them. 'We need to get him.'

Leila nodded at her words, her face pale, sweat beading her forehead.

The Americans didn't respond. The chopper kept climbing. It flew away from the mountains. A span of blue in the distance.

'Caspian Sea?' She recognized it. 'Aren't we getting Zeb?'

'We have got to get to international waters as soon as possible,' Beth said grimly, 'before Iran sends fighters to stop us.'

Zohra's belly clenched. They weren't out of the woods yet.

'What of Zeb?' She clutched the younger sister's sleeve.

'He'll make his way out.'

'We are leaving him behind?'

A vein twitched on her temple. Meghan looked at them, her face tight and then returned to the low-voiced conversation she was having with Broker and Roger.

'Are we deserting him?' she yelled.

'No,' Chloe ground out, 'but we need to get you and the package to safety first.'

'Over and out,' a voice filled the chopper.

It took Zohra a moment to recognize Zeb's voice, filtered through the helo's speakers, over the rushing of the windstream.

'Zeb,' Beth shouted, a note of pleading in her voice.

Zohra gripped Leila's hand instinctively, knowing something was being unsaid between her American friends. A strange expression on the younger sister's face that she recognized with a chill was fear and helplessness.

'Over and out,' Zeb repeated firmly and didn't say anything more.

Zohra peered through the door. She couldn't see his parachute.

'What does he mean?' she asked, fearfully.

Beth closed her eyes and looked away. Bwana and Bear's faces remained rock-hard and expressionless.

Chloe's shoulders drooped as if she was carrying an invisible weight. 'Zeb is going after Farhad.'

Zohra blinked. It took a while for her to make meaning of the words. 'Farhad? Why? We have the Xenosine.' She knew her voice was sounding shrill but she didn't care.

'Because as long as he is still alive, Emad could be revived.'

Zohra moaned low and fell back in Leila's arms as she worked out what that meant.

Zeb Carter, her baradar, her friend, would be alone in Tehran, with no back-up, no support as he attempted to stop the weapons program for good.

She reached out instinctively and felt Beth and Chloe's palms curl around her forearm and she closed her eyes and prayed for him.

III

Zeb landed in a clearing on Polur Plain in between a clump of rocks. He felt the jacket to unfasten the canopy and then slipped out of it when he couldn't find the release mechanism.

He removed his helmet and examined the garment and the parachute curiously. The canopy was a variant of the MC-1C parachute that was used by some special-ops teams. It folded neatly into the jacket to make it wearable. He couldn't help smiling as he fingered the nylon. *Beth and Meg ... they are continually checking out what equipment they can add to our gear.*

He folded the chute and shrugged out of his coveralls. He transferred his spare magazines and grenades from its pockets to his cargo trousers, and looked around to get his bearings.

The Bell was nowhere in sight. *Somewhere over the Caspian Sea, in international airspace and heading to Baku,* he hoped.

It was nearing eight am. Barely three hours since he had woken up in the hospital's garage. It felt like a lifetime ago.

I must have jumped off at around three-thousand meters, he looked at the sky and guessed, going by the four minutes it had taken him to hit the ground.

The narrow road from where he had shot through was a

distant line on the mountain. The flashing lights of the police vehicles were tiny, blinking dots.

I've got to get out of here before they send choppers.

Polur Plain was vast and rugged with rocky terrain and high-altitude meadows. He had landed near Lar National Park which was popular with outdoor enthusiasts.

It's also where the Iranian army conducts their maneuvers, he thought grimly, as he set off at a ground-eating pace that he could sustain for hours.

He needed cover. He needed a ride and soon, he would need water.

He checked his satellite phone. It worked. No messages from his team, which was expected. His *over and out* meant there would be radio silence between him and his team unless there was an emergency.

The woods were five kilometers away to the south. Haraz Road which was also known as Route Seventy-Seven was the way out of the mountain range to Tehran.

Zeb took stock of himself as he jogged. His shoulder hurt from when he had clung to the ladder. His body ached. However, no bones were broken and no ligaments were torn.

He was in better shape than he expected.

That was a bonus.

He didn't know how he was going to take out Farhad and exfil from Tehran.

Those were details he would work out later.

What was more important was to get to the city without being apprehended.

112

Naser was expecting Gholamreza to rage at him. He stood ramrod-stiff at his boss's desk and waited in silence after he and Abid had finished narrating Carter and Hashimi's escape from Mount Damavand.

'So,' the Sepah leader hissed, 'they have the Xenosine, Navid's notes and they got away in some kind of Hollywood-style stunt?'

'Yes, agha,' Naser said and braced himself for the angry words. He expected to be sacked and had told his family to leave Tehran immediately and go into hiding.

'We have been out-maneuvered every time and been made to look like fools. We are Sepah, the most feared organization in the country, but two women and a bunch of Americans have outsmarted us and set back our country's most secret weapon program. I don't need to spell it out for you what this means.'

Here it comes, Naser thought.

'The three of us are unlikely to have a job by the end of the day,' Gholamreza continued. 'However,' his hawk-like eyes rested on Naser, 'we might be able to partly salvage the situation.'

'If we get Carter,' he said after a moment.

'We know he is somewhere in Polur Plain,' Naser began. 'I

will send choppers and vehicles to cover every inch of the area. He cannot escape. He has no back up—'

'No,' the Sepah chief said harshly. 'There is no need for that. If we fail, and going by your track record that is highly likely,' he sneered, 'that will make our predicament worse. The president will accuse us, that with all our resources we were unable to nab him. No, don't send any men or choppers. I know where he will be.'

'You do, agha?' Naser couldn't hide his surprise.

'It's not hard to work out, Saeed,' Gholamreza said bitterly. 'Carter will come to Tehran. He wants to kill Navid. He knows, just as we do, that without Navid there is no Emad. In fact, I know how to bait him.'

'Organize a press conference,' the Sepah head got to his feet. 'Navid will give it from outside his lab. He will accuse the Americans of sabotaging his research because they don't want an Iranian to get the Nobel Prize. Arrange it for this afternoon. Carter will come.'

Gholamreza opened his palm. 'And when he does,' his fist closed, 'don't let him escape. It is our last chance.'

113

Zeb reached Lar National Park without incident.

Which worried him.

Why haven't choppers landed and surrounded me? The police and Sepah vehicles on Mount Damavand would have seen where my chute landed. It wouldn't have been hard to mount aerial surveillance and then send troops to capture him.

However, he hadn't encountered anyone in his run to the forest.

It remained in the back of his mind as he picked his way through the thick woods.

Got to find some hikers.

He found a running stream and cupped his hands in it to bring the water to his lips. It had a faint bitter taste to it, but it was cool and refreshing, the first drink he had since he had left the garage that morning.

He bathed his face, dried himself with his sleeve and continued through the woods.

He came across the campers forty minutes later.

It was the smell of smoke that alerted him of their presence and when he ghosted from tree to tree, he came across their tents in a clearing. Two of them, zipped shut, from within which he heard light snoring. The remains of a fire which was the source of smell. Emptied tin cans and paper bags tied in a plastic bag which hung from a drooping branch.

It was the Hilux that caught his attention. The truck was facing a faint track. Faded white in color, scratched and caked with dust.

He tried the door to the cab. It opened with the smallest protest. Zeb held his breath and searched inside. Cracked leather seats, grime on the floor mats. Empty soda cans. Glove box stuffed with insurance documents and at the bottom, a key.

It fit in the ignition and at the half-turn, the dashboard lit up. Three-quarters of the tank was full.

Zeb crept out and slipped a wad of Iranian Rial beneath the tent through which the snoring was the loudest, hustled to the Hilux, fired up the engine and shot out of the camp.

Gotta swap this ride for another one, he thought as he raced out of the forest, following the dusty track. His sat phone was mounted on the windscreen stand that the owners had helpfully equipped the vehicle with.

Two hours to Tehran.

Zeb turned on the radio as soon as he got a signal and heard about the city-wide hunt for terrorists.

A smaller news item made him reflexively ease his foot off the pedal.

Professor Navid Farhad would be giving a rare press conference outside his lab that afternoon.

114

Ten am.

Zeb turned into a supermarket's parking lot near Pardis. He looked at himself in the rear-view mirror and removed his false ears and nose. He went to the salon next to the store and got his hair styled with blond streaks.

Warm food and chai at the store's café gave his body fuel. He bought a pair of cargo pants, a Tee and a loose jacket. Changed into them in the bathroom, bought a new pair of shades on the way out and returned to his ride.

He re-applied the prosthetics and drove around the parking lot casually until he saw what he wanted.

A lone man heading towards a white Toyota with bags in his hands.

Zeb looked around. The market wasn't busy that early in the day. There didn't seem to be security cameras either.

He hurried to the man who looked up at his approach.

'I need your help,' he smiled disarmingly, got into the shopper's personal space and before he could react, applied a choke hold and squeezed until the man went limp.

He dragged the man to his Hilux and dumped him in the shotgun seat. Fished out the Toyota's key from his pocket, rummaged through the vehicle's tool box and found a screwdriver.

He went to the neighboring car and swapped its plates with the Toyota and drove out in the stolen ride.

Zeb was counting on normal human behavior. Very few car owners looked at their vehicle's plates. They identified their rides by shape and color and didn't pay attention to anything else.

The Toyota's owner would call the police but they would be looking for the wrong plates.

Another car swap at Omid Town using similar tactics. This time he got a Ford and stole four plates to further confuse the police.

The radio was thick with updates about the hunt for the terrorists. The police were confident that the recent attacks were linked. They suspected it was a foreign state behind the shooters.

'No one else will have a helicopter, a Ducati and a Stinger missile,' an officer declared. 'They must be Mossad killers.'

There was an increased police presence when he reached Tehran. Cruisers patrolling the streets. Armed officers on foot. Choppers in the sky. Banners on billboards demanding answers. 'POLICE SLEEP WHILE TERRORISTS TAKE OVER TEHRAN.'

Zeb grinned. He checked his phone when it buzzed briefly.

SAFE! His smile grew wider at the message.

His team along with Zohra and Leila were in Baku.

Need a plan to get close to Farhad.

That press conference is an opening.

It might have only journalists.

There was no way he could score a reporter's identity.

He thought briefly for a moment and when another police van passed him, the idea came to him.

He drove to the hospital in Eram and wasn't surprised at the number of armed officers. They must have discovered we used the garage as a base.

He parked his stolen car, put on a concerned look and hurried to the entrance.

Two Sepah vehicles near the portico. Three officers near them, idly chatting. Two of them were similar to his build.

Can I take out all of them?

He had no choice. He was too close to them to back out.

'I saw some suspicious people,' he whispered, jerking his head towards the far end of the parking lot where his stolen car was. 'They were carrying something long. I think they were guns.'

That word did it. The officers didn't bother to check him out closely. They straightened. They gripped their HK G36s.

'Show us,' the captain, the senior-most among them, ordered.

Zeb could see it in their eyes. *They're already anticipating headlines and the recognition they will get.*

'There,' he pointed. 'Come quickly. They might leave soon.'

'How many were there?'

'One man and two women.'

The Sepah men exchanged a knowing look.

Gholamreza must have circulated our details.

'Anyone else?'

'I didn't notice, agha. I got scared as soon as I saw the guns.'

Zeb hurried to the remote area in the parking lot which was less busy because of the large waste bin in its corner.

'There,' he pointed to his Ford whose trunk was visible behind the metal waste container.

'Stay here,' the captain ordered as they crouched behind another car.

There wasn't anyone else nearby.

'Ali, Kamran, you go from behind. I will back you up. Shoot if they resist.'

'Yes, agha.'

The men straightened. They emerged from cover, crouched low and ran towards the Ford.

Zeb drew his Glock out and raised it.

The captain sensed his move and started turning. He collapsed heavily when Zeb struck him on the temple viciously and crashed his gun again on his face for good measure.

Zeb grabbed his HK and lunged towards the Sepah officers who started spinning around.

His swung the German weapon and caught the first officer on the face and jabbed the second in the throat. He was on top of them instantly, driving the butt of the rifle, breaking their noses and jaws.

His blows were savage, controlled bursts of aggression, swiftly executed with no room for them to retaliate.

'You should have split up,' he panted. 'One of you should have gone around that waste bin to come at the Ford from the front.'

They were beyond hearing him.

He dragged their bodies behind the Ford, stripped them of their weapons and cell phones and bound their wrists with their belts. He tied their ankles with their laces and jammed their socks in their mouths.

He was sweating by the time he had squeezed them in the back of his Ford and made them look like they were sleeping sideways.

He returned to the captain who was stirring.

Zeb dragged him to the Ford as well and jabbed him in the throat with the HK. 'What are you doing here?'

The captain opened his mouth and Zeb jammed a rag in it that he had found on the ground.

'You won't live if you shout. Your best chance of surviving is if you answer my questions. What were you doing here?'

'It's our shift,' the captain groaned.

'How long does it last?'

'Till evening.'

'Who else is with you?'

'Just the three of us.'

'How often do you check in?'

'Check in?' the captain gasped. 'We don't do that. We report if anything unusual happens otherwise we get relieved in the evening.'

Zeb knocked him out with a blow and stripped him of his uniform. He removed his clothes and got into the captain's. Secured the unconscious man with his belt, laces and socks and squeezed him in the shotgun seat of the Ford.

He was perspiring heavily by the time he had finished. He thanked his good luck that not a single person or vehicle had come his way during the takedown.

He wiped his face, studied himself in the mirror and removed his false nose. The misshapen ears could stay. He jammed the captain's cap on his head and inspected himself. He would pass on a cursory look.

He pocketed the man's wallet, which had his identification card. He took his phone and radio, locked the Ford and returned to the portico.

He straightened his shoulders and put on an arrogant look.

Carrying off a look was even more important than the disguise. People took in a person's bearing and most of the time didn't look closely beyond the uniform.

Zeb drove out of the hospital in one of the Sepah vehicles.

That, along with his captain's uniform, would gain him entrance to Farhad's event.

No one stopped Sepah in Iran.

⁂ 115 ⁂

Zeb's assumption was correct.

There was a significant police presence at the university's entrance. The officers checked the students' identities and those of visitors.

They didn't check his.

They didn't even look at his face.

He had the captain's cap jammed low over his head, his shades over his eyes, but the officers didn't even look at him. They took in the identity card he had thrust out and waved him inside.

The university seemed to be crowded. The parking lot where he had picked up the Ducati was full. The maintenance van wasn't around. He drove to the sewage tank. It was closed. No police tape around it.

Gholamreza doesn't want to admit the Xenosine was in the university all along. He might not even have told the president about it.

There were signs to the press conference stuck to pillars and the sides of buildings.

Zeb parked his Sepah SUV near a bunch of other police vehicles. He nodded when soldiers saluted him.

He strode into the university building without looking at

anyone in the eye. Civilians were meaningless to the Revolutionary Guards officers. They didn't matter.

Zeb acted the part as he went down the corridor.

This must have been the one Zohra fled down.

The biochemistry lab was at the end. Its doors were shut. *Those will be made of toughened glass.* Two soldiers stood in front of it, alert.

He didn't get close to them.

My disguise won't get through them. Zohra said they don't allow any visitors unless they are personally approved by Gholamreza.

The lab's outside looked to be newly painted. There was nothing to distinguish it from other such research centers other than the Sepah presence.

A lectern was in front of the doors with several chairs facing it.

That's where Farhad will brief journalists.

It was one pm. Zeb had no plan in mind.

I could toss a grenade through the lab as soon as he returns inside. How will I exfil? The Sepah guards will shoot me. There will be too many people for me to escape safely.

I could take him out with a Stinger or a Barrett.

He had neither, however.

He decided to play it by ear.

If an opportunity presented to take out Farhad, he would grab it, or else, he would use the event for recon.

The corridor started filling up.

More Sepah soldiers arrived and lined both sides of the seating arrangement.

Zeb hung back.

Journalists started arriving.

They showed their passes to the soldiers who pointed them to various chairs. TV crews arrived and took position. Students, professors and visitors lined the back of the corridor.

Navid Farhad was a local celebrity. What he had to say was of interest.

At two pm the lab's doors opened.

The professor stepped out in a dark suit. His goatee, silvery hair and spectacles gave him the right academic look.

He beamed at the assembled crowd and went to the lectern.

He adjusted the mic.

'Welcome, my friends,' he began. 'This is a highly unusual press conference for me because I am not here to talk about my research breakthrough. I am here to tell you about a threat to our country.'

A murmur swept through the crowd.

The journalists leaned forward.

Zeb's phone buzzed.

He brought it out and read the message.

EVAC IMMEDIATELY. LAB WILL BE DESTROYED IN FIVE MINUTES.

116

Zeb knew his team didn't use hyperbole. The language they used in their communication was precise.

If Meghan, who had sent the message, had used the word *DESTROYED*, she meant it.

He started backing out unobtrusively and then stopped.

There are civilians here!

The thought translated to instant action.

He brought up the HK and pointed it at the ceiling.

His move caught the eyes of several Sepah soldiers who straightened.

'EVACUATE!' Zeb shouted as he fired a long burst. 'THERE ARE TERRORISTS IN THE CROWD.'

His shooting had the desired effect.

The crowd erupted in screams and yells. Chairs were upturned as the journalists dived out of the corridor. The students and professors broke away.

Two of the Sepah soldiers caught Farhad's elbows and hustled him inside the lab.

Zeb fired once more and plunged into the fleeing crowd. A few Revolutionary Guards soldiers tried to come to him but the panicked journalists got in their way.

He leapt onto the lawn and sprinted towards the exit. Thought of getting to his stolen ride but one look at the crowd convinced him the vehicle would hinder him.

Every student in the university is escaping. They will clog the roads. No vehicle will be able to move fast.

He was more than hundred meters away from the lab, when he heard what sounded like a swarm of angry, buzzing bees.

He looked back and was stunned at the sight of a flock black birds coming over the neighboring building and flying to the lab.

Drones!

'RUN!' he shouted. 'BOMBS!'

The drones detonated an instant later.

Zeb felt the shock wave like a strong draft of wind.

He snatched a glance. The lab was obscured in smoke. He heard more buzzing.

The drones are coming in waves!

He joined the fleeing crowd as the second explosion blew out windows and made the earth shudder.

Two more blasts followed when he was at the parking lot and a bigger one when he was nearing the exit to Enghelab Street.

The police officers and Sepah soldiers at the gate and at the sides had no chance of containing the crowd which was streaming from every building and had packed the road.

They stood back and let the panicked civilians flee.

Zeb reached Enghelab Street. Two Sepah vehicles to his left, near the sidewalk, parked in a line.

A man crashed into him and sent him off-balance and near the edge of the fleeing crowd.

Another civilian cursed and shoved him out of the way.

Zeb lost his cap.

His shades fell away as he stumbled. His false ears dropped to the ground.

He was close to an officer who was on the phone.

The Sepah man took him in casually.

His eyes widened. He drew his phone away and his hand clutched his waist.

He has recognized me!

'IT'S HIM!' the officer shouted.

A shadow moved inside the vehicle.

Zeb shot the officer.

117

Zeb shot him again in the chest.

The fleeing crowd didn't respond to his firing, so intent were the panicked civilians on fleeing.

The shadow inside the vehicle burst out of the rear door.

Zeb spun around to see a uniformed soldier lunge towards him. He saw the man's name, Abid Khan on his chest, and then he ducked from the rifle that swung at him and fell back when the officer body-slammed into him. His rifle dropped to the ground.

Can't drag this out, he thought dimly as he took a blow to his neck. *That other vehicle might have more soldiers. They will trap me.*

Zeb grimaced when a bony knee crashed into his thigh.

'GET AWAY, AGHA!' the man screamed. 'THE OTHERS MIGHT BE NEARBY.'

Agha? Who's in the other vehicle?

Zeb let his body slide down when Khan cocked his fist. The punch landed on the vehicle. The officer grunted and drew his hand back and clawed.

Zeb had enough.

His Glock was still in its shoulder holster. However, Khan was crowding him and he didn't have room to draw it.

He caught hold of the officer by the waist and threw him bodily away.

Khan rolled against the vehicle and started raising his HK.

Zeb dived at his feet as the hail of bullets ripped over his head.

He slapped the rifle away with one hand, caught his chin with the other and smashed the man's head against the SUV.

The other Sepah vehicle fired up. It started moving. Its window rolled down. Naser appeared in the frame.

Can't let him get away again.

Zeb rabbit-punched Khan's throat with his knuckles and yanked the HK from his loose hand and fired it point-blank into his chest.

He lunged to his right and fired through the open window at Naser.

The Basij leader's face disappeared. His SUV mounted the street.

Zeb got his hand on the door and pulled himself forward as the vehicle started speeding up. He hooked his elbow inside and gritted his teeth as he started losing his balance.

Something smashed his fingers, but he held on and took long, bounding steps to try to keep up with the vehicle. It couldn't speed up since the fleeing crowd was around it.

He got close to the door and fired indiscriminately at the driver and then the door swung open suddenly and he lost his balance and still clung on, dragged on the street with his hand attaching itself to the door.

Naser, on the rear seat, clawing at his waist to bring out his revolver.

Zeb lost his HK when its barrel snagged against a street imperfection. He drew his Glock, but his grip was loose and it went spinning into the air when the door swayed in the wind and he had to clutch desperately to the frame to keep latched on to it.

Naser's gun rose.

Zeb dug his heel and flung himself upwards and pivoted in the air using the door as leverage and got his legs inside the vehicle and then the rest of his body was coiling inwards as well.

Naser's round blasted through the confined space. It grazed his neck.

Zeb kicked his belly.

The Basij leader shouted in agony.

Zeb reared forward and punched his face, caught his gun hand and twisted desperately when he sensed movement behind him.

The driver, who thrust an HK backwards with one hand.

Zeb crushed Naser's trigger finger. The Basij head's gun bucked, its rounds star-bursting the windshield.

Zeb kicked the driver's HK away savagely, its rounds ripping into the seat's leather and blasting out of the open door. The rifle fell out of the vehicle.

The vehicle careened before the driver got it under control.

Zeb smashed his elbow in Naser's throat and yanked his gun away.

It came up in his hand.

Naser's face was twisted in rage. He was cursing and swearing, a litany of furious words that streamed out of his mouth as he twisted and kicked and punched.

Zeb took the blows, felt something prick his neck and swung sideways to see the driver jab a knife backwards.

Naser took his opportunity.

His arm snaked around Zeb's neck. His second hand locked the first, trapping the operator.

He started squeezing.

'KILL HIM! he roared.

Zeb kicked at the blade but missed. He reared backwards and crashed his legs at the driver's seat.

The man jerked forward. The vehicle swerved. A honk sounded.

The knife fell to the carpet.

Naser grunted and squeezed hard.

Zeb's vision started darkening.

He searched the floor mat as he kept kicking at the driver's seat to throw the man off-balance.

His fingers felt the sharp edge of the blade.

Naser's arm lock was like a vise, driving out the air from his body.

Zeb knew he couldn't last long.

His scrabbling fingers found purchase on the blade. His palm cut on its edge.

He ignored it.

His grip loosened from the blood streaming out of his hand.

He gritted his teeth, tightened his fingers on the blade and plunged it in Naser's shin.

The Basij man howled.

His arm lock eased.

Zeb reached high and plunged the blade backwards, into Naser's side.

The brigadier general's arms fell away.

Zeb twisted around, let the blade slide in his palm until his hand gripped its hilt and thrust it deep in Naser's neck with all his strength and removed it with a squelch and twisted around forward and dived to puncture the driver's chest in short, furious jabs and returned to plunge it repeatedly in Naser's chest until the light escaped his eyes.

Zeb threw the knife down.

His eyes landed on the notepad and pen that had fallen to the floor mat.

He scribbled on it, tore the page and pinned it to Naser's chest with the knife.

A blaring honk sounded.

He looked up to see the careening SUV head straight towards a truck.

Zeb grabbed Naser's handgun and dived out of the door.

He rolled onto the street, groaning when his cut palm burned on hot asphalt.

The SUV crashed into the truck.

He rolled to the edge of the street and then felt another vehicle come up from the university.

He recognized the Sepah emblem on its hood and raised his weapon.

The SUV came abreast.

A uniformed, masked officer leaned out, caught his wrist expertly and twisted his gun away. His rounds fired harmlessly in the air.

Another figure reached out, caught his jacket and yanked him inside the vehicle.

Zeb charged at the two figures.

'STOP!' one of them yelled.

That voice!

The person yanked their face mask away, reached behind their head and loosened their hair.

'You are with friends, Zeb,' Carmel grinned at him.

118

Zeb blinked his eyes open when the vehicle jolted over a pothole.

He sat up.

Carmel and Dalia looked at him concernedly. 'You lost consciousness as soon as we rescued you,' the former said.

He drank from a bottle of water she gave him and wiped his lips.

He looked at the dressing on his palm.

'Yeah,' Dalia grinned, 'you didn't even feel the tetanus shot we gave you.'

'I was running on adrenaline,' he made a face and took them in.

Both of them in Sepah uniforms, sporting false, men's names on their chest plates. Carmel had fastened her hair behind her head and hidden it underneath her cap.

The driver and passenger at the front were men, outfitted in the same uniforms.

'The drone attacks were yours,' he guessed.

'Ken,' Carmel nodded.

'You coordinated with my team?'

'Yes.'

'The lab?'

'Destroyed.'

'Farhad?'

'Turned to ash.'

'Civilian casualties?'

'We don't think there are any,' Dalia said somberly. 'Your warning got the crowd away. Sepah guards died, but we are reasonably sure no student, professor, journalist or visitor was killed in the attack.'

'What's on the news?'

'Confused reports. What's known is the lab does not exist anymore. We packed the drones with nuclear-bunker-busting charges. No building would have survived them. Wave attacks on top, to reduce the lab to the ground.'

Zeb's neck itched. He reached up and felt another dressing where Naser's bullet had grazed him.

'Superficial cut,' Carmel said. 'You got lucky. Who were you fighting with inside that vehicle?'

Zeb raised his eyebrows. 'You didn't see?'

'No. Abid Khan was the officer you took down. He's a fast-rising star in Sepah.'

'Was,' Dalia corrected her.

'Was.' Carmel agreed. Her lips twitched. 'Tell us you took out a few more high-profile officers.'

'I didn't.'

'I took out only two men,' Zeb smiled at her disappointed expression. 'One was the driver. The second ...' he paused to draw it out. 'Sepah will need a new deputy leader.'

'Naser?' Dalia gasped.

'Ken, it was him.'

He drank water again. Looked out of the darkened window and recognized the route to Mehrabad International Airport. 'How did you know where I would be?'

'How?' Carmel snorted. 'We, both your team and us, had eyes on you all the time. Meghan shared your phone's location with us. We were tracking you continually. In addition,' she pointed to the sky, 'we have eyes up there. A surveillance drone that the Iranian military isn't aware of. Super-stealth.'

'That's how you have carried out other attacks,' he referred to the reports of other drone strikes Mossad had executed.

'Ken.'

'You provided the Bell,' he sat up abruptly. 'Meghan was mysterious when I asked her about exfil.'

'Yes,' Dalia grinned. 'But the chute, the Ducati, that escape,' she kissed her fingers and blew in the Italian gesture of approval, 'that was all you and your friends.'

They reached the airport where a uniformed guard checked their driver's passes and let them in.

They drove inside the private entrance and rolled up to an aircraft.

Zeb eyed the Iranian military insignia on its side.

'It's the real deal,' Carmel said proudly as they hurried to the airstairs. 'Real aircraft that we stole. Our flight plan is officially recorded. Passenger manifest shows us as high-ranking military officials on a diplomatic visit to Azerbaijan.'

The jet rolled to the runway and leapt into the sky after its take-off run.

Carmel drew Zeb's attention to the blob of smoke in the city. 'Farhad's lab,' she said.

'Emad is dead,' Dalia declared, reached beneath her feet, drew out a flask and poured chai for all of them.

119

Baku

It was the same drill, but in reverse, when they landed in Baku at four pm.

The military aircraft taxied to a private concourse and stopped.

Carmel rolled out the airstairs and was first out. Dalia followed and then Zeb.

He reached the ground when a whoop sounded.

Zohra and Leila burst out of the glass-fronted building and barreled into him. They hugged him hard and then withdrew instantly when they looked at the Mossad operators.

'Who are they?' Zohra asked uncertainly as she caught Leila's hand, prepared to run.

'Friends,' Carmel said in Persian. 'You don't have to fear us. You are safe.'

'You will always be,' Bwana boomed out as the rest of the operators joined them.

Beth sized Zeb up. She took in the dressing on his palm and his neck. 'I would punch you,' she said and wrapped her arms around him, 'but I am just glad you got out.'

Alive. He knew the word was on the tip of her tongue. He held her close and inhaled deeply.

The smell of life.

'Don't ever do that again,' Meghan warned him. 'Don't do the lone-wolf thing. That's not us. That's not how we work.'

'I won't,' he promised, fist-bumping her and meaning it.

The rest of his friends back-slapped and high-fived him and then Broker and Roger did their thing.

They looked at his outfit, brushed invisible lint from their pristine jeans and shook their heads mournfully.

'The package?' Zeb chuckled.

'Over there,' Chloe cocked her head as their Lear taxied to the building, its jet engines screaming.

Zeb was the last to board the airstairs. He clasped Dalia's hands and embraced her and then shook Carmel's hand.

'We won the battle,' she said.

'Yes,' he agreed.

'Tell us everything,' Beth demanded as soon as they were in the air.

He laid it out for them, Zohra and Leila hanging onto every word.

'I overheard what that woman said,' the psychology student said. 'About winning the battle. She meant the war against Sepah, didn't she?'

'No, Zeb said. 'She is correct. Naser's death is a setback, but Gholamreza will appoint another deputy. Farhad is dead and Emad is finished, but as long as there are hard-liners in the government, they will find ways to build other, secret weapons. All we can do is react and sometimes we will win. Like today.'

'You make it sound so bleak.'

Covert ops are like that. We live in the shadows and have incremental success.

He didn't articulate his thoughts, however.

'Change will happen,' he told her confidently. 'It will be slow, but it is coming. The protests you and thousands of other students and civilians took part in and are organizing, the awareness of how freedom looks, tastes and feels ... that will force every hard-liner run country to change for the good. It won't be easy. It won't be smooth. What will evolve won't be everyone's definition of a free society, but it will be better.'

'And this,' he pointed to Leila and Zohra's joined hands, 'is a definite win.'

'Hell, yeah,' Bear asserted.

'What did you write on that note?' Meghan asked.

'Something that will terrorize Gholamreza.'

Their shouts of laughter, when he explained, carried them back home.

120

Tehran and USA

GHOLAMREZA HAD TO BE THERE.

The optics wouldn't look good if he wasn't seen at Naser's body.

He ordered his men to leave his deputy's body untouched as soon as he heard the news, got into his official vehicle and got driven to the scene of the killing.

His face was grim, his lips tight, his face expressionless when he alighted.

He could smell and taste the acrid smoke from the bombed-out lab. He knew that Navid and all the Sepah soldiers inside it had died.

Emad was dead too.

He hadn't taken any calls even though his phone had been ringing non-stop.

He knew what would be coming. He would be fired and would disappear from public life.

He was going to face the future on his terms

But firstly, he was going to show himself in public.

Gholamreza didn't look at the line of Sepah men who formed a barricade and kept back the curious onlookers and the few journalists and TV cameras who covered his approach.

He went to Naser's vehicle and glanced inside.

He remained bent for long, respectful moments and then removed the knife from his deputy's chest.

He tossed it to the floor and reached his hand out for a clean handkerchief that his aide passed.

He wiped his palm, picked up the note and presented his profile to the cameras.

He couldn't control his hands from shaking when he read the line

You are next.

He was going to crumple and throw the note away when he saw the smaller lettering at the bottom.

Turn over.

He turned the sheet over. It was filled with words.

Farhad didn't tell you the truth.

We have his notebook.

He was working on another viral weapon that would show no symptoms.

He was a patriot which is why he signed up for Emad, but he was also a mercenary.

He was going to sell the weapon to other countries and terrorists.

He had created its vaccine.

Zohra stole that viral weapon as well as the antidote.

We have it.

Bad news.

Everyone who came within five meters of Naser's body are now infected.

The TV cameras were broadcasting live.

The entire country watched Major General Mehrdad Gholamreza's panic attack.

He was sacked two days later and wasn't seen or heard of again.

President Morgan acted swiftly. He briefed an emergency special session of the United Nations and accused Iran of playing fast and loose with humanity's survival.

President Hossein retaliated by saying the intel was a fabrication by America and Israel and that the two countries were responsible for Professor Farhad's death and the university explosion.

Amidst the word slinging, two news items got barely any attention. Behnam Ali and Javed Reza were found dead in mysterious circumstances.

Mossad's cleaning up, Zeb thought as he read the article on a news site. He shut down his screen, put on his jacket and went out of their Columbus Avenue Office.

He took a deep breath when he reached Central Park.

The world hasn't changed that much but for now, it's a better place.

With that thought, he started jogging towards his friends who were teaching Zohra and Leila baseball.

MORE BOOKS

Download The Watcher, a novella exclusive to Ty Patterson's newsletter subscribers here: https://bit.ly/3mDhpCO

Check out Primer on Author's store, the next Cutter Grogan thriller

Join Ty Patterson's Facebook group of readers

BONUS CHAPTER FROM PRIMER

New York

Cutter Grogan had his feet up on his desk as he unwrapped the sandwich he had bought from the deli.

Loft office on Lafayette Street. His name on the outside door.

Cutter Grogan. Private Investigator.

Alright, it was old school in a time when firms like his went for fancy names.

He didn't need fancy, however. He got his clients through referrals. Business had never been a problem for him. If anything, he often had to turn clients down.

Someone thumped his door and then pressed the bell repeatedly.

A fancy firm would have a door camera and mic through which visitors could communicate. It would have a reception desk which would take such calls.

He was old school. He didn't have an executive assistant.

'I AM BUSY,' he yelled and hoped the visitor could hear him. There was a reception area immediately inside the entrance and then a semi-transparent door that led to his office.

Office? It was a single room. Walnut bookshelves on the wall. A large oak desk on which was his laptop, a landline phone that had never rung – who needed them – and his cell phone charging on a wireless mat. A globe in the corner. Colored rugs and throws on couches.

It had a warm, comforting look. Cutter couldn't take credit for the décor.

That was Meghan and Beth Petersen's doing. Friends of his. Twins. Snarky as hell, a trait that they delighted on unleashing on him. 'We have taste, you have none,' Beth had said and she and her sister had taken over refurbishing the interior of his office.

They had also installed elaborate security systems. Like the ceiling-mounted camera that had a good view of the door. He could see who was battering down his door if he wished.

He didn't want to.

He liked to be surprised.

He was on his third bite when he heard the door open.

Which meant either the visitor had picked the lock or had a key.

He went for the latter because the twins had also installed a high-end lock which had biometrics and couldn't be easily beaten.

So, the visitor had a key.

Which meant they were a friend, because he had given keys only to them.

He was a PI. Such deductions came easy to him.

He saw two figures through the glass door. He stopped chomping. Beth and Meghan? Nope. The twins would have let themselves in without the pounding.

He sighed audibly when the door slammed open.

NYPD Detective First Grade Gina Difiore entered. FBI Special-Agent-in-Charge, Peyton Quindica, followed her. The latter led an FBI-NYPD Joint Task Force. JTF for those who loved acronyms. Difiore was her deputy. Her partner in real life.

Their titles didn't reflect their seniority. Both were heavy-hitters in their respective organizations and had track records that ran into pages.

'I'm busy.' Cutter resumed eating.

'Yeah, we can see that,' Difiore sneered. She slapped his shoes away from the desk and planted herself in one chair while Quindica took the other.

She shot up instantly, eyeing the paper bag on his desk.

'Is that from Lin Shun?'

Lin Shun, the deli, that only those in the know in New York were aware of.

She grabbed the bag before he could answer, dipped her hand inside and brought out a pastry.

Gina Difiore rarely smiled at him. A scowl, a frown, a grimace, cold-flat-dead eyes, were her usual expression when it came to him.

She grinned at the pastry and bit into it.

She dipped her hand and brought out another and gave it to her partner.

Cutter watched as his visitors finished his delicacy.

'You are welcome,' he growled.

He had done a favor to Lin Shun some years ago as a result of which she insisted on not taking payment from him. Forever. He was equally stubborn and didn't take freebies. They came to a compromise. He paid for his meals but got the pastries free.

Cutter was sure murders and kidnapping had been committed over her delicacies, such were their quality.

And here, Difiore and Quindica had consumed them without as much as a please and thank you.

The detective airily waved away his growl. She dabbed at her lips and wiped her hands on a paper towel. Poured herself and Quindica generous shots of the juice on his desk and sipped.

'Its my mistake,' he shook his head.

'What is?' Quindica cocked her head at him.

'Giving you my office keys.'

Difiore made a noise that suspiciously sounded like *pshaw*. 'Drop everything you have,' she ordered. 'We have a case for you.'

AUTHOR'S MESSAGE

Thank you for taking the time to read *Tehran*. If you enjoyed it, please consider telling your friends and posting a short review.

Sign up to Ty Patterson's mailing list and get *The Watcher*, a Zeb Carter novella, exclusive to newsletter subscribers. Join Ty Patterson's Facebook Readers Group.

BOOKS BY TY PATTERSON:

Zeb Carter Series

Twelve books in the series and counting

Cutter Grogan Series (Zeb Carter Universe)

Seven books in the series and counting

Zeb Carter Short Stories

Three books and counting

Warriors Series (Zeb Carter Universe)

Twelve books in the series

Gemini Series (Zeb Carter Universe)

Four thrillers in the series

Warriors Series Shorts (Zeb Carter Universe)

Six novellas in the series

Cade Stryker Series

Two military sci-fi thrillers

ABOUT THE AUTHOR

Ty has been a trench digger, loose tea vendor, leather goods salesman, marine lubricants salesman, diesel engine mechanic, and is now an action thriller author.

Ty 's books are read on all continents by thousands of readers.

Ty lives with his wife and son, who humor his ridiculous belief that he's in charge.

Printed in Great Britain
by Amazon